Firm Appleton

Appletons' Summer Book

For the seaside, the forest, the camp, the train, the steamboat, the arbor, and the

watering-place

Firm Appleton

Appletons' Summer Book
For the seaside, the forest, the camp, the train, the steamboat, the arbor, and the watering-place

ISBN/EAN: 9783337409807

Printed in Europe, USA, Canada, Australia, Japan

Cover: Foto ©Andreas Hilbeck / pixelio.de

More available books at **www.hansebooks.com**

APPLETONS'
SUMMER BOOK.

FOR THE SEASIDE, THE FOREST, THE CAMP, THE TRAIN, THE STEAMBOAT,
THE ARBOR, AND THE WATERING-PLACE.

NEW YORK:
D. APPLETON AND COMPANY,
1, 3, & 5 BOND STREET.
1880.

CONTENTS.

APPLETONS' SUMMER BOOK.

OUR SUMMER PLEASURE-PLACES.

On the Eastern Shore.

SO various in character and large in number have become the places to which
we resort for recreation and rest during the
summer solstice that many books have to be
written to suitably set them forth.* How, as
one turns over the pages of some of these captivating volumes, he ever succeeds in deter-
mining which of the thousand claimants upon his attention shall give him the benefit of
its freshening airs, is puzzling to understand.
And, even if the indefatigable summer pleasure-seeker resolves to enjoy them all successively in turn, he must depend upon the years

* Appletons' Hand-book of Summer Resorts. Illustrated. 8vo. Paper. New York : D. Appleton & Co.

1

of a centenarian to accomplish his purpose. The dozen or so leading "resorts" are, of course, quickly compassed; but the ambitious youth who thinks to carry his knapsack into all the places that parade large hotels, or rejoice in a mountain, a glen, a trout-stream, a lake, or a prospect, little knows the legion that awaits his coming.

Nature has certainly done wonders for us in the way of glorious scenery and inviting sheets of water; when man has effectually done his part in the hotels that he sets up and the loco-motion he provides, the summer resorts of America will be endeared to every heart as so many happy paradises.

Their variety is fairly endless. They skirt our sea-border; they nestle among our hills and mountains; they line our river-courses; they take possession of our islands; they make gay our lakes; they hang over our glens and cascades; they marshal in all places that have a natural grace. The weary town-worker who pants for green hills and shady dells, or longs for

Cliffs at Mount Desert.

the tonic of tumbling sea-waves, may find his health-giving rest at any point to which he may turn.

Away on the coast of Maine are many notable places. First, on its remotest border, and without its dominion, is the island of Grand Manan, the home of fishermen and sea-fowl, with rugged and towering cliffs, and rude, primitive life, but with every condition to attract the artist, the sportsman, and the adventurer. It is not easy of access, being reached only by fishing-vessels from Eastport; but this may prove its chief attraction in the estimation of some tourists. Its cliffs are the highest on our shore, rising four hundred feet; and altogether it is a wild, weird place, the home of storms and fogs, a favorite summer haunt of the artist, and the "very theme of the bold and romantic." Nearer than Grand Manan, and with some of its characteristics, is Mount Desert, also an island, lying a little over a hundred miles from Portland, in Frenchman's Bay. As it has an area of a hundred square miles, its separation from the main shore implies no unpleasant limitation of space. Mount Desert

The Isles of Shoals.

is girdled by cliffs and crowned with mountains, the latter come down to the sea. The resources
the only instance on our Atlantic shore in which for the pleasure-seeker are therefore many:

Cliffs, Portland Harbor.

there are fine sheets of water for boating, and excellent marine fishing; the mountain-paths on the island are wooded and picturesque; and the sea-cliffs, cut by the tireless waves into many fantastic forms, hewed out into caves, shaped into obelisks and columns, and sometimes dragged down by the elements into a chaos of titanic blocks, supply an endless variety of picturesque objects. The only drawback is the lack of surf-bathing.

From Mount Desert all the way to Cape Cod are innumerable places to charm the lover of the

Scenes on Lake George.

seashore. Casco Bay, on the southwest extremity of which stands Portland, the commercial metropolis of Maine, is one of the most picturesque on the coast. Like Lake Winnepesaukee, it is popularly supposed to contain 365 islands, and its green archipelago abounds in good fishing-places, in charming picnic resorts, and in snug, solitude-haunted retreats. On the larger islands are spacious summer hotels, and Portland itself looms beautiful from the water, rising in terraced lines along its hills. South of the harbor the surf-beaten promontory of Cape Elizabeth projects its rugged cliffs into the ocean; and southward of this, stretching away toward quaint old Portsmouth, are Old Orchard Beach, the most frequented and fashionable in New England, after Swampscott and Rye, Wells Beach, covered with snipe and curlew, and a great rendezvous for sportsmen, and the long Ogunquit Beach, between which and York Beach is the remarkable rocky promontory known as Bald Head Cliff.

Twelve miles off from Portsmouth are the famous Isles of Shoals, a sea-girt group of little islands furnished with good hotels, where one may fancy himself, even when upon the firm-set earth, far out on the bounding ocean. Here all the air is salt; the sea-spray moistens the beard and hair; and one sleeps to the murmuring of the waves. One who would forget the turmoil, the parched highways, and the dust-laden airs of the land, can at the Isles of Shoals isolate himself from all past experience, and with every breath inhale fresh sensations of pleasure.

But the Eastern shore abounds with places that allure the summer traveler. The shore intermingles beach with rocks, so that with fine bathing-places are many curious rocks with their weather-worn surfaces, and caverns and caves with their wealth of strange marine life. Rye Beach, Hampton Beach, and Salisbury Beach, levies each its annual tribute of pleasure-seekers; there are the fashionable resorts of Swampscott and Nahant; the quaint old fishing-towns of Marblehead and Gloucester; Newburyport, with its relics and mementos of a former maritime importance, now lost; and Salem, with its haunting associations of the witchcraft delusions—in fact, this entire shore is replete with varied beauty, full of historic interest, and a tourist might with vast delight and pleasure spend a long summer upon its sea-beaten rocks and in its antique towns.

But we have as yet only begun to enumerate all the seaside resorts. The breezes and quaint places about Cape Cod are not to be forgotten: the superb Martha's Vineyard far down Buzzard's Bay, where throngs of visitors crowd the spacious hotels, and where the Methodists congregate every summer in vast numbers for camp-meeting purposes, has all the salt savor of a sea-surrounded place; and Nantucket, some thirty miles farther out in the Atlantic, we all know as once a great whaling-place, but still retaining, amid the stimulating bustle of a growing popular resort, the quaint characteristics of an isolated people accustomed to go down to the sea in ships. Here come now every season the lovers of shark-fishing, rapidly becoming a favorite pas-

time for those who love robust and exciting sports.

From Nantucket and the Vineyard, a short excursion westward toward the mainland brings us to the spacious Narragansett Bay, in a picturesque nook of which nestles Newport, "the Queen of American watering-places," the most select and exclusive of summer resorts, the most interesting for its historic and personal associations, and one of the most charming for its scenery. At the mouth of the bay, and possessing one of the finest beaches on the Atlantic coast, is Narragansett Pier, another popular watering-place; and thence westward, along the northern shore of Long Island Sound, is a fringe of old towns, each of which has its clientèle of summer visitors, and all of which are too well known to require mention.

Off the mouth of Narragansett Bay, full amid the ocean-surges, lies Block Island, favorite of many; and then comes the eastern portion of Long Island, where we cease to find rocks, but instead conglomerate cliffs of pebbles and sand. Long Island ends in two spreading prongs, between which lies the superb Peconic Bay, a noble sheet of water, capitally adapted for boating and fishing. At the inland boundary of the bay is Shelter Island, where the land rises to fine wooded hills, and where recently large hotels have gone up. Sag Harbor is an old whaling-town; Greenport is a new, green, shaded village on the northern prong, inhabited by prosperous fishermen; East Hampton, on the ocean-side, is one of the most charming and picturesque vil-

Lake Champlain.

lages in the country, to which come every summer many lovers of green lanes and rural solitude. The open downs on eastern Long Island, where many cattle are grazed, and over which always sweep pleasant breezes from the sea, have an indescribable charm. The southern shore of

the island is protected for long distances by nearly continuous ridges of sand-dunes, within which are bays admirably suited for boating. Fire Island is here, where those fond of trolling for bluefish come in great numbers. There is no scenery but the sand and the ocean; but sands and sea and boats have an ineffable charm, and an ample hotel extends its welcome to the busy idlers whose holiday-making must keep them within easy reach of the metropolis.

Nearer that metropolis, of which it is practically a summer suburb, is Rockaway Beach, whose arid sand-wastes the enchanted wand of capital has transformed into a vast pleasance for the pleasure-seeking thousands of the heated city. Here spacious hotels and ample eating-saloons fling wide their hospitable doors; and here the visitor may enjoy excellent surf-bathing on one side of the narrow beach, and equally fine still-water bathing on the other, where the placid expanse of Jamaica Bay ex-

tends a perpetual invitation to all who have a propensity for boating and yachting. At Coney Island, still nearer the city, just outside the entrance of New York Bay, are vast hotels and bath-houses, restaurants, pavilions, and promenades, which offer their competing attractions to the visitor. Here the surf-bathing is unsurpassed; here throughout the summer evenings, the sounds of music and revelry are commingled with the monotonous refrain of the waves as they trample upon the beach; and here the thronging thousands constitute in themselves one of the most striking features of a spectacle which, as a whole, is unequaled on the continent.

Crossing now the mouth of the beautiful New

Lake Memphremagog.

York Bay, and glad of an excuse for avoiding the heated and tumultuous city, we reach the shores of New Jersey, where Long Branch, Cape May, and Atlantic City flourish to the knowledge of all the world, and woo the attention of those gregarious pleasure-seekers whose recreation is best appreciated when it is flavored with a spice of social excitement. At Barnegat Bay will be found the characteristic features that are so attractive on Long Island; and in the vicinity are the favorite haunts of the sportsman. At the Highlands, near Long Branch, one may find the seashore, a picturesque inland river, with fine fishing, and high, beautifully-wooded banks—these features not elsewhere coming together on our coast.

Below New Jersey, the low and storm-fretted coasts of Delaware and Maryland present no inducement to a pause until we enter the ample roads where the noble Chesapeake Bay debouches into the Atlantic. Here, near the entrance to the Chesapeake, is Fortress Monroe, or Old Point Comfort, where there is every facility, we are told, for bathing, boating, and fishing, and which forms the southern terminus of seacoast places visited in the summer season by the Northern pleasure-seeker. From the cliffs of Grand Manan the distance is some eight hundred miles. How varied the scene, how multifarious the pictures, how abundant the means of pleasure! South of Newport, as we have already said, there

Scenes at Newport.

The Beach at Long Branch.

are no rocks; but the shore and the sea, no matter what the conditions, have ever a penetrating charm. The advance of the waves is life; a single white sail upon the expanse of water makes a picture; the salt savor of the breeze carries tingling pleasure to the veins; the pebbles upon the shore and the strange forms of marine life that abide under the sand and within the caverned rocks are full of interest; even the old wrecks that the sands are ingulfing make fancy-kindling pictures. Hundreds of thousands are enjoying the scenes; they congregate in vast numbers at Cape May, at Long Branch, at Coney Island, at Rockaway, at Newport, at Swampscott; they people all the intermediate places, hang upon every cliff in Maine, clamber every rock and explore every recess on the Eastern shore, and their feet press on the sands of Long Island and New Jersey—a vast army of votaries at the footstool of Old Ocean.

But the mountains and the lakes press forward to dispute the supremacy of the sea. They, too, can point to their multitudes of pilgrims, of those who love the exaltation of the hill-tops, the ripple of the lakes, the music of the waterfalls, the solitude of the forests, the flowers of the meadows, or who come to medicated springs for their healing waters.

In number and measurement the inland places greatly outdo those of the shore. They extend from the Saguenay and Ottawa of the North to the mountains of North Carolina, and reach from the Atlantic Ocean to the Pacific. Our space is brief, and we can do no better now than cata-

Lake Erie.

logue some of their names; but even the mere enumeration of our vast resources of this nature excites the imagination. Mere statistics sometimes have glow and eloquent speech! Our mountains in the far West reach the splendor of the Alps; our lakes outnumber those of any other land, and some of them equal the beauty of the Swiss; our rivers are rivaled only by the Rhine and the Danube; our forests retain their primitive supremacy; and scattered everywhere are beautiful valleys, sylvan dells, grand cascades, embowered villages! The only difficulty is, that many of these places can not be reached and enjoyed, save with great discomfort. Our ill-ballasted railways suffocate us with dust, and our hotels are too often huge barracks, in which the art of living has not yet found its best form.

But let us glance at the more important places that invite the summer tourist, who has come to the wise conclusion that the attractions more than counterbalance the discouragements, and who is willing to place himself on more familiar terms with Nature. Far up in Maine, on the verge of the great Maine forest, is Moosehead Lake, a sheet of water forty miles long, in which trout abound. There are good hotels here, and the usual accommodations for visitors; but some sojourners prefer to taste the wilder sweets and more piquant flavor of camp-life, and to such the facilities in the way of guides and outfit are ample. Mount Kineo overhangs the shores of the lake, with a precipitous front over six hundred feet high. "These," says the author of "Appletons' Hand-book of

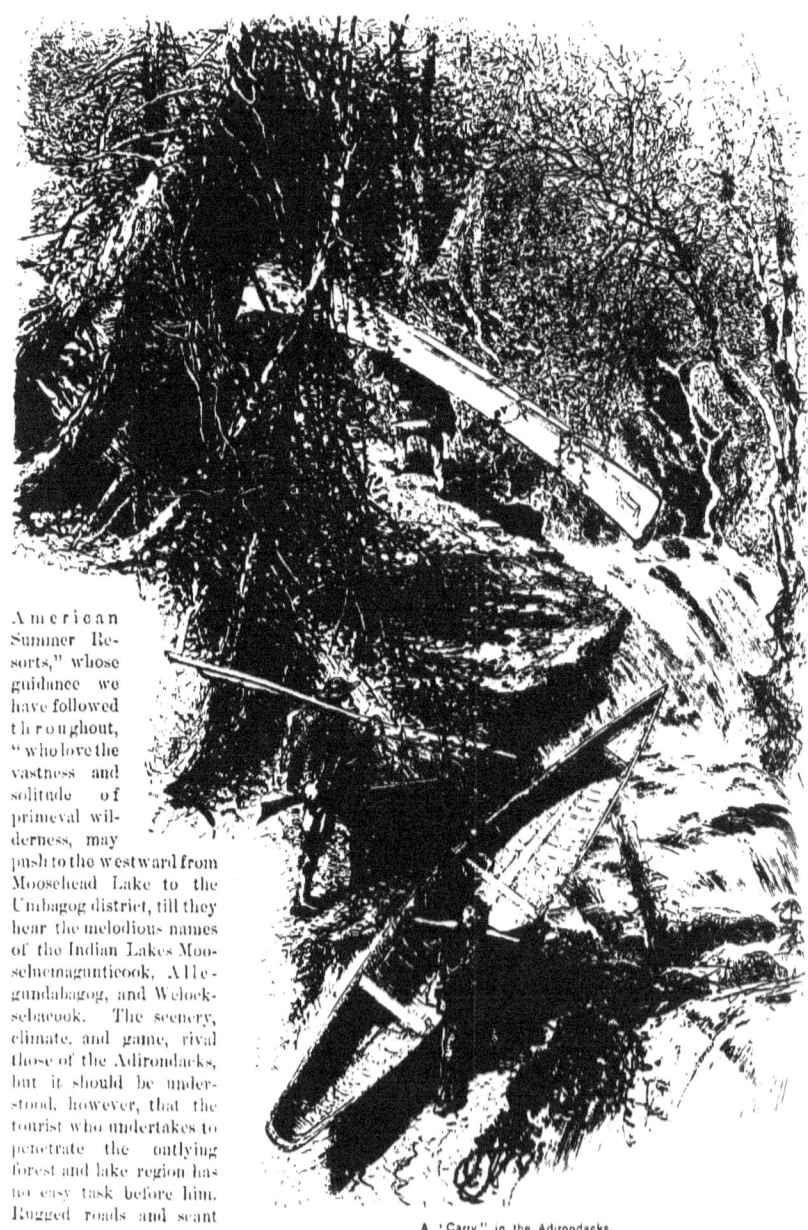

American Summer Resorts," whose guidance we have followed throughout, "who love the vastness and solitude of primeval wilderness, may push to the westward from Moosehead Lake to the Umbagog district, till they hear the melodious names of the Indian Lakes Mooselucmagunticook, Allegundabagog, and Welocksebacook. The scenery, climate, and game, rival those of the Adirondacks, but it should be understood, however, that the tourist who undertakes to penetrate the outlying forest and lake region has no easy task before him. Rugged roads and scant physical comforts will not be the most severe trial;

A "Carry" in the Adirondacks.

for in many places he will not find a road or inn at all, but must trudge along on foot, or by rude skiff over the lakes, and trust to his rifle and his rod to supply his larder." This is just

The Catskill Mountain House.

those thirsting for woodland adventure. It is also said that an enjoyable route for the adventurer is from Moosehead lake, by a two miles' portage, down the west branch of the Penobscot. Mount Katahdin, the great mountain of Maine, may be ascended from the river-shore.

Still farther west and north, just within the borders of the great forest region, are the remote and romantic Rangeley Lakes, the only remaining portion of our Eastern States that can be truly called "the paradise of sportsmen." The chain known collectively as "the Rangeley Lakes" consists of several distinct lakes, connected by narrows and streams, extending from the Oquos-

the picture to fascinate some adventurous spirits, and hence we quote it as a tempting bait to all soe or Rangeley Lake to Lake Umbagog, forming one continuous water-way for a distance of nearly fifty miles, embracing eighty square miles of water-surface, and abounding in blue-back trout and other game-fish. From the cold and limpid waters of these lakes trout are often taken weighing as much as ten pounds; and in the adjacent forests deer and other game reward the efforts of the hunter.

From Moosehead and Rangeley on our flight southward we pause at Lake Winnipesaukee, lying just south of the White Mountains, with a magnificent outlook on that noble range. Edward Everett has left on record the opinion that he has seen nowhere abroad a lovelier scene than this lake presents. The waters are pure; it is dotted with islands, and lofty hills and mountains close it in; all charming, but it lacks, at least, the snow-capped peaks and the delightful villas of the Swiss lakes. Near it is Squam Lake, a much smaller but scarcely less beautiful sheet of water. Up on the northern border of Vermont, extending into Canada, is Lake Memphremagog, a superb, mountain-inclosed sheet of water, some thirty miles long. Numerous other lakes diversify the surface of the Eastern States, but we are on the borders of New York, which ought to be called preëminently the Lake State. The great Ontario forms a large part of its western and northern border; the superb Champlain separates it from Vermont; and it holds within its bosom that gem of all our inland sheets of water, Lake George, and the scarcely less beau-

tiful Cayuga, Seneca, Skaneateles, Canandaigua, Otsego, Oneida, Cazenovia, Chautauqua, Mohonk, Mahopac, and the several score of lakes that lie among the Adirondacks. Singularly enough, our lake-region lies wholly in the North and West. Neither the Alleghanies of Pennsylvania, the Blue Ridge of Virginia, nor the mountains of North Carolina and Tennessee, have lakes, picturesque and beautiful as many of their mountain-streams are. There is not one of the New York lakes that is not a delightful summer place for the town-wearied searcher for wholesome air and pleasant scenes. A sheet of water would seem to be almost indispensable for true beauty in a landscape, especially if the view be an extensive one. There is always a charm in swift streams flowing through shadowed forests; but if one emerge upon an open landscape the eye searches for an expanse of water, and is delighted in seeing one as it mirrors the hills and forests that encompass it, reflects the blue depths and moving clouds of the sky, and holds suspended upon its surface the onr or the sail of the pleasure-seeker. Lake George only lacks the white-capped peaks of the Swiss lakes to equal them in beauty, if its three hundred or more islands are not a feature that more than compensates. They probably do more than compensate those on summer vacations, as they offer admirable camping-grounds. To break away from civilization and live out-of-doors is one of the intense desires of many people; and hence on these dry, shaded, breezy islands of Lake George, with

Catskill Mountains.

glorious hills, charming water expanse, and excellent fishing, camp-life abounds and has every nomadic felicity.

To these *petit* gems stand in contrast the gi-

gantic lakes of the West. In Lake Erie are the Wine Islands, recently become favorite resorts, where the life and the scene have their novel features, and which are gay with animated groups of boating and picnic parties. Far up in the strait between Lake Huron and Lake Superior is Mackinac Island, which is only some three miles long, but full of interest. It is an old military post of the United States; was originally settled by the French; has an antiquated village; is marked by high and picturesque rocks; and the waters that surround the island are wonderfully clear, and teem with fish of delicious flavor. The fisherman sees the fish toying with his bait, and the active little Indian boys on the piers are always ready to dive for any coins the visitor may throw into the water for them. If report speaks true, this is a very gem of an island, and, great as the distance is, would reward the summer tourists that visit it.

From Mackinac we pass to the shores of Lake Superior. A steamer carries the passenger over the lake, giving him glimpses of its bold and striking shores; but, if one would enjoy all their wild and rugged aspects, he must command a vessel that will land him where he lists.

Corduroy Bridge, Mount Mansfield Road.

Excursions to the Pictured Rocks, and other striking features of the southern shore, can be made from the town of Marquette; and the more picturesque and majestic north shore, more than half of which belongs to the Hudson Bay Company, whose hunters, trappers, and *voyageurs* are almost its sole frequenters, may be visited during the summer from Duluth or Port Sarnia. Lake Superior invites the attention of the explorer; there is the fascination of the dangerous and the unknown; the life is wild, the adventures racy, the experience exhilarating and health-giving.

And now, as to the mountains. We would say nothing of the White Mountains, because every one is familiar with them, either by personal experience or by description; nor need

we dwell upon the Catskills, which come next in the affections of tourists and artists. The Green Mountains of Vermont are scarcely inferior to them in altitude, and, as their name implies, the vigorous and verdant forests that clothe their sides give them supreme beauty. Mount Mansfield is the highest; a road from Stowe ascends to the top, along which can be noted, in the ravines below, grand forests. There is a smuggler's notch, similar to the great caverns of the West, that is certainly wild and eminently picturesque. In the Catskills, the Clove Road is one of the most charming highways in the world; High Peak commands a view unsurpassed in reach and variety; picturesque roads descend in every direction through rugged gorges from the plateau to the plains below; murmuring trout-streams wind through primeval forests; to the west lie the profound glens of Lexington; and all through the region are spots immortalized by the artists.

The Adirondacks of recent years have been the fascinating theme of all lovers of the wilderness. People hurry to them by the thousands to enjoy a taste of nomadic freedom. The lakes are covered by their boats, and the forests that border the lakes are animated by their camping-grounds. But there are parties who penetrate into the interior, put the keels of their boats upon fresh waters, and set their feet in places where the primitive wilderness has remained uncontaminated by the presence of man. Rich in adventures, in experience, in life, in health, in beauty, are these interior Adirondack journeys; and if the labor is sometimes severe—such as a "carry" of boats and effects over rugged forest passes from one lake to another—still the rewards are manifold.

Our space is nearly occupied, and yet innumerable places remain to be mentioned. The mountains of Pennsylvania are lofty, green, and beautiful; the Upper Susquehanna runs through a wild region with many trout-streams, and places for the accommodation of anglers; the Alleghanies have their many summer hotels and their sequestered retreats; the Upper Delaware is glorious in picturesque beauty, and at the Dela-

Mount Holyoke, Massachusetts.

ware Water-Gap there is every charm of river and mountain scenery. A little way above it the romantic Raymondskill and Sawkill attract the angler and the artist. The Connecticut Valley has its hundred points of interest; the Genesee flows into Lake Ontario through picturesque shores; the Berkshire Hills of Massachusetts and the valley of the Housatonic wear the crown of sylvan beauty; the Hudson, the Highlands of which are famous the world over, and whose shores are lined with places of wonderful beauty; the Thousand Islands of the St. Lawrence invite the dreamer, the poet, and all who love to sit contentedly in boats and be wafted amid green-fringed isles; the Ottawa and the Saguenay of Canada offer stupendous cliffs and somber forests; far away in the West are the wonders of the Yosemite, the geysers and waterfalls of the Yellowstone, and the peaks and parks of Colorado; in Virginia lies a picturesque region of mountain-springs; while farther south, in western North Carolina, the great Appalachian chain rises to heights not attained by any other mountain-peaks east of the Mississippi.

Our seashore, our mountains, our lakes, our rivers, as we have seen, are wonderful in beauty; and then for scenes of gayety what places can excel our Saratoga, the metropolis of watering-places, to which famous men and brilliant women come from every social center; or Long

Scenes in Saratoga.

Branch, that dashing summer city on the sea; or Newport, the social elegance of which is so exclusive? Infinite is the variety; and let us say, finally, that it is a mistake to suppose that our summer resorts have not, each in its way, a legitimate purpose to serve. To some brain-fagged men the brilliant gayety of Saratoga or Long Branch is a tonic; their ideas are freshened, and their whole nature stimulated by this free contact with their fellow-beings; with others a watering-place only repeats the experience of the town, and such long for the seclusion of the woods, the exhilaration of the mountains, or the rough life of the sea. He must be dull of imagination or sluggish in his sympathies who can not find in mountain or water-ing-place, seashore or forest, the place that will serve the purpose of a summer resort—freshness to the mind, strength to the body, and recreation to the whole nature.

Rocks at Mackinac.

WONDERS OF THE SHORE.

Oh, what an endless work have I in hand,
To count the sea's abundant progeny!
Whose fruitful seed far passeth those in land,
And also those which wonne in th' azure sky.
For much more eath to tell the stars on high,
Albe they endless seem in estimation,
Than to recount the sea's posterity;
So fertile be the floods in generation,
So huge their numbers, and so numberless their nation.
—SPENSER.

THE varied attractions which the seashore offers to seekers after health and pleasure, to those who are getting rid of the "long leisure of summer days," to lovers of the majesty and the awfulness of the ocean, and to those who, like Dr. Syntax, are in search of the picturesque —all these attractions have been often enough pointed out and emphasized; but the riches and the wonders which it possesses not merely for the student of natural history, but for whoever will open his eyes to what almost obtrudes itself upon his notice, have hardly as yet been even mentioned. Of all the departments of natural history there is none more curiously interesting, or more inviting to enter upon, than marine zoölogy; and, while such a portion of it as the sojourner at the seaside would care to acquaint himself (or herself) with would present scarcely any difficulties, there can be no doubt that it will furnish a really enjoyable resource to many who become fatigued after a time with the vapid amusements and dull routine of watering-place life.

This fact has long been understood and appreciated in England, and there are several popular and charmingly written guides to the zoölogy of the English coasts; but Mr. W. E. Damon's "Companion for the Seaside"* is, we believe, the first attempt that has been made to direct the attention of the non-scientific to the more varied wonders of our own shores. Mr. Damon's little book itself touches upon only a very few of those multitudinous forms of life which throng both the ocean and the shore; and, as we can cite but a few even of those instances which he records, what we shall say in the present article must be regarded as merely hints or suggestions of the exhaustless wonders that offer themselves to the observer.

Anemones, or Sea-Flowers.

flowers, says Mr. Damon, "rival in beauty the choicest treasures of the garden or conservatory. But added to their loveliness of form is the superior attraction of their vitality; for these sea-flowers are living animals, breathing, eating, digesting, and capable of changing their forms at will. Would not a pink be more curious if it could walk? a rose awaken greater interest if it could reach after its necessary nourishment, and take care of its own buds? Well, this is what the flowers of the sea do."

Some of the anemones are detached, swimming about freely when undisturbed, and all have some capacity for movement; but the habit of most is to attach themselves to some firm object, as a rock or a section of coral, or the back of a crab or other crustacean. "In fact, when free they swim backward, and wherever their base encounters a firm object, no matter what, there they will fix themselves by suction, and as a general rule contentedly remain. There are two species, however, which show a marked preference for the back of a crustacean. One is called the parasite anemone, and its favorite home is on the hard shell of the hermit crab (the *Pagurus*

Beginning with those baffling organisms which occupy the border-land between the animal and vegetable kingdoms, Mr. Damon devotes an interesting chapter to the anemones, or sea-flowers, of which every sea possesses some representatives, and which are found upon all our shores, usually adhering to rocks, but sometimes attached to the timber of our docks. Many of these animal-

* Ocean Wonders: A Companion for the Seaside. Freely illustrated from Living Objects. By William E. Damon. New York: D. Appleton & Co.

2

Bernhardus) ; and as these crabs are great travelers, and have the peculiarity of frequently changing their residence by taking possession of the empty shells of other animals, this parasite anemone is likely to see far more of the world than its more modest brethren. There is one other genus which cultivates the parasitic habit, the

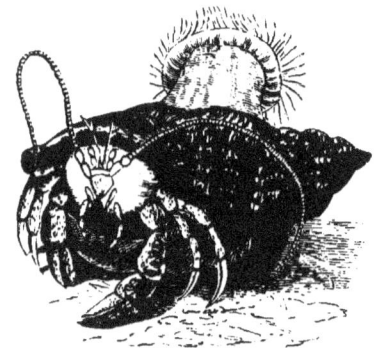

Hermit-Crab with Sea-Anemone on its Shell.

Adamsia, which selects the crab *P. Prideauxii* for its place of abode. This habit is known as commensalism, as they are presumed to dine at the same table."

The sea-flowers differ greatly in size, form, and color, and also in special peculiarities of development and function ; so that a large collection would have the appearance of an animated flower-garden, composed of carnations, china-asters, dahlias, daisies, etc. "The beauty of many species," says Mr. Damon, "is greatly enhanced by the fact that several colors are combined in individual specimens. Thus sometimes the main body or column will be green with white or golden tentacles, and the base buff with a pink disk or tips, or crimson with azure spheroids ; sometimes the whole animal will be of one color, varied by different tints and shades. Down below, in the caves of the sea, these wonderful creatures have for untold ages anticipated our modern 'combination-suits,' and have appeared dressed in all the glory of scarlet and gold, pink and gray, blue and white, green and crimson ; their exquisite taste always selecting accords or pleasing contrasts, and avoiding all discordant shades which would clash or 'kill' each other, such as we sometimes see in human productions."

The column-shaped body of the anemone is soft, but usually tough and tenacious, and consists of a simple sac or cavity, commonly broadened at the base and open at the top or mouth. The upper chambers of the cavity are prolonged

into tentacles or feelers which extend in a number of rows around the mouth, forming, when they are all extended, a beautiful crown. "If these tentacles or feelers are touched, or if the creature is in any way alarmed, they are instantly contracted, and all the parts sink down and are drawn together into a compact mass. This is effected by the exudation of water from the cavities or chambers through a series of small openings connected with the central cavity. Expansion takes place by the reversed action, filling these cells with water." Sometimes the power which they possess of altering their shape appears to be exercised for the mere pleasure of the thing. Now they will contract themselves into balls, partially elongated and expanded ; then they will stretch out their fringes or tentacles to their widest extent, like a polypetalous flower in full bloom ; and again they will encircle themselves with belts or girdles, drawn more or less tight and shifting up and down, involving changes of form every minute.

"In addition to the tentacles," says our author, "these curious creatures are armed for attacking their prey with what we may call fine thread-like lassos, of arrow-like sharpness, called *cnidæ* (from a Greek word meaning a nettle), from which is transmitted a powerful stinging and benumbing sensation, deadly to small prey, the victim being affected as by a shock of electricity. This I know by experience, for, some years ago, when in Bermuda, while attempting to take a large actinia from a rock, one of these soft-looking beauties gave me a shock which disabled my arm for hours. It will easily be understood that this concealed battery enables the sea-anemones to conquer much larger and stronger creatures than they could hold simply by the tentacles ; they often seize large shrimps and crabs far beyond their own size. Occasionally, however, if one of these finds an anemone weakened from any cause, it will take up a position upon the edge of its mouth, keeping it distended, and with its claws pluck out the food from the victim's sac and appropriate it to its own use. Sometimes, when such an attempt is made, a combat ensues, and then woe to the marauder if he has mistaken the strength of the sea-anemone! He will surely fall into his own trap."

Mr. Damon gives much curious and interesting information about the structure, habits, and modes of propagation of the anemones, but for further details we must refer the reader to the book, only inviting his attention for a moment beforehand to the coral, which is closely related to the anemone, being placed by naturalists in the same group of organisms. Unlike the anemones, however, the coral is not distributed over every sea, its natural habitat being the warm waters of the tropics; yet among the discoveries of our Coast Survey is the fact that coral grows on our North Atlantic seaboard. One variety, at least, the *Astrangia Danæ*, has been found on the shores of Massachusetts and Connecticut; but these are rare, and the coral is seen to advantage only at the Florida Keys, some parts of the West Indies, and at the Bermudas.

From the earliest times the coral has attracted the attention of naturalists and travelers. The Greeks named it "Daughter of the Sea," but do not seem to have investigated its nature and mode of growth; and ever since their time the coral has been the subject of a number of popular errors—as that it is a vegetable formation, and that it is soft while in water and only hardens on exposure to air. Mr. Damon remarks that he has heard public speakers, in search of an illustration, speak of "the wonderful *labors* of the coral *insect*"! and points out that in this short statement are involved two fundamental errors, the coral-producers being neither laborers nor insects. "Their simple and sole business," he says, "is *eating*; and that a strong stony structure is the result is no more creditable to them than it is to a maple-tree to secrete sugar, nor does it indicate any more effort."

"Another very common mistake," he adds, "is the supposition that they are exceedingly minute—even microscopic—in size. This is far from being the case. Having had several varieties under observation in my aquarium for years, I can assure the reader that they are not only large enough to be plainly seen by the naked eye, but that they sometimes elongate themselves nearly an inch above the upper edge of their cell, measuring one third of an inch in diameter.

"But some one may ask, 'If the coral-producers are not insects, what are they?' We answer, mainly polyps, with some hydroids and soft mollusks of the lowest class. These are all soft-bodied organisms, consisting of many varieties, having the organic function of secreting carbonate of lime, which, with some other ingredients, as silica and small portions of sand, composes the hard substance called coral.

"The body of the polyp consists of a cylindrical skin, with an inside sac, which is the stomach, and is furnished at the top with thread-like appendages, with which it draws in its food. Whatever it does not wish to retain in the stomach it rejects by the mouth, having no other resource, as the lower end of the polyp is affixed to the stony substance. When expanded, these thread-like tentacles around the mouth give them a flower-like appearance. It is between the outer skin and the sac or stomach that the

limestone is secreted which forms the coral substance.

"It will thus be seen that the polyp does not gather or collect from external sources the material of the coral—does not in any correct sense work or 'build' any more than a tree may be said to work as it grows into wood. Nature has

Cluster of Coral-Polyps in various stages of expansion.

simply provided that, in receiving its food, the polyp selects from the ingredients of the sea-water that which is capable of being reduced by simple functional processes into coral; just as a plant selects and secretes from the earth that kind of nourishment which makes stems, leaves, and buds.

"Each mature polyp, when fixed in its cell, may be considered as resting upon the tombs of its ancestors; and, when it dies, its descendants will repeat the process over its remains, and its own body, within which its share of coral has been secreted, will be the base for a new living descendant. . . .

"The large, massive forms of coral, whether of the dome, reef, or tree-like shape, would never reach the magnificent proportions that they do were it not for that peculiar provision of Nature in regard to the zoöphytes, of life and death both proceeding simultaneously and successively; each, combined and singly, aiding in one and the same object. This curious condition of growth favors the coral aggregation by allowing the living polyp, as it secretes the calcareous matter, to mount upward on that which it has already secreted and deposited. From the successful execution of this ascending process, we are led to infer either that the creature has the power of indefinite elongation, or that it must desert the precipitated portion of the corallum as growth proceeds; and, in fact, this last is what actually occurs. In some instances a polyp of only an inch in length, and even less, has been found at the top of a stem many inches in height; for the whole substance of what is called 'living coral' is in reality dead, excepting the extreme surface or point of each branch occupied by the little animal. The living tissues which once filled the cells of the lower portion of the corallum have been consumed by natural processes, and have disappeared as growth went on above. . . . "The final solidification of the coral mass is aided by the increased secretion by the polyp shortly before its death, filling all the pores with this stony matter in proportion as the vital tissues occupying them shrink and dwindle. This last deposit greatly aids in strengthening those tree-like or branched coral growths which, though so slender of form, are really very strong."

When first born the young larvæ are worm-like in form, and are very agile, darting about in all directions, and apparently enjoying themselves greatly. But this life of freedom soon comes to an end; their base becomes attached to some stationary object; and their gay youth is exchanged for a sedentary life, with no other changes than that of eating and digesting their food. "There are few natural objects," says Mr. Damon, "more pleasing than an association of these corallets; for, as the polyps rise above their cells and extend their fine, long tentacles, resembling threads of pure white silk, waving them to and fro like the radiated petals of a fairy-flower swayed by a gentle zephyr, or, again, like a minute feather fan slightly concave at the edge, they present an exceedingly animated and elegant appearance. Sometimes, when nearly at rest, and the filaments are more contracted, they suggest the appearance of a dense frost settled upon a bed of moss."

Next to the anemones in interest and in their abundance on our shores are the star-fishes, of which the most common variety is called by sailors "five-fingered Jack." Says Mr. Damon: "One of the most common objects to be met with at Newport, Nahant, or almost any point along the Massachusetts coast, are the so-called 'star-fishes,' though, scientifically speaking, they are no more fishes than is a rabbit or a bird; yet, for convenience and to save circumlocution, we may adopt the popular name in speaking of them. At low tide these curious 'stars' may be seen by thousands, sometimes clinging to the rocks, sometimes on the gravelly bottom, or perhaps attached to the sea-weeds."

In examining one of these "stars," it will be found that it has *two distinct sides*—an upper, slightly convex, and an under or oval side. The upper is rough and tuberculous; the under is soft, and contains all the vital and locomotory organs. The "rays" or fingers are usually on the same plane, but the animal has the power of raising them so as to progress over obstructions

which may be in its way. Extending one of these rays, it is made fast by suction, while the remainder of the body is drawn forward, the mode of progression being something like that of a ship dragging its anchor.

As star-fishes are found upon the shore, they often appear to be quite dead when they are really alive; they are the opossums of the sea. "Take up one of these fellows who is lying perfectly still, and put him into fresh sea-water, and he will very likely soon be traveling about as well as ever. However, as the dead and living, when left stranded by the tide, present so nearly the same appearance, it may be well to have some test by which to make sure of their true condition. There are two modes of ascertaining this with a reasonable degree of cer-

Star-Fish on a Rock.

tainty. If, on taking up a star-fish, he hangs loose and limp, he *is* dead; but, however dead he may look, if on touching it there is a firmness and consistency in the substance, he is only 'playing 'possum,' and will revive in the water. The other mode of trial is to lay our starry friend on his back, when, if he is alive, you will soon see a number of semi-transparent globular objects beginning to move, reaching this way and that, as if feeling for something; these are the locomotory organs or ambulacra, seeking to regain their normal position. If there is no movement of these, you may conclude that he is an extinguished star."

One of the most interesting traits about this lowly-organized creature is the care it bestows upon its eggs, which are contained in pouches situated at the broad base of the rays. But their mode of reproduction is not limited to eggs. "They have the strange capacity and frequent habit of detaching one or more of their rays, when each of these cast-off members becomes in time a perfect star. I have seen this operation performed many times, almost incredible as the statement seems to those unfamiliar with the vagaries of the zoöphytes and radiates. For instance, an arm or ray would, perhaps, be accidentally broken off close up to its point of junction with the central portion of the body. The animal, instead of appearing to be disturbed or annoyed, as it would be at the loss of its eggs, appears to mind the disappearance no more than if it were a cast-off garment, and goes about as happy with its remaining rays as if the whole had remained intact. Perhaps, if we could replace a lost arm as easily as our star, we should be nearly as indifferent to such a loss; for what do we see next? Only a little protuberance where the lost arm was separated. But look again in a week, and we shall see some little suckers or ambulacra projecting; the parts by degrees enlarge, and at the end of a few weeks a somewhat smaller but apparently quite perfect arm takes the place of the lost member! Its spines, water-tubes, tentacles, pedicellariæ, etc., are all in perfect working order, and its normal functions are fulfilled with all the precision of the elder rays. It is not, however, quite equal to the original; besides being smaller, it is of a more delicate texture, and its color of a lighter shade. It is very interesting to watch this extraordinary effort of nature in the development of the new member. The last one I had in my collection was just fifteen weeks in producing a new, full-grown arm."

This curious faculty is of no small practical importance, for the star-fish is very fond of oysters, which it eats by inserting its stomach between the edges of the shell and gradually sucking the substance out. When brought up in the

Serpent, or Brittle Star-Fish.

nets, rakes, or dredges, as they often are, fishermen are in the habit of cutting them up by drawing cords around them and throwing the pieces

overboard—the result of which is to multiply their enemies fivefold.

Belonging to the same group (*Echinodermata*) as the star-fish, and, in fact, very closely related, are the brittle star-fish (*Ophiopolis*) and the basket-fish, both found in Massachusetts Bay. The former has long, slender arms, nearly cylindrical in form, attached to a small disk-like body. These arms seem to be very loosely attached, and are often thrown off when the creature is fright-

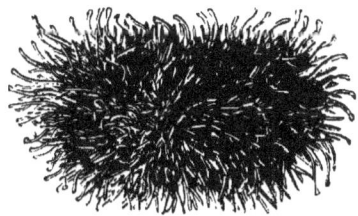

Sea-Egg, or Sea-Urchin.

ened, readily growing again afterward. Similarly related, though not quite so closely, is the sea-urchin, or sea-egg, a curious animal, spherical in form and covered all over with long, beautifully shaped spines, like those of the hedgehog. When alive sea-urchins are very shy, concealing themselves in holes and crevices of the rocks, or covering themselves with bits of sea-weed and the like, so that they must be closely looked for. As usually found, dead on the shore, the urchin is devoid of spines, and presents something the appearance of a melon, the surface being marked off into ten zones or divisions. "The urchin's relationship to the star-fish," says Mr. Damon, "may be illustrated by supposing that we bring all the five points of the star together, filling up the interstices with a similar substance: we have then a complete urchin minus the spines. Or, take the peel whole off of an orange, divide it into fifths, and bring the points up together, sticking needles in to simulate the spines, and we have an urchin, at least in shape." The color of the sea-urchin is usually reddish-brown or black, and while the body or ball part is not larger than a hen's egg (which it much resembles in shape) the spines are sometimes a foot long. "These animals," to quote Mr. Damon again, "are voracious vegetarians, eating off large fronds of the sea-lettuce and other plants, and cleaning a tank of every vestige of vegetation in a very short time. Their motion in swimming is slow, and when walking on the side of a glass tank, which they do with perfect ease on their long, slender legs (which are terminated by cup-shaped disks, constructed on the same principle as a surgeon's cupping-instrument), and aided by the spines, they are certainly an attractive sight, especially when all the spines and numerous pedicellariæ are fully distended. To the cursory observer they look no more capable of ascending a smooth surface like glass than a chestnut-bur does of walking up the side of a house."

A more modest relative of the urchin is the "sand-dollar" or "sand-cake," which, instead of being spherical, is flat, and when at rest looks something like a circular cake of sand (of a reddish-brown color) about the size of a silver dollar.

Also belonging to the same group is the sea-cucumber (*Holothuria*), a curious cylindrical animal, varying in length from an inch to between three and four feet, and found in several varieties on our shores. "They inhabit deep water, but when found near the shore are usually partly imbedded in the muddy bottoms. Their outside covering is a tough, leathery skin, plentifully studded with short, hairy spines. The mouth, a circular opening at one end, is furnished with a wreath of beautiful plume-like appendages, which

Sea-Urchins lodged in the Rocks they have excavated.

are extended at will for the purpose of grasping food and conveying it to the mouth; but, the food being brought within reach, only one of these tentacula is occupied in actually introducing it within the orifice, while the others remain passive, and appear to be waiting their turn to do the same service. Mrs. Agassiz has likened this group of tentacula in the sea-cucumber to some of the delicate sea-weeds, for their fineness of structure and the richness of their colors." These animals, besides the curious power of multiplying themselves by fissure, have the still more remarkable capacity of emptying themselves of nearly all their internal organs, and after a brief time of reproducing them and living on as comfortably as ever.

The numerous family of hydroid medusæ, jelly-fish, and the like, is very copiously represented upon our shores. Of one variety of them (the *Sertularia argentea*), Mr. Damon says: "Specimens can almost always be found which have been washed ashore, lying high and dry, at Coney Island; and, in this state, I venture to say that not more than one person in a thousand who

Sea-Cucumber.

pick this up supposes it to be anything but a vegetable production—some kind of sea-weed; but it is altogether animal, built up by millions on millions of little hydroid polyps, almost invisible to the naked eye, but developing a world of beauty under the microscope. In its dead and dried condition it is of so fine and elegant a texture as to take the place of honor among dried ferns, and other delicate plants or algæ, usually without exciting the least suspicion in the minds of its preservers that they are carefully *cherishing an animal skeleton.* The *Sertularia pumila* does not grow in such large masses as the former; it may be found attached to the lower sides of stones, or creeping along the sides of fucus, eel-grass, and different kinds of sea-weeds, and is a most beautiful object for the aquarium."

The general principle upon which all these kinds of animals are constructed is that of a floating bladder, which

"The general name of *Medusæ,*" continues Mr. Damon, "was given to this class of animals

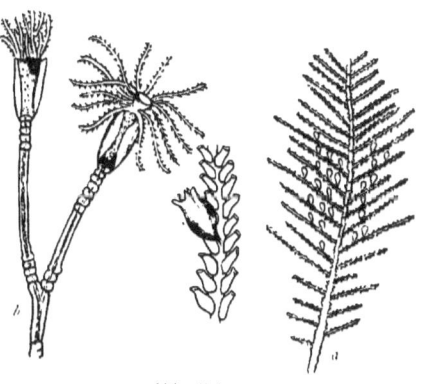

Living Hydrozoa.
Sertularia pinnata: a, natural size; *b,* enlarged.

can be filled or discharged of water at will, with a greater or less number of tentacula, and long, stinging filaments, and some appendages as sails with which to trim these bladder-boats, or else cilia to act as oars or means of propulsion. Some of them are so slight in their structure that they can not be submerged, though they are often thrown upon the shore, and in that manner suffer shipwreck. "When taken intact," says our author, "they will at first weigh surprisingly heavy for such transparent-looking objects, yet the weight consists almost wholly of nearly pure sea-water; but when the animal is stranded and dies this water all escapes, and nothing is left upon the sand but a filmy, gelatinous skin, scarcely observable, or looking like flakes of dried varnish in the sun. Some of them when distended with water will weigh ten or twelve pounds; others are so small that a few ounces of water will contain thousands. Some of these animals have a much denser fibrous organization than others; some are so extremely delicate that one would feel no substance if moving the hand through water in which they were sailing and actually coming in contact with them; while others are not only gorgeously colored, but of a very definite consistency to the touch. Almost any day at certain hours may be seen stranded on the clean sands at Manhattan Beach hundreds and thousands of these shining little balls of life, varying in size from a pea to a marble. Sometimes so many of these are blown ashore by the ocean-waves, that it is impossible for the multitude of people who visit this grand and popular seaside resort to avoid walking upon them."

on account of the snake-like filaments which they all possess, and which are highly suggestive of the snaky locks of the Greek Medusa, one of the three Gorgons. And the petrifying power of the latter is practically exercised by their marine namesakes; for, if their looks are less terrible, their embrace may prove as fatal. And yet how beautiful they look as they move with a sort of pulsating motion through the water, generally borne by the tides and currents, but appearing to ride them voluntarily! Sometimes hundreds of them may be seen floating along, showing every shade and tint, from the brightest to the most delicate opalescent hues.

"How different is their appearance, thus disporting themselves, from the wretched aspect they present when stranded on the sands! But then the fine tissues, which in fact form the framework of the animal, can be examined at leisure; and it will be found that in nearly all there are four elongated oval marks crossing each other nearly at right angles, variously tinted with some shade of red, and which are the seams or lines of juncture of the slight, sac-like skin which holds together this unsubstantial aqueous animal. But the best way, if possible, is to secure the medusa alive if one would see the *modus operandi* by which this slight epidermis and these trailing threads resolve themselves into a beautiful form, which seems to hold the secret of the prism within its dilated cuticle. If, then, our medusa can be dipped up in a bucket, or some vessel large enough to secure it unmutilated, and the water drained or poured off, in a short time the animal will shrink away to a mere fibrous remnant. If now, before it actually dies, a new supply of water is added, a little at a time, the whole process of distention will be readily seen, and the animal will presently rise with something of that pulsating movement which may be observed in a balloon during the process of filling it with gas. When nearly full it tugs at the cords, anxious to get into the aërial space; and, as the medusa fills all its cellules with the fluid which gives it shape and consistency, it leaves the bottom of the vessel, floats gayly to the top, and once more revels in the air and light of the surface."

One species of the Medusæ, popularly known as "the stinger" (*Cyanea capillata*), is so dangerous, and so abundant upon our coasts, that Mr. Damon thinks that to it may be attributed some of the sudden drownings, apparently otherwise inexplicable, which have occurred with expert swimmers when at no great distance from shore. The long, poisonous filaments touch and paralyze the bather while the body of the animal is yet a considerable distance away; and a gentleman who nearly lost his life from this cause at Long Branch a few years ago gives the following advice: "If the bather or shore-wanderer should happen to see, either tossing on the waves or thrown upon the beach, a loose, roundish mass of tawny membranes and fibers, something like a very large handful of lion's mane and silver paper, let him beware of the object, and, sacrificing curiosity to discretion, give it as wide a berth as possible; for this is the fearful 'stinger,' the *Cyanea capillata*."

Other numerous and most interesting groups of seashore animals are the Mollusca and the Crustacea, which comprise the countless generations of the shell-fishes, and some representatives

The Dancing Scallops.

of which are found on every coast. These are so well known and so easily found that we shall not pause to describe them, but will content ourselves with a reference to one or two of the most noteworthy.

The common *scallop*, or "St. James's shell," is almost as familiar a sight in our markets as the oyster; but, though chiefly regarded for its edible qualities, its interesting habits render it peculiarly attractive to the zoölogical connoisseur.

Says Mr. Damon: "The finest jewels of our fairest belles can be no brighter than the natural adornments of this common mollusk. In their native element alone the scallops show to perfection all the beauties Nature has lavished upon them, especially when seen in motion. They move in a rapid zigzag fashion, and with the speed of an arrow, the propelling force being secured by the rapid opening and shutting of their valves. One can scarcely see a lovelier

Crab eating a Clam.

sight than that of a large number of these pretty creatures, with shells of every hue, from purest white to black, enlivened with shades of pink, yellow, fawn, and other tints, darting about in the clear water, up, down, here, there, everywhere. In their flight-like movements, vertical, horizontal, east, west, north, and south, they are more suggestive of a flock of winged animals than of bivalves of which to make a meal. When at last they dispose themselves to rest, sinking to the bottom for that purpose, and there remaining passive for hours at a time, they will in the aquarium, if not properly managed, come to anchor by tying themselves with their byssus to the rocks; and, if that occurs, they will entertain us no more with their lively and amusing habits."

Perhaps the most fantastic creature of all the crab tribe is the sea-spider, or decorating crab, which, according to Mr. Damon, unites the animal creation to the human, "for he has certainly one of the first instincts of civilization, namely, that of attempting to cover himself with extraneous and ornamental garments. . . . He is the dandy of the sea," continues Mr. Damon. "Bits of sea-weed are his great reliance, but small objects of almost any kind he will appropriate, even to pieces of stone or wood. One of mine showed considerable taste and an idea of style, preferring always the most gaudy colors which he could find in the tank. These animals will spend hours every day at their toilet, appropriating with their hand-like claws bits of sea-weed, *Sertularia*, sponge, or *Tubularia*. One will perhaps place a bit on the tip of his nose, or suspend from it a long ribbon-like strip of red or green algæ, or affix similar fragments to his legs, elbows, or knees, as we may call them. He does not appear to take these pieces at random, but has the air of selecting them with care, and then leisurely cutting them off from the large fronds with his own nippers, of which he has two pairs, one upon each of his two foremost arms. Having severed the desired portion, he takes it up in one of his hands (for his nippers serve for hands as well as shears), and, placing one end of it to his mouth, evidently deposits upon it a species of mucus or marine cement, which secures the object in the position in which his lordship sees fit to arrange it, and in which matter he is somewhat fastidious. This mucus must have great strength, for in his

The Decorator.

native element he will walk about thus arrayed, without any danger of his ornaments being washed away even by the rolling surf. In the tank, when his toilet is completed, he will advance to the front or most conspicuous spot he can find, and as near to the spectator as he can conveniently get, with a self-satisfied air, as much as to say: 'I'm in full dress now; how do you like my style?'"

These are but a few even of those "wonders of the shore" which Mr. Damon finds room to treat of, and of course are but an infinitesimal proportion of the five hundred thousand recognized varieties of marine animal life. As we said at the outset, however, our aim has been to furnish only hints or suggestions, and if what we have written prove sufficient to arouse intelligent curiosity, and show the way to gratify it, we shall have accomplished all we hoped for and all the reader can reasonably expect of us. Those who desire more are advised to provide themselves with Mr. Damon's handy little volume; and such as would like to prolong the pleasures

derived from their inquiries and researches are recommended to the article which appears elsewhere, entitled " A Miniature Marine Aquarium."

TROUT-FISHING.

FROM the time of old Izaak Walton and Charles Cotton until now, no pursuit or pastime in which man can engage has been the theme of such enthusiastic and appetizing writing as angling; and, by all the votaries of the art, trout-fishing is conceded to carry off the palm. If we may believe Dr. Prime, for example, there is no other way in which we can be so sure of reaching that innermost shrine where Nature utters her mysterious oracles directly to the spirit of man; and Mr. George Dawson, in expounding the "Pleasures of Angling with Rod and Reel for Trout and Salmon," finds it necessary to consider the subject in its relation to health, happiness, morals, religion, love of nature, serenity of spirit, and the like. Mr. John Burroughs, too, mingles his melodious notes with the general chorus, and devotes some of the most delightful of his ever-charming essays to enchanting us with " the legend of the wary trout."

From one of these essays (on "Speckled Trout") we shall quote a few passages which will awaken a responsive thrill in those who have had experiences and sensations kindred to those described, and which to those who are unfamiliar with the " legend " will serve to convey an idea of the fascination which it exercises and the enthusiasm which it can inspire.

"I have been a seeker of trout from my boyhood," says Mr. Burroughs, "and, on all the expeditions in which this fish has been the ostensible purpose, I have brought home more game than my creel showed. In fact, in my maturer years, I find I got more of nature into me—more of the woods, the wild, nearer to bird and beast—while threading my native streams for trout than in almost any other way. It furnished good excuse to go forth; it pitched one in the right key; it sent one through the fat and marrowy places of field and wood. Then the fisherman has a harmless, preoccupied look; he is a kind of vagrant that nothing fears. He blends himself with the trees and the shadows. All his approaches are gentle and indirect. He times himself to the meandering, soliloquizing stream; its impulse bears him along. At the foot of the waterfall he sits sequestered and hidden in its volume of sound. The birds know he has no designs upon them, and the animals see that his mind is in the creek. His enthusiasm anneals him, and makes him pliable to the scenes and influences he moves among.

"Then what acquaintance he makes with the stream! He addresses himself to it as a lover to his mistress; he woos it and stays with it till he knows its most hidden secrets; it runs through his thoughts not less than through its banks there; he feels the fret and thrust of every bar and bowlder. Where it deepens, his purpose deepens; where it is shallow, he is indifferent. He knows how to interpret its every glance and dimple; its beauty haunts him for days.

"I am sure I run no risk of overpraising the charm and attractiveness of a well-fed trout-stream, every drop of water in it as bright and pure as if the nymphs had brought it all the way from its source in crystal goblets, and as cool as if it had been hatched beneath a glacier. When the heated and soiled and jaded refugee from the city first sees one, he feels as if he would like to turn it into his bosom and let it flow through him a few hours, it suggests such healing fresh-ness and newness. How his roily thoughts would run clear! How the sediment would go down stream! Could he ever have an impure or an unwholesome wish afterward? The next best thing he can do is to tramp along its banks and surrender himself to its influence. If he reads it intently enough, he will, in a measure, be taking it into his mind and heart and experiencing its salutary ministrations. . . .

"The trout like meadows; doubtless their food is more abundant there, and usually the good hiding-places are more numerous. As soon as you strike a meadow the character of the creek changes: it goes slower and lies deeper; it tarries to enjoy the high, cool banks, and to half hide beneath them; it loves the willows, or, rather, the willows love it and shelter it from the sun; its spring-runs are kept cool by the over-hanging grass, and the heavy turf that faces its open banks is not cut away by the sharp hoof of the grazing cattle. Then there are the bobo-links and starlings and meadow larks, always in-terested spectators of the angler; there are also the marsh marigolds, the buttercups, or the spot-ted lilies, and the angler is always an interested spectator of them. In fact, the patches of mead-ow-land that lie in the angler's course are like the happy experiences in his own life, or like the fine passages in the poem he is reading: the pas-ture oftener contains the shallow and monoto-nous places. In the small streams the cattle scare the fish, and soil their element, and break down their retreats under the banks. Wood-land alternates the best with meadow: the creek loves to burrow under the roots of a great tree, to scoop out a pool after leaping over the pros-trate trunk of one, and to pause at the foot of a ledge of moss-covered rocks, with ice-cold water dripping down. How straight the current goes for the rock! Note its corrugated, muscular ap-pearance! It strikes and glances off, but accu-mulates, deepens with well-defined eddies above and to one side. On the edge of these the trout lurk and spring upon their prey.

"The angler learns that it is generally some obstacle or hindrance that makes a deep place in the creek, as in a brave life, and his ideal brook is one that lies in deep, well-defined banks, yet makes many a shift from right to left, meets with many rebuffs and adventures, hurled back upon itself by rocks, waylaid by snags and trees, tripped up by precipices, but sooner or later re-posing under meadow-banks, deepening and ed-dying beneath bridges, or prosperous and strong in some level stretch of cultivated land, with great elms shading it here and there.

"But I early learned that from almost any stream in a trout country the true angler could take trout, and that the great secret was this: That whatever bait you used—worm, grasshop-per, grub, or fly—there was one thing you must always put upon your hook, namely, your heart. When you bait your hook with your heart the fish always bite; they will jump clean from the water after it; they will dispute with each other over it; it is a morsel they love above everything else. With such bait I have seen the born angler (my grandfather was one) take a noble string of trout from the most unpromising waters and on the most unpromising day. He used his hook so coyly and tenderly, he approached the fish with such address and insinuation, he divined the exact spot where they lay; if they were not eager, he humored them and seemed to steal by them; if they were playful and coquettish, he would suit his mood to theirs; if they were frank and sincere, he met them half way; he was so patient and considerate, so entirely devoted to pleasing the critical trout, and so successful in his efforts—surely his heart was upon his hook, and it was a tender, unctuous heart, too, as that of every angler is. How nicely he would mea-sure the distance! how dexterously he would avoid an overhanging limb or brush and drop the line in exactly the right spot! Of course, there was a pulse of feeling and sympathy to the ex-tremity of that line. If your heart is of stone, however, or an empty husk, there is no use to put it upon your hook; it will not tempt the fish; the bait must be quick and fresh. Indeed, a certain quality of youth is indispensable to the successful angler; a certain unworldliness and readiness to invest yourself in an enterprise that don't pay in the current coin. Not only is the angler, like the poet, born and not made, as Walton says, but there is a deal of the poet in him, and he is to be judged no more harshly; he is the victim of his genius. Those wild streams, how they haunt him! He will play truant to dull care, and flee to them; their waters impart somewhat of their own perpetual youth to him."

That is very captivating, is it not? But it is well that the author remembers to mention before he closes that there is another side to the picture. "People inexperienced in such matters," he says, "sitting in their rooms and thinking of these things, of all the poets have sung and romancers written, are apt to get sadly taken in when they attempt to realize their dreams. They expect to enter a sylvan paradise of trout, cool retreats, laughing brooks, picturesque views, balsamic couches, etc., instead of which they find hunger, rain, smoke, toil, gnats, mosquitoes, dirt, broken rest, vulgar guides, and salt pork; and they are very apt not to see where the fun comes in. But he who goes in a right spirit will not be disappointed, and will find the taste of this kind of life better, though bitterer, than the writers have described."

This is no doubt true, but Mr. Burroughs might have added that much of the disappointment felt by beginners is due not merely to absence of the "right spirit," but to mistakes produced by their inexperience, and to ignorance of a few practical details which it is essential for a would-be angler to know, and which are rarely furnished by the rhapsodists. The more important of these practical details, therefore, we shall now proceed to furnish.

OUTFIT FOR A CAMPING EXPEDITION.

The late Bayard Taylor, than whom few can have had a wider experience, has said somewhere, in effect, that the art of traveling comfortably is dependent upon the art of limiting one's baggage; and this great truth is especially applicable to that sort of travel which is involved in camp-life and "sport." Not only are the elaborate outfits with which novices usually equip themselves a foolish waste of money, but he who takes such a one into the woods is condemning himself to an amount of toil at which a hod-carrier would rebel. Nothing is more cumbrous and difficult to pack than personal luggage of this sort, and, as guides have very distinct ideas of what they can be expected to do, the sportsman may be sure that any superfluous *impedimenta* will fall to his own share. Moreover, there is no surer sign of the "greenhorn"; and, as too obvious a greenhorn is apt to be treated as such by all whom he meets, the very outfit which has cost him so much pains and money will prove the chief drawback to his attaining the objects of his ambition.

According to those who know from long experience, the following list comprises all the "essentials" in the way of clothes that one man will need for a two months' trip in the wilderness, beyond what he wears in:

A complete undersuit of woolen or flannel, with a "change."

Stout pantaloons, vest, and coat.

A felt hat.

Two pairs of stockings (woolen).

Pair of common stout winter boots and camp shoes.

Rubber blanket or coat.

A pair of pliable buckskin gloves, with chamois-skin gauntlets tied or buttoned at the elbow.

Hunting-knife, belt, and a pint tin cup.

To these should be added a pair of warm woolen blankets, *uncut*, and a few toilet articles, such as towel, soap, etc.

The above is a good serviceable outfit, and, with the exception of the blankets, can easily be packed in a carpet-bag, which is readily stowed in a boat or carried over "portages." Of course, but a small portion of this outfit will be required by those who make their headquarters at some convenient hotel or farmhouse; but, one of the first things that a beginner learns is, that fishing worth the effort can seldom be obtained in places that are easily accessible.

TACKLE.

The following is Mr. W. H. H. Murray's advice regarding tackle:

One light single-handed fly-rod, with "flies."

In respect to "flies," do not overload your book. This is a good assortment:

Hackles, black, red, and brown, 6 each.

Avoid small hooks and imported "French flies."

Let the flies be made on hooks from Nos. 3 to 1, Limerick size.

All fancy flies discard. They are good for nothing generally, unless it be to show to your lady friends. In addition to the "Hackles,"

Canada fly (6), an excellent fly.

Green drake (6).

Red ibis (6).

Small salmon flies (6), best of all.

If in the fall of the year, take

English blue-jay (6).

Gray drake (6)—good.

Last, but not least, a large stoutly-woven landing-net.

This is enough. I know that what I say touching the salmon-flies will astonish some, but I do not hesitate to assert that with two dozen salmon-flies I should feel myself well provided for a six weeks' sojourn in the wilderness.

If you are unaccustomed to "fly-fishing" and prefer to "grub it" with ground bait (*and good sport can be had with bait-fishing, too*), get two or three dozens short-shanked, good-sized hooks, hand-tied to strong cream-colored snells, and you are well provided. If you can find worms, they make the best bait ; if not, cut out a strip from a chub, and, loading your line with shot, *yank* it along through the water some foot or more under the surface. I have had trout many times rise and take such a bait, even when *skittered* along on the top of the water. To every fly fisher my advice is, be sure and take plenty of casting-lines; have some six, others nine feet long. There are lines made out of "sea-snell." These are the best. Never select a bright, glistening gut. Always search for the creamy-looking ones.

1. Whenever you see a small stream, cold to the touch, and rippling clear over clean, smooth, or mossy stones—especially if it is near mountains or in woods—there are probably trout in it, unless they have all been fished out or otherwise destroyed. Of course, the more remote the stream is from "settlements" and the more difficult of access, the more likely it is to contain fish in abundance.

2. Always fish *down stream*, if possible.

3. The art of successful trout-fishing is, to a great extent, the art of keeping out of sight of the fish. An expert angler knows almost by instinct where to drop his hook while remaining concealed behind a bush or a rock.

4. The mistake most often made by beginners is in thinking that fish are only to be caught in holes or pools. Most brook-trout are caught in those rippling shallows where the water flows swift over barely concealed stones.

5. The trout-fisher must not be afraid of wet feet. Where the banks are difficult or afford little concealment, the best way to fish is to walk along in the stream, letting the hook run far down ahead.

6. When fishing in a party, never fish close together. Portion off the stream, and keep out of sight of each other.

7. Ordinary earth-worms (not too large) are usually the best bait. Put plenty on the hook, and as soon as the bait looks ragged or whitish take it off and put on fresh. The eye of a freshly-caught fish is good bait ; better still is the anal fin ; best of all (especially for large fish) are the little bullheads or darts (an inch and a half or two inches long) found in clear, still shallows. When none of these are obtainable, a bit of bacon, or bread, or white cotton will often answer.

8. Trout are as whimsical and coquettish as young ladies. At times they will bite anything as rapidly as it is offered. Again for hours or days together, nothing can induce them to bite. When reluctant, try them with different kinds of flies and bait. Sometimes they will accept one lure when nothing else seems to tempt them.

9. In small brooks, the best time to fish is just when the water is running clear after a good, hard, or long rain.

10. The best time of day to fish is usually in the early morning or forenoon. After dusk trout can seldom be induced to bite.

11. The smallness of a stream need not discourage. Any water deep enough to conceal a hook is deep enough to contain trout.

12. Small fish afford less sport in the catching than large ones, but those about six to eight inches long are perhaps the best eating of all.

13. In trout-fishing, as in all other fishing, patience and quiet are the supreme requirements.

BIRD-SHOOTING ON THE COAST OF NEW JERSEY.

THE entire ocean-front of New Jersey, from Sandy Hook to its corresponding point known as Cape May, is made up of long lines of sandy deposits, occasionally broken by inlets, and diversified by bays and lagoons, presenting a strange, and at first sight repulsive, combination of shallows and bars, mingling in interminable confusion. The water sometimes becomes confined in small harbors, into which empty miniature rivers, some of the largest of which afford tolerable navigation for boats of very small proportions. Against this low, broken coast the surf of the stormy Atlantic, even on the calmest days, beats with inquietude, and, when the storm rages, the angry waves plunge spitefully into the low banks, twisting the sand-heaps into every variety of form, and, in a night, in the wantonness of its power, often changing the very face of the landscape.

In the "olden times" the lighthouses, placed here and there along the "desolation," were not supposed to be erected to welcome the homeward-bound vessel to a safe anchorage, but to announce *danger*, for there was no hospitality to ships at Absecum or Barnegat.

The lands in the vicinity have apparently but little soil worth cultivation ; there are spots to be occasionally met with, which, by an inundation of "moss-bunkers" and "horseshoes," change from aridity to suggestive loam ; but, when the fertilizing qualities of these "queer fish" escape in fetid gas, or disappear through the bottomless sand, the fitful dream of vegetation vanishes away. Then assumes again the supremacy of salt-ribbed grass, which is not only valueless to man or quadruped, but even defies the nippers and untiring industry of the fiddler-crab.

But with time there has been found a charm about these waste places which makes them, to the constantly increasing populations which gravitate in and around our great metropolis, a haven

Bird-Shooting in Absecum Creek, New Jersey.

of never-ending consolation. The strong, untiring arms of steam have almost robbed the coast of much of its marine terrors, while the jutting banks of sand are being crowded with costly residences. Taste and fashion have carried their votaries down to these surf-beaten shores, that they, the votaries, may be invigorated with the fresh, life-inspiring breezes which come across the sea. The surf, which was formerly the harbinger of evil, is now the nursery of health; while the repulsive coast, in addition, is found to be the center of "feeding-grounds" which attract the inexhaustible wealth of the ocean, and the lagoons and sluggish streams are alive with every variety of feathered aquatic game that tempt the appetite and encourage manly sports.

While the seacoast of New Jersey has become known to the fashionable world within a comparatively recent date, the country in its isolated condition was, and has been for scores of years, the center of a primitive people, who have lived pleasantly and thrived abundantly; who, without being sailors, are pretty good seamen, and, without being husbandmen, glean treasures from the earth—a kind of amphibious humanity, almost as much at home on dry land as its representatives are on the water. These primitive people find a paying business in furnishing New York City and much of the outside world with fish, are kind and hospitable, and not given to the indulgence in conventionalities which are considered so essential where more artificial manners prevail.

The amateur and accomplished sportsmen have alike an admirable field for their pursuits on this southern Jersey coast; independent of the unsurpassed fishing, the number of aquatic birds, which visit the vicinity each successive month of the passing summer and fall, is almost beyond calculation. Hence it is that the true Nimrod finds no difficulty, in company with his well-trained setter, in selecting his field and his game, and, sauntering away from the busy crowd, he indulges his love for Nature and gratifies his ambition for sport, by finding the reward of his

Curlew-Shooting.

labors at nightfall to be a well-filled bag, each individual specimen contained therein suggesting some reminiscence of a good shot, or of an unexpected trait of sagacity in his faithful hunting-companion, his dog.

The tyro who, pent up in the city the long year, very sensibly rushes into the wilds we speak of to spend his short vacation from business, and who knows little of the practical use of the gun, finds no difficulty, after he has overloaded his weapon with powder and shot, in bringing down innumerable victims to his prowess, for fortune most frequently favors him with the privilege of firing into great flocks of curlews, snipe, or meadow-larks. To this excitement is added the novelty of threading the creeks and watercourses in some primitive skiff, or dug-out, the awkwardness of their construction and diffi-

culty of their management adding relish to the expedition.

Among the few birds which are abundant in summer, the snipe is the most delicious to eat, and most individualized in its peculiarities, and so easily approached, if any attention is paid to its habits, that the sportsman must be most indifferent who fails to meet with some success. The red-breasted snipe, which is a favorite with amateurs, because less wary than other shore-birds, come in flocks, and settle upon the mud-flats and sand-bars, and soon become so engaged in the business of procuring food, that they will often allow a boat to approach sufficiently near to give its occupants an opportunity to fire with destructive effect. Yet, for all this easy killing of the game we speak of, "a crack snipe-shot," that is, a person who will take them singly and successfully, is good against all other birds. The curlew is also a favorite, and combines in its capture some of the excitement attending the chase after fish. With a favorable breeze, to send the well-trimmed boat over the bay, and the curlews plentiful enough to be brought within gunshot, hours of enjoyment are obtained that leave pleasant reminiscences for the remainder of one's life. If hunted in the lagoons and marshes, they are exceedingly shy, and difficult to approach; but, if a curlew happens to be wounded, its screams of pain and for succor will bring its companions to its rescue, and their devotion under these circumstances is often the cause of their untimely death.

After Reed-Birds.

The meadow-larks, which we naturally associate with the high and dry fields, find attractions in the barren places of New Jersey, and, along with that traditional glutton of rice and other farinaceous seeds, the reed-bird, make the vicinity of their temporary homes musical with their sweet notes, and afford most animated sport.

Common to all regions filled with game, there is the hunter, who, regardless of the healthful excitement and the unfoldings of the secrets of Nature enjoyed by the refined and cultivated sportsmen, makes the pursuit one of business, and to whose unsentimental industry the people of our cities are indebted for so much palatable food. These men are generally possessed of good-nature, are quiet, and fond of being alone. They work hard, and are satisfied with moderate gains. They are great favorites with "hunters," who exhaust their energies in talking about the pleasures of wading through the swamps, plunging across mud-banks, fighting mosquitoes, and shooting on the wing, when in search of game, but who really have no other actual ambition than to waste their time in idleness, in their hearts the while

Shooting Robin-breasted Snipe.

Meadow-Larks near Tuckerton.

laughing to scorn the enthusiast who works all day for game that, they say, can be bought for a song. Let one of these idlers come suddenly upon a "pot-hunter" at work in the woods, who will dispose of the fruits of his industry for moderate reward in money, and you will witness the next hour an addition to the "settlement" of "a knowing one," who, overborne with game, will, for long hours, grow eloquent over his extraordinary experiences, accidents, and escapes, suffered by him while securing the contents of his well-filled bag.

The country-store, dignified with the possession of the post-office, in these amphibious towns, is the true center of gossip—set up in some old-fashioned building erected in part of pine scantling and the wrecked pieces of stranded ships, while the cozy manner the goods are all stored away is highly suggestive of the economy of space so observable in the cabin of an Albany sloop. Salt and silks, tenpenny nails and gay calico, sweet crackers and pickles, tacks and nutmegs, sugar and carbolic soap, all mingle in general confusion. Here are carried on traffic and gossip, and the successful magnate, who has suddenly filled his pockets to overflowing by some unusual luck in catching sheepshead or Spanish mackerel, will spend his money with the most gentlemanly disregard of economy, and gossip for hours, stretched on a pile of merchandise or the counter, so that the corroding effect of saline fogs and salt-water on jeans, satinets, and cowhide boots, may be conveniently studied by the casual customer.

The "old inhabitants" of this Jersey coast take great pride in their

The Hunter.

locality, which is often illustrated in very characteristic ways. It was at one of these country-store gatherings that a learned cockney from New York attempted a general lecture on the voracity of animals of the feline species, more especially of the tiger-kind. A representative of Barnegat beach, who was present, listened a while with unconcealed impatience, and finally broke forth after the following fashion :

" Thar's no use to talk to me about them tigers for fighting and biting; they ain't anything that may be compared to a well-grown blue-fish. He's an animal, if he hasn't got claws, that can whip anything of his size, and something over. In fact, a regular blue-fish is a natural enemy of every fish not superior to him in size, and goes about, as Satan does in Scripture, seeking whom he may

The Knowing One.

devour. Nothing swallowable comes amiss to him. He gorges himself with bits of sea-weed and junk-bottles, and then gobbles up clam-shells and gravel-stones to aid his digestion. The tiger is nothing to a blue-fish, in t'aring things to pieces. Why, a shoal of moss-bunkers or porgies, disporting in the sea, will be cut to shreds in no time by a dozen blue-fish. He's clipper-built, he is ; and, when doing his work, will spring at his fodder, dash around it like a mad cat, and, in a few seconds, kill, waste, and devour more than his own weight, driving every living thing from the vicinity but the tautog—that black rascal having sense enough to hide away in sand-holes and under the rocks until the yarthquate is over. And when the blue-fish has got a surfeit, and you would suppose you couldn't drive a point of a knife into his body with a hammer, he will dash at a bone bait, seize it, and, when you haul him up, he will

give you a few nabs at your hands and legs, just to let you know that his appetite is insatiable even in death. Talk about tigers! what are they for fighting and eating, to a clipper-built blue-fish ? "

The game pursued is, for the most part, not native to these shores, visiting the coast only as annual trysting-places. and hence can scarcely be exterminated. Each year it comes in abundance, and hence hunting and fishing must remain a permanent attraction of these sandy shallows. Absecum Creek and Beach, the scene of our illustrations, are near Atlantic City, in the county of the same name. They may be reached from New York by the New Jersey Southern Railway to Atco, thence by the Camden and Atlantic road, or from Philadelphia direct by the latter route.

AIR-PAINTING.

" I HAVE seen a gallery of many pictures," said one who had been sitting on the sea-shore watching the sunset. There had been fleeting clouds, ships that came and went, and varying skies that now shrouded the scene in gray, now flooded it with yellow or rosy tints ; and the sails of the vessels, as they continually formed into new groups, at one moment became superb foci of light, at another shadowy phantoms. Those who have eyes to see need not go in search of new landscapes ; there is always a succession of changes coming to him if he will but attentively watch the gallery that Nature keeps always open to those who can see. One of our best landscape-painters declares that landscape-painting is *air-painting* ; that a veil hangs over every scene, which is different at different times, and it is this veil, this medium of atmosphere, that gives to every picture its true quality. " One day," he says, " we go out in the morning, and, looking up and down the street, take no note of the sight ; we are not impressed ; but another day there is a slight change in the density or clarity of the atmosphere, and lo! what before was a commonplace view has become extremely beautiful. It is the change in the air that has made the change in the object." There ought to be a great deal of philosophical comfort in this theory to all who have to stay at home. Every one has observed how a distant mountain changes its aspect during different hours of the day, and noted similar transformations on the sea ; but few, perhaps, have fully realized how every view, however apparently ordinary in character, has its succession of changes ; how completely it proves to the studious observer an ever-varying gallery of pictures, each of which has its peculiar quality and its subtile beauty.

WITH rhythmic chime
  Our oars keep time
Adown the rapid river;
  On groves of balm
  And bays of calm
The hues of sunset quiver.

  Oh, glad the song
  That lilts along
From hearts so fondly yearning!
  For them afar
  Night's fairest star—
The lamp of home is burning!

  And sweet the thrill
  Of hearts that still
Await night's radiant cover,
  That lips may press
  In tenderness
Their weary, hunter lover!

  All day we clove
  Past isle and cove,
And pine-trees' fringy branches,
  And where the stream
  Danced, all agleam
With foamy avalanches!

'Neath rocky steep
Where mirrored deep
Were caverns black and glossy,
And we have dipped
Our oars, and slipped
By meadows mild and mossy.

But shadows fall,
Night covers all,
And we are landward going;
Our toils are past:
Give way! and fast
Now, comrades, be our rowing!

Oh, day may fail,
And night may pale,
And stars may one by one set;
But lights of home,
Howe'er we roam,
Burn brighter at the sunset!

GEORGE COOPER.

A MINIATURE MARINE AQUA-RIUM.

IN his charming little volume, "Glaucus, or the Wonders of the Shore," the late Charles Kingsley gives the following practical directions for forming an "aquarium," such as the least ambitious can put in practice, and which any one can derive pleasure from possessing:

"Buy at any glass-shop a cylindrical glass jar, some six inches in diameter and ten high; wash it clean, and fill it with clean salt water, dipped out of any pool among the rocks, only looking first to see that there is no dead fish or other evil matter in the said pool, and that no stream from the land runs into it. If you choose to take the trouble to dip up the water over a boat's side, so much the better.

"So much for your vase; now to stock it.

"Go down at low spring-tide to the nearest ledge of rocks, and with a hammer and chisel chip off a few pieces of stone covered with growing sea-weed. Avoid the common and coarser kinds which cover the surface of the rocks, for they give out under water a slime which will foul your tank; but choose the more delicate species which fringe the edges of every pool at low-water mark: the pink coralline, the dark-purple ragged dulse (*Rhodymenia*), the Carrageen moss (*Chondrus*), and above all, the commonest of all, the delicate green ulva, which you will see growing everywhere in wrinkled, fan-shaped sheets, as thin as the finest silver-paper. The smallest bits of stone are sufficient, provided the sea-

weeds have hold of them; for they have no real roots, but adhere by a small disk, deriving no nourishment from the rock, but only from the water. Take care, meanwhile, that there is as little as possible on the stone, besides the weed itself. Especially scrape off any small sponges, and see that no worms have made their twining tubes of sand among the weed-stems; if they have, drag them out; for they will surely die, and as surely spoil all by sulphuretted hydrogen, blackness, and evil smells.

"Put your weeds into your tank and settle them at the bottom, which last, some say, should be covered with a layer of pebbles; but let the beginner leave it as bare as possible, for the pebbles only tempt cross-grained annelids to crawl under them, die, and spoil all by decaying; whereas if the bottom of the vase is bare you can see a sickly or dead inhabitant at once, and take him out (which you must do) instantly. Let your weeds stand quietly in the vase a day or two before you put in any live animals, and even then do not put any in if the water does not appear perfectly clear; but lift out the weeds, and renew the water ere you replace them.

"Now for the live-stock: In the crannies of every rock you will find sea-anemones (*Actiniæ*); and a dozen of these only will be enough to convert your little vase into the most brilliant of living flower-gardens. There they hang upon the under side of the ledges, apparently mere rounded lumps of jelly; one is of dark purple, dotted with green; another of a rich chocolate; another of a delicate olive; another, sienna-yellow; another, all but white. Take them from their rock; you can do it easily by slipping under them your finger-nail, or the edge of a pewter spoon. Take care to tear the sucking base as little as possible (though a small rent they will darn for themselves in a few days, easily enough), and drop them into a basket of wet sea-weed; when you get home turn them into a dish full of water and leave them for the night, and go to look at them to-morrow. What a change! The dull lumps of jelly have taken root and flowered during the night, and your dish is filled from side to side with a bouquet of *chrysanthemums;* each has expanded into a hundred-petaled flower, crimson, pink, purple, or orange; touch one, and it shrinks together like a sensitive-plant, displaying at the root of the petals a ring of brilliant turquoise beads. That is the commonest of all the Actiniæ (*Mesembryanthemum*); you may have him when and where you will. But, if you will search those rocks somewhat closer, you will find even more gorgeous species than he. See in that pool some dozen large ones, in full bloom, and quite six inches across, some of them! If their cousins, whom we found just now, were like *chrysanthemums*, these are like quilled dahlias; their arms are stouter and shorter in proportion than those of the last species, but their color is equally brilliant. One is a brilliant blood-red; another, a delicate sea-blue, striped with pink; but most have the disk and the innumerable arms striped and ringed with various shades of gray and brown. Shall we get them? By all means, if we can. Touch one. Where is he now? Gone!

Marine Tank, Front View.

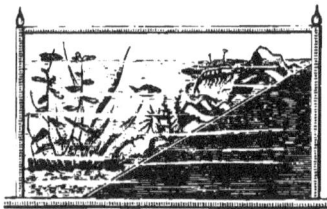

Marine Tank, Side View.

Vanished into air or into stone? Not quite. You see that knot of sand and broken shell lying on the rock where your dahlia was one moment ago. Touch it, and you will find it leathery and elastic. That is all which remains of the live dahlia. Never mind; get your finger into the crack under him, work him gently but firmly out, and take him home, and he will be as happy and as gorgeous as ever to-morrow.

"Let your Actiniæ stand for a day or two in the dish, and then, picking out the liveliest and handsomest, detach them once more from their hold, drop them into your vase, right them with a bit of stick, so that the sucking base is downward, and leave them to themselves thenceforth. . . .

"But you will want more than these anemones, both for your own amusement and for the health of your tank. Microscopic animals will breed, and will also die; and you need for them a scavenger. Turn, then, a few stones which lie piled on each other at extreme low-water mark, and five minutes' search will give you the very animal you want, a little crab, of a dingy russet above, and on the inner side like smooth porcelain. His back is quite flat, and so are his large, angular fringed claws, which, when he folds them up, lie in the same plane with his shell, and fit neatly into its edges. Compact little rogue that he is, made especially for sidling in and out of cracks and crannies, he carries with him such an apparatus of combs and brushes as Isidor or Floris never dreamed of; with which he sweeps out of the sea-water at every moment shoals of minute animalcules, and sucks them into his tiny mouth.

"Next, your sea-weeds, if they thrive as they ought to do, will sow their minute spores in millions around them; and these, as they vegetate, will form a green film on the inside of the glass, spoiling your prospect; you may rub it off for yourself, if you will, with a rag fastened to a stick; but, if you wish at once to save yourself trouble, and to see how all emergencies in nature are provided for, you will set three or four live shells to do it for you, and to keep your subaqueous lawn close mown.

"That last word is no figure of speech. Look among the beds of sea-weed for a few of the bright yellow or green sea-snails (*Nerita*), or Conical Tops (*Trochus*), especially those mottled pink one spotted with brown, which you are sure to find about shaded rock-ledges at dead low tide, and put them in your aquarium. For the present they will only nibble the green ulvæ; but, when the film of young weed begins to form, you will see it mown off every morning as fast as it grows, in little semicircular sweeps, just as if a fairy's scythe had been at work during the night. And a scythe has been at work; none other than the tongue of the little shell-fish.

"A prawn or two, and a few minute star-fish, will make your aquarium complete; though you add to it endlessly, as one glance at the salt-water tanks of the Zoölogical Gardens, and the strange and beautiful forms which they contain, will prove to you sufficiently."

The author then goes on to explain that there are two more enemies to guard against—dust and heat. If the surface of the water becomes clogged with dust, aëration can not take place, and the animals will die. The best way to prevent this is to stir the surface of the water occasionally, or tie a piece of muslin over the mouth, or simply lay a sheet of brown paper over it. This last is best of all, perhaps, because its shade also protects against the next great evil, heat. If the vase is left in a sunny window long enough for the water to become tepid all is over with your pets, and half an hour's exposure may frustrate the care of weeks. And yet, on the other hand, light must be abundant, or the sea-weeds will neither thrive nor keep the water sweet. Choose, therefore, a south or east window, but draw down the blind, or throw a handkerchief over all if the heat becomes fierce. The water should always feel cold to your hand, let the temperature outside be what it may.

Next, you must make up for evaporation by adding a little *fresh* water, as often as you find the water in the vase sinking below its original level. Otherwise the water would soon become too salt, for the salts, remember, do not evaporate with the water.

Where, from any cause, the water has become spoiled, and fresh sea-water is not procurable, the following formula (Mr. Gosse's) may be used for making artificial sea-water:

	Parts.
Common table-salt...	81
Epsom salts	7
Chloride of magnesium	10
Chloride of potassium	2
Total	100

One pound of this mixture carefully dissolved in water, and then filtered, will make about three gallons of sea-water.

For those who would like something a little less primitive than the glass jar, a marine tank, such as that shown in the cuts, will answer admirably, and make a very beautiful display. The front is of glass, the back and two ends are of marble, slate, or well-seasoned wood, and the bottom is an inclined plane rising from the lower corner in front to above the water-level behind. The purpose of the sloping bottom is to afford the anemones, etc., which move seldom and slowly, to approach the surface and recede from it at pleasure. The bottom may be covered to the depth of an inch or two with sand and gravel, and rocks and shells may be arranged on the slope above. In selecting and arranging the plants and animals the suggestions given above will apply. The animals should be fed twice a week with finely cut fresh mussels, oysters, or raw beef; and, in the case of mollusks, actiniæ, etc., etc., food should be placed within reach by means of a small glass rod. When the supply of oxygen is deficient the fishes approach the surface often to breathe.

HOW TO MAKE AN HERBARIUM.

THE first thing to do is to collect the plants. They should be carefully dug up with a trowel, so as to preserve the root intact, as, to form a good specimen, it is necessary to have the root, leaves, flowers, and fruit. It also adds to the value of a specimen if the seedling is shown, the autumn tint of the leaves; if a parasite, the plant on which it grows, etc. When going on a collecting expedition, it is a good plan to carry a few sheets of newspaper in a portfolio, and to place the plants flat between the pages as soon as they are dug up. If this is not convenient, they will keep fresh for some time if placed in a tin case or vasculum. To dry them, the surest way is, to lay them between a good many sheets of blotting or newspaper, with a board at the top and bottom of the pile, and a heavy weight placed on the top of all. Change the papers every two or three days, and take care to keep the plants quite flat and with a good many sheets of paper between them, or the thick stems will crumple and bend the thinner ones. The sheets of paper on which to mount the plants must be rather stout and of a uniform size—16¼ inches by 10½ inches is a useful size; but of course this must depend on the taste of the collector. Botanists differ very much as to the best method of attaching the specimens to the paper. Some attach them by means of strips of paper secured with pins, others gum or glue the specimens, others fasten them with gummed straps of paper, or sew them with a needle and thread to the paper. The best plan, however, is to combine the last three methods, and to secure plants of a medium size, such as the buttercup, with narrow gummed strips of paper; thick, woody plants, such as the oak, with glue; and such delicate plants as ferns and grasses should be tacked to the paper by means of a needle and thread as much the color of the specimen as possible. Weak gum may be used for the large petals of flowers, and for large flat leaves; but when it is used the plants must be again laid under heavy pressure to dry, or they will shrivel. The plan followed in foreign herbaria is to lay the plants between a double sheet of paper, without fastening them to the paper at all. When managed in this way they are more easily examined; but the great disadvantage of this plan is that both the plants and their labels are very apt to become inserted in the wrong sheets among specimens of totally different species.

When fastening the plants to the paper they should not all be arranged precisely in the center of the page, but should be fastened more at the sides, otherwise, when the plants are laid one above the other, the packet will not be nearly flat, but will be higher in the middle than at the sides. With regard to the names of the plants, they may either be written on the sheet itself or on printed labels sold for the purpose. If the herbarium is to be an aid to the study of botany, and not a mere ornamental collection of gayly tinted plants and flowers, it will be found very convenient to inclose a flower, fruit, bud, etc., of the plant in a little envelope fastened at one corner of the paper, so as to avoid touching the rest of the plant for the purpose of examination. These little envelopes may be made on the same plan as those used by tradesmen to inclose change, or may simply consist of a piece of paper folded so as to form a small flat case, similar to those in which seedsmen inclose seeds, and druggists powders, etc. The labels must contain a brief history of the plant, thus: its technical and common names, habitat, by whom collected, where and when, and the order to which it belongs. After the plants have been fastened down and labeled, the next thing is to poison them, or the insects will soon find them out, and it will be observed that they show their good taste by feeding solely on juicy, succulent plants, scarcely ever touching the dry, sticky plants. The best poison for this purpose consists of one pound each of corrosive sublimate and carbolic acid to four gallons of methylated spirits. The great drawback to the preparation is its disagreeable smell. The plants are simply painted with it after or before fastening down; if it is done before, they require to be pressed while the poison is drying. The best way of preserving the color of flowers is to dry them quickly, either by placing them between sheets of paper, tying them together firmly, and drying them near a hot fire, by laying them among dry sand, or by pressing them with a warm flat-iron. This is an excellent plan, but great care must be taken not to have the iron too hot, or the plants will become brittle. No varnishing is requisite in forming an herbarium; if the plants are properly dried and stuck down they look better without it. When the plants have all been duly affixed to their respective sheets and labeled, they are ready to be placed in covers, so as to be handy for reference. Each genus should have a separate cover, which should be of stouter paper than that on which the plants are mounted. The name of the genus should be written distinctly in the bottom right-hand corner.

ABOUT FISHING:

TROUT-FISHING, BASS-FISHING, BLUE-FISHING, SALMON-FISHING, COD-FISHING.

BY BARNET PHILLIPS.

AS a grand center, whence a fisherman can enjoy all the delights of sport, New York has few equals. Good angling may be found not only within an hour of him, but, if he has time and means, in half a day, or at most two days, he can cast his line amid the trout in almost a primeval country. If he wishes to fish in his own country, the streams and lakes are countless. If he has the impulse to seek nobler game, such as the salmon, the Restigouche and other Canadian or Provincial streams are almost as near to New York as Quebec. If not inclined to fresh-water angling, and he be desirous of sea-fishing, he can find, not fifteen miles from New York, in ordinary seasons all the sport and amusement he requires. The writer of this has often been in doubt, through pure *embarras de richesse*, whether he would catch a striped bass or a bluefish, as both were possible within three hours' journey from his house in New York.

To define what are game-fish is somewhat difficult. Those fish which are handsome to look upon, which take hold vigorously, which require skill to capture, which resist and show fight, are called game-fish. A trout or a salmon is considered as representing the type of the game-fish; a sucker or an eel the opposite. There is one fish —the pike, pickerel, or the muscalonge—whose title to the nobility of a game-fish has been de- nied. Still, Professor Goode classes them among the game-fish of America. Those who argue against the gameness of the whole *Esox* family will tell you, and quite rightly: "The muscalonge is a craven fish. Yes, he will strike with vigor of a shark; but, once you have him on your squid, he gives up like a whipped hound. It is nothing more than to haul him in hand over hand. He shows no fight. He is dead beat at once." A game-fish is, then, one which requires especially skill and judgment in the catching of it. Looking at the matter philosophically, it rather speaks to the credit of the fisherman than otherwise that he should make these distinctions. The mere pleasure of catching fish might be accomplished by means of a fish-weir, if quantity alone were desirable. It is, then, the pleasure an angler feels in overcoming the wiles of the fish which enhances the character of his sport. Game-fish, in order that they should be caught, have called forth the ingenuity of the rod-maker. Man's inventive faculty, the possibility to devise tools which will accomplish his purpose, have necessarily been combined with personal dexterity. There has been just as much care bestowed upon a modern trout-rod to-day as on a Stradivarius violin in the seventeenth century. To accomplish the greatest amount of work with the lightest material and with the most elegant form of rod, has been the happy fortune of the American angler in 1880. It is a bold and sweeping remark, but English rods are not so good as American ones. They make no pretensions to elegance. They are dreadfully heavy, without any gain of strength. The modifications they have undergone, quite notable ones during the last eight years only, are merely such changes as were made by our best rod-manufacturers in 1865, and abandoned in 1870. We work through our rough streams, both in the United States and in Canada, with our delicate rods, and are prepared to catch and land bigger fish, from a trout to a salmon, than are to be found in England, Ireland, Wales, and Scotland. Our tackle is lighter, stronger, and better adapted to the work. As to our flies, the best English lures, those of their crack makers, are not a whit more perfect than ours. As to variety, we manufacture ten different kinds to their one. Here before me is a book of English flies, just imported. It is true, duty and all, they are a trifle cheaper than ours. But here the comparison ends. These English flies are dreadfully solid, too compact. If I used two of them, I could not, I think, throw them either lightly or well. Now, I may or may not be an adept in such things; but here is a fly which is handsome enough, and has not exactly that beefy, ponderous look which most English things possess. Here is my little test-piece of leather. I slip the bit of morocco (it has a slit cut in it) over the knob of a door in my room.

Bass-Fishing in Rapids at Hell-Gate.

I am lucky enough to be working in a fairly large room. I make a short cast from my six-and-a-half-ounce rod, and strike my leather at the second trial. I give a slight jerk, and out come all my pretty feathers and the hook, too. I have not struck harder than if I had hooked a two-pound trout. Then I remember the wail that Mr. Froude sent up some months ago, when he wrote a charming bit of history about the Russel family and fly-fishing. Though England might all be going wrong, his greatest complaint was just then in regard to the bad workmanship of the English fly-maker, and how his (Froude's) heart was broken almost when he lost fish after fish, because his flies were poorly tied and fashioned.

There can be no positive rule about the weight of rods. A rod is like the woman a man lives with, he must find one to suit himself. A rod is something on a par with a gun, and weight has to be considered, with only this difference, that you can see your bird and not your fish. You might be taking leisurely enough one-pound fish in an Adirondack lake, and your feather-weight rod would respond admirably to the slight strain put on it, when lo! the grandfather of the Salmonus, a five-pound fish, might fancy your fly. Then, if your rod be not perfect in material and make, you have a splintered joint, a broken rod, and your day's sport is marred by the loss of the crack trout of the season. Putting expensive rods in the hands of younglings is often a mistake, and accidents happen; but, supposing a father, with the angling instinct, is sire to a son with the same fancies, a first-class rod does no

harm. It teaches a lad early to be deft and handy; and I have found that, though my boys will dog-ear some of their best books, and mine

Trolling for Blue-fish.

too, as for that, their fine rods, after two or three years of work, are almost in as good order as when on a certain Christmas they were presented to them.

With April trout-fishing commences. The proximity of the fishing-grounds to New York has been commented upon. All along Long Island there are fairish fishing brooks and creeks, belonging, however, to private persons. Clubs composed of gentlemen with angling proclivities frequent these grounds. We may state that fishing here is generally poor. It is quite wanting in *couleur local*. Fish are small. A one-pound fish is a marvel. This year one fine fish, said to have been a four-pounder, was caught; but this is unusual. These creeks owe their fish mostly to the efforts of the fish culturists. It may not be exactly like a *battue*, for the fish are not plenty enough for that, but still it is a tame affair. If the season happens to be a cold one, and thin ice in the streams, the sport is only disagreeable, without any of the pleasurable excitement one finds in the wild woods. It may be considered as rather the *réunion* of gentlemen who have got very tired of a winter passed at the clubs, and who leave their counters at the whist-table for a day or so, to play with the fish in the brooks.

Any one, who has fished but during the brief

holiday of a week in some of those unknown streams in the Adirondacks which flow between the Raquette and the Upper Saranac, would prefer one hour there to a month on Massapiqua Pond in Long Island. There, in those wild north woods, there is perfect freedom. The last splotch of ink that has sullied your hand has been washed out, scrubbed away, as you plunged your hands in the silver white sands that border these wild streams. It is up at daybreak with Bill Hartly, the guide. You carry your canoe one mile (you think it ten), and launch her in some quiet blue water, all silent save for the flutter of some far-distant flock of wild ducks. Bill (he was always a skeptic) looks askance at your seven-ounce rod, and slowly whistles. "He don't keer about fishing, but is just going to see you try it on with that 'ere straw-stalk of yourn." He paddles out through the water-lilies, and is so clever at it that he makes no ripple. "I've seed a big one around here. Just you cast from thar toward the shore." You have taken a dull fly—a Quaker-gray wound with honey-yellow hackles with just a smatter of oriole blue—only one—and you swing out the line. It is a fair cast, though fully three yards farther than you wanted to flirt it. You are a little excited, and have used just a shade too much exertion. Well, let it go! You trip the fly toward you. The water is so sweet and calm that, as your fly skips along, great oval swells of water with their circular films are formed, and cross one another. Ha! There is just a little boiling up there. Can it be? Up starts a livid bit of gold and silver: you raise your hand just a shade, but he will not be fooled. He follows, vaults four inches full out of the water, and takes the fly, and away he is. You let him have his way. It is your first fish, and you must get him. The reel is spinning as he tries to bolt for the water-lilies a hundred yards off. You stop him, but not too suddenly. He shakes to right now, then to left. But line and leader, rod and reel are sound, and so are you. In he comes, inch by inch. Bill smiles, and says, "Not a big one; but he is a handsome fish." You say, "Pound and a half?" as Bill puts a landing-net under him, and Bill nods his head. You cast again, and in fifteen minutes you have four more fish, all smaller ones. It is a pleasant beginning. Your wife and party are at some farmhouse, ten miles away, and you will send the fish to her, and they will arrive by nightfall. You count on thirty fish at least. You cast, and cast, and there is not another fish. As the day brightens, you try other flies. You fish for two hours more, and have nothing. Bill is asleep, for the canoe is anchored. It is monotonous. You pull up the stone, and let the canoe drift. You get near the shore, just a good long cast to the edge of the lake. You silently drop the anchor, you take a fresh fly; it is done with deliberation. You have seen General Hooker—you remember him? Here is a fly called after that brave old fellow. It is green, with faint-yellow reflections, and a dash of red, and a shading of ruffed grouse. It is a trifle large, you think, still it looks tempting. One wing of the fly is a little crumpled; you moisten your finger between your lips, and smooth it, and think of the boy's luck, and wonder how much saliva has to do with it. You look close at your reel. It is all right. It is a big cast to make. Now, Seth Green has taught you a trick, but not in a canoe. You gather yourself up, and try to throw so as not to rock the canoe and throw yourself out, nor to wake up Bill, who walked twenty-five miles last night to meet you. You have done it well. The rod responds like a bow, and out flows the line as cleverly as if you were a Japanese prestidigitator playing with his ribbons. It does fall just about where you want it. Bill is snoring, and is happy. Along dances the fly. There is now a gentle breeze, which comes soughing through the great, gaunt fir-trees. There is air enough to belly out your line. It works itself, the fly tripping along from crest to crest. You let out more line. You have a very—very long line, and you judge that half of it is out. If

Salmon-fishing in Canada.

the wind keeps on, in five minutes you will be in the spatter-docks. Well, time enough, then. Whist! You can see a little blue swell, heaving up of the water. A fish—a fish! Not greedy, but watchful. Let the fly sail on. It may tantalize him, so that he may clutch it yet.

In a minute more you will be fouled. Well, let us run the chances. But the wind dies out, and, as you lift the rod ever so lightly, the fly comes in. He has struck. It is not a vicious lunge, rather an unguarded snap, but he smarts with the hook. He is an old fellow, up to all kinds of dodges; has lived there about those reeds for years, and will play you a trick. That he is a big one you are sure. You never can let him have all that line. He is mad now, and you have to hold him. You have been dancing in that boat, and Bill wakes, sees the situation at once, and takes to the paddles. "A whacker!" says Bill, sententiously. "Take the canoe in not more than three lengths, and hold her there!" you cry. Working on the reel slowly, cautiously, you get nearer to him. Now he is for the weeds again; fortunately he don't jerk, but pulls steady like a horse. He finds it is of no use, so he suddenly darts to the right, slanting off for the shore. He comes so fast that, with a little slant upward (when you check him to the left of the boat), you see a superb head and a bit of the dorsal fin. Now he sulks, getting his wind, and Bill looks slightingly at the rod, which is quivering in your hand: "It's a baby thing, nary good." "It is the best rod in the world, and I will get that fish," you cry angrily, for your blood is up. He zigzags, but has given up his bolts toward shore. You will have your hands full for a half-hour. The line twangs at times, and, as he stops fighting, just as suddenly is limp again. He must be kept tight hauled all the time. Though he is dogged still, you rule his destinies. Bill is all excitement, and has been fingering the landing-net for some time. At last, when you have him only a canoe-length distance from you, there comes the final combat. He has been saving himself for this. Nothing but a good rod, taxed to its utmost capacity, could have saved that fish. It fairly buckles as the fish tries to get under and past the canoe. If he does that, you are gone. Give him all the butt you can, and hold so tight, that the wrapping on the last joint of bamboo splint marks the palm of the hand. He is stopped, and is docile, lamb-like now. Bill has the anchor up, and paddles along now slowly, but it is not necessary. "Bully rod, mister," he says, "and I wouldn't have believed it." "And nothing about the fisherman?" you ask. "It's the rod," says Bill. The trout is yours. He comes up slowly, quite exhausted. Bill can almost put his fingers in his gills, but he has him in the landing-net. "He is five pounds full, and the biggest fish of this year!" cries Bill. "Five pounds? He is six! Here, Bill, in that coat, left-hand pocket, is a spring balance: weigh that beauty." "Most five and a half pounds," cries Bill. This is fishing—only a page taken from a book kept of

such exploits, more to note excellence of rod than with any attempt to extol personal skill.

Trout-fishing has its delights, but hardly less so are those of bass-fishing. I can speak of the pleasures of striped-bass fishing off Newport, though of late all good places have been so pre-empted that it is difficult to get a locality for love or money. It is the noblest of American sports, and the most exciting, requiring great skill—I think even greater skill than for the salmon. You want for the *Roccus lineatus* the best of rods, but not a delicate one—not a rapier, nor exactly a broadsword. About an eight-foot rod is ample. It must be fairly stiff, capable of standing a great strain, with a line of fully four hundred feet in length. Every thing about this tackle must be of the best, with a reel that works on agates. You may use a live squid, or a sand-eel, or a bit of bass-skin. If you know how, you can throw your line out one hundred feet—I have seen it more than once thrown one hundred and fifty. If he feels like it, the striped bass is a ferocious biter; and, once he has the hook, from his size, and the strength of the jaws, he is not likely to tear away. But for long manœuvring, for watchfulness, for steady tugging, for give and take, for courage and endurance, the striped bass, as a game-fish, stands the first. There is a capriciousness about a trout or a salmon which a striped bass does not possess. He fights from the very instant he is struck, and has no give up in him. I do not take kindly to spinners, metallic baits, as I have never seen them bring in big fish. I have, watch in hand, counted fifty minutes of hard fight between the striped bass and an adept angler, and he one of the most adroit fishermen I have ever known.

It is in blue-fish that New-Yorkers can indulge the most readily. Last season was a particularly bad one, as the *Pomatomus saltatrix* was not abundant. The most pleasant way to go blue-fishing is in a sail-boat. Vast schools of blue-fish, which eat up their weight almost every day in other fish, flock on shore after the shiners and moss-bunkers, and thus fall victims to their own greed. It is about August that the blue-fish may be found from Chesapeake Bay up to Vineyard Sound, Nantucket. In October he will weigh ten, even twelve pounds. Your squid or jig has a white rag tied to it, and, as your boat moves along with the wind, your line trailing away far behind you, the greedy fish strikes. A six-knot breeze is fast enough. You want for this fishing, if it is active, rubber finger-stalls, or your fingers will be lacerated. Be careful how you take your fish from the hook when you have him, for, if he sets his teeth in your fingers, you will be pretty sure to feel it. It is a goodly sport, requiring no special skill, when hand-lines are used; but, when it comes to rod-fishing, that is a different thing. It is then the jolliest of sports. Use an eight-foot rod and a stiff one, for the *Pomatomus* is a vigorous fish, and will smash your elegant trout-rod into smithereens. He is a game fish, and fully entitled to the name. About this same time, the weak-fish, the squeteague (the *Cynoscion regalis*), also affords ample sport. With the tide they come in to the Narrows, and of a good day you can catch many of them near Fort Richmond. Some fish with rods and tackle, and four-pounders sometimes turn up. Off Fire Island, at half-ebb, you can catch him with a hand-line and a squid, and glorious sport it is.

Another fish is the kingfish, by far the most delicate of our table-fish. You can use for the kingfish a three-jointed rod of ten feet long; you want a sinker which will withstand the sweep of the tide. A shedder-crab a kingfish especially loves; when he is hooked he works differently from most other fish. He will hurry far away under the water, and suddenly break when seventy-five feet away. He is a sturdy fighter, and, though a three- or four-pound fish is a very large one, he will have a tussle with you of an hour.

As to salmon-fishing and choice of rod, I want to fish with a twenty-foot rod, and not with one an inch less. I want to cast in impossible places. I can scramble on a rock and sight a pool below, yet can not get within twenty yards of it with a short pole. I must take every

Cod-fishing.

advantage of the situation. Nature makes the salmon-streams wild and brawling, and the shores inaccessible. You can't keep dropping your fly, and teasing salmon as you do trout. He takes it at once or not at all. Keep on sweeping with a long rod as you would for trout, and in a short time you tire of it. It is the play, the headlong dash of the salmon, that fatigues you, but when rest comes it is a glorious lassitude. You want a braided silk line, water-proofed for this fishing, and it must be sound, or good-by to your fish. You look at a Gaspé district fisherman, and be sure he knows what he is about. His rod is a New York one—though he lives in Montreal—but it is as perfect as can be. It is just as long as an English rod, but is a full three eighths of a

pound lighter, which is an immense advantage. That reel of his is not an ounce too light, though it does assume horological proportions. I think fancy flies for salmon-fishing, have gone very much out of repute of late days. There is a certain fly, "the Nicholson," that is said to have especial charms. I do not think there is any very great difference between a trout and a salmon fly, save that the latter must be the larger. A great many flies for both trout and salmon fishing are made pretty, rather as ornaments than for actual use. An elaborate, gaudy fly, save on special occasions, when the day is very dark, I have thought, frightened all the fish that swam in those deep pools of the Nipisiquit, Restigouche or Cascapediac Rivers. It is not all of us who have either the time or the money to spend, both of which are necessary, and specially much of the latter, for salmon-fishing. Still, for those who can afford it, it is a noble sport, but not any better than striped-bass fishing.

There is one kind of fishing which New-Yorkers should be acquainted with. It is perhaps the sole one which removes a man entirely from his surroundings and makes him live a new life. Such a happy change is not difficult to procure, nor is it expensive. It is rough, it is true, but it has its natural charm. Go codfishing—not for yourself, but for a market. This opportunity, by a little adroit management, you can obtain at any time. Every two or three times a week, during the fall, there leaves from the Fulton Market slip a smack going out to Vineyard Sound and Nantucket for cod and haddock. Engage passage on board. The cost is slight. You may, if you are an epicurean, send on board a dozen claret, a ham, and some canned meats; but these are not necessities. You will be almost certain to find everything clean and sweet on board. You take your oldest clothes and stow away your razor. You are to rough it for a week or ten days. You can have a good berth, and the most honest and simple of fare. Off you go, and pass rapidly through the Sound. Ten to one your smack is a clipper, and nothing but a yacht can catch her. By and by you make Point Judith, and in a day more you are off Nantucket. Away you bowl along, cross the tides which swirl through the Sound there, and you are on the cod-banks. Now the fun begins. As fast as you can open your clams, you must bait your line, heavy with a two-pound sinker. You have two, three hooks, and down she goes. You fish at thirty fathoms, maybe sixty. There is a tug—a slight one. You haul up, and find an ugly dog-fish! The boat's crew smile. You are too much on the bottom. You will get the hang of it after a while. Better luck next time. Another clam or two on your hook, and you are at it once more. Up again comes your line. You have just touched bottom, and you have two codfish. One is a fifteen-pound fish, the other ten. They do not struggle, but come up even light, at least in your excitement you think so. You take them off, and, while you have been doing this, your neighbor the captain has caught ten fish. And so it goes on. You fish until your arm aches. There are muscles in the hand that you have never before this called into play; a special lot of cords, belonging to your anatomy, run along your forearm,

which before this you were ignorant about. Your hand begins to swell, from absolute overwork. Still, you are excited and keep at it. You drop your line after a while, having caught in an hour and a half thirty fish, certainly two hundred pounds dead-weight, and now you recognize what really hard work it is; but you enjoy it. Soon a beautiful phenomenon takes place. A soft, downy fog settles on the ocean. You can hear the birds—the gulls—squawk, but can not see them. In the distance you listen to the chatter of voices—a laugh—the beating of a tin pan. It is a neighboring craft, though you can not see her. All is quiet and subdued-like. The deck is now fairly littered with fish. They are flapping all around you. Here come haddock tumbling on board. You must have a haddock. You look at your hand, which hurts; but you try it again, and two haddock come up at every haul. After you have caught a half dozen at three hauls, you remember your hand and give it up. Ah! what has your neighbor got? He gives a steady pull, and it is all he can do to keep at it. He beckons to a fisherman, who seems to understand what is the matter at once. The captain gives the man his line, and goes for a good stout stick of wood with a strong steel hook in it. Can that be a gaff? Now the fisherman works for ten minutes on that fish, or whatever it is. Maybe he is pulling up the sea-bottom! No! now, as you look over the taffrail, you see a huge white surface, like a big sheet of paper, coming up. Now it turns, and is black—now it is white. His head is above water. You know now it is a halibut. The captain makes a lunge at him with the hook; two men get hold of the wood of the gaff, and he is lugged on board; and for the first time alive (or rather in a comatose condition, for no sooner is he on board, than the handle of the gaff is given him with a heavy blow across the head) you see the *Hippoglossus Americanus*. It is a big one, will turn the scales at ninety pounds, and he is a white one, and quite a find. Your captain says: "We catch them occasionally, but they are small, chicken-halibut. This would be a fair halibut for the Georges." A week passes in this sport You go to your bunk tired out, and sleep as you never slept before. You forget newspapers and books, and are happy because neither letters nor telegraphic dispatches can reach you. If the sport tires you, there are every day craft within call, going to Nantucket or Gloucester or New Bedford, and you can be in New York within ten hours.

A TRIP UP THE HUDSON.

Day-Boat on the Hudson.

tire and most striking exception. Many, indeed, are willing to admit that, in varied and picturesque charm, it excels the world-famous Rhine; and one who has seen both has not hesitated to record the opinion that "the Rhine is monotonous compared with the Hudson. Its course," he adds, "is winding, but its shores are uniform in character, and the hills are denuded of trees, while the river has not that varying succession of broad expanse and narrow pass that gives to the Hudson a peculiar and untiring charm." Still more emphatic is the testimony of Mr. George William Curtis: "The Danube," he says, "has in part glimpses of such grandeur, the Elbe has sometimes such delicately-penciled effects; but no European river is so lordly in its bearing — none flows in such state to the sea."

The surpassing beauty of the Hudson, indeed, cannot be gainsaid; and it is beautiful under any of its aspects. Seen by soft moonlight from one of the spacious "night-boats" which ply in summer between the metropolis and Albany, one can hardly resist the conviction that its weird and

THE fault commonly found with American scenery by traveled foreigners is that in its grander aspects, especially in the far West, its wildness is almost terrible, while in its gentler phases its unkempt ruggedness repels the admiration which its picturesque beauty might otherwise excite. To such criticism, however, the Hudson River is always confessed to be an en-

supernatural charm can not possibly be repeated under the garish light of day; and yet, to see it

ly granted, will endeavor to add to his enjoyment by pointing out, not too obtrusively, the more salient features of the double panorama which will speedily begin to unfold itself.

Seated now in our chosen positions, secured by being early on board, we turn from the arid defiles of the city streets and the serried ranks of houses; and, looking out upon the broad, palpitating river, we remind our companion that he is viewing, perhaps, the most animated harbor-scene in the world. Nowhere, we assure him, can be seen such a picturesque variety of craft, from the huge steamships that link the Old World with the New, down to the snorting, restless little tug-boats and the diminutive yachts and pleasure-boats, a unique feature being given to the whole by the uncouth ferry-boats swinging from shore to shore, and the great tows of canal boats and barges.

The Palisades and Palisade Mountain-House.

to advantage for the first time, the tourist should take one of the morning-boats, whose sumptuous appointments go far to justify the epithet of "floating-palaces" so often applied to American river-craft. On a midsummer's day, when the great city about to be left behind is panting and reeking in its stifling atmosphere, the cool, aromatic breath of the river seems to be wafted straight from the "Isles of the Blest"; and the umbrageous green of its banks invites eye and mind to serene enjoyments and contemplative repose.

Supposing the tourist to have consigned himself to one of these day-boats, and secured a good position on the forward-deck, whence both shores can be seen at a glance, we will ask permission to accompany him, and, if the permission be kind-

For the first few minutes after starting, the western or Jersey shore is decidedly the more interesting. Far down at the mouth of the river are the clustering houses of Jersey City. A little nearer is the village of Hoboken, where the bank rises steeply, crested in the foreground with the Stevens mansion on Castle Hill. Adjoining it, on the summit of the heights, are the famed Elysian Fields, which are rapidly losing their elysian character; and then come the Weehawken hills, at the base of which Burr put a nation in mourning by his murderous duel with Alexander Hamilton. The wooded quiet of these hills is grateful to the eye after the glare and tumult of the city, but, turning for a moment to the New York shore, we observe with interest the dense lines of piers and warehouses which testify to the presence of one of the great commercial marts of the world.

Even while we look, the scene changes; the houses of the city become more scattered, the attention is caught for a moment by the spacious edifice of the Orphan Asylum at Manhattanville, and then the eye rests with pleasure upon the tree-clad Washington Heights, crowned with the lofty Deaf and Dumb Asylum and covered with the beautiful villas of wealthy New-Yorkers. Here the city properly ends, though its "legal limit" is still far above; and here the characteristic features of the river scenery may be said to begin.

Opposite the Washington Heights, on the other bank of the river, is the picturesque promontory still called Fort Lee from its Revolutionary associations,

Palisades above Nyack, with Distant View of Sing Sing.

but now completely denuded of its warlike aspects and become one of the most popular pleasure-resorts of the metropolis. At this point begin the Palisades, a continuous wall of nearly perpendicular cliffs from 300 to 600 feet in height which line the western bank of the river for nearly twenty miles, and form one of the most striking features of its scenery. While the face of the cliffs is bare and rugged, the summit is thickly wooded, and consists of a level table-land, not more than three quarters of a mile wide in some places, separating the Hudson from the Hackensack Valley. About four miles above Fort Lee the Palisade Mountain-House crowns a tall escarpment of the cliff, and here and there cottages and villas peep through the trees of the plateau; but in general the solitude is unbroken, and the precipice, as viewed from the steamer, looks as lonely and desolate as the cliffs of the Saguenay.

After gazing for a time upon this silent procession of cliffs, one is apt to declare it to be monotonous and forbidding; and yet if we use our eyes to any purpose we are compelled to admit that, aside from its own wild and austere beauty, it serves as an admirable foil to the softer and more civilized scenery of the other shore. The eastern river-bank, indeed, for upward of thirty miles, might fairly be described as a con-

tinuous suburb of New York, whose citizens have crested its hills with innumerable villas and cottages, and whose wealth has converted its undulating and tree-clad slopes into an almost continuous panorama of the most exquisitely kept lawns and gardens. Here and there, at frequent intervals, the houses cluster into villages and hamlets, and at Yonkers and Tarrytown the dimensions of considerable towns are attained; but even the towns do not lose the rural and verdurous aspect which pervades the whole, and the largest of them reminds us quite as much of a park as of a city.

The first town seen after leaving the city is Riverdale, which is simply a group of elegant mansions without a shop or other common feature to mar its aristocratic exclusiveness. Just above, between it and Yonkers, is Mount St. Vincent, from the crest of which the vast, bare

Croton Point

building of the convent-school of the Sisters of Charity stares down upon the river. Adjoining this building and completely dwarfed by it is the quaint castellated stone structure known as "Fonthill," formerly the residence of Edwin Forrest, the tragedian. Although now seen at a disadvantage, it could never have been a very pleasing because incongruous feature of the scene amid which it is placed. Much more attractive, because more obviously harmonious with the life and habits of the people, are the villas and mansions which occupy every advantageous spot upon the shore in this vicinity, and some of which are really imposing by reason of their size and situation, if not for any special architectural merit.

A few miles above Yonkers, on the same side, is the pretty town of Hastings-upon-the-Hudson, near which is the stately old Livingston Manor-House, renowned as one of the oldest residences in the valley, as the headquarters for a time of

Washington, and as the scene of the official conferences about the British evacuation of New York in 1783. Opposite Hastings, at Indian Head, the Palisades reach their most picturesque point; and a short distance above, at Piermont, where a pier nearly a mile long extends from the western bank into the river, they end, or rather recede from the shore and cease to form one of the features of the river-scenery. At this point, too, the river broadens into a noble bay, ten miles long and two to five miles wide, known and renowned as the Tappan Zee.

As the steamer plows its way toward the middle of this lake-like expanse, the scene on either hand is most beautiful. On the western margin extends a line of undulating, richly-wooded hills, at the foot of which nestles the picturesque town of Nyack. On the eastern shore, which rises by long, receding slopes to the height of two or three hundred feet, are the prosperous villages of

Irvington, Tarrytown, and Sing Sing, while costly villas and other residences are exceptionally numerous on the intervening hills. Just below Irvington, the classic portico of Nevis, the home of the Hamiltons, and the striking Cottinet mansion, built of Caen stone in the Renaissance style, are passed. A little above Irvington and near the river, though hidden from view by the dense growth of trees and shrubbery, is Sunnyside, which as the home of Washington Irving has become famous the world over, and which is now one of the classic spots of American literature. Still above and close at hand are the mansions of Bierstadt, William E. Dodge, Cyrus W. Field, and other wealthy citizens of New York. Near the shore is seen the tapering tower of Cunningham Castle; while on a conspicuous promontory just below Tarrytown is the Paulding Manor, one of the finest specimens of the Tudor style of architecture in the country. Tarrytown and its vicinity are perennially interesting from their intimate association with the life and genius of Irving and with memorable events connected with the Revolutionary struggle. Above Nyack, on the western shore, the Palisades come down once more to the river-edge, and form a high and precipitous bluff which bears the name of Verdrietigh Hook—also called Point-no-Point, owing to its deceptive appearance, when seen from the river above or below, of a grand headland. In pass-

Entrance to the Highlands.

ing Sing Sing a fine view is obtained of the massive stone buildings composing the famous Penitentiary.

At the upper end of the Tappan Zee the river narrows sharply, and the vine-clad Croton Point separates the Tappan Zee from Haverstraw Bay,

4

West Point.

Point on the east and the historic Stony Point on the west contract the river to a comparatively narrow channel, their forms and outlines have become quite distinct.

We are now at the entrance to the Highlands, and, in face of the scenery which begins to present itself, the attention of the tourist will hardly be secured for the Revolutionary memories which cling about all this region; even the famous exploit of "Mad" Anthony Wayne in capturing the fort of Stony Point, held by a superior force, at the point of the bayonet and without firing a shot, will be apt to awaken but a languid interest; and Peekskill will be regarded with a similar apathy, though we assure him that it is one of the prettiest and most romantically situated towns on the Hudson.

The very steamer seems to be conscious of the superior interest and beauty of the scenery to which it is approaching, and, turning swiftly into that sudden bend of the river to the west, known as "The Race," hastens with eagerness toward the Dunderberg or Thunder Mountain, whose precipitous front almost

which is another lake-like widening of the river, with the village of Haverstraw on its western shore and a long line of white limestone cliffs producing a million bushels of lime every year. As the steamer crosses this beautiful bay, the Highlands begin to loom up boldly in the distance; and at its upper end, where Verplanck's overhangs the water on the left, while the loftier peak of Anthony's Nose (1,128 feet high) confronts it on the right, and forms the twin outpost of the Highland region on the south. At the base of Dunderberg is a broad and deep stream known as Montgomery Creek, on either side of which in Revolutionary times stood Forts

Montgomery and Clinton to protect the boom and iron chain which were stretched here across the river in an unsuccessful attempt to arrest the progress of the British fleet. Just above Dunderberg, near the mouth of the Forest-of-Dean Creek, is the grape-abounding Iona Island, a favorite picnic resort, three hundred acres in extent, and containing extensive vineyards.

Following the river now in its curve to the northeast, a fine view is obtained on the right of the symmetrical cone of Sugar-Loaf Mountain (865 feet high), at the foot of which, in a small cove, is seen Beverly Dock, and near it Beverly House, where the traitorous Benedict Arnold was breakfasting when news came to him of André's arrest, and whence he fled to the British vessel anchored in the stream below. From this point also a distant view is obtained of the ruins of Fort Putnam, of Revolutionary fame, crowning the heights on the left, and a short distance above, also on the left, we come in sight of Buttermilk Falls, descending over inclined ledges a distance of one hundred feet, and forming at

Cro' Nest and Storm-King Mountains, from Cold Spring.

times a fine cascade, though the heats of summer are apt to dwindle it to insignificance. On the summit of the cliff above is the spacious Cozzens's Hotel, one of the favorite summer retreats of pleasure-seeking New-Yorkers.

Just beyond Cozzens's, on an elevated plateau in the heart of the Highland Pass, is West Point, the site of the great military school of the Republic, and one of the most picturesque spots in America. From the pier where the steamer pauses for a brief interval, all that can be seen is the dusty road hewed out of the cliff-side, and leading by a gentle grade to the plateau above, where tantalizing glimpses are obtained of spacious buildings and grassy slopes; but, if the tourist should take our urgent advice and stop over for a day or two, he will be surprised at the romantic charm and varied fascinations of the locality. If so inclined, he can examine into the organization and discipline of the military school; can see the morning roll-call and the evening dress-parade; can pass a fruitful hour or two in the Library, the Observatory, the Picture-Gallery, or the curious Museum of Ordnance and Trophies; and at the proper hours can amuse himself with the cavalry exercises in the Riding Hall. When the interest of these is exhausted, he can wander over the spacious parade-ground, smooth as a lawn, level as a floor, and commanding at every point novel and beautiful views; can search out the romantic and sequestered nooks, such as Kosciusko's Garden and Flirtation Walk; can ascend the winding path to the picturesque Cemetery; and, by climbing still higher, can obtain from the crumbling ramparts of Fort Put-

nam a view the memory of which shall remain with him as long as he retains a taste for the grand and beautiful in scenery. If his visit happen to occur at the time of year (July or August) when the cadets are in cantonments, the social gayeties of a summer resort will be added to the other attractions of the place; and, however exaggerated may have been the praises of West Point that he has heard, he will be apt to admit that the reality surpasses any anticipations they may have raised.

As we have already said, West Point is only half-way through the Pass of the Highlands, and some of its grandest features, as viewed from the steamer, remain to be seen. Just above West Point, on the same side, is Cro' Nest, one of the loftiest of the Highland group (1,428 feet high), and still above is Storm King (formerly known as "Butter Hill"), which is 1,529 feet high, and the last of the range upon the left. Between Cro' Nest and Storm King, and in the laps of

The Catskill Mountains.

both, lies the lovely Vale of Tempe; and opposite, on the other side of the river, is the picturesque village of Cold Spring, from which a noble view is obtained of the heights across the river. Behind Cold Spring rises the massive granite crown of Mount Taurus, which is a modern euphemism for "Bull Hill"; and on an elevated plateau a little to the north is Undercliff, the home of the late George P. Morris, the poet and journalist. Immediately above are the jagged precipices of Breakneck Hill, which is 1,187 feet high, and which terminates the range on the east side. Traversing the narrow channels between this height and Storm King opposite, the steamer passes Cornwall Landing, on the west, the most frequented summer resort on the river, with fine scenery and drives above upon the Terrace; and enters upon the broad expanse of Newburgh Bay, whence the view back toward the Highlands is singularly impressive.

After the unapproachable beauty of the High-

lands, the scenery of the upper river will be apt to seem tame and uninviting; yet there are portions of it which but for the superior glories of the renowned Pass would be expected to arouse the enthusiastic admiration of the beholder. For more than fifty miles above the Highlands, the river-banks on either hand are high and varied, rising here into bold and sweeping hills, and dropping there into gentle, verdure-clad slopes, many of which are still crested with stately villas, while picturesque towns nestle at their base or look down from the summit of the plateau. Some of the handsomest and most populous places along the river are to be found on this portion, such as Newburgh, rising in terraced lines on the west side of Newburgh Bay; Poughkeepsie, the largest city between New York and Albany, built on an elevated plain 200 feet above the river, with a background of high hills; Fishkill, a pleasant village opposite Newburgh, on the east side of the Bay; Hyde Park,

Source of the Hudson

a high-lying village above Poughkeepsie, nestling amid trees; the busy commercial cities of Rondout and Kingston, lying close to each other on the west shore; and Rhinebeck Landing, opposite Kingston, where is the ancient Beekman House, nearly two hundred years old, and the best specimen of an old Dutch homestead to be found in the valley of the Hudson.

Nor is the more distant landscape unworthy of the immediate foreground. Immediately upon leaving the Highlands and entering Newburgh Bay, far away to the west are seen the Shawangunk Mountains, stretching northward in a dim blue line; while to the northeast are the Matteawan Mountains, the dominating peak of which (the New Beacon) commands a magnificent view, extending even to New York City. Poughkeepsie has been left behind but a few miles when a first glimpse is obtained of the blue peaks of the Catskills on the northwest; and from this point to Hudson, a distance of thirty miles, an almost continuous panorama of majestic mountain-scenery, to which distance seems only to lend enchantment, may be enjoyed.

Beyond Hudson, which is a flourishing city on the east side, one hundred and fifteen miles from New York, the scenery is flat and monotonous, and nothing demanding notice presents itself until the steeple-crowned heights of Albany announce the approaching termination of a voyage which, if taken for the first time, must prove a memorable event in the life of the traveler.

At Troy, six miles above Albany, tide-water ends, and above this the Hudson is a rapid, rocky river, navigable only by sloops and smaller craft. By taking the railway to Glenn's Falls, however, on the road to Lake George, the tourist may see the river again in one of its more picturesque aspects, where, as a brawling mountain-torrent, it rushes in a series of tumultuous rapids and cascades down eighty feet of stony and precipitous descent. And if, leaving railways and steamboats far behind, he place himself face to face with Nature in the Adirondacks, there, in the inmost heart of that lonely wilderness, in the stupendous gorge known as the Indian Pass, in whose cold depths the ice of winter never melts entirely away—there, in a crystal spring whose waters trickle waveringly through dim crevices and plash softly on the stones, he will find the "Source of the Hudson."—What a contrast does the vision bring up! At one end a crystalline spring where the wolf, the wolverene, the wild-cat, and the panther quench their thirst; at the other, only three hundred miles away, a noble river, bearing upon its opulent bosom the commerce of a continent! Such is the Hudson; and from one of its extremes to the other the tourist can pass in the space of forty-eight hours.

THE THOUSAND ISLANDS.

AS SEEN BY AN ENGLISHMAN.

MY wife and I are camping out for a fortnight among the Thousand Islands. Our friend the Colonel has offered us the hospitality of his steam-yacht and his hut; so here we are, on a charming little domain of four hundred yards square, living the primitive life of squaws and braves—fishing, shooting, boating, swimming, and flirting unconscionably—in total oblivion of Pall Mall or Piccadilly, and ready to fling politics and propriety, like physic, to the dogs. And this is how we have got here:

Our friend the Colonel is a *compagnon de voyage*, whom we picked up in the Clifton House at Niagara. He does not seem to be a military man, but apparently holds his title as a sort of brevet rank. He lives at Detroit, so he tells us; and, from hints which various other members of our little party let drop from time to time, I strongly suspect that the Colonel's true vocation lies rather in the dry-goods line. However, our host has plenty of money, a pretty little steam-yacht, and an island of his own among the famous thousand; so the only wonder is that he has not long since been elevated into a general or a judge. Handles to one's name go cheap in republican America, and every man with five hundred a year or upward receives honorary promotion as captain or commodore at least.

The Colonel is hospitality itself. We wandered about Niagara for a week with him and Mrs. Colonel (such a style of address is *de rigueur* in transatlantic society); and at the end of that short acquaintance the good soul positively insisted that we should accompany his party to the Thousand Islands, and become members of a camping-out expedition. For all he knows, we may be bank-swindlers or pickpockets; nay, worse, he may be introducing into the bosom of his family a pair of English runaways, anxious to avail themselves of the easy deliverance afforded by the divorce courts of Illinois; yet he accepts us unhesitatingly, on our own authority, as mere traveling Britishers on a scientific mission, desirous of seeing as much of America as we conveniently can in a three months' trip. Upon my word, good, kindly Western brethren, when I bethink me of your warm hearts and your childlike confidence, I feel ashamed of myself for sometimes hinting that your voices sound a trifle nasal, and that your manners smack a trifle of the aboriginal backwoodsman.

But what and where are the Thousand Islands? asks my country reader. Now, dear reader, don't be angry because I have found you out. Confess that you have only the very haziest notion of where this delightful region may be, and I will confess to you in turn that I had not the slightest idea myself until I came here. Which of us knows anything about geography except by traveling? We have a clear conception as to the whereabout of Paris, and Brussels, and Cologne, and Milan, and Naples, because we have all been there; but can you answer me whether Delhi is on the Ganges or the Jumna, and whether it lies to the north or to the south of Agra? In what State of the Union is Chicago, and on which of the Great Lakes does it stand? You know you can't tell me; and I couldn't have told you three or four years ago. In topographical matters seeing is believing; for eyes, as good old Herodotus puts it, happen to be better witnesses among men than ears. So allow me first to tell you what and where these Thousand Islands are, and then I shall try to picture for you our life in their midst.

Just at the point where Lake Ontario empties its waters into the great river St. Lawrence, a barrier of granite rock bars its course. Through the grooves and depressions in this rock the river winds its way by a hundred different channels; while all the higher masses rise above the surface of the water as tiny islets, crowned with brushwood and Canadian pines. Ages ago, during the great glacial period, the ice wore down the summits of these rocky bosses into smooth, rounded domes; and now they appear upon the river's edge like basking whales or huge elephants' backs. You may trace the markings of the glacier on the scratched and worn granite, just as you may trace it on the *roches moutonnées* of Swiss valleys, or on the grand slopes of our own Llanberis and Aberglasllyn. Sometimes the water has washed away the side into a mimic cliff; but, more often, the rounded boss rises in a gentle curve above the blue waves, showing its red seamed structure near the edge, and covered toward its summit by mold, on which grow low bushes or tall and stately trees.

Some of the islands are big enough to afford farms for the industrious squatter, who has made himself a title by the simple act of settling down bodily on his appropriated realm. Others, however, are mere points of granite, on which a single pine maintains a struggling existence against wave in summer and ice-floe in winter; while not a few consist only of a bare, rocky hog's back, just raised an inch or two above the general level of the water. But the most wonderful point of all is their number. Most people imagine that the term "Thousand Islands" is a pardonable poetical exaggeration, covering a prosaic and statistical reality of some fifty or a hundred actual islets. But no, not at all—the popular name really understates the true features of the case. A regular survey reveals the astonishing fact that no fewer than *three thousand* of these lovely little fairy-lands stud the blue expanse to which they give their name—the Lake of the Thousand Islands. All day long you may wander in and out among their intricate mazes, gliding round tiny capes, exploring narrow channels, losing your way hopelessly in watery *culs-de-sac*, and drinking in beauty to your soul's content. Fairy-lands, I called them just now, and fairy-lands they veritably seem. Their charm is all their own. I have seen much variety of scenery on this planet of ours, north, south, east, and west; but I never saw anything so unique, so individual, so perfectly *sui generis* as these Thousand Islands. Not that they are so surpassingly beautiful; but their beauty is so unlike anything that one may see anywhere else. Tiny little islands, placed in tiny little rivers, crowned with tiny little chalets, and navigated by tiny little yachts; it all reminds one so thoroughly of one's childish dreamlands, that I declare I should hardly be surprised to see Queen Mab or Queen Titania step down, wand in hand, to the water's side, and a group of attendant fairies dance around her in a grassy circle.

Among such scenery it is that we glide these delicious summer mornings, disporting ourselves in the Colonel's yacht, and drawing in fresh life with every breath. All the world here seems to own a steam-yacht; indeed, the possession of that costly piece of property appears as necessary a mark of respectability among the islands as a chimney-pot or a card in Mayfair. Up and down they go perpetually, snorting defiance from their shrill whistles, with a note whose excessive treble seems to surpass all the resources of acoustics; saluting without end the endless bunting which waves the stars and stripes from every tent, hut, or cottage with that effusive loyalty peculiar to the great American people; and getting into interminable trouble upon shoals or reefs, fouling, grounding, colliding, but, by the mercy of some special Providence, never capsizing.

The Colonel brought us here from Kingston, in his own specimen of these quaint little craft, some ten days ago. Kingston stands to the islands in the same relation as Chamouni stands to Mont Blanc or Oban to the Western Highlands. It forms the starting-point, the center, and the rendezvous. To Kingston we came from Niagara and Toronto by steamboat, across the wide waste of Lake Ontario, a shoreless sea, whose low banks form one endless expanse of growing, waving corn. Corn in vast sheets for fifteen miles inland, as the country slopes away upward from the lake-side; corn in the foreground of our voyage, rising up for ever before us as we moved on; corn sinking below the horizon as we looked back over the distance already covered, and shaking its myriad heads in the breeze to the utmost limit that the eye could see. No hedges, no copses, no parks, no trees, nothing but corn, corn, corn, till one begins to disbelieve in the possibility of famine, and to wonder where all the millers and bakers will ever come from. The good Canadian farmer—that mild modern Vandal with a tinge of Methodism—has cut down the pine-woods right and left before his utilitarian axe, leaving only a Philistine paradise of agricultural wealth, and prosperity, where every man eats roast beef and plum-pudding under his own vine and fig-tree, while nobody troubles his head about useless trifles like the picturesque and the beautiful. If it be true, as they say, that good Americans, when they die, go to Paris, then I am sure that, by parity of reasoning, the soul of William Cobbett must be comfortably housed on the desecrated shores of Lake Ontario.

It was delightful after ten or fifteen hours of this monotonous scenery to find ourselves at last in the pretty little open harbor of Kingston. A wooded country stretched around us on every side, while the outliers of the Thousand Islands lay within sight to the south and east. In front, a basking blue stone-built town glowed in the foreground, its roofs all covered with tinned iron, and shining like gold in the morning sun. I could almost fancy myself in the East once more, looking out upon some domed and minareted village of the Bosporus. Building after building of a quaint, debased American - Byzantine style, propped on pseudo-Doric pillars and surmounted by a false Italian dome (wood, tinplated), stared out upon us boldly, unabashed by its own pretentious absurdity. Incredibly monstrous they all are, if taken separately—perfect models of the avoidable in architectonic art, which Mr. Ruskin would rejoice to pillory, and Mr. Fergusson would delight in demolishing—yet, looked on in the mass from the water-side, they really compose a pretty and harmonious picture. The effect is much heightened, too, by a few scattered martello-towers, standing straight out of the shallow water, with red-rusted iron roofs, which contrast finely with the sun-gilded domes; while a grim European - looking fort crowns a slight eminence eastward, and spreads its brown-burned glacis down to the water's edge. Altogether, rather a pleasant oasis in the desert of white-and-green American towns; for this quiet old Kingston is no bantling of yesterday, like Buffalo or Toronto, but the lineal descendant of Louis Quatorze's Fort Frontenac, quite an historical city for the New World.

Onward from Kingston the Colonel escorted us in person on board his aforesaid yacht, the General Jackson, to Mathison Island, his own peculiar domain, some ten miles off, in the very heart of that beautiful miniature archipelago. We reached our destination at six o'clock on a lovely evening. The whole party, some seven gentlemen with as many ladies, were ranged ready to receive us on the landing-place, a rapidly shelving granite step, where the water stood ten feet deep close under the shore. Above the rock, a tall white pole bore aloft the inevitable bunting, provocative of a fresh loyal display from every wandering steam-whistle that passes throughout the day. "Salute the flag!" says the Colonel, with a military air; and the stoker turns on a hideous blast which stuns our ears like ten thousand claps of thunder. Then the little craft sidles gently against the solid natural pier, and we step lightly out at last on the shore of the Thousand Islands.

The ceremony of introduction follows—and oh, what a ceremony! I almost fear to tell the tale, lest I should be accused of exaggeration. The Colonel takes me by the hand gravely and trots me out in front of the assembled party. "Mr. Doolittle," he says to the eldest of the group in a sepulchral tone, "allow me to present you

to Mr. Wilson, a British gentleman now on a scientific visit to America."

I bow distantly to Mr. Doolittle, after our European fashion; but such is evidently not the custom of the country. Mr. Doolittle advances three paces mechanically, as one would advance in a quadrille, grasps my hand firmly, and holds it while he says in the same sepulchral voice: "Mr. Wilson—sir, I am proud to make your acquaintance. Welcome to the Thousand Islands!" Having said which words as a child repeats its lessons, he drops my hand mechanically, and retreats three paces, quadrille-fashion, once more, into the general line.

Then the Colonel begins again. Taking the second in age among the gentlemen he observes, tone and manner as before: "Dr. Koerber, allow me to present you to Mr. Wilson, a British gentleman now on a scientific visit to America."

Dr. Koerber takes his turn, steps forward his three paces, grasps my hand exactly as Mr. Doolittle had done, and then observes, in precisely the same regulation tone: "Mr. Wilson—sir, I am proud to make your acquaintance. Welcome to the Thousand Islands!" The hand drops: three paces to the rear again, and Major Greely Robbins comes to take his turn.

Through all the seven gentlemen the same pantomime takes place with admirable gravity, and then through all the seven ladies. Meanwhile, Mrs. Colonel has taken my wife in hand, and, beginning with the ladies, presents the whole fourteen persons to her with exactly the self-same speeches on either side. Having done which, the party suddenly unbends, becomes natural, and begins to talk like rational creatures, not like highly trained poll-parrots. For my own part, I felt myself blushing fiery red, for a terrible fear possessed me that my wife would misunderstand this ceremonial, and laugh outright with her hearty, silvery, English laugh. But I learned afterward, when a moment of intercommunication turned up, that she had been in equal fear lest *my* gravity should prove unequal to the occasion: so happily no harm came of it in either case.

"You see, Colonel," said Mr. Doolittle, leading the way to the huts, "we have succeeded in erecting the flag of our country since your departure."

"I observe you have, Sheriff," answered the Colonel (of course, it was imperative that Mr. Doolittle should possess a title of some sort, and this was apparently the special form which the respect of his fellow-citizens had assumed)—"I observe, and I trust our British friends will enjoy the full freedom and security which that flag never fails to afford." Uttering which sentiment like a copy-book maxim, the Colonel took

The Thousand Islands.

us on to inspect the preparations made for our reception. I really often wonder whether these people possess independent minds like our own, or whether, after all, they form a sort of hereditary unconscious automaton.

Assuredly, camping out is a much more luxurious proceeding than the ordinary Britisher could easily conceive. They know how to make themselves comfortable, do these children of the Great Republic, and their cousins in the Dominion over the way. The "huts" in which we were to house ourselves turn out on closer investigation to be two large and airy rough wooden buildings, looking very much like overgrown barns, but pleasant enough in their internal arrangements. No glass adorns the empty windows, which are really the etymological wind-doors of our early English ancestors; but the light and the breeze come through them readily enough, and at night we close them up securely with rough pine-wood shutters against possible bad weather. One of the huts accommodates the male members of the party, who have permanent beds fitted up on the grassy floor; actual feather beds, erect upon four iron legs, with a flexible chain *sommier* to support them. The second hut, which does duty as dining-room during the day, acts as general ladies' bedroom at night. The Colonel poetically refers to it as the Bower, but the other men of the party profanely christen it the Hennery.

Supper stands on the table at the moment of our arrival, and we are seated in our places before we quite know where we are. The table consists of several long planks, set carelessly on some trestles; but a snowy white cloth covers it from end to end; and pretty common earthenware graces it with a homely grace. *Simplex munditiis* is the motto of the Hennery, and the supper of a surety deserves that high commendation. There is capital tea from a steaming kettle (the fire still smolders outside), with cream—real cream, for we keep a cow on the island; there is bread, and there are hot cakes, and fresh whitefish, and ham, and cold beef, and boiled eggs. Above all, there is appetite—healthy, robust appetite, the result of abundant air and proper exercise. We eat our supper with a will, amid much laughing (a wee bit nasal), much chatting, and no small proportion of wild flirtation. But we are no ascetics, not a man or woman of the company, and we all enjoy a supper, a laugh, and a good flirt, as well as heart can reasonably desire.

But, to avoid vain repetition, I had better tell you at once how we spend a sample day. In the morning, we men are all astir at seven or before, the ladies never rising till half-past seven. We go down to a sequestered spot on one side of the island, shaded by Canadian cedar, and hemmed in by tiny granite cliffs; and here we take our morning dip. The water is deep enough to allow of a delicious header, and so clear that you may see the fish scuttling out of your way in alarm as you dive among their astonished shoals. By half-past seven we have all returned to the Club, as we call the men's hut, and have endued ourselves in garments fit for the eyes of womankind. Then, and not till then, the ladies may show themselves, which they promptly proceed to do, and the work of the day begins at once. Into the mystery of the ladies' ablutions I can not proceed—indeed, I have no authenticated accounts upon which to base a veracious history. The Doctor asserts that the ladies have a bathing-place of their own at the opposite end of the island, sheltered from possible intruders by a canvas screen; while two chains, set across the narrow channel, prevent the access of "foreign" boats. But how this may be I can not answer from personal experience: I only know that a rope has been fastened from tree to tree at the ladies' end, which a law, like that in Tennyson's "Princess," forbids any man to pass on pain of death: and of course no one of the party has ever at any time laid himself open to capital punishment on this account. In England, the curiosity of the younger members might lead them to transgress during the small hours of the night, just to settle the problem; but the self-restraining American, always courtesy embodied where women are in question, would never dream of overstepping the appointed limit.

The day's labor begins with lighting the fire and boiling the kettle on a rough hearth of heaped-up stones. That task completed by the men, the housewife community makes the tea and lays the table. Fresh provisions arrive every second day from Alexandra Bay, by yacht, and, more marvelous still, the mail, including the New York papers. When breakfast has been set, we all fall to, and make short work of the various good things provided for us. Then sentence of banishment is proclaimed against the men, while the Club is cleared out and the beds made. After that performance, the excursions of the day are organized, and we separate till two-o'clock dinner. Sometimes we boat among the surrounding islands, and lose our way among the little channels, only to recover it by some red-painted number, which indicates a special landmark. At other times we improve the commissariat by a catch of rock-bass or speckled trout. Some of us sketch or paint in water-colors; others botanize or gather snail-shells; the Doctor has a mania for butterflies; while the Major consumes most of his time by lying on his back in the shade, and smoking innumerable cheroots. So in various ways we while away the hours, every man in his humor, till two o'clock brings dinner.

From dinner to supper passes in much the same manner as from breakfast to dinner, with this difference, that peradventure we work a little less and flirt a great deal more. Practical divorce has been imposed on us by the laws of the community, coupled with a kind of Platonic communism. You stroll off after dinner with some one of the seven pretty girls or women, to any sequestered nook on the island or one of its neighbors, and there you go through a farce of fishing or sketching, which really serves as a transparent pretense for a downright American flirtation. You lie on your back and discuss everything, nothing, everybody, nobody, philosophy, society, and love. Unhappily, the islands are so very small that you invariably find your own wife, with *her* companion, intervening at the exact moment when you have asked a most telling question, and are gazing with a capital imitation of boyish and poetical ardor into a pair of swimming blue eyes in front of you. But such little *contretemps* are really the very making of the flirtation. Without them, it might become "quite too awfully real"; but, as we have all got thoroughly accustomed to surprising one another in the midst of tragi-comical pseudorotic passages, we have learned to regard the whole transaction as a vast and harmless joke, in which nobody means anything, and nobody expects to escape being laughed at.

Of course, in dear, prudish, tittle-tattling Old England, such freedom would be impossible. Ineffable scandals would arise, and become themes for Mrs. Grundy's tea-table throughout the next half-century. But then England, with all her virtues—and I am one of her most devotedly affectionate sons—can not be acquitted of a tendency toward scandal-mongering, like a majestic old Aunt Tabitha as she is. America, on the other hand, is rich in that charity which thinketh no evil. *Honi soit* might be just as truly her motto as that of her suspicious mother-country; and, to say the truth, I think she applies it a great deal better. The self-respect of men and women and the universal chivalrous courtesy shown to the weaker sex prevent the necessity for all those conventional barriers with which we in England fortify ourselves against Paul Pry and Mrs. Candor. Young ladies receive their own visitors in their private drawing-room, and mamma never dreams of intervening to do propriety. Engaged couples start alone to spend a week at some hotel among the Hudson Highlands or the Adirondacks, and no New York society is convulsed by their shocking conduct. The result is that American women, perfectly independent and free in their outward movements, are hedged round by a cordon of self-constraint and self-possession which the boldest Lothario would

never venture to transgress. If you want to know what were the emotions of a Greek who felt himself turning into stone under the petrifying gaze of the Gorgon Medusa, you have only to watch the freezing glance of an American maiden who faintly suspects you of a contemplated incursion beyond that magic and circumscribed circle.

Thus, between love-making, real and pretended—for of course some of our young couples have an eye to serious business, and a camping-out excursion offers splendid opportunities for rigging the matrimonial market with little fear of competition—our day passes away pleasantly enough, and six o'clock brings supper. Tea, we should call it at home—the good-old fashioned high tea which still lingers in remote counties; but the American mind follows the traditions of its Puritan ancestors, and speaks of it by the still older English name of supper. It is interesting to note how the habits of a simple colonial farmer community still cling about this great, wealthy, thoroughly sophisticated, ultra-civilized mercantile people. They dine early almost to a man: and the terrible institution of an early dinner, which might really be substituted for the treadmill in modern prisons, derives some mitigation among the Islands from the abundance of fresh air which we imbibe between whiles. They sup at six, with a portentous prodigality unknown to older lands. They seldom wear a swallow-tail coat, the decent black frock being considered sufficient for almost any solemnity. And they carry about five hundred minor farmer tinges through all their doings, which survive to mark the creature from which they have developed, just as Mr. Darwin and Professor Huxley tell us that the tips of our ears and the rudimentary caudal appendages of our vertebral column still survive in man to mark our descent from "an arboreal quadrumanous mammal"—*Anglicè*, an ape.

After supper comes the delicious coolness of Canadian eventide—Canadian, I say, for, though our island lies on the republican side of the imaginary boundary, the archipelago as a whole belongs in its geography and its climate to Upper Canada. We sit in front of the huts, on chairs or sward, and the Doctor strums his violin, while a young man from Skaniateles (orthography guaranteed) accompanies on the flute, and one or other of the nymphs in muslin sings some appropriate verses. The music lingers over the waters, and rings back again from the granite bosses in a dozen dying echoes, each one farther off and fainter than the last. Then the daylight fades, the fire-flies begin to glimmer among the cedar-trees, the calm water mirrors back their flashes, the violin and flute subside, a single *Eng-*

lish voice pours out a lower, richer, fuller flood of music, and the heart of man waxes dreamily poetical till all is silent. The shrill whistle of a passing yacht happily intervenes to save us from the approaching wave of sentimentality; and about ten o'clock sees us all turned off to our bachelor quarters, where we lie eight or nine in a room as big as a ballroom, and are soon snoring at our ease, to begin again the same aimless, listless, delicious, do-nothing life to-morrow morning.

A few more words about the other islands, and then I must quit the little group, perhaps for ever. Now and then we start in the yacht to explore the surrounding channels, and to discover "kings and islands new," like the great Rear-Admiral Bailey Pip in Mr. Gilbert's masterpiece. For kings abound here as well as kingdoms. Numbers of wealthy New York merchants or Chicago shippers have bought an island, and built upon it a pretty little cottage, sometimes rising to the pretensions of a mansion. Mr. Pullman, the lucky inventor of drawing-room cars, has raised himself a perfect palace in the outward semblance of a chalet, grown out of all recognition, but still retaining the deep eaves and fancy woodwork of its toy-shop original. Many another celebrity has displayed his taste (or his want thereof) in ornate buildings, perched upon little rocky knolls, and always surmounted by that ubiquitous square of bunting, which proclaims the aggressive nationality of its loyal possessor. On the whole, most of these cottages are in perfect harmony with their surroundings, and add to the picture rather than detract from it. Indeed, the Americans, who generally fail with an absolute magnificence of failure in the higher walks of architecture, have considerable taste in domestic buildings, while in landscape gardening and the laying out of parks or ornamental grounds it must be at once conceded that they "whip creation."

Every one of these island realms has its own landing-place, often a regular pier, where the yacht lies moored during the greater part of the day. The little craft bring down their masters at the beginning of the season, and carry them about during the summer months in search of the picturesque. The cottages are furnished in true American style, with satin, mirrors, and gilding; and they contain a company during the season not unlike that of an English country-house, accent and manners always excepted.

Other islands, like the Colonel's, belong to mere campers-out, who prefer to rough it in simpler style. Even these, however, as will have been seen already, are far from devoid of the luxuries of life; and I must say my first feeling was one of disappointment when I found *pâté de*

foie gras and champagne included in the bill of fare. Civilization pursues us nowadays, as Horace used to tell us black care pursued the wealthy, till at last we are reading English scientific weeklies, twelve days after publication, in a summer camp among the Thousand Islands.

Here and there, however, we come upon some more genuine campers, in the shape of a young men's party, who have appropriated an unoccupied island for the nonce, and are really living under canvas. These hearty young fellows turn out as a rule to be Canadian students or military cadets, for the true Yankee loves civilization too well to forego roof or bed, except upon dire necessity thereto prevailing. Your genuine camper also lives largely on the spoils of his gun and his rod, often taking with him no more than a bag of Indian meal, which he kneads into damper with water from the river, and bakes rudely upon a flat stone. But, alas, *luxuria armis sævior incubuit;* and I fear me that the honest Canadian stripling himself has begun to indulge in tinned provisions, while I can assert from personal experience that brandy-and-soda is no unknown beverage, even under primitive canvas. When the first Japanese ambassadors came to Europe in quest of civilization, they were duly regaled at the Mansion House with a civic banquet. As the interpreter's glass was filled again and again with bubbling Veuve Clicquot, that excellent functionary exclaimed many times with much fervor, "How I *do* like civilization!" Japan is not the only country, apparently, which is ready to accept the precious boon in the same limited sense.

One other island positively claims attention from its local coloring, its perfect raciness of American feeling. A good many hotels line the shores of the little archipelago, but for many years no island had been specially set apart for religious services. At length, an enterprising body set on foot the notion of a permanent campmeeting. No sooner said than done. Wells Island and was opened for the purpose; a meetinghouse was built, a landing-place was provided, and appropriate services were devised. The enterprise proved an enormous success. Numbers of good souls, who regarded picnics as worldly and camping out as little short of sinful, accepted the invitation to visit the islands for prayermeetings and missionary sermons. You hire "a location" on Wells Island for the season just as you rent a pew in church. Steamers call at the landing-stage on their voyages up or down; the good people disembark, while the less good go on to livelier shores; and nowadays Wells Island does a roaring trade, from spring to autumn, in spiritual consolations and material provisions, not including alcoholic stimulants. The whole notion is deliciously redolent of American character, with its quaint and shrewd mixture of godliness and money-making.

As a parting word, let me say to all readers, if you are tired of that eternal round—Cologne, the Rhine, Switzerland, the Italian lakes, Rome, Paris, and London—why not run across the Atlantic? And, if you run across and can spare a week or so in the sultry summer weather, be sure you don't forget to try the Thousand Islands. You must be a very difficult fellow to please if you don't thank me heartily for the hint on your return.

THE BIRDS OF THE BROOKSIDE.

By Ernest Ingersoll.

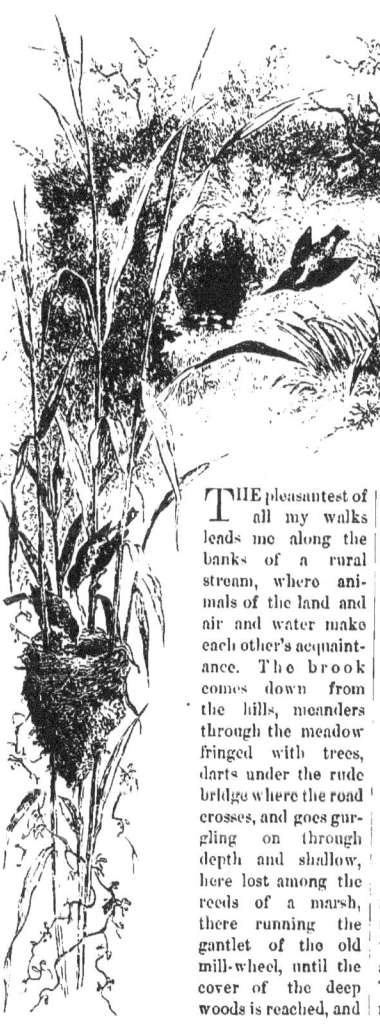

THE pleasantest of all my walks leads me along the banks of a rural stream, where animals of the land and air and water make each other's acquaintance. The brook comes down from the hills, meanders through the meadow fringed with trees, darts under the rude bridge where the road crosses, and goes gurgling on through depth and shallow, here lost among the reeds of a marsh, there running the gantlet of the old mill-wheel, until the cover of the deep woods is reached, and

it can afford to saunter slowly under the quiet shade of the elms and sycamores. I am impelled to seek its banks by the same constant instinct which led Thoreau always to walk toward the southwest. He thought this inscrutable impulse in him was a part of the settled migratory instinct of the race, insisting on national and individual progress westward. But the avenues of entrance to new continents have always been by its rivers, so it may be that my impulse, also, is owing to the prevailing tendency of humanity; yet I only think of it, if I consider it at all, as the quickest way of withdrawing into the wilderness.

A walk along the edge of a stream in the country, following all its curves, stepping from stone to stone in its shallow bed, or better yet its navigation, furnish sensations akin to those felt by original explorers. The border of rushes, shrubbery, and trees shuts out the civilized landscape, the sounds of distant industry are lost in the near prattle of the water, and the vista is as primitive and wild as when no keel but that of the birch canoe had cleft its waters. There are the hope and exhilaration of discovery in rounding every bend.

In the course of a mile along such a stream you may study the whole of geography: on either hand are continents; the stream is an ocean, or inland sea, or river, or brook, as your fancy dictates; the hills form a *terra incognita* where are the hidden sources of this Nile; the mill and bridge are the towns of its world, the meadow and pasture the plains and highlands by which it passes; it has islands and peninsulas and isthmuses, capes, promontories, and reefs. The teacher of the district school at the crossroads can plant a firmer lesson in the restless young minds under her charge, by an afternoon's stroll along this stream, than by a month's study of atlases and definitions.

Thither goes the ornithologist on sweet June mornings when the spring torrent has subsided, and the dogwood is launching its large petals on the brook. The long-roll of the kingfisher summons him, and he finds a gay company of birds hardly to be met with elsewhere.

As I follow the path where the cows go down by the side of the bridge to drink, a little Quaker-dressed object shoots past my face, and I stoop under the old timbers and look for the home of

THE PHŒBE-BIRD.

Here it is, plastered on the shelving upper side of this unbarked and dusty beam, so close underneath the planks that the bird can only squeeze in—a wonderfully pretty and modest nest!

It is shaped like a very thick half-bowl, or the quarter of a citron, cut lengthwise, made of mud mixed with moss to give it greater strength, and is fastened up by its broken edges; or like one of the little basins for holy-water built against the pillars at the entrances of cathedrals. It is green with moss on the outside, and lined with hair within. The phœbes build nowadays under bridges more than anywhere else, and are known only as "bridge pewees" in many sections, but in unsettled regions they plaster their bracketed homes upon the sunny side of a cliff, in a cave, or even against the upturned roots of a fallen tree in the woods. Sometimes the phœbes save labor by building upon the flat surface of a rocky ledge, where they only need raise a rim of mud round the bed upon which the eggs lie to keep them from rolling off their bed of hair. So pleased with this economy were one family of phœbes I knew of that they returned to the same ledge three summers in succession.

Mr. Minot tells a remarkable story of a pair, which, being behindhand in their work, constructed two nests side by side on a beam in a shed, and, as soon as one set of eggs was hatched, the female immediately began to lay a second set in the other nest, while the male fed the first brood. If undisturbed, they seem always to return year after year to their old quarters, getting back among the earliest in the spring, and sometimes raise three broods in the season.

The phœbe (*Sayornis fuscus*) has several small relations belonging to the family of true fly-catchers, which are much like it and each other in appearance, but vary curiously in their architecture, although all agree pretty closely in respect to their pointed, creamy eggs, sparsely spotted with lavender and deep crimson.

Look at the nest of the wood pewee. The bird is nearly as large as the phœbe, yet its exquisite structure is not one quarter the size of that bird's. It is balanced upon the upper side of an horizontal branch, often of an apple-tree, and seems merely an excrescence upon the bark; for, while the inside of the nest is padded with the downy blossoms of the cottonwood, the outside is veneered with silver-gray lichens. It is just such a nest as the humming-bird's, and looks as though it grew there. Now, a still smaller brother, the green-crested or Acadian pewee, does not take all this trouble, but in the remote beech-woods gets together a few long straws, out of which he weaves a shallow cradle across the fork of some low, drooping branch. These two, however, do not nest before the last week in May, at least, by which time the phœbe is feeding her young.

While I am under the bridge looking at her snug home with its furniture of wood lichens and household of eggs, the mother-bird perches upon the railing of the bridge, nervously flirting her tail, and watches me, anxious lest all her treasures are to be lost, or at least lest she shall not be permitted to return until her eggs have grown so cold that all her warmth will not resuscitate them. As I move away I see her joined by her twittering mate, and watch them as they survey the premises, clinging to the edge of the nest with clinching talons and whirring wings, and I fancy I understand their rejoicings as she settles carefully upon the shining eggs, and the loving husband darts after a gnat.

The olive-green bird is so near the color of the deadened moss of which her couch is composed that she hardly needs the cover of the bridge-planks or the shelter of a cave to keep her from the eyes of hawks. It is a beautiful example of the protection afforded to most small birds by the tints of their plumage assimilating them with surrounding objects, and thus making them almost invisible. I have frequently discovered one of these nests against a vine-trellised cliff, and, removing my eyes from it for an instant, have had to search long and sharply before I could recover the sight of it; the bird meanwhile remaining absolutely still, as though well aware that the smallest movement might betray her presence. "The rock seemed to love the nest and to claim it as its own," I said. "What a lesson in architecture is here! Here is a house that was built, but with such loving care and such beautiful adaptation of the means to the end that it looks like a product of nature. The same wise economy is noticeable in the nests of all birds. No bird paints its house white or red, or adds aught for show."

The color of the lower parts of the phœbe-bird

is dull yellowish-white mixed with brown on the chin and sometimes across the breast; the tail is brown, with the outer edge of the outer feathers white; the brown wing-feathers are edged with white, and the bill and feet are black.

On the Pacific coast our phœbe-bird is replaced by a brother—the black pewee—whose habits are almost precisely similar, and which is equally dear to all philornians.

Just below the bridge, where there is a sharp bend, the brook eats through a high bank, and, by eating it away at high water, keeps the face of the cutting bare and vertical. Approaching this bank I rarely fail being roused from my reverie by a sudden splash and noisy cry, and raise my eyes to catch a silvery gleam as of sunlight flashing from a spear-point. It is the successful dive, and the triumphant shout, and the glistening prey of

THE KINGFISHER.

We all know him with his jaunty crest and blue waistcoat, and admire him, too, as he shakes the bright drops from his plumage, and looks sharply down from some high sycamore ready for a new victim. Woe to the luckless fish who swims under the range of his piercing eye! He is a diver who brings up living pearls.

The design of much of classic mythology seems to have been to account for the appearance of favorite animals upon the earth. Prominent among these myths, and one of the most beautiful, is the touching story of Halcyone, the fond wife, who, awaiting the return of her husband from his long voyage, one day beholds his dead body tossing in the surf. Overwhelmed with grief she springs to snatch him from the sea, but ere she touches the water is changed into a kingfisher, and with her husband, alike transformed, she floats away over the billows. Many a time after are they seen resting upon old Ocean's bosom; and, whatever the violence of the storm, around their buoyant nest the sea is always tranquil. What wonder that mariners protected and venerated Halcyone, the kingfisher, and that even yet we call serene, peaceful seasons halcyon days?

But for these old fables we have little room. Over the winds and waves the humble *Ceryle alcyon* of our day has no control. "Its nest is neither constructed of glue nor fish-bones, but of loose grass and a few feathers; it is not thrown on the surface of the water to float about, but snugly secured from the winds and the weather in the recesses of the earth. Neither is its head or its feathers believed, even by the most illiterate of our clowns or seamen, to be a charm for love, a protection against witchcraft, or a security for fair weather. It is neither venerated like the kingfishers of the Society Isles, nor dreaded like those of some other countries; but is considered merely as a bird that feeds on fish, is generally fat, relished by some as good eating, and is now and then exposed for sale in our markets."

Thus prosaically the usually poetic Wilson brings us back from romance to reality, and cautions against anything but *facts!*

The belted kingfisher ranges from the Rio Grande to Labrador, but everywhere is more conspicuous than abundant. In the northern portions of the Union he is migratory, flying away to the South on the approach of winter, and returning by easy stages in the spring as fast as the ice thaws in the rivers. Yet he does not altogether follow the river-courses, but often wings his way straight across the country thirty or forty miles, his flight consisting of a series of six or seven slopes, followed by a long slide on motionless wings. Thus progressing he reaches us by the first of April in ordinary seasons, and loses but little time before pairing. A mate is soon found, and together they seek out a soft, steep bank, usually near the water, where they dig a straight, sometimes winding, hole, three or four inches in diameter, and from four to ten feet in depth, near the enlarged extremity of which a little carpeting of loose grass and feathers, if anything at all, constitutes the nest. (It is the English species that makes a nest of fish-bones.) Both sexes work with bill and feet at this burrow, "turn and turn about," and progress so fast that, if the bank be of soft sand, the hole is sometimes completed in twenty-four hours. Then the eggs are laid, one a day, until there are six or seven, nearly round and crystal white. Should the nest be robbed, the parents will again and again renew their labor; and it is their custom to return year after year to the same bank to breed.

They live almost or quite exclusively on fishes, plunging after them in a swift, curved line from some dead limb over the water, and flying off with their prey to their perch, or to the entrance of their nest, before eating it. The fish is swallowed whole, and after digestion the hard parts are disgorged. When the young are in the nest they are fed mainly at night, and, as each capture is heralded by the loud r-r-r-r—rallying-cry of the parent, this peculiar and stirring sound, which Wilson aptly likened to a watchman's rattle, is more often heard after dark than during the day. How keen must be the vision distinguishing fishes in the water at midnight, and how sure the aim which can catch them through the gloom!

The kingfisher seems to me to be a wonderfully capable, self-reliant bird. He shows it in his erect, vigilant attitude and brave crest. He knows he is the King-fisher, and is proud of his skill. He holds up his head like a soldier, and the crest on his cap and the broad red band across his breast are his regalia. Knowing he can take care of himself, he defies, is solitary, taciturn, and exclusive. It is rare to see two pairs within a mile of each other, and it may be because each feels no need of the other's company. The dashing torrents he loves are congenial to his heroic nature, notwithstanding the reputation of his mythical ancestors, who may yet be patrolling the blue Ægean.

Opposite this crescentic bluff where the bank-swallows and kingfishers breed, is a broad gravelly beach which, during spring freshets, is inundated, as is shown by the muddy drift-wood entangled in the lower branches of the willows and alders. Whenever I come here my ears are saluted with a soft, little bird-squeal—*pee-weet, weet, weet,* and a tiny object sends off on swift, slender feet, or gray wings, trailing downward from its body as though broken, carry it away in a circuitous sweep, just skimming the surface of the water. This can only be

THE SPOTTED SANDPIPER.

He is another independent little fellow, scuttling, in his ridiculous way, from the tropics to the Arctic Zone and back every year. Unlike most of its allies, this species is not confined to the seashore nor does it congregate in flocks, but spreads all over the country, following those natural paths—the rivers—until adventurous ones reach even Alaska and Labrador, scale the sides of the Rocky Mountains, and make their nests in the fens far north of Lake Superior. Meanwhile thousands, less energetic or more economical of time and strength, stay with us in every State, and, in the southern portions of the Union, succeed in raising two families before being warned by comrades returning from the North that winter is at their heels.

It breeds as abundantly in the depths of the Maine forests as on the low, sandy islands, or in the marshes by our seacoast. The female, about the first week in April, scratches a hollow in the sandy earth by some pond, or sometimes in a corn-field or orchard, lining it with a few pieces of straw or moss, and lays four eggs, which she adjusts with their small ends together in the middle of the nest; these eggs are usually abruptly pyriform, sometimes a little lengthened, are clay-color, marked with blotches and spots of umber and sienna, thickest at the greater end, where they are sometimes confluent, and measure about one and a third inch in length by one inch in width.

Its nest presents so little to catch the eye that you may look long and not discover that it is close to your feet. The young appear during the first days of June, and run about with wonderful speed as soon as they leave the shell, being covered with down of a dull-gray, marked with a single streak of black down the back, and another behind each ear. Their cry is weak and plaintive. The parents are greatly distressed on the approach of any person to their nest, and exert themselves by counterfeiting lameness and by other frantic movements to lead the intruder away and prevent its exposure.

Mr. William Bartram—America's White of Selborne—told Wilson a pleasant story of how he saw one of these sandpipers defend her young against the attacks of a ground-squirrel—though it seems to me that it is not the ordinary habit of chipmunks to attempt to devour young birds: "The scene of action was on the river-shore. The parent had thrown herself, with her two young behind her, between them and the land; and, at every attempt of the squirrel to seize them, by a circuitous sweep raised both her wings into an almost perpendicular position, assuming the most formidable appearance she was capable of, and rushed forward on the squirrel, who, intimidated by her boldness and manner, instantly retreated; but, frequently returning, was met as before, in front and on flank, by the daring and affectionate bird, who, with her wings and whole plumage bristling up, seemed swelled to twice her usual size. Her young crowded together behind her, apparently sensible of their perilous situation, moving backward and forward as she advanced or retreated. This interesting scene lasted for at least ten minutes; the strength of the poor parent began evidently to flag, and the attacks of the squirrel became more daring and frequent, when my good friend, like one of those celestial agents who in Homer's time so often decided the palm of victory, stepped forward from his retreat, drove the assailant back to his hole, and rescued the innocent from destruction."

This bird is not uncommonly found also in western Europe, and winters in Central and South America and the West Indies, whither it departs in October.

The spotted sandpiper is small—about seven and a half inches long—but has a straight, slender bill an inch in length, and grooved on each side; the legs and toes are reddish-yellow and rather long, the outer toe connected with the middle one by a large membrane. The color of the upper parts is brownish-green, with a somewhat metallic or bronzed luster, and numerous lines, arrow-heads, and spots of brownish-black, also lustrous; the under parts, and a line over the eye, white, with numerous circular and oval spots of brownish-black, largest on the abdomen; wings greenish-brown, crossed by a narrow bar of white; outer feathers of the tail tipped with white, and barred with black. Its systematic name is *Tringoides macularius*.

Following the windings of the growing stream down below the meadows to the woods, where it prowls about the bare roots of old trees, and plunges over a rocky bottom between banks covered to the water's edge with thickets and fern-brakes, we are pretty sure to find one or two little birds that rarely leave such sequestered spots. These are the two cousins of the oven-bird—

THE WATER THRUSHES OR WAGTAILS.

Very pleasant little folks to know are both of them, although it is not at all easy to make their acquaintance, since they are shy of being watched, and hide themselves in the most out-of-the-way places, but always in the close vicinity of the water. The small-billed or New York wagtail —for water-thrush is an incorrect and, consequently, a bad name—is not uncommon in the northern parts of the United States through the summer, while it slowly moves in the winter to the Gulf coast and the West Indies. The large-billed, or Louisiana wagtail, on the contrary, is best known at the South, where in summer it extends northward to southern Illinois in the West and to Connecticut in the East. Each finds its food in the insects and their young which live among the wet leaves and rank weeds flourishing along river-banks, and in those aquatic species that cling to stones in the bottom of the stream. On land they have a graceful, gliding walk, not hopping, as do most woodland birds. Both are very fine singers—the finest of all the warblers. The small-billed does not seem to have its full share of credit as a vocalist on account of its modesty, and the fact that its songs are all of love to its mate, seeming never to be wasted on any other occasion than wooing, although then often continued into a moonlit serenade. An enthusiastic writer describes this song as beginning with a startling outburst of melody, clear and ringing, as if surprised by a sudden joy, after which it keeps falling until you can hardly hear it; the strong tones are yet very sweet. But, if you want to see the little minstrel, you must go carefully in a boat to near the place where he secretes himself with his mate.

The large-billed is more prodigal of his music and not quite so cautious about listeners. In the picturesque little "runs"—"trout-brooks" in New England—that find their way down the tangled ravines between the lofty hills of West Virginia, I used often to come upon them, and, by ordinary caution, could easily watch them at work or play or when singing. They seemed to choose to loiter about the pebbly shallows just above the cataract, where they could jump from stone to stone, or run along the drifted logs, rather than to retreat to the dark brakes beloved of the small-billed wagtail. They were never still a minute. Even when standing they seemed to stand unsteadily on their legs, as if their thin, transparent tarsi were too weak to hold them, and were incessantly jerking and "wagging" their tails, not depressing them as the pewees do, but flirting them in a nervous way. The large-bill's song is uttered while the bird stands on some log or stone—for it rarely alights upon a branch—and is full of fire and bright melody, yet it is hardly so accomplished a musical performance as that of his brother. If he gets the idea that he is wanted to grace your cabinet, he vents his indignation in a little *chick* like the noise made "by striking two pebbles together," and is off to some secure retreat in a twinkling. "Come upon him suddenly, however, as he is running nimbly along the margin of some great pool or rippling eddy, and at times he will seem to pay little regard to your presence, and you may have a fine chance to observe his motions and sandpiper-like ways as he wades knee-deep into the water, or splashes through it in hot pursuit of some aquatic insect." Thus pleasantly writes William Brewster, with whom it was my privilege to climb those rugged West Virginia hills and thread those charming valleys in search of feathered friends.

All three members of this genus are aptly called oven-birds, because of the covered, oven-like nests which they build upon the ground. That of the common golden-crowned wagtail is well known to all of us. The northern home of the small-billed is very similar, except that it usually builds beneath a pile of drift or some such object, and so saves itself the trouble of putting a roof over its nest. In the dense cedar-swamps of Maine an excavation is often made under a decaying log, and a warm bed of firmly woven mosses and soft fibrous materials is tucked into it. Could one imagine a snugger resting-place for the red-spotted eggs?

Although the Louisiana wagtails were so common in West Virginia, we never found one of their nests; but it was my good luck to discover its home near Norwich, Connecticut, where it is very rare, and very much farther northeast than it had ever before been known to breed.

I was walking up the bed of the Yantic River one day in the latter part of June, stepping from stone to stone, and searching the overhanging branches for nests, when a little bird I did not at once recognize darted from under the roots of a beech-tree growing on the sheer edge of the steep bank, and flew straight away, uttering alarmed chirrups. Feeling interested, I concealed myself near by and patiently waited, confident that the

5

strange bird would return. In twenty minutes I was rewarded by its reappearance, and then I saw, with delight, that it was a female large-billed wagtail, and that she had her home under the roots of the beech : but she seemed to have forgotten all about the disturbance, and to be in no haste whatever to resume her sitting. By these signs I concluded that her eggs were fresh, for when she is driven off during the latter days of incubation she rolls and tumbles about, uttering piteous cries to attract your pursuit. When at length she disclosed its position, I found the nest sunk behind a cushion of moss and into the rotten wood among the roots in such a manner that it was covered over completely.

It was rather loosely and carelessly constructed of fine grass and some dead, fibrous moss ; but, beneath and about the outside, particularly in front, many dead leaves were put as a sort of breastwork, the more thoroughly to conceal the sitting bird. It was a typical nest, except that often it is more conspicuously placed. The four eggs were of a beautiful rosy tint (becoming pure white after being blown), and were profusely spotted all over with dots, specks, and obscure zigzaggings, of two tints of reddish-brown and faint lilac, the spots being most crowded at the large end. The female is said to sit fourteen days, and when ten days old the young leave the nest and follow the mother about until they are able to fly.

In order to distinguish these two species apart, and from the golden-crown (*Seiurus auro-capillus*), a somewhat minute description of each will be necessary.

The small-billed wagtail (*Seiurus noreboracensis*) is six and one fifth inches in length, with the bill about as long as the skull. The plumage above is olive-brown, with a shade of green ; beneath, sulphur-yellow, brightest on the abdomen. There is a brownish-yellow line over the eye, a dusky line from the bill through it, and the throat and chin are finely spotted. All the remaining under parts, except the abdomen and sides of the body, are thickly streaked with olivaceous brown, almost black on the breast.

The large-billed wagtail (*Seiurus ludovicianus*) is slightly larger than the other, and its bill is longer than the skull. The upper parts are olive-brown, with a greenish shade ; under parts white, with a very faint tinge of pale buff behind. There is a conspicuous white line over the eye, a brown one though widening behind, and a dusky line backward from the mouth along the side of the throat ; the fore part of the breast and sides of the body are covered with brownish arrow-shaped streaks, but the chin, throat, belly, and vent are unspotted.

VACATIONS IN COLORADO.

By WILLIAM H. RIDEING.

WE can feel for him who has but one vacation in a whole year, and who has that spoiled by inclemency of weather or the iniquity of hotel-keepers and guides. But the vacation tourist is usually egotistically exacting, and is dissatisfied if his choice of a resort is not most felicitous, or the time which he chooses does not prove the very best of the year. If he should happen to strike continuous cold or rain, never afterward is he willing to believe that the climate is not persistently wet or bleak. He may not flatly contradict you if you describe a different experience, but there is a dubiousness in the smile with which he listens that is more provokingly negative than any explicit denial.

There are some who will tell you. supposing that you have not been there, that, in order to conceive the sensations of life in Colorado, you must rub yourself and your clothing with brick-dust ; that you must imagine your lips cracked and hands blistered and teeth for ever on edge ; that, if you are susceptible to the despondent moods of nature, you must be in heart-breaking gloom from the unspeakable influence of the vast gray peaks ; that, if you associate with coal-heavers and oyster-openers, and never take a bath, and never feel cheerful, you will have the usual "first impressions" of a tourist in Colorado.

But, though all this is so obviously extravagant, it is entertained by some who are not ordinarily violent, and whose prejudices are based on the discrepancy between too brilliant anticipations and imperfect fruition. Let us confess ourselves. We believe in Colorado—in the salubrity of its air and the ennobling expansiveness of its influence, in the wonderful beauty of its mountains and the healing balsam of its pines. But we can understand the inimical position of one who at the end of twenty-four hours on the plains between Omaha and Cheyenne finds himself deposited in that arid little offspring of civilization while a searching wind is shrieking from the mountains, which are concealed in a whirling dust ; who, as he travels southward to Denver and gazes disconsolately upon the fallow undulations of land without verdure, is told that this

A Glimpse of Denver.

is Colorado, and that the deep wall of blue occasionally visible in the west is that range which he has heard of from childhood with the greatest veneration: who lands in Denver when the streets are ribbed by sand like the seashore, and the air is so parched that a wet handkerchief flung in it becomes dry in a few moments; who is sensitive to the brusqueness of some of the people with whom he has to deal, and whose purse is not so plethoric that he can endure every demand upon it without wincing; who limits his excursions to the foot-hills and Monument Park, without learning the grandeur of the peaks, and who is pursued during all his sojourn by the dust. We car

Monument Park.

pure exuberance of Nature — days when a quick gladness dances in the eyes of the ailing, and all beings respond to the vitalizing influence, and feel a strength that makes idleness insupportable. It is no *dolce far niente* —the pleasure is in movement and exertion; and he who would in other climates care little or nothing for pedestrianism feels a tremendous longing to stride out toward one of the distant and defiant peaks. There are days, also, of trailing mist which play hide-and-seek with the mountains, and which bring out upon them new wonders of shade and shine, and days of that marvelous lucidity which accentuates every notch in the outlines and every knoll on the slopes. The nights are more spacious and luminous than any nights we know of elsewhere, and the sunsets have a passion and a splendor that are only rivaled by those of the mid-ocean. Let us not forget, either, the Alpine lakes in the regions of perpetual snow where the ice melts every morning in midsummer, and where flowers of the most delicate hue and form lift themselves out of the white and arctic imprisonment; or those still glens high above the plain, through the arching branches of whose foliage dim glimpses are had of a deep country below, between which and us are insurmountable cliffs; or the mellow-colored thickets of cottonwoods whose every leaf seems dancing at the faintest breath of air.

understand how, as the clovered pastures and waving corn-fields of Kansas and Iowa are being traversed in the homeward journey, he looks back in contrast to the ashy grasses and loose soil of Colorado, and proclaims that sand-paper and pulverized bath-brick well applied to the clothing and skin will give a fair idea of what it feels like to be out there. Sometimes the wind and dust *are* unpleasant in Colorado; the air is bleak, and the whole effect of the scenery is dispiriting. Such a " spell " of weather to one who has read of the country as a paradise—who is nervous, irascible, and unprepared to wait for a change—justifies the expression of disappointment if it does not sanction the inimical generalizations we have alluded to. We remember to have been in Denver when it has seemed that any place in the world, under any condition, would be preferable. But there are days in Colorado when the air is like wine in its exhilarativeness, and when all that is bitter in the world is lifted off the mind by the

No; Colorado is not a paradise, nor could it seem so even to a select party traveling in a special director's car, with a commissary attached, and *carte blanche* as to time and speed. It embraces among its features absolute sterility and unloveliness; the winds on the foot-hills and plains are apt to be mistaken for fogs from the quantity of dust they carry with them; but we who have traveled beyond the beaten path know that Colorado is not only a revelation to him who can enter into the subtiler moods of Nature, but that it has attractions in a bracing climate, and the simple charms of wood, valley, ravine, and mountain. Pleasure is to be commanded, and he who is defeated in his search for it may charge his discomfiture to his own lack of resource. Come to Colorado prepared for wind, and well supplied with glycerine; come, not expecting the *menu* or attendance of a fashionable club; come to be content, and then you shall not go away disappointed.

We have already briefly indicated some of the specific charms, and we may now look at them in detail. First, there is the journey over the Plains by the Union Pacific Railway from Omaha, or by either the Atchison, Topeka and Sante Fé, or the Kansas Pacific from Kansas City. The merits of the three are about even, and we should advise the tourist to go by the Union and return by the Kansas Pacific or Atchison, though the scenery on each is singularly alike. To the traveler who has never been west of the Missouri before, the departure is quite a different thing from leaving Boston or New York for Chicago or St. Louis. He has an awe-inspiring sense of approaching the remote and unknown. There is only one through train each day, and the ultimate destination of that train is the misty shore of the Pacific, a point between which and Omaha there are one hundred and twenty hours of continuous travel. The train itself has an imposing largeness and dignity—an extraordinary number of mail and express cars and sleepers. It is the business of the day to dispatch it. The " overland," as it is called, is no common conveyance, and the old-fashioned sentiment of leave-taking is touched as it ponderously sweeps out of the depot. Whether we travel by the Union Pacific through Nebraska or the Kansas Pacific through Kansas, the first few hundred miles out present the same features of a teeming and developing agricultural country, with a greater activity of labor and luxuriance of woodland in the latter than in the former. There are a breeziness and an extent of horizon, a massiveness of cloud-forms, and withal a brilliance of light, that in some indefinite way

force upon us the recognition of an uncrowded, abundant land, and an atmosphere for men to thrive in. But, before evening, the verdant farm-lands are succeeded by the Plains, which are the same whether seen from the Union Pacific, the Kansas Pacific, or the Atchison. Billow follows billow of land, the prevailing color of which is a yellowish-green, jeweled with patches of wild verbena. Occasionally the land sinks into a basin surrounded by hogs'-backs, a form of rock which has a steep and rough escarpment on one side, and on the other side slopes off by easy gradations to the level. But no great elevation is visible to convey an idea of space by contrast, and the impression received by the spectator is one of contraction rather than immensity. At intervals of between ten and twenty miles, a red tank, with a creaking windmill, marks a water-station, and, still farther apart, some white little towns, with names suggestive of frontier life, tell a story, to which the mendicant Indians crowding the depots are a graphic antithesis. Between the towns the plains rise and fall, keeping the traveler's interest only half-awake by prairie-dog villages and small herds

Tower of Babel, Garden of the Gods.

of antelope. The buffaloes have entirely disappeared.

From the novel but tedious landscape we are glad to turn to our fellow passengers, who discard the formalities of conventional life, and are quick to make acquaintance with one another. Notes are compared and plans are broached. As the sun leaves the vast land " which few beholding understand," as a Western poet says, all outer things are obliterated by what seems like utter darkness, while within the " sleeper" the crimson upholstery, the yielding seats, and the soft lamps remind us of the sanctum of a friend who has learned how to make the most of home. Individual characteristics stand out with the broad relief they have on shipboard, and a feeling of intimacy springs up which vents itself in confidences as to whom we are, what we are, and whither we are bound. There is a good deal of euchre, whist, and casino playing, and, when the ladies have retired, there are several old travelers who bring forth odorous bottles, of which the odor is not the strongest nor the better part. The objects that have momentarily united us are as

dissimilar as the traits of the persons who entertain them. There is a young earl traveling for pleasure, with unlimited means; a delicate man who is leaving the austere climate of New England for better things in southern California, and who, as we accidentally discover, is so poor that he depends for subsistence on the contents of an old millinery-box ; a weather-beaten miner who has not yet exhausted a lucky " strike "; a Japanese student from Yale, who is always bland and courteous, and thirsty for information; an animated little cockney who is bound for New South Wales; a brisk, fluent, anecdotal man from Ohio, who has abandoned the cares of a country newspaper office for the emoluments of a consular appointment at Tahiti; a star actress engaged to play an engagement in California ; a complacent millionaire of the Comstock lode ; and a frail, almost transparent, little woman, whose strenuous breathing shows her suffering from asthma. There are travelers bound over this iron pathway across the continent to Vancouver's Island, to Chili, Peru, and Mexico, to the Sandwich Islands, to Japan and China, to Alaska, and to Siberia! The Golden Gate has become a door to nearly all quarters of the globe. But it is not for us to follow all of the passengers to their destinations. Our special interest is in the persons going to Colorado, among whom we discover that mild little invalid aforesaid, whose object is relief from her complaint; a substantial English squire and his wife who propose to "do " the country without leaving the beaten path, and half a dozen young men and women from New York, who have come to rough it, to avoid hotels, and to camp out. If we follow those, we shall see what Colorado offers to different classes of visitors; and the fact of the matter is, that the State is so enmeshed by railways and stage - lines nowadays, that a " transient " like the English squire, who has only a few weeks to give to it, can see nearly all the varieties of scenery without exposing himself to any hardship or danger. There are hotels and cities now, where a few years ago the tent of the explorer or the prospector was the only habitation in an area of a hundred miles. True, the squire can not know the solitudes of the moun-

Major Domo, Glen Eyrie.

Rainbow Falls, Ute Pass.

mit of the Sangre del Cristo Mountains after six hours of labor. Tall pines cast their long shadows on the slopes, and moaned as the rising wind stirred among their straight and dusky branches. Now and then an Alpine bluebell nodded at us, or a wild rose peeped out of a thicket. The valleys lay under a dense growth of shrubbery as leafy and as lustrous as the arbor-vitæ. We toiled over the innumerable foot-hills—the lowest loftier than Mount Washington—and far away could see the snowy spires and domes of the Sierra Blanca, and the smooth, precipitous gray walls of Baldy Peak. No sooner had we attained the crest of the hill than another still higher appeared, and our outlook expanded every minute. We followed the trail through a deep grove, and glanced down through a natural clearing in the pines and aspens on ninety miles of country, in which the more distant mountains looked like islands in a wide ocean. The life-limits were not far above, and the wind roared among the trees with the sound of a tremendous cataract. Whole forests of pines were prone on the slopes, torn from their beds by the tempests of the previous winter, and in all the

tain-peaks, or the cragginess of the preëminent cliffs, but, without once putting his portly person to distress, he can see all the other phases of Nature, which are many, in this Western wonderland. Five years ago, we stood on the sum-

outlook there was not a cabin or a house to be seen.

A railway now encircles this same summit. "Up, up," that charming author, "H. H.," has written, "nine thousand feet up across a neck of the Sangre del Cristo range itself, down the other side, and out among the foot-hills to the vast San Luis Valley, the plucky little railroad has already pushed. It is a notable feat of engineering. As the road winds among the mountains, its curves are so sharp that the timid and inexperienced hold their breath. From one track running along the edge of a precipice, you look to another which you are presently to reach; it lies high on the mountain-side, four hundred feet above your head, yet it looks hardly more than a stone's-throw across the ravine between. The curve by which you are to climb up this hill is a thirty-degree curve. To the non-professional mind it will perhaps give a clearer idea of the curve to say that it is shaped like a mule-shoe—a much narrower shoe than a horseshoe. The famous horseshoe curve on the Pennsylvania road is broad and easy in comparison with this. There are three of these thirty-degree curves within a short distance of each other; the road doubles on itself, like the path of a ship tacking in adverse winds. The grade is very steep, two hundred and eleven feet to the mile; the engines pant and strain, and the wheels make a strange sound, at once sibilant and ringing on the steel rails. You go but six miles an hour; it seems like not more than four; the leisurely pace is so unwonted a one for steam-engines. . . . From the mouth of the pass to the summit is, measured by miles, fourteen miles; measured by hours, three hours; measured by sensations, the length of a dream—that means a length with which figures and numbers have nothing in common. One dreams sometimes of flying in the air, sometimes of going swiftly down or up endless stairways without resting his feet on the steps; my recollection of being lifted up and through the Veta Pass, by steam, are like the recollections of such dreams. The summit is over nine thousand feet above the sea-level—the highest point reached by a railroad on this continent."

When we looked down from here we likened our sensations to those of Vasco Nuñez de Balboa "alone on a peak in Darien," as Keats sonorously puts it; but now there is a tourist standing on the porch of the Summit House and sending the incense of a cigar to heaven, as if he were posted at the window of his club in Fifth Avenue!

What more can the squire see? A three hours' jaunt from Denver brings him to Monument Park, and there he may study those abnormal geological developments which are a pro-

dominant feature of the far West—a region which strikes one as being the creation and abode of some fanciful race of goblins, who have twisted everything, from a shaft of rock to an old pine-tree, into a whimsical and incredulous shapelessness. The eroded sandstones impress us as the result of a disordered dream—the preposterous handiwork of a crack-brained mason, with a remembrance of Caliban's island lingering in his head. Those in Monument Park are ranged in two rows lengthwise through an elliptical basin. They are cones from twelve to twenty-five feet in height, and may be said to resemble mushrooms at the first glance, though a more imaginative person than the squire is apt to find himself transfiguring them into odd-looking men and animals. Think of several sugar-loaves, such as are seen in grocers' windows, with plates or trays nicely balanced on their peaks, or of several candle-extinguishers with pennies on tops, and you may obtain an idea of what these geological curiosities are. Each pillar is capped with a conglomerate of sand and pebbles cemented by iron, and, this being so much harder than the underlying yellow sandstone, has resisted the eroding influences, and in some cases extends continuously over several pillars, thus forming a natural colonnade.

In the Garden of the Gods, Glen Eyrie, Cheyenne Cañon and Williams Cañon, all of which are as accessible from Denver as Hampstead Heath is from London, other rock phantasies of a grander sort may be seen, but the abnormal is not a lasting source of pleasure, and the squire gladly passes from it to Nature in her sublimer moods. He visits the three cañons of the Boulder, and is awed by their vertical walls of basalt and granite, which are exalted from the narrow bed of a stream to tremendous heights and occasionally split by transverse chasms into which a ray of sunshine never creeps. The locomotive whirls him through Clear Creek Cañon, with its sheer and overarching cliffs and rushing stream. The Concord coach with six horses conveys him to steep defiles into Leadville, where there is all the urgency of a city among mountain-tops. He visits Chicago Lakes in the saddle—two crystal basins held on the slopes of Mount Rosalie, within a few feet of twelve thousand above the sea-level, which at night are crusted with ice even in midsummer—ice that melts as the days warm, and admits the vision in twelve or fifteen feet of dazzlingly pure bluish water while the snow presses on the margin and from it spring delicate flowers of marvelously soft colors. Near the lakes he finds Idaho Springs, the curative properties of which relieve him of a threatening touch of the rheumatism, and at Manitou Springs he falls into a curious little world of fashion with

Clear Creek Canon.

"hops" and like festivities, night after night. From Manitou he ascends Pike's Peak, on the topmost pinnacle of which he lets his heart fill with the emotion that the outlook invariably inspires—an outlook that embraces in a glance the silent billows of the plains and the chaotic, gashed, knife-like peaks, before whose feet those endless yellow waves have ceased to beat, like an eager living creature struck with despair at omnipotent opposition.

All these things the squire sees without any more fatigue than a delicate woman could endure, and without barbarianism of any sort. Every night he sleeps in a secure and well-furnished bedroom; his meals are served in clean if not luxurious dining-rooms by polite attendants; he is not once shot at, and no attempt is made at his scalp—indeed, he does not meet one Indian in all his peregrinations; and, though at Denver there are shops filled with bowie-knives and six-shoot-ers, buckskin breeches and moccasins, he perceives that these things are more in demand as memen-tos of adventures (never experienced) by tourists than by the natives of that interesting and pro-gressive " Metropolis of the Plains," as it loves to be called.

After the squire's fashion, Colorado with its most salient features may be embraced in a charming summer excursion lasting only a few weeks. But, if one has more time to spare,

Grey's Peak.

and is young, strong, and sound, and can get a few congenial companions, who will not mind a bed of boughs and a supper without a table-cloth, the example of the camping-out party that we met in the Pullman is the one to be followed. The quality of hotels—whether this *cuisine* be good or that indifferent—the departures of trains, all the cares of routine travel, then become the shadows of an unreal dream, and the miserable conventions of society are cast aside with an ex-hilarating sense of relief.

There are camping-out parties and camping-out parties. We have seen a cavalcade of ladies and gentlemen leaving Denver with an outfit so elaborate that it has excited the risibility of small boys to a convulsive degree—with wall tents for each member, patent stoves, spring beds, easy-chairs and such a quantity of *impedimenta* that more than one pack-animal has been necessary for each person in addition to his own "mount.", We don't despise spring beds nor easy-chairs—ah, no! we have felt the rough edge of too many campaigns for that; but all these things limit the movements of the party, and that complete change of life which is supposed to be the peculiar advantage of camping out becomes impossible. A camp may be established among the woods, and the balsam of the pines may be breathed to the full. What sort of a camp is it, however, where all the members sit down on stools to a covered table, and eat a dinner of pretentious canned stuffs? It is a garden-party, no more nor less!

perhaps beneficial—no doubt very enjoyable, but it is expensive, yet circumscribed, and it is not the real thing; it is a fastidious imitation, and, except that the roof is canvas instead of shingles, there are many taverns among the foot-hills where the same advantages could be had at a much smaller outlay.

Now, let us see how our acquaintances of the Union Pacific manage it. The three ladies are simply dressed in strong flannels with short petticoats and thick-soled boots with flat heels. Their experience is only new as to the country, not as to the manner of life, for they have already done the Adirondacks and the Rangeley Lakes with

Idaho Springs.

their husbands, and they know that tent-life under ordinary conditions will not be too severe for them—something that it is desirable every woman should understand before entering on an expedition of the kind. They can walk sixteen miles a day without straining themselves, and they can listen to the rain pattering on their tents without dreading a cold to-morrow. The men are vigorous, courageous fellows, with a keen zest for sport, who, instead of feeling that the presence of their wives will embarrass them in their pursuits, are aware that these ladies can angle and aim almost as well as themselves, and will make camp-life far more happy than it possibly could be

without them. The more essential prerequisites of success in camping out are in the dispositions of the members of the party, and herein they are indicated. Nervous, delicate, fidgety people can only enjoy themselves by a prodigious effort of the imagination.

The less elaborate the outfit the more movable the party, and our six friends dispense with everything that is not necessary. Two V-tents suffice for all, one for the three ladies and the other for the three men. The "kitchen" is packed in a box less than two feet square; the only provisions taken are canned vegetables, tea, coffee, flour, sugar, condiments, and baking-powder. The men mean to find the rest. The whole equipment can be carried by three *burros* (*Anglicè*, asses), and now behold our party with a guide and a packer in the field!

They are absolutely independent of all the world: they travel for days together without meeting a stranger; they enter valleys wherein the primitive sanctity of Nature still remains; they pitch their tents on summits known only to surveyors, and they have all the exhilaration of discovery, for what they find has no mention in any guide-book. There are long, vitalizing days spent along the margin of lakes whose boundaries are the granite and basaltic peaks of the main range, and whose surface is silvered while the sunlight lasts by the quivering reflections of snows that never melt—lakes which yield them trout by the score; other days there are of swift-flying cloud and high winds, when all the earth seems to be in visible motion and the pulses beat with eager responsiveness—days in wildernesses of pine where it is always afternoon; days in the silent and spacious "parks" where the verdure is soft and abundant: days on the peaks themselves; days of toil ending with views of unutterable splendor, and nights so calm that the throbbing of the stars seems audible. It is one thing to stand on a summit like that of Pike's

Peak, which has been trodden down by men's feet—which nearly every day in summer is the resort of excursion parties—and it is another to gaze out upon a vast country from an apex which may never before have been overcome, and upon which, at least, no sign of man exists. There are a grandeur and exaltation in the isolation, and the vesture of earth seems to fall away from us in the contemplation of it.

After the toil and sights of the day, moreover, comes repose of a sort for princes to envy. Before erecting the tents the men dig out three shallow troughs, in the space to be covered by each—three troughs seven feet long and three wide—each of which they fill with small cuttings from the pines, which form a springy and aromatic mattress. Over the branches they spread successively a sheet of heavy canvas, a rubber blanket, and three California blankets, which together make a bed that gently hurries the person lying on it into sweet and immediate sleep. We can not specify all the pleasures these adventurers experience. They dine on brook-trout and venison steaks, lunch on cold grouse, and sup on toasted quail and potted rabbit. When we think of them, we decide at once that this is the best way of seeing Colorado; and, one way or another, Colorado ought to be seen by every American.

THE STRAWBERRY PICKERS.

FROM "ALICE OF MONMOUTH," BY E. C. STEDMAN.

I.

THE strawberry-vines lie in the sun,
  Their myriad tendrils twined in one;
Spread like a carpet of richest dyes,
The strawberry-field in sunshine lies.
  Each timorous berry, blushing red,

Has folded the leaves above her head,
  The dark-green curtains gemmed with dew;
But each blissful berry, peering through,
  Shows like a flock of the underthread—
The crimson woof of a downy cloth
  Where the elves may kneel and plight their troth.

II.

Run through the rustling vines to show
Each picker an even space to go,
Leaders of twinkling cord divide
The field in lanes, from side to side;
And here and there, with patient care,
Lifting the leafage everywhere,
Rural maidens and mothers dot
The velvet of the strawberry-plot:
Fair and freckled, old and young,
With baskets at their girdles hung,
Searching the plants with no rude haste
Lest berries should hang unpicked, and waste,
Of the pulpy, odorous, hidden quest,
First gift of the fruity months, and best.

III.

Crates of the laden baskets cool
Under the trees at the meadow's edge,
Covered with grass and dripping sedge,
And lily-leaves from the shaded pool;
Filled, and ready to be borne
To market before the morrow morn.
Beside them, gazing at the skies,
Hour after hour a young man lies.
From the hillside, under the trees,
He looks across the field, and sees
The waves that ever beyond it climb
Whitening the rye-slope's early prime;
At times he listens, listlessly,
To the tree-toad singing in the tree,
Or sees the catbird pick his fill,
With feathers adroop and roguish bill,
But often, with a pleased unrest,
He lifts his glances to the west,
Watching the kirtles, red and blue,
Which cross the meadow in his view;
And he hears anon the busy throng
Singing the Strawberry-Pickers' Song:

IV.

"Rifle the sweets our meadows bear,
Ere the day has reached its nooning;
While the skies are fair, and the morning air
Awakens the thrush's tuning.
Softly the rivulet's ripples flow;
Dark is the grove that lovers know;
Here, where the whitest blossoms blow,
The reddest and ripest berries grow.

"Bend to the crimson fruit, whose stain
Is glowing on lips and fingers;
The sun has lain in the leafy plain,
And the dust of his pinions lingers.
Softly the rivulet's ripples flow;
Dark is the grove that lovers know;
Here, where the whitest blossoms blow,
The reddest and ripest berries grow.

"Gather the cones which lie concealed,
With their vines your foreheads wreathing,
The strawberry-field its sweets shall yield,
While the western winds are breathing.
Softly the rivulet's ripples flow;
Dark is the grove that lovers know;
Here, where the whitest blossoms blow,
The reddest and ripest berries grow."

V.

From the far hillside comes again
An echo of the pickers' strain.
Sweetly the group their cadence keep;
The vines are stripped and the song is sung,
A joyous labor for old and young—
For the blithe children, gleaning behind
The women, marvelous treasures find.

HOW TO PRESERVE AUTUMN LEAVES.

OF all the methods by which we attempt to keep the glories of one season before our eyes throughout the year, there is none more attractive, and, if the leaves have been successfully preserved in all their delicacy and variety of tint, none more effective than that afforded by "autumn leaves." Nearly every one has made the experiment at one time or another of gathering them; but their beauty is evanescent unless fixed by some appropriate method of drying and preserving; and so few of the methods commonly employed yield satisfactory results, that many persons refrain from collecting leaves which they have learned by experience will only be spoiled on their hands. From a lady whose success in this and similar matters has obtained for her quite a local reputation, and the product of whose skill we have ourselves admired, we have been fortunate enough to secure the following description of her method. We quote directly from her letter, though it was not designed for publication:

"From my own observation," she says, "I think it a mistaken idea that frosts are needed to brighten and deepen the tints of autumn leaves. 'Leaves have their time to fall' is as certain as any of Nature's marvels, and they do it much more gracefully in the mellowing sunshine, ripening day by day, every day showing new tints and beauties, until they fall, their mission accomplished. To preserve their coloring, they should be gathered from the trees *before frosts* (getting all the shades and tints possible, of course), singly and in sprays suitable for pressing, and at once placed between the leaves—not too near together —of books or newspapers, and several pounds' weight laid upon them. They should be kept, while pressing, in a cool place, and as often as every other day (every day is better during the first week) changed into new books. This is important because the paper absorbs the dampness from the leaves, and they soon become discolored if allowed to remain.

"They should be kept in press until thoroughly dry—between two and three weeks—otherwise they shrivel; they are then ready for a coating of oil or varnish. I find a mixture of three ounces of spirits of turpentine, two ounces of boiled linseed-oil, and half an ounce of white varnish preferable to either alone. Get a perfectly smooth board, large enough to lay a spray upon with no reaching of the leaves beyond the outer edges, or in an unlucky moment comes the wail, 'How could I be so careless as to break off the very loveliest leaf!' I have done it more than once, and have thereby learned that autumn leaves are brittle things and require tender handling. Take a piece of soft cloth to apply the dressing—a brush does not do it as evenly—and there must be no streaks left; they are a blemish when dry.

"After the application, the leaves must be laid carefully on boards or papers (not overlapping each other) until dry, and then disposed of as taste suggests, avoiding as much as possible a stiff, unnatural arrangement. They charm me most in sprays and groups on curtains and walls, with or without ferns; but they can be arranged very artistically on the panels of doors, using starch for holding them in place. I have seen them used with evergreens in winter decorations with great effect; the stem can be broken off and a fine wire fastened in its place, which makes them a little more yielding to handle. There is beauty for some in a wreath, so called, of autumn leaves, but I have always failed to see it, more especially if under glass; they have such a helpless, imprisoned look, the beauty all flattened out of them.

"Not long since I read the maledictions of an individual on a newspaper; he had read in it, 'To preserve autumn leaves, put a little white wax on the surface and pass a warm iron over them.' He said he sat up till after midnight ruining a bushel of the loveliest leaves he ever saw; 'it left them the color of an old felt hat.' I have had some experience in the ironing process, and can truthfully say it spoils both leaves and temper.

"The leaves of sumach and the Virginia creeper, or five-fingered ivy, will retain their beauty for a time, if pressed, and can be used to advantage with other leaves; but after drying they have not much substance, and soon 'the grace of the fashion of them perisheth'—as do so many other beautiful things."

NEW HAVEN SKETCHES.

By George T. Ferris.

I.

WEST ROCK AND ITS ENVIRONS.

THERE are very few cities in the country better known to cultivated people than the Elm City, the seat of one of the two greatest universities in the United States. What at the beginning of the century was little more, judged by modern standards, than a superior academy, has become a noble seat of learning, rivaling Oxford and Cambridge in England, Göttingen and Jena in Germany. Here every summer, when the magnificent elms have their full gala-dress on, and the beautiful scenery which tempts the visitor to stray in every direction is at its brightest, at least two thousand strangers congregate to see sons, brothers, and lovers step from youth to manhood from the threshold of cloistered study. Every State sends its delegation, and perhaps few conventions so fully represent the social and intellectual worth of the country.

The streets are thronged with the young and beautiful of both sexes; the very air is alive with the music of mirth. In every rustic lane may be seen parties of pleasure-seekers enjoying the picturesque landscapes which variegate the environs of the beautiful college town, dreaming amid its ancient trees, and sedate with the atmosphere of student-life.

Yet, in spite of this annual visitation, which to the alumni of the college and the friends of the student is almost like a pilgrimage, there are so many who are ignorant of the charming surroundings of the Oxford of America, that we are tempted to make some brief sketches of tradition, life, and landscape, which are not intended to be complete pictures, but only off-hand studies.

Let us wander out of the city proper, with its clean, wide, solemn streets, arched with the umbrageous roofs of elms one and two centuries old, northwest of New Haven, and observe the beautiful villas, alternated with substantial and cozy farmhouses, that meet the eye at every turn. About all these there is an atmosphere of culture and refinement. We see no such monstrous caricatures of architecture as those with which the *nouveaux riches* so often disfigure the fair face of Nature in building country-seats. The rich residents of New Haven have mostly been so for several generations, and a certain solid æsthetic culture has come down to them with their money-bags. The same characteristic may be noted in the farmhouses. The buildings are often old-fashioned, many of them ancient as the Pequot war. But now here can we see any of that slattern carelessness so often found about American farmhouses. The yards are trim, and, in the open, sunny spaces where the trees do not shut out the light and warmth, the eye is very apt to remark beautiful flower-beds evidently guarded by loving hands. One noticeable feature, too, is the multiplication of splendid box-wood hedges, an eminently classic taste, as we may gather from the descriptions of the magnificent Roman villas which covered Italy in the time of the emperors.

West Rock.

In the suburb of Westville is the residence of Donald G. Mitchell, who seems of late years to have rested on his laurels as a writer, and to have devoted himself to landscape-gardening. "Ik Marvel" years ago was the delight of the young people of his generation, and some of us have not yet forgotten his "Reveries of a Bachelor." It is questionable whether we have been altogether repaid for the loss of the literary products of this genial writer's fancy in its application to the practical yet poetic pursuit of landscape-gardening; though such an example of æsthetic culture, in a field generally barren in America, is never without its good results.

Edgewood farm, as Ik Marvel calls his home in honest, simple fashion, is deservedly one of the show-places of New Haven. Certainly not on account of the beauty of the residence itself, for it is a simple, old-fashioned, squarely built house, with rambling wings overgrown with creepers, and with clumps of fine trees on the not very extensive lawn. There is a hearty, almost picturesque, homeliness in the house and its surroundings, yet not indicative of aught more than the residence of the scholar and the country gentleman. It is in the farm itself, a rocky, broken, rolling sweep of several hundred acres, from whose higher ground there is a noble view of the shining waters and delicious stretches of landscape, that the attraction exists. The owner has taxed all the resources of his art, and of a singularly rich and original fancy, to make a "pleasance" such as that stately lover of forest and garden, Lord Bacon, would have delighted in, if we may judge from one of his best and most pregnant essays.

Mr. Mitchell has refrained from interfering with Nature except under the guidance of a severe and intelligent taste. The forest portions have been carefully trimmed out, every bit of underbrush removed, and the deep, soft turf is like velvet. Here and there open spaces let a flood of sunlight into the solemn darkness of the umbrageous shadow. The rough stones of the fields have been built into the semblance of woodland temples, and every possibility of suggestion borrowed to deepen the somber yet artistic aspect of the forest interior. Wherever a brook, in its sinuous route through the fields, gives opportunity, it has been transformed into a miniature lake or waterfall. On the higher elevations of ground quaint summer-houses look off toward the bay, and noble hedges or fences, made of huge gnarled roots interlocked and overgrown with creepers, everywhere meet the eye of the visitor as he wanders over the beautiful grounds. It is in the harmony and unity of design, however, that the chief charm of Edgewood lies. So well has the artist-owner accomplished his purpose, that there is not the least sense of discrepancy in the appearance of the Swiss chalet farmhouses, constructed of rough stones yet wonderfully picturesque in style, which have been built for the workmen.

From beautiful and highly cultivated Edgewood it is not many minutes' walk to the bold, lonely steep of West Rock, consecrated, in the minds of the sons of the Puritans, as the hiding-place of Goffe, Whalley, and Dixwell, when the three stern regicides were obliged to hide like wolves and foxes from the pursuivants of Charles II. This wild spot, where the flavor of romance and savagery still lingers, for its immediate vicinity is as desolate and forbidding as in the days when it sheltered the slayers of a king, is about four miles northwest of the New Haven State-House.

On one side, facing the south, it is a lofty, broken bluff, a mass of yellow shale and sandstone, which the winds and rains have beaten against so insidiously that it seems a crumbling ruin. On the other sides thick forests with tangled undergrowth guard the approaches. Altogether a gloomy, wild, somber spot, it seems a fit place to have been chosen in the olden time for the purpose which tradition assigned to it. The outlook from the summit commands a view of Long Island Sound for many miles. Not a sail can approach the harbor but what, far away, it may be seen from the rocky pinnacle. The visitor now gazes on a beautiful and populous city, villages dotting the country far and wide, the stacks of manufactories belching forth towers of smoke, clusters of farmhouses thickly sown every quarter of a mile, fields richly dressed by the thrift of man coöperating with the kindliness of Nature, the bright waters of the Sound bearing on their silver surface innumerable vessels skimming along like sea-gulls—everywhere the marks of a highly advanced civilization lending its final touches to the naturally picturesque.

What a contrast to the spectacle that met the sad and straining vision of the three regicide judges, when daily they climbed from their rugged cave to the top of the rock watching for the vessel which, perchance, might bear the king's colors and the king's warrant, the sure passport to a scaffold and a tomb! Let the imagination uncover the past with its successive layers of events, like the writings on a palimpsest, and stand with Whalley, Goffe, and Dixwell on their eagle eyrie.

Stern, savage, yet romantic and striking as their own dark fate, is the outlook. Crouched in the little valley at the head of the harbor is the sturdy Puritan settlement of New Haven, Quinepiack as it was first named, and Red Mount as it was known to the Manhattan Dutch. No lofty spires, glittering roofs, or factory-chimneys stand out against the sunshine, only a few low-built, square, beetling houses, each one of which is half a fortress. Here and there a more pretentious dwelling, though hardly distinguishable in the distance, marks the home of one of the magnates of the colony. With a spy-glass, perhaps, could be distinguished the whipping-post, pillory, and stocks with some poor unfortunate expiating in their embraces the crime of cooking a dinner or driving a horse on the Sabbath. A homely, solid edifice in the center of a large inclosure marks the "meeting-house," where the austere religionists veritably wrestle with God in prayer, and feast on sermons two hours long. Not far from the Long Wharf of to-day a massive block-house or fort frowning with culverins speaks of constant readiness for attack. The Puritan ancient was as prompt with the temporal as with the spiritual weapon.

In other directions the three exiles can see little except a wild solitude: lonely waters on the south, a wilderness with an occasional cluster of houses west and north, and the tiny settlement of Milford standing like a vidette outpost of the mother colony.

The cave in which the fugitives were con-

cealed, about three quar-
ters of a mile from the
southern extremity, was
well chosen for shelter.
The huge, broad pillars
of stone, twenty feet in
height, fence in an in-
closure forty feet square,
and rude, flat slabs and
inclined masses of rock
arch it above. Lofty
trees, until recent years,
secluded the entrance.
By thatching the open-
ings in the roof with
leaves and boughs, it
was made a barely habit-
able retreat. Here for
four months the hunted
exiles gnawed their own
sad hearts in silence and
isolation, for their friends
hardly dared visit them,
from fear of revealing the
secret.

At last they disap-
peared as suddenly as
they had come, Dixwell
excepted, who lived in
New Haven under the
name of Davids till the
time of his death. Goffe
and Whalley died at Had-
ley, Massachusetts, some
years afterward, and
were buried in the min-
ister's cellar, whence
their bones were finally
transferred and placed
by those of their brother
exile. Three stones in
the rear of Center Church
now indicate their rest-
ing-place. They are
marked: " E. W. . . .
1678 " ; " M. G. . . .
1680 " ; and " J. D.,
Esq. . . . 1688."

The pretty suburb
of West Haven, which
hugs the west side of
the harbor, is a perfect
garden. Here we find
a succession of highly
cultivated market-farms,
which are models for
imitation in their com-
pleteness of appliances
and their arrangements.

6

West Beach.

Thence early vegetables are shipped in large quantities, not only to New Haven and adjoining towns, but even to New York, Boston, Hartford, and Springfield. Most of these market-gardeners are Germans or Scandinavians, and many of them have become rich through their thrift and industry. Wine-growing has of late been introduced and extensive vineyards planted, the soil and exposure in some parts of the township being peculiarly adapted to this crop.

The visitor to West Haven, however, will find his most agreeable rambles along the beach which stretches in picturesque and diversified curves for about four miles to the mouth of the harbor. Its great width at this part and the fact that it is not landlocked cause the waters of the bay during southeast storms to roughen their ordinarily serene expanse into giant waves, and the beat of the breakers on the western beach can be heard many miles rolling like continuous thunder. In serene weather the harbor and its surroundings are very beautiful. Symmetrical in shape, its borders agreeably diversified with costly villas, spacious farmhouses, and a happy combination of grove and meadow, hillside and level, we know of few arms of Long Island Sound, famous for its charming estuaries, more attractive. At ebb-tide both beaches may be seen dotted with bending figures, raking the sand for soft-shell clams; or farther out on the mud-flats, "proggers," as they are known in the local patois of New England seaside places, searching for quahogs. These two varieties of shell-fish, though less prized elsewhere, are dear to the heart of "Down East" gastronomes, for do they not furnish the material for those dainty and succulent feasts known as clam-bakes? And who that has been at one does not treasure it in memory alongside even of the Apician banquet, where all of the artifices of the cook have been exhausted to excite the appetite of the jaded epicure?

At no time does the bay present a more picturesque view than when the college racing-boats are out on Wednesday or Saturday afternoons for the exercise of their crews. The collegians have some dozen or more rowing-clubs, and when these are on the water, as they not unfrequently are, all together, the bright uniforms and flashing oars give peculiar touches of color and brilliancy to the outlook, as the spectator gazes from the beach.

II.

EAST ROCK.

The English, in pursuing the broken and demoralized Pequot tribe from east to west, after they had inflicted on them the first terrible de-

feat, realized the beauty and fertility of the country between Saybrook and Fairfield. On these fair reports Theophilus Eaton and a few associates, who had come from London in 1637 to Plymouth, determined to make the present site of New Haven the establishment of a new colony. Eastward of New Haven the hostile Indians had been thoroughly crushed, and it was only between the new colony and the borders of Manhattan that the savages, who were for the most part tributaries of the Mohawks, were specially dangerous. The latter redoubted tribe, the leading sept of the confederacy of the Five Nations, had thus early acquired a potent feudal ascendancy over all the savage clans east, west, and north. It was perhaps fortunate for the Connecticut colony that the attention of the most dangerous of the Indian nations was absorbed in quarreling with the sturdy Dutch, or it might have had a harder foe to battle than was found in that Hannibal of the New England savages, King Philip.

The immunity of the country, eastward of Quinepiack, from the dread of midnight attack and massacre, caused many little thriving settlements to be made within short distance of the parent colony. These were the nuclei of the prosperous and busy towns which the visitor to the top of East Rock, one of the two giant buttresses guarding either flank of New Haven Harbor, may see lying apparently almost within a stone's-throw of his lofty perch. Here multifarious factories turn out all kinds of articles, from buttons and pins to steel rails and locomotives—nearly everything, in short, except the wooden nutmegs, which the facetious jokers of other States attribute to good old Connecticut as a favorite product.

We will ask our readers to follow the example of the stranger visiting New Haven, and take a look from the stately observatory which commands so bright and pleasing a landscape.

The drive from New Haven is a beautiful one, passing through a section of the city notable for its elegant villas, for it seems a veritable rus in urbe. This aspect is given by the extensive and picturesque grounds which inclose many of these fine mansions. One of the most costly of these is the residence, we believe, of the President of the Whitney Arms Company, a descendant of the original inventor and founder, Eli Whitney, the inventor also of the cotton-gin. Villa after villa flanks the broad, winding street, all the taste and culture of wealth giving finish and variety to the advantages of nature. A drive of about two miles and a half from the college buildings, and the visitor is at the foot of East Rock, a geological relic from some far-distant period, when the silent but fatal action

East Rock.

of water gradually ground down the highlands between two parallel ranges of hills into a beautiful valley.

New Haven Harbor is formed by the confluence of three streams—West River, and the Quinepiack, or Wallingford, and Mill Rivers on the east. Both the latter branch off like huge cords of silver, and may be seen from the top of the rock, meandering many miles through fertile meadows and prosperous towns. The number of mills driven by them would almost astonish the computation of those not familiar with the thrift and ingenuity which in the New England States utilize every drop of water-power. Near the mouth their resources are taxed in another sort, for every square inch of the current, as far as the rivers are influenced by the salt tides, flows over an oyster-bed.

The last visit made by the writer to East Rock, one of the classic memories of the whilom Yale student, was on a bright fall day, which rendered all the surroundings of the drive peculiarly agreeable. The rock itself is a huge, scarred, shambling mass of sedimentary formation, its lower face worn and eroded by the same influences which have battered its twin brother on the other side of the harbor. The lower portion of the rock is covered with thick, scrubby underbrush, through which the road winds its way around, with a most obstinate predilection to select the difficult and rugged portions. If the livery-horses of New Haven could speak their minds, they would probably condemn East Rock most fervidly to a hotter region than can even be found under the equator. After twenty minutes of puffing and straining, the top is reached, and the visitor finds himself in a beautiful grove, covering a great flat shelf, inclosing, perhaps, several acres of land. This grove, in the center of which is a large, half-ruined stone mansion, is fenced in by high pickets, and the weather-stained sign-board warns off trespassers in rude and significant language which evidently "means business."

The old tumble-down house has passed through some queer vicissitudes. It was built a matter of thirty years ago, perhaps, and was designed by the sanguine but unlucky speculator as a summer resort. Want of custom, however, soon ruined him, and a very atrocious murder, committed there under circumstances which thrilled the community with horror, gave a moldy and unsavory odor to the place. Superstition lent its uncanny atmosphere to the lonely grove, with its house standing there like a huge stone tomb, and after the latter became empty an appalling ghost-story grew up out of the tradition of the rock. The farming and fishing folk became afraid to go to the summit after nightfall.

It is not uninteresting to notice in this place the peculiar tendency of the Puritan mind, even as shown in the instincts of modern New England, to lay stress on the supernatural. New England is to-day, *par excellence*, the home of schools and colleges, the seat of the most uniformly intelligent population in the United States. Yet how numerous are the accredited tales of haunted houses, apparitions, and similar shadows of mediæval credulity. The days of Salem witchcraft have projected some distant reflection even into the clear light of the present. In the writer's college days, not very many years since, there were at least half a dozen "haunted houses" in and about New Haven.

East Rock finally passed into the hands of a proprietor—a rude, ignorant man—who found means to exorcise the ghost. The grove was laid out as a sort of pleasure-garden, with swings, tables, etc., and the house became a great Sunday resort for the lower orders. Here were such gatherings of the more vicious and dissipated, such outrageous orgies, that the authorities at last revoked the proprietor's license, for the establishment had degenerated into a crying nuisance. It was even suspected that it was a regular thieves' den and "fence."

The owner, however, still clings to his high perch, and his moldy and mossy old stone ruin, and it is to this Cerberus that the searcher after the picturesque must pay tribute. For, perhaps, two weeks in the summer this source of revenue is a franchise of some value, but all the rest of the year it must furnish slender pickings.

Indeed, the individual who comes shambling and shuffling out of the rear wing of the house, which alone is inhabited, looks seedy, surly, and disreputable in the extreme. It is only after repeated calls that he has been made to crawl out of his shell and open the padlocked gate, for it is through this portal that the visitor must pass to reach the brow of the precipice, whence he gazes on as lovely a landscape as the sun ever gilded.

A shock head of tow-colored elf-locks, skin shriveled and tanned into the semblance of parchment, bleary eyes, huge horny hands, and naked feet, thrust into shoes gaping at every seam, an exceedingly filthy woolen shirt with an odor surpassing description, lower integuments of a similar kind, fastened together by tow strings, and exposing the lean shanks—such is the aspect of the *genius loci*, who gazes at us with a look as suspicious and truculent as that of the half-starved dog that trots after him.

Without a word he extends his grimy fingers. The gesture is enlightened by the sharp, avaricious glance of the eyes. Fifty cents deposited in his palm softens the unhandsome face into something like a smile, and opens the mouth, down which run streams of tobacco-juice.

"Let ye in sooner if ye'd rung the bell," he said, pointing to an old, cracked bell, hanging over the gate, half hidden by a tall tree.

"Stranger about yer, I guess. Not many as comes up to the rock now. Folks hain't got much stamps now, or else they're gettin all-fired stingy. Come from York way or Hartford way? Chap up here last summer gave me two dollars" (this with a reproachful look at the half-dollar he had just received).

"Raise anything up here? Yes! Used to raise the devil some afore the cussed justices took away an honest man's means of living. Now can't raise much but a little garden-truck."

"Do you find much else to do except rent out the landscape?"

"No!" said he, sullenly; "except when some gentleman is dry, and wants a taste of good apple-brandy. Got some of the best stuff in the State, 'ily as butter and sweet as milk. Perhaps ye'd like to have a drink—sell it cheaper than they do in town?"

On signifying a desire to taste some of his nectar, he preceded us into the rear of the house, where this Yankee Ganymede decanted from a broken jug into two glasses a liquor whose vile smell did no injustice to the taste, for it scalded the throat like vitriol. His face relaxed again grimly as the *douceur* for the poison was given to him. To step out once more into the open air and bright sunshine was a relief after this assault upon the senses.

A few steps through the trees bring us to the brow of the steep cliff, with its bird's-eye views of many miles. New Haven, with its steeples and spires, looks to be almost at the foot of the rock, and a little way to the southeast Fairhaven, the busiest center of the oyster-traffic, Baltimore excepted, in the country. Toward the east and northeast we may see the towns of Wallingford, Bradford, Bethany, Woodbridge, and Hamden, thriving factory and farming towns, and one of the loveliest valleys in the State. On this charming autumn day a golden haze softens the landscape with a peculiar glamour, and lends a luscious,

Old Fort, New Haven Harbor.

half-tropical languor to what would be otherwise suggestive of energy, industry, and toil. The spectator lingers long on this noble lookout, and tears himself away from its visions with regret.

Ten minutes' sharp drive from the foot of East Rock brings us to the village center of Fairhaven. The wide, well-shaded street, which ends in the great oyster-mart, is lined with pleasant and tasteful residences; for some of these oystermen are men of large fortunes, and have fished out of the waters snug packages of United States and railway securities, wallets fat to bursting with

greenbacks, houses, and lands. The Fairhaven man transposes the swelling vaunt of Hardolph into—

"The oyster is my world, which I
With my knife will open."

An exceedingly ancient, fishy smell greets the nose, becoming more and more decided till the river is reached. Here are extensive warehouses and canning establishments, whence oysters are sent all over the world, some firms doing business amounting to hundreds of thousands of dollars a year. Nearly every one is engaged in some line of business having to do with the luscious bivalves, from the urchin to the staid burgher. The river-wharves are lined, two and three deep, with well-appointed smacks, and a ship-yard does a very large business in building these vessels. Not a few of the oystermen employ as many as ten or a dozen. The water property, for several miles' distance from the shore, is far more valuable than the land acreage, and not the least important feature in the litigation of the New Haven courts is that involving the extensive oyster-beds which yield so rich a harvest to their owners. The culture of the oyster as a scientific process is one of much interest, and but few people are aware of the care, study, and labor necessary to meet the enormous demand for this king of shell-fish. It is said that the crop harvested in New Haven waters, and finding its mart in the busy little burgh of Fairhaven, is from 5,000,000 to 8,000,000 bushels annually.

The average citizen of Fairhaven, as is natural with one engaged in an engrossing occupation taking in all of his fellows, has his idiosyncrasies of appearance. He is essentially a waterman. The oyster has stamped the *physique* of his capturers. He does not, like Jack Tar who sails the deep-blue waters, roll along like a ship in a swell, but there is a certain swing in his movements that tells of one much on the water. A fresh, weather-beaten complexion, a square, set posture in standing still, as of one bracing himself for a grip of the oyster-tongs, the potent weapon with which he makes war on his victims, a drawling speech, and a tendency to garnish his sentences with the strong condiments of language, mark the tiller of the oyster-beds, who is, nevertheless, an excellent, staid, worthy citizen, saying his prayers once a week as devoutly as any other Christian.

A pleasant drive of a couple of miles over well-kept country roads, with many a fine mansion on either side, finds one at Fort Hale, the only harbor-defense, we believe, which New Haven possesses. It is a small work, designed to mount about twenty guns, and to accommodate a garrison of three or four hundred. It was originally built as a mere earthwork, at the time of the Revolution, when the traitor Benedict Arnold ravaged the shore of the Sound so mercilessly. New Haven, however, fortunately escaped the polite attentions of the whilom druggist, who mayhap had some lingering tenderness for his early home.

During the war of 1812 the fort was enlarged and elaborated, but afterward allowed to tumble into ruin. During the late civil war repairs to the extent of several hundred thousand dollars were carried on, and a heavy artillery regiment

kept in garrison. At present the work is entirely unused, and the guns have been for the most part removed. The fort has no function now except to serve as a picturesque reminder of war-like possibilities, or become the objective point of a pleasant walk or drive. Certainly, a shot has never yet been fired at it, and probably never will be, unless it is selected for target-practice to test our own heavy ordnance.

WITCH-HAZEL.

WHAT time the dainty darlings of the Spring,
   Summer's ripe beauties, and gay Autumn's train
In swift procession trooped o'er hill and plain,
Through grove and vale, while every bird did sing
His fitting song, we had no thought of thee,
O gloomy sorceress of the dark, dark woods,
Waving aloft thy flowerless magic rods,
And whispering to the winds mysteriously!
But when the merry carnival is o'er,
The banners furled, the bright robes laid away,
How joyously we greet each little ray
That gleams from thy well-hoarded golden store!
The witchery of thy wands astounds not more
Than these pale stars that light the wintry day.

E. T. F.

MOUNTAIN-CLIMBING.

AN experienced pedestrian and climber gives the following practical advice on mountain-climbing: "When you climb a mountain, make up your mind for hard work, unless there is a carriage-road, or the mountain is low and of gentle ascent. If possible, make your plans so that you will not have to carry much up and down the steep parts. It is best to camp at the foot of the mountain, or a part of the way up, and, leaving the most of your baggage there, to take an early start next morning so as to go up and down the same day. This is not a necessity, however; but if you camp on the mountain-top you run more risk from the cold, fog (clouds), and showers, and you need a warmer camp and more clothing than down below.

"Often there is no water near the top; therefore, to be on the safe side, it is best to carry a canteen. After wet weather, and early in the summer, you can often squeeze a little water from the moss that grows on the mountain-tops.

"It is so apt to be chilly, cloudy, or showery at the summit, that you should take a rubber blanket and some other article of clothing to put on if needed. Although a man may sometimes ascend a mountain, and stay on the top for hours, in his shirt-sleeves, it is never advisable to go so thinly clad; oftener there is need of an overcoat, while the air in the valley is uncomfortably warm. Do not wear the extra clothing in ascending, but keep it to put on when you need it. This rule is general for all extra clothing; you will find it much better to carry than to wear it.

"Remember that mountain-climbing is excessively fatiguing; hence go slowly, make short rests *very* often, eat nothing between meals, and drink sparingly.

"There are few mountains that it is advisable for ladies to climb. When there is a road, or the way is open and not too steep, they may attempt it; but to climb over loose rocks and through scrub-spruce for miles is too difficult for them."

To this may be added a suggestion or two from the excellent work of Dr. Elliott Coues on "Field Ornithology," a work which is full of useful information for the naturalist or sportsman: "The secret of *safe* climbing is never to relax one hold until another is secured; it is in spirit equally applicable to scrambling over rocks, a particularly difficult thing to do safely with a loaded gun. Test rotten, slippery, or otherwise suspicious holds, before trusting them. In lifting the body up anywhere, *keep the mouth shut, breathe through the nostrils, and go slowly.*

"In crossing a high, narrow footpath, never look lower than your feet; the muscles will work true if not confused with faltering instructions from a giddy brain.

"Take care never to check perspiration; during this process the body is in a somewhat critical condition, and the sudden arrest of the function may result disastrously, even fatally. One part of the business of perspiration is to equalize bodily temperature, and it must not be interfered with. The secret of much that is said about *bathing* when heated lies here. A person overheated, panting it may be, with throbbing temples and a *dry* skin, is in danger partly because the natural cooling by evaporation from the skin is denied; and this condition is sometimes not far from a sunstroke. Under these circumstances, a person of fairly good constitution may plunge into the water with impunity, even with benefit. But, if the body be already cooling by sweating, rapid abstraction of heat from the surface may cause internal congestion, never unattended with danger.

"Drinking ice-water offers a somewhat parallel case; even on stopping to drink at the brook, when flushed with heat, it is well to bathe the face and hands first, and to taste the water before a full draught."

SUMMER PICTURES.

ALL along our far-stretching shores, in the shady places by the banks of our streams, on the rocks that abut from the hillsides, in the cool depths of our woods, on the surface of our countless lakes, there are in the soft, summer days many idyllic pictures—lovers dreaming as they watch the sky and listen to the murmur of the sea; happy children playing on the sand, and letting tiny waves ripple over their white feet; maidens musing in hammocks, and catching on their cheeks the fresh breezes that deepen the roses there; merry groups in mountain-places and on the shore picnicking, with quip and jest and hearty laughter; the white sails of boats with damsels at the helm; wandering fair ones who gather flowers by the brooks or in the meadows; artists beneath their white umbrellas studying the contours of the hills; groups of men and women tumbling gayly in the surf—these and endless other scenes hourly enact themselves in the wide spaces of our land. It is a holiday-time, and holiday-making goes on in a thousand different forms, by sea and forest, on plain and hill, wherever men and women consent to put off care and surrender themselves to the sweet aspects of Nature. It was at one time commonly said that Americans had very little talent for out-of-door enjoyment. This allegation may have possessed once some small measure of truth, but now it is essentially false, for every summer the whole community nearly goes to the seashore or the mountains, and lives with vast delight in the open air. The seacoast from the upper part of Maine to North Carolina is fairly lined with pleasure-seekers, and all the mountains, all the wooded valleys, all the rivers and lakes are fairly alive with multitudes bent upon enjoying out-of-doors. During July and August at least we are a nation of holiday-makers.

Our artists have limned a few of the captivating pictures that grace the pleasant places of the land. What a serene and charming sea-shore group is this that Darley has depicted for us! A young girl and two children have come down to a sweet, quiet nook on the shore, with their pets and playthings, to enjoy the air and the water; to rest a little, romp a little, and paddle in the warm, pleasant flood. Many times the scene will come back in wearisome winter school-hours to the imaginations of the little ones, and they will pant for the returning sum-

A Noon on the Shore.

mer that is to restore to them such free and
happy hours.

"The artist in the country" is nowadays a
common scene in many sections. From the
first swelling of spring buds, through all the
changing periods of Nature's panorama, until
dark November is reached, there is no time that
the painter does not seek for new aspects of Nature for his sketch-book, or can not find it profit-
able to plant his camp-stool, erect his umbrella,
set up his easel, and surrender himself to the
study and the reproduction of hazy skies, or waving foliage, or far-off, mellowing hill-tops. As to
the painter's companion in the sketch, we must
let our readers frame what romance pertaining
to her they may please. A love-story could
easily be woven out of the situation.

But numerous are the love-dramas enacted
under our summer suns! Are these lovers that
we see seated beneath this huge cedar-tree? Is

the happy fellow reading aloud dulcet verses to his fair listener? One feels the air fresh from the far expanse of the sea; he hears the gentle zephyrs murmur in the gnarled branches of the tree; he breathes the soft, aromatic air, and the gentle murmur of the waves and the leaves. The reader's voice rises and falls with the tender cadence of the poet's lines. In this picture the cedar-tree must divide our interest with the living group. It is a portrait of a famous cedar at Cape Ann, Massachusetts. Along the wild and broken coast of New England the native vegetations of our forest struggle for a place. Occasionally the seeds of the cedar will fall upon some ocean-washed rock. "The feeble plant will for long years scarcely lift its head above the surrounding level, and then only to find itself shadowed by precipices that rise into the very clouds. Throwing out its delicate suckers, it clings to its native barrenness, even more closely for its poverty. The searching winds of a thou- sand storms straighten its tendrils; the impacted snows of each returning winter scarcely disappear before the summer's heat, ere our cedar is again bound in an icy tomb. But silently, steadily, perseveringly it grows. In time it reaches its head into the noonday sunshine, and its sappy trunk is chafed and gnarled by the ever-recurring hurricane. Sometimes, when the great pines in the perturbed depths of the mountains groan and fall under the hurricane, our cedar clings to its native rock, though lashed as a whip-cord, but still intact. A limb occasionally falls from the effects of these persecutions of the elements, or it is stripped of its feather-like foliage, but the tree struggles on, growing more majestic, more grand, and more as if possessed of a mental history; for there is something suggestive of humanity in its scarred and wrinkled front. On the coast of Cape Ann, under the results of having a comparatively flat surface for display, is a memorable specimen of one of these

An Artist in the Country.

Under the Cedar-Tree.

'storm-kings' of the vegetable world. It has drawn its substance from the flinty gravel and adamantine rock, and its great, gnarled trunk looks as if it were made of ligatures of brass.

The most superficial observer of the grand works of Nature insensibly stops and regards this tree, while the true artist beholds it as an inspirator. It is a noble and natural monument of the weird waste it adorns, and a sentinel for observation on the rock-bound coast of New England."

Our next illustration is an inland scene—a pond shadowed by forest-trees, and a fair flower-gatherer by its side. These summer rambles into shaded places, searching for wild flowers and ferns, are among the most agreeable of our vacation experiences. Our rambler in this instance is alone, communing sweetly, no doubt, with her own thoughts. We may suppose her dreaming of an absent one, or thinking only of her flowers, in "maiden meditation fancy free." A poet has asked the question in this wise:

FANCY FREE.

Wealth of starry bloom;
Sun, and leafy gloom;
Whispers of the glossy stream;
Is she lured by these,
Or the melodies
Wandering in her waking dream?

Fancy Free.

A Picnic at the Isles of Shoals.

Blissful melodies!
Lily argosies
Rise and fall in checkered light ;

They but mirror there
Fancies quaint and fair
Floating in her vision bright!

Is it love? Ah, well,
Who is there to tell?
Oh, the dream that's dearest yet!
Does it come to bless—
Is it sought unless
With it falls a sweet regret?

Hands will meet her own,
Lips in loving tone
Woo her soon to low replies!

Will it—will it be
Where the birds may see
All the story in those eyes?

Ever may her hand
Cull as fair a band :
Queen of all the dewy dell!
Will a lover fair
Keep with tender care
One sweet flower—her heart as well?

" All in the gay and golden weather."

Oh, the hours are brief!
Bird and falling leaf
Soon will tell the glory past ;
Dreams will never stay.
Live, then, while we may :
Sunny days will never last!

In the picture that follows we have a scene full of agreeable associations, for who has not picnicked on the rocks by the sea, and found an indescribable delight in the adventure? This picnic-party is gathered on the rocks of Star Island, one of the islands of the " Isles of Shoals," of late years a much-sought summer resort. The Isles of Shoals lie some ten miles beyond the splendid harbor of Portsmouth, New Hampshire, in the broad, open sea, directly opposite the State line which divides New Hampshire from Maine. They consist of eight islets or rocks, the largest of which, Appledore, contains three hundred and fifty acres, and here there is a capital hotel. Near Appledore is Smutty Nose or Haley's Island, low, flat, and dangerous, on whose reefs many a luckless vessel has been dashed to pieces. A quarter of a mile distant is Star Island, the scene of our picnic. " Here sturdy New England fishermen, more than a century and a half ago, made their homes, built themselves houses of the wrecks of vessels, created a village, made it attractive by the spire of a miniature church, and named this little marine prodigy after the ancient English town of Gosport, where for centuries has been a ferry that crosses to Plymouth in Hampshire. The inhabitants of the Isles of Shoals depend upon the ever-abundant treasures of the sea for subsistence; they are expert fishermen, and are alike at home when pursuing the herring or the whale. For vegetables and fresh meats they rely upon the mainland, exchanging their fish for such-named necessaries of life. Sometimes the Isles of Shoals will be for days enveloped in deep fogs, and the inhabitants seem to be as comfortable under the infliction as do the fish in the surrounding sea. But it is not always desolate and stormy in these bleak regions. In the midsummer, the restless Atlantic even will have days of repose. Then it is that the bright sun pours down its uninterrupted rays upon the islands, making them in the distance look like amethysts and garnets set as mosaics in glistening emerald."
But, after all, is there a more delightful summer experience than floating on gentle waters with some fair companion? This is an incident that artists have always delighted to sketch, and so we may believe that it is a picture that other people delight to look upon. There is a sense of romance and of poetry in scenes of this kind ;

and, if lovers are ever to love, it must be when they are together in a boat, whether gliding under spreading branches, flecked with radiant spots of sunlight, or floating over placid open waters, bathed in the rich glow of the " circumambient air." A poet writes :

" All in the gay and golden weather,
    Two fair travelers, maid and man,
Sailed in a birchen boat together,
    And sailed the way the river ran.
The sun was low, not set, and the west
Was colored like a robin's breast.

.   .   .   .

And they were lovers, and well content,
Sailing the way the river went."

Many of us could be content to " sail the way the river went "—to float along through rocky glens, by grassy banks, under shadowy arcades, between sunny meadows, listening to the ripple of the current, and dreaming of a life full of sweetness, like the stream we float upon.

THE SKIES.

IN the old days, when fancy wrought
    Bright fables of the stars and skies;
When men like children dreamed and thought,
    And wore the raiments of the wise;

When heaven was all a golden space
    Hung in the abysm of the air—
A wide and lordly dwelling-place
    Which gods had grandly fashioned there—

No light, of all the lights that flowed
    From worlds that circled through the night
In countless myriads, dimly glowed
    Upon men's blind and barren sight.

But now, when lifting up our gaze
    To the blue heavens, our eyes behold
The omnipotence of a God whose ways
    Are strange, and vast, and manifold—

We know—for we are wise indeed—
    That all around us vaguely lies
The infinite spirit of our creed,
    The ethereal beauty of the skies;

And that our world is but a star
    Amid the perfect stars that gleam
Like hopes of sweeter life afar,
    Faint as the substance of a dream.

GEORGE EDGAR MONTGOMERY.

"CAMPING OUT."

By R. R. Bowker.

THERE is a something about "camping out" that can't be carried on the point of a pen. I suppose it is the getting down to first principles —shaking hands with Nature, as it were. Nobody can describe how Joe or Jeannette shakes hands: there are an honesty and heartiness in the grip that win you and make you feel more of a man, and give you a better idea of the world at large, a firm conviction that life *is* worth living—and that is all you can say. Other people shake hands with a limpness and flabbiness that take all the starch out of you. There is the same difference between living out-of-doors and living in a house, not least if the house has all manner of *bric-à-brac* in it and the people all wear their best clothes to dinner. It is comfortable to get down to first principles once in a while, and find out what a comfort it is not to have comforts.

I know one set of city men to whom the first of January is only a dividing-line between camps. Up to that time their talk, when they are themselves, is all of the last camp; and after that it is all of the next one. Incidentally, they prate in courts of law, or cure or kill, or help to make newspapers, or practice other means of getting a living, and they date their letters by the Julian calendar; but the chief object in life is to get to camp. It is as near as we can come, I suppose, to the garden of Eden, and perhaps that accounts for it. Adam and Eve were always sorry they ever broke camp—and the whole race after them.

It is one of the mysteries that, while it *is* so difficult to tell other people just what the delights of camping are, the camp-fever is nevertheless so infectious. They will ask you all sorts of impertinent questions that you can't answer—what the fun is of staying out all night in the cold ? why you like sharp twigs under your tired back instead of spring-mattresses ? what you do all day ? —when for the life of you you can't tell. And yet the most satiric of the scoffers will be found the next year eager to become martyrs themselves, and making anxious inquiries as to all the thousand-and-one details of how not to do it.

There is a first time to everything, and the inexperienced camper must expect to gain a realizing sense of "ad castra, per aspera" (or "per castra," as it is also written), in his early attempts. "Through camps—and pretty rough camps—to the stars," is the plain English of it. Particularly if he is to do his own cooking, and has never been tied to his mother's apron-strings when she went into the kitchen. I know one man who never will forget the strong conviction that there was something in civilization, after all, which came upon him when he tasted the dreadful mouthful of clear starch that resulted from his first attempt to make a corn-starch pudding. And who of the early days of "Camp Manhattan" will forget the direful day when the whole camp took turns, for unnumbered hours, picking off by hand the pin-feathers of the two chickens that, after all, had to be boiled and skinned, because no one had the sense to remember that in the ordinary methods of civilization it is done in a jiffy with a bit of flaming paper ? But such tribulations as these, and even the drenching and dreary storms that so dampen the ardor of the inexperienced camper, are not sufficient to deter him, if there is any "gumption" in him, from wanting to try it again, and ever again.

Mr. Stockton's famous camping-party, in "Rudder Grange," proposed to camp out in their own back-yard, and did settle down a few rods off, resolutely refusing to take shelter under their own dry roof even when the floods came and the milk-boy didn't. Others cherish the superstition that they can not properly camp out except some hundreds of miles away from home and amid dense wilderness. The earth is wide, and happily there are a number of good camping-places upon it, not so very far away from one's own home, wherever that home may happen to be. At some of the beaches of the New England coast there is a growing fashion of "camping out" in shanties which may be hired for the purpose ready-furnished with the few necessary articles. There are like summer settlements on the Great Lakes, and the great camp-meetings are now so many that almost every one has heard of the life in those improvised yet permanent summering-places that gather nominally, at least, around the preaching-platform. All this, however, is only half-way camping out. You don't quite get the flavor of the real thing until you give up the house altogether, and live with only the thickness of canvas between you and the stars.

There is no reason why this should not be done near home, except the unaccustomedness of it. I mean for people who can not get to the Adirondacks, or the White Mountains (now almost too much a thoroughfare for camping), or the seashore, or the borders of the Great Lakes, or Leadville. In the very midst of the denseness of the virgin forest, or within ear-shot of the sounding sea, is, of course, the ideal place for camping ; but to reach these places costs often more time and more railroad-fare than most people can afford. And, while change of air and change of scenery are of great good and delight, the mere change of life from in-doors to out-doors and change of daily routine are what many people want most. There are in many parts of the country pretty little lakes, with pleasant groves upon their shores, sufficiently isolated yet sufficiently convenient to a base of supplies, that would delight the eye of the camper if a few hundred miles away from home, but are quite snubbed by people near by who are "dying" to camp out at any place quite out of their reach. I know of very

The Camp.

pleasant camps founded under just such circumstances.

Those who can have what they want will, of course, take the money and the time, and do that best thing of changing their whole environment. In general it is, doubtless, best for coast people to seek the mountains, and for inland people to seek the sea; but this question can only be fully solved on individual grounds and by individual experience. The chief care should be to avoid absolutely malarial places, which is not so easy nowadays in this country, since the great wave of this mysterious infliction has been pushing its front even across and up the Connecticut Valley. Damp ground, or any in the neighborhood of swamps, should especially be shunned. Water and woods are among the first requisites for a fully enjoyable camp, though the seashore or the forest, either by itself, is not to be despised. But the camp should not be hidden among the trees so that the sunshine and the free winds can not get to it; rather in the open, where it may bask in the sun all the morning and have the welcome shade in the hotter afternoon. It should not be in clayey soil, but where there is good drainage through the earth, and on slightly sloping ground, that there may be surface drainage as well. To prevent this through the tent, which is *not* delectable, a shallow trench is often usefully dug around the outside of the tent or shelter. This must itself drain down the slope. On sloping ground heads must be always up the hill in "turning in." Next to a good base a good outlook is an important thing for real enjoyment, and should be had in mind in pitching a tent.

The tent is on the whole the most satisfactory camp. The board-shanty is but a poor apology for an orthodox house; a tent is a different thing altogether. The permanent "camps" that are found along the Adirondack trails, sometimes individual property, but more often dedicated to the service of whosoever may happen along, are commonly rude log-houses, with no door, and with a square aperture at top for chimney; or else the "hunter's shelter" of a mere roof made of poles, covered with bark or boughs, closed at the back, where the poles are ingeniously pitched on stakes, and opened to the weather at the higher front. I have myself slept comfortably, during a wet night, in a camp improvised hastily, wigwam-fashion, in an hour or two, by stacking up hastily-cut poles half around a big tree, and covering them with boughs the trees being so wet that no bark could be peeled off to make a bark shelter. Indeed, I have slept comfortably under the stars, with a great trench dug along our feet and filled with fire, keeping us warm to the top of our heads. But a tent is on the whole the best, and often the warmest, and the best tent is what is called the wall-tent. This, like the A tent, is raised on two perpendicular poles supporting a ridge-pole, but the roof, sloping on either side, instead of reaching the ground, stops short about four feet above, where it meets perpendicular walls of canvas, which may be fastened down by loops fitting upon stakes, or by rolling stones upon the edges. In bright weather, or to air the tent of a morning, these walls are rolled up and tied to the edge of the canvas roof, which is made fast by guy-ropes, that must invariably be loosened out when the rain begins to draw them up, and which

should *not* be used for clothes-lines. The last should be hung from tree to tree within reasonable distance of the tent, not at the points of view, which must be dedicated to the hammocks, where-in the sweet idleness of camp-life has its apotheosis. A "fly," or second great sheet of canvas, thrown over the ridge-pole and guyed so as to be a little higher at the edges than the roof of the tent, is an exceedingly useful thing to keep out rain, whether from a leaky or a dripping tent, either of which is sufficient botheration. The tents oftenest used in camp are the "shelter-tents" of the army, strips of canvas with buttons or buttonholes at the respective edges, of which each of the party carries one, and which can be buttoned together to make tents of various shape and size, or to make flies. These are commonly used for peripatetic camps.

Since we are talking about the tent and its immediate surroundings, we may as well step down to the kitchen, which may be a gypsy fire under a stack of three sticks supporting the inevitable kettle and taking the inevitable frying-pan to its bosom of flame; but much better, an old stove-top, if civilization be sufficiently near to permit, resting on built-up stones. Too breezy a spot won't do. For the other extreme, an apology for a refrigerator, a hole in the ground covered with a board serves well, provided the wild or tame beasts are not allowed to get at it. For dining-room find the loveliest spot about camp, within easy range of the kitchen, that the inner man and the outer man may be satisfied together. The after-dinner hours are often the height of enjoyment of the day. Many of these arrangements depend, of course, upon whether the camp is large or small: in the first case, a cook is absolutely desirable, unless, as in the Adirondacks, there are guides who take that as part of their work.

But, after all and before all, the first prerequisite of the right kind of a camp is to have the right kind of people in it. There is no better trial of friendship than the close test of camp-life, and woe be to that party which has despised this fundamental rule! One bore, or one Miss Nancy, or one weakling, will easily spoil the pleasure of an entire camp. You want people who will not pout on rainy days or over a week of rain; who will not be afraid of spoiling their clothes or die of dampening their feet; who will not talk all the time, but sometimes; who will do their share of work as well as of play; who will not fume over bad dinners or no dinner at all; in a word, people who are cheerful and cheery, and who go knowing that even the rainbow has tears in it. As to number, it is well to reckon by twos, and to remember that a large company is not easy to provide for, at indefinite distances

7

from grocery-stores, unless you are sure of a base of supplies. Four or six is the best number for experiment. If you have both ladies and gentlemen, a large camp is usual and agreeable, and ladies are a blessing in camp if they are the kind who take to it kindly. It requires a large tent, however, to afford room for a canvas center-wall, and two tents are by all means better. If the ladies are afraid to stay by themselves in a house of their own, they are of the sort who will do better to stay at home altogether. But it is a comfort to have them about camp, and not only because they know better than most men how to wash the dishes! A friend of camping experience, nevertheless, insists that it is well, once in a year, to break away from all such social ties, and get a company of clean-spoken men together by themselves, for the sake of the entire change. The incompleteness of man without woman is then the more fully appreciated when one gets back again. There is philosophy in this; but, then, the ladies can scarcely revel in a similar exclusiveness, and it's a poor rule that don't work both ways.

In getting up the personal outfit for camp-life there is apt to be more danger, with greenhorns, of taking too much rather than too little—I mean not of a dram, but of dress. The particular mistake most people make, however, especially in going north in summer, is in taking thin instead of thick garments. Nights are cool, and apt to be cold, in the northern woods or by the lakes. A change of not too thin woolen underclothing is the first *sine qua non;* then a pair of laced boots that fit (too large are quite as bad as too small), and a pair of slippers for a change and to sleep in, which may seem an absurdity, but is a very practical comfort. A change of flannel *negligée* shirts, loose-necked and long; one coat that will serve as an overcoat; pantaloons that neither tear easily nor catch burrs and dirt—blue jeans is capital material, though not handsome nor very warm; woolen stockings, and a hat that shades the eyes, are the other necessaries for the outer man. In a tramp the pantaloons should be tied about the ankles, not too tightly. Ladies are best off with simple mountain-dresses, short-skirted, of dark flannel or waterproof. It is a practical suggestion, worth noting, that pockets in camp-apparel should always be arranged to button up, because things do "spill 'round" dreadfully in camp. Thread and needles are items that masculines can not afford to forget. For these things and toilet articles the light rolling toilet-cases are very convenient, because they serve as a memorandum in keeping your things together, and can be tied up at the side of the tent over your sleeping-place. A stout jack-knife, a water-tight match-safe, and a compass, are absolutely indispensable. Writing-material and

postage-stamps are "a great nuisance when you don't have them"; and a guide-book and the best map that can be had should be somewhere among the party. Don't forget towels and soap, which are individual rather than camp properties, but apt to be overlooked because of the doubt. In a capital little book, called "How to Camp Out," by John M. Gould, an old army-man and an experienced camper, is a check-list of all the things you are likely to want, and a great many more than you ought to want, that it will be useful to run .over. Guns and ammunition, and rods and flies, must depend on the locality in which the hunting or fishing is to be done.

A light rubber blanket is needed ; those, called *ponchos*, with an immense buttonhole, so to speak, in the middle, to put your head through, serve in the night *and* overcoat by day. A pair of light-weight army-blankets (the two woven continuously, so as to fold at your feet), costing from three to five dollars, complete the bed. In a permanent camp some take a ticking-sack, which they may fill with straw or leaves, but most will prefer the fragrant mattress of hemlock-leaves, although it is abominable work picking enough of them. All this "kit," for a movable camp, should not count up to so much as twenty pounds, which is a sore load for most travelers. They can be made up into a pack in the rubber blanket, fastened with carrying-straps, which should be broad at the bearings on the shoulders; or into a long roll, similarly wrapped, and tied into a ring, to be carried first over one shoulder and then over the other ; or packed in a knapsack, of which those of light waterproof cloth, such as are made in London for the Alpine Club, are the best.

For cooking utensils, a frying-pan, coffee-pot, water-pail, hatchet, large knife, and knife, fork, spoon, plate, and cup for each person, are necessaries. There are beautiful camp-kettle affairs that combine everything you can possibly want, in no space at all, but in these cases all is not gold that glitters. Particularly in a movable camp, they are of more bother than the primitive articles, which can be distributed among the various members of the party. As to provisions, it is difficult indeed to give general advice ; it depends on the country. An Adirondack guide commonly contents himself with salt pork, corn-meal, coffee, a little tea, potatoes, salt and pepper, in addition to his gun and rod. Self-raising flour, crackers, and canned goods, especially soups and vegetables, come handy in a permanent camp ; for it must not be forgotten that fresh vegetables are not procurable north until late in the season. Such things can most economically be bought in the large cities before starting, and freighted up as far as possible. Lemons are a great desideratum in camp. But "everything depends." If the camp is to be permanent and not far from roads, much more can be carried; a servant is then desirable, at once for the care of these things, to cook, and to keep camp. With small parties, moving about, a servant is less desirable. The Dartmouth College boys had a way of camping about the White Hills peripatetically, hiring a wagon for their camp-luggage, and buying an old horse at the beginning, which they could sell at not much loss at the end. Such a plan limits you, but saves much hard work. In the Adirondacks, the journeying is mostly by water; but, when you do come to the "carry," it is a great bother to have so much luggage that the guide, after walking off like a great beetle with the boat on his head and part of the "kit" underneath on his shoulders, must go back for a second load.

Enjoyable and healthful camping should be leisurely—not an attempt to do ever so much or make ever so many miles a day. The laziness of it is a great boon. Yet there must also be exercise. In walking, a dozen to twenty miles a day is enough for any one, and it should be done morning and evening, before eleven and after four. It is a good plan to laze one day and "do" the next, alternately. To one who manages wisely, camp-days become thus the most enjoyable in life.

Camp recreations are more varied than stay-at-homes suppose. One warning must be given: Don't permit any misguided four to form a whist "series"—from that hour they are lost to the camp. Even rainy days may be made bright in camp. A favorite amusement of one camp I know of was the comb-orchestra dish-pan-onion combination, which did the "Tännhauser" overture in a way that would have taught Herr Wagner something in the way of effect a little beyond him. Another Adirondack camp published a newspaper in MS.; "The Fly-Sheet," I think, was its name. It was for the benefit of this rural journal that a tournament of verse was held, which would have done credit to the Minnesingers themselves. Here is the contribution of one member of that camp, a New York publisher, who prints other people's poetry and not his own, to the competition for a rhyme with "venison":

"'Tis sweet by woodland lake to rest,
   Enjoying Nature's *benison*,
Mayhap a book to lend a zest,
   Some pastoral of *Tennyson*,
And some fair maid whose faithful breast
   'Tis safe to bet one's *pennies on*.
So placed, one tastes the joys of life,
   And need not envy *any son*
Of man who midst the toil and strife
   Of cities rests a *denizen*.

"And though those halcyon days are past,
And now we mourn the *many sun*-
—Dered ties with friends that might not last,
And joys we've had in *plenison*,
We still can keep our courage stout,
Throw off dull care, if *any's on*,
Renew our dreams of lusty trout,
And feast off boughten *venison*."

Ah, the delight it gives an old camper to look back upon the days that are gone, and to dream of the days that are coming! I remember a first time—the hap-hazard start for Lake George in general and nowhere in particular; the landing just where the good-natured captain of the little steamer chose to put us off; the delightful novelty of that first life in the open air, the not delightful novelty of our own cooking; the jolly time it proved to be when all was over! I remember how, year after year, we pitched our tent in the same spot, with the very same rocks under our backs, and every rock dear to us! I remember the forced camp on old Black Mountain, when, coatless and supperless under the frosty stars, we lay spoon-fashion to keep warm, with the long trench of fire blazing at our feet! I remember the Berkshire and the White Hills tramps—the long pulls in the fresh morning, the splendid mountain-tops at night, the pine forests and the moonlight, the figures trudging along in the shadow and in the silence, the whiff of odorous balm, the sense of nature! I remember, above all, that lonely night in the midst of the Adirondack wilderness, when, caught in the pelting rain, we built ourselves a lodge of boughs, and set ablaze a hollow tree, till we had so grand a sight of pyrotechnics as never city man saw on the Fourth of July: the pillar of fire as the great tree opened with the heat, beautiful with violet and rosy and purple flame, the wet leaves shining back like stars, the thunderous fall—and silence! Days and nights like these, supperless though they might have been, are now refreshment that never fails. Indeed, he who has not known something of camping has not quite found out to the full how well worth living is life, or what life is!

ALONE BY THE SEA.

, FROM RÜCKERT.

HERE! where no nightingale's quick melody
   Showereth from bloomy dell, by bubbling spring:
Where overhead the sea-gulls wheel and cry,
   And underneath the waves crawl murmuring,
I couch on bed of spray-dewed rosemary,
   And hear the winds and solemn waters sing,
A ceaseless song, monotonous, forlorn,
On which dear distant names are faintly borne.

BLAKE'S FERRY.

By JAMES T. McKAY.

IT was a lovely spot. Harlan stood on the platform and looked about him as the train slid on out of sight. It was near the twilight, and very still. Every footfall of the passengers trooping down the long plank walk to the ferry was distinctly audible. Then the pattering ceased; the little ferry-boat steamed out upon the placid, darkling river, and he was left alone.

It seemed but just now that he had left the glaring, breathless city, and the contrast made the scene doubly grateful. The river-bank, the heights that rose steeply above him, and the more gentle slopes across the water were dense with foliage and dark with cool shadows. Above the crest of the opposite hills hung one gorgeous cloud, and its rich light tinged even the shadows with a tender radiance not to be described.

The young stranger stood watching the enchanted picture till the color burned out; then he looked in at the waiting-room and asked to be directed to Mr. Stillfleet's. A boy came a little way with him and pointed out a path leading toward the river above the ferry, and he walked on, loitering slowly.

Two years before, Ned Harlan had gone one night to Marian Stilfleet and told her that his firm had offered him the charge of a venture that would take him to South America for a year at least. He was excited and in doubt, and it was necessary to decide quickly. He could not bear to leave her, yet if he went it would be for her sake; the salary would be considerable, and the experience and knowledge acquired of value to him on his return. But he would do just as she said. The decision was hard for both, but Marian Stilfleet was not the girl to let any weakness prevent her advising in the end the course that seemed manly and prudent. So they had parted sadly but hopefully, without effusive grief, or fondness, or protestations of fidelity, but with entire confidence and affection for one another. And neither faith nor affection had flagged in the years of separation.

Only a short time after Harlan's departure, Marian's mother was taken sick and died in the fall. Mr. Stillfleet had many years before been nearly ruined by a passion for drink, and now in his grief the old craving revived, and it seemed as if nothing could stop him for a while, until some consequent disastrous speculations brought him face to face with degradation and want. At that juncture his distracted daughter bethought her of an old friend of her mother's, of whom they had lost sight for a good while, General

Hilgate, President of the Due North Railroad, and she went to see him at the railway-office. He was busy in his private room, messengers and visitors going in and out, and the President's commanding voice coming through the opening door to her now and then, as she waited for an opportunity to speak alone with him. Her heart almost failed before she was shown in, and quite sank as she stood for a moment till the stern-looking old gentleman should turn and see her. But, when he looked up from his desk sharply, his face softened, and he exclaimed in a low tone:

"My God! It's Marian Lincoln!"

"Marian Lincoln's daughter," she said softly —"Marian Stillfleet."

"Yes, yes," he answered, coming to meet her, "of course, of course! Come and sit down. Do you know, you are the picture of your mother at your age? I knew your mother when she was younger than you."

He drew her to a chair near his own and sat looking at her, still holding her hands. "Dear me, dear me!" he soliloquized. "And this is Marian's daughter. I knew she had a little girl, but I never thought of her but as a baby. I don't know how I had forgotten so; I haven't seen Marian Lincoln for years and years. Is she well now—your mother, is she well?"

Marian shrank, and her lips trembled. Her eyes filled and fell, but, after a little, she lifted them and answered, in an unsteady voice:

"Didn't you know? My mother is dead."

"Dead! Oh, that's too bad!"

He got up and turned away, with his head bent and his thumbs in his side pockets. A clerk who looked in met his frowning face and sharp order to shut the door and not to open it till he was called. How strange that, at that time of day, with grown sons and daughters of his own, and his head gray, that forgotten wound should open and rankle afresh at sight of Marian's child! The thought of her death pierced him with a pang so keen that the perception of it infected Marian, and caused her to shake and sob quickly in spite of herself. Seeing that, the old man came and patted her cheek, and bade her not to cry. He sat down again and talked to her, telling her of her mother in her young days, and asking her questions about these later years. And Marian dried her eyes and cleared her choked voice, and told him of the strait she and her father were in, encouraged by his unwonted gentleness to be quite frank with him.

"I thought," she concluded, "if my father could get some situation that would employ his time and thoughts, and especially if it were away from his present associations, it might be the best thing for us that the money is lost."

The general pulled the bell and ordered the attendant to look for Mr. Hilgate, and ask him to come in. In a few minutes a young man entered, a handsome, athletic, slow-moving fellow, with an air of reserve and command.

"Tom," said the General, turning in his arm-chair, "who is superintendent of the ferry at Blake's now? Can we do anything else with the man? I want the place."

"His name is Whitelaw," the young man answered; "we can put him somewhere, I suppose."

"It's just the place you want," the general said, turning back to Marian. "Let me introduce you to my son." Then to that gentleman: "Tom, you will see Miss Stillfleet's father and arrange the matter. Give them any help they need, and make it comfortable for them. If it costs you anything in time or money, let me know."

He showed Marian out to the street-door, and parted from her with great kindness, bidding her always to come to him when she needed advice or assistance; and Marian could only express brokenly the gratitude she felt.

In a fortnight from that time they were installed in a very pleasant cottage at the ferry, the father occupied with his duties at the landing, or at his accounts in the little room overlooking the river, which they had made into an office, and the daughter busy with her house-keeping, and happy as the birds among the trees by the river-side, which she enjoyed as much as they. There were only two or three houses, a store, and the station at the ferry, and the nearest town or tavern was a mile from the landing across the river ; so that there was no immediate temptation to undermine the man's determined effort, and, though it was a hard fight enough, he persevered, and Marian did all that watchful love and care could do to cheer him on.

Under the circumstances, to induce Mr. Stillfleet to undertake the office, and then to establish him at the ferry, had been no simple affair, and Marian recognized thankfully how greatly she was indebted to young Mr. Hilgate's respectful persistence and kindness. The General had a summer place on the river, half a mile above the ferry, and his son continued to drop in upon Mr. Stillfleet, by day or evening, as long as he could be of any use in explaining the system of checks and settlements between the ferry company and the railroad ; and, by the time that necessity was passed, he had earned a friendly

footing in the cottage that he showed no disposition to abandon, and which the father and daughter were far from grudging him. There was never any special familiarity between him and Marian : though polite and gentlemanly, Hilgate was naturally reserved and somewhat taciturn, and Marian, while quite conscious that his thoughtfulness and constant attention had been of great service to her father and herself, and grateful to him personally, still could not forget that it was through his father's orders and as his agent that the son had undertaken to assist them, and that idea kept her from feeling any peculiar obligation toward the son, or dreaming of any troublesome complication. A tacit friendliness and confidence grew up insensibly between them. He came often, and was always respectful and unofficiously serviceable, the extremely considerate representative of the company which her father served ; and Marian found these good and sufficient reasons for liking to have him come, and was glad to see him, and looked and said it sometimes in her modest, candid way.

And in time Hilgate came to find her looking and saying that the pleasantest thing in his world ; to see and hear it far away among thronging people and thundering trains, and to hanker for the repetition of that sight and sound. He enjoyed his position in the cottage too much, and had too much self-control, to be in haste. From a mere boy he had been accustomed to command men, at first in the army and then on the railroad ; he had been always exercising authority under his father, the General, and had acquired as an instinct both the determination and assurance of success, and the intuitive perception that there are times when calm persistence is better than promptness and decision. The very habit of mastery that made him quick and unswerving as lightning when the decisive moment came, made him quiet and reticent at other times, and wary of taking a risk against too great odds. There were no young men in the neighborhood of whom he felt any fear, and his watchful eye assured him that none of the Stillfleets' few visitors were before him in the race. So he took his time, not doubting of the end, and finding the way so pleasant that he was quite content with loitering. The winter came, and he moved his quarters into town, with the family, but he did not come the less to the ferry. Spring followed speedily, and now again it was summer.

Only the evening before this of Harlan's arrival, as Hilgate and Mr. Stillfleet sat smoking together on the piazza of the cottage, looking out upon the river and inhaling the tropical fragrance of the honeysuckles, the older gentleman had asked the younger if he could find out for them on the morrow when the steamer Chimborazo was expected to arrive; and, in answer to Hilgate's glance of inquiry, had explained briefly that they were looking for a young friend by her from a two years' absence, and hinted very plainly that he would some day be more than a friend to him and Marian. Hilgate made no comment, and showed no mark of surprise or displeasure, but there were an increased taciturnity and an earlier departure than usual. But to say that he was surprised and displeased would be a very mild way of expressing the fact.

As he opened the paper on his way to town in the morning, his eye fell on the shipping news, and glancing down he saw the Chimborazo among the arrivals. He read no more; but, after thinking darkly awhile, got out at a station and telegraphed, "Chimborazo in the lower bay last night. Be up to-day."

The Stilfleets were at breakfast when the message came. Marian's father saw the eager flutter it put her in, and an unexpected yearning toward Harlan came over himself. The young fellow seemed suddenly a part of his lost, happy past coming back to him.

"Marian," he said, "I ought to go to town about that mortgage business soon; suppose we go to-day and meet Ned?"

And Marian assented joyfully.

Arriving in the city, Mr. Stilfleet stopped to ask Hilgate to give an eye to the ferry, and left the cottage key to let him into the office. They sent a message for Harlan, to his sister Jessie's, to inform him of their whereabouts; but, toward evening, were vexed to receive answer that he had only run in and started directly for the ferry before their note was received. Mr. Stilfleet could not leave his unfinished business for another day, so they were obliged to make the best of it.

Meanwhile Harlan arrived at the ferry as we have seen, and sauntered along the path from the station toward the Stilfleet cottage, as the shadows deepened and the dusk drew on.

For months past the thought of thus coming back to Marian had been with him, or very near him, by night and by day. She had described the ferry in her letters, and he had thought of her there till he fancied he knew it well. His eagerness for this day had increased insensibly till it became a passion; many a time he had thought how he should leap from the car and hurry along the path and spring on the cottage porch. She would not know just when to expect him, but would know his tread and come quickly; he could see her glad flush and smile, and hear himself laugh aloud as he caught her and held her fast. So he had thought and dreamed. And now the time had come; and, as the starving castaway turns sick at the sight of the food over which he has gloated in his thoughts and

dreams, Harlan felt a strange, vague sinking and reluctance come over him when he stepped down from the train. The place was not just what he had pictured it: the station was on the wrong side, and the path to the cottage led the wrong way. His heart misgave him strongly. But he knew it was only the natural recoil of the feeling that he had unconsciously strained to breaking, and that the sight of Marian would set all right again.

He came to the gate. Through the shrubbery he saw a light in the little west room; his heart leaped up: that must be the office, and doubtless father and daughter were there together. While he lingered, the light was put out, and he heard footsteps—a strange man came out and locked the door, and walked down the path toward him. Harlan stepped back to let him pass; he stopped in the open gateway, and the two young men stood face to face.

"Does Mr. Stilfleet live here?" Harlan asked, touching his hat.

Hilgate continued to eye him with a deliberate, searching scrutiny, and the immovable face and form thus confronting him communicated to Harlan gradually an undefined sense of alarm, which was increased by an unwonted depth in the habitually deep and commanding voice that answered:

' Yes, but he is not at home. He and his daughter have gone to the city, and will not be back for a day or two."

Harlan said, "Thank you," mechanically, and turned away, lingering a minute to think what he should do next; he felt vexed and hurt.

"Wait a moment," the other said in the same deep, deliberate tone. "Your name is Harlan, I believe? My name is Hilgate."

Harlan glanced at him sharply, taking a stronger and stronger dislike to him.

"Yes, I have heard the name," he answered carelessly, and would have passed by him to return to the station; but Hilgate persisted:

"Where are you going now? There's no place here where you can spend the night, and the boat won't be back till morning. I've got a skiff down here, and I'm going across; and, if you like to come with me, I'll show you the way to an hotel."

Harlan remembered Marian's writing him how kind young Hilgate had been in executing his father's friendly offices, and reflected that it was foolish to start upon ill terms with a person whom he would have to meet as a friend of her father and herself; and, besides, he knew not what else to do. So he said:

"Well, I am in rather a tight place, and shall be obliged to you."

So they took a path through the cottage

grounds down to the shore and embarked. The river, dammed up by the hills here, spread out like a lake. A mile below, it broke through a narrow gap to the eastward, full of falls and rapids; and around this impassable channel a canal had been constructed to the south. Harlan knew these facts from Marion; and he asked his companion about them as they crossed the pleasant, rippling current.

"I suppose that is Partridge Island? And that must be the gate—that dip in the hills there? And whereabout is the canal?"

Hilgate answered briefly but politely in the same grave, unmoved manner, rowing with a grace and power that Harlan could not but admire. Half-way over, he stopped and let the boat drift a little way, just dipping the oars and keeping the prow up-stream. Harlan glanced at him but took no further notice, and presently he turned the boat's head again and sent her quivering to the westward shore. Beaching the skiff and making her fast, Hilgate led the way up a steep path till they came to a stone fence with a stile. Hilgate leaned against the wall, and Harlan was glad to sit a moment on the step after the climb. He looked back at the sloping fields and the river placid in the moonlight, beyond the black border of shadowing trees. Hilgate said:

"Mr. Harlan, I am going to ask you a question that will seem impertinent to you. Before I ask it, I want to disclaim anything of the kind. I never heard of you till last night; I did not know till then that there was such a person in the world, and I tell you plainly I wish there was not. But I suppose that's no fault of yours, and I want if possible not to quarrel with you or treat you otherwise than as one gentleman treats another. Have you come back with the expectation of marrying Miss Stilfleet?"

Harlan sat very still. The steadiness and deliberate, full voice of the other had the greater effect upon him as things foreign to himself; he was of a rather slight and nervous constitution, impressible, susceptible of enthusiastic ardor, but of panic as well. Whatever courage he had was moral, and his coolness that of habit and self-control. He was startled by the calm, chosen words of his questioner, but he did not show it. His eyes did not turn from the moonlit river, and after a minute's silence he answered low and distinctly:

"I certainly have."

He stood up and looked for the way beyond the stile, but Hilgate held him with his eye.

"I don't intend that you shall," he said, in the same deep, low way.

Harlan put up his foot on the stile.

"Wait!" Hilgate commanded, with a move-

ment and a ring in the word that mutinous railroad hands knew and seldom disputed, and Harlan waited, with an inward tremor.

"Don't cross me lightly," Hilgate went on, falling back into his former controlled manner. "I tell you I don't want to quarrel with you; I know nothing against you; I want to treat you like a gentleman. But you and I stand in such a position toward one another that it's as much as we can do if we manage to keep the peace. I shall be frank and open, and I expect the like treatment from you. For your own sake as well as mine, I seriously advise you not to trifle with me, or make light of what I say. I am talking with you under great self-restraint, and am hardly my own master. I made Miss Stilfleet's acquaintance a year ago and more, as you may have heard; but you can't have heard that I admired her the first time I saw her more than any one I ever knew; that I have seen her almost daily ever since, and that my regard for her has increased day by day till there is nothing in the world or out of it that could tempt me to give her up, and very little that I would not do or endure to prevent it."

His manner was impressive, and Harlan was not the less moved by it that he stood so still himself and met the other's steadfast look and speech with unshrinking eyes and face. And after a moment Hilgate went on:

"I advise you to go away; I can not answer for myself if you stay here. Consider well before you decide. I think it will not be good for either of us if you remain—for either of us or for her. But I don't want to seem inconsiderate. If you consent to go peaceably, I will do anything in my power for you. If there is anything you can think of, you have only to name it; but I will make you a definitive offer. I hope you will not regard it as offensively mercenary or otherwise. I don't look at it in that light at all. It is quite impossible that any one should care more for Miss Stilfleet than I do, to put it moderately, and I am equally sure that there is no one who does. I mean no offense; I am trying my best not to offend you. I simply mean that I can not conceive of any gain or success that could induce me to think of leaving her for two years. If the facts were different, there would be no shame in it; but, as they are, they give me some rights. If you concede that, I can see no reason why you should not accept some consideration for the great favor you would do me. In so many words, our company has an enterprise out there where you have been, as you probably know. Your experience makes you of value to us; if you will go back there, I can give you a very good position and almost any salary. Take time to consider, and name any figure in reason."

Harlan then for the first time withdrew his eyes from the speaker's face and turned about. He had a swimming sensation and a sudden yearning toward Marian, with the feeling that she was sliding from him and he grasping vainly after her. He wheeled around slowly without pausing till he looked again into Hilgate's face, and, though his voice was low and not very steady, he answered:

"It would not be worth your while to offer me less than a million or two."

He crossed the stile quickly and went on without looking back, came to the road, and followed it till he found the village and an inn.

He felt uneasy and excited all the evening, and had a restless, troubled night; but with the daylight came back confidence and determination.

In the morning he learned from the clerk of the ferry that Mr. Stilfleet would be back that day and resolved to wait. He got a waterman to take him out upon the river. They rowed down to the mouth of the canal, passing to the west of Partridge Island, and as they came back Harlan wanted to go round the island on the east side, but the boatman said it was hardly safe.

"You can see it lays square acrost the Gate, and the water eddies in there from both ways and makes it kind o' whirlpooly. I've been round there, but it's rough and wet anyway. It's smoother further in; the water jest crowds and piles to get through the Gate, and it runs like Ned when it's in till it comes to the falls—that's the sound of them you can hear now. I don't calc'late," the man gossiped on as he rowed, "that nobody's never been as fur in there as Tom Hilgate; but I reckon he'll go once too often some day and not come back."

And he went on to narrate the lives and adventures of people who had been carried down the fatal passage.

After the early dinner, Harlan had still a couple of hours on his hands. The landlord's son, young Raymond, had a handsome horse standing before the hotel, and, Harlan admiring it, Raymond asked him to ride with him two or three miles up the river. The miles proved long, and they were a good while getting back. It was warm, and, as Harlan got down at the hotel door, Raymond asked him to hand his coat into the little room off the bar. Seeing water and towels there as he hung up the coat, Harlan pulled off his own to wash his hands, and hung it up for a moment beside the other, noticing that they were very much alike.

About three that afternoon, Hilgate saw Marian and her father take the train for the ferry, and he entered another car and came with them, but without being seen by them. Arriving, he walked down to the landing, again avoiding the Stilfleets, whom he saw getting their key from the agent with whom he had left it. He talked with the ferry clerk a minute or two, and then went and got his skiff and crossed the river.

When Harlan had washed his hands hastily and paid his bill, he hurried down to the river, to find the ferry-boat just gone across. He looked for some one to row him over, saw a boat below the wharf with the oars in it, and ran round to get it. As he cast about for the owner, Hilgate came down the bank in his leisurely, agile way, passed by him, and stepped into the boat.

"Get in," he said, standing and steadying the rocking skiff with an oar.

Harlan stepped back.

"Are you afraid?" Hilgate said slowly.

The blood flew into Harlan's face. Without answering, he got in, and Hilgate pulled off. As soon as they were well afloat, Hilgate turned and crept forward and hung the anchor just over the bow, fastening it with a running knot. He brought the slack-rope back with him and took a turn of it round his foot as he sat at the oars; then he headed the boat south and pulled rapidly down-stream. Harlan lounged in the stern and looked on, but there was that about the set face and the way the boat formed through the water that kept him from making any remark. But, though he made no sign, he looked away across to where the cottage above the ferry peeped out from its trees and vines, and a line of "Horatius," which he had not seen since he spouted the ballad at school, came into his mind with a sudden heart-sick apprehension of the old Roman's feeling when, with the bridge down and "thrice thirty thousand foes" behind him, he looked across the flood, and

"He saw on Palatinus the white porch of his home."

Without a word on either side, they swept swiftly and smoothly down the same course Harlan had gone in the morning, past the west side of Partridge Island, and toward the mouth of the canal. But then, with a broad sweep, they headed back again. Harlan lay looking behind, seemingly interested in the southward view, but perfectly conscious that Hilgate was pulling a straight course without looking ahead. Suddenly his attention was aroused to the fact that the water was growing rougher and a shadow drawing over them. He sat up quickly, making the boat rock, and saw that they were passing around the southern point of the island and taking the eastern passage. He was quite sure Hilgate had not once turned his head to look forward, and he asked sharply:

"Do you know where you're going?"

Hilgate looked at him but kept on rowing, and answered evenly but with a peculiar note in his voice like that of the night before when he had bidden Harlan "Wait!"

"1 know what I'm about, and if you don't want to upset this boat you'd better not try jumping round again like that. Sit still and keep the skiff trimmed."

The high rocky islet drew between them and the low sun; on every other hand the heights frowned over them. The crowding, concentering currents, that swirled darkly about them and tossed their light craft, lapped and fretted against the barring hills, and in the course of time had cut away and undermined all loose and friable material from their steeps, and left to all appearance only precipitous walls of bare rock, shagged and crowned with clinging masses of evergreens.

The heights approached one another gradually toward the east, hemming the river into a narrower and narrower bed till it reached two lofty opposing cliffs, strikingly like a Titanic gateway. The whole scene, to one coming suddenly from the quiet beauty of the outer river, was one of such impressive and gloomy grandeur that it distracted Harlan's attention till he perceived with a start that they were in the center of the converging currents, and that, though Hilgate had headed the boat westward and was pulling steadily, they were drifting sternward slowly but surely in toward the dark defile, whence came distinctly now the roar of rapids and falls. He felt the blood ebb out of his face, feet, and hands, leaving them cold; then as suddenly it came back with a hot rush of resentment, and he looked all about and up the cliffs, then bent forward and spoke to Hilgate with a fierce calmness:

"What the devil are you about?"

Hilgate did not quicken his stroke or change his attitude or expression, as he answered:

"1 wouldn't call on the devil now if I were you; you'd better call on God. No man who went down there was ever found again, dead or alive. And, if you keep jumping about, you'll go down a little sooner than there's any need."

He laid himself to the oars then for a few strokes and made perceptible headway, then let the boat fall away again. He repeated this every minute or two after that, gaining a little always when he put forth his strength, but steadily drifting in on the whole, till they lay fairly under the gigantic gateway, to pass which was certain death.

Harlan crouched in the stern, in a still and helpless desperation, looking into the chasm, and by degrees comprehending how utterly he was

in this man's power. Not only was he overmatched twofold in weight, strength, and assurance, but his only hope of escape lay in that very strength and dexterity of his enemy. He could do nothing; to attack, to interfere in any way, even to move quickly, was to precipitate the worst he had to fear. But, under the very shadow of the dread gate, Hilgate, by a powerful effort, gained a few yards, and then suddenly slipped the anchor with a motion of his foot. It plunged and then dragged, caught, the oars keeping the boat from drawing too sharply and snapping the rope; it slipped, then caught again and held. Hilgate slackened his stroke gradually, trying the boat's behavior under the strain, then ceased and crossed the oars carefully before him.

He was somewhat blown with the exertion, and he sat bent forward a little while over the oars, while he got his breath. The tug of the anchor on the bow sunk the skiff's head deep in the water, and the swift current lapped and gurgled past them, communicating to the boat a tremulous vibration, as if she sympathized with its eagerness for the rush and leap of the falls. Far down the dark and narrow gorge, whose high walls echoed with the reverberation of the plunging waters, Harlan could see now dimly an evermoving, ghostly whiteness which he knew was a cloud of spray.

Hilgate took up the loose end of the anchor-rope, which Harlan saw with a start controlled the running knot that alone held it fast at the bow. Then Hilgate spoke in a slow, predetermined manner and deep, clear voice:

"Now, listen to me. You will never go out of here unless I take you. If I jerk this rope, this skiff will shoot in there, and in three minutes you will be over the fall. But promise me to take the first train south and not to come back, and I'll land you safe in half an hour from now. Decide which you prefer."

Slowly there rose in Harlan a burning, fierce desire to spring upon him and throttle the life out of him. He clutched the boat's gunwale in his hot impatience, but the consciousness of its futile madness sufficed to hold him still, and then crept over him with a benumbing sense of faintness and soreness that made him feel like rolling into the deep, cool current, where at least there was room to stretch out. He was obliged to push himself forward so that he lay at length in the boat, his shoulders only resting on the sternseat, and his arms behind his head. To Hilgate it seemed an attitude of defiance. He looked down at him a minute or two, then took out his watch and glanced at it, and said as before:

"How much time do you want?"

"If I go down there," Harlan answered, "what good will it do you? You will go, too."

"Perhaps so," Hilgate returned, "perhaps not. There are places where it is possible for a good swimmer who knows them perfectly to land. Don't trouble yourself about me; I'll take my chance. There would be no chance for you."

"Only a coward would take such an advantage!" Harlan retorted hotly. "Even among gamblers it is considered dishonorable to bet upon a certainty."

Hilgate winced perceptibly, but recovered at once. He answered evenly:

"I don't choose to discuss the point with you. How much time do you want?"

Harlan sat up. He was quite close now.

"I'll tell you one thing," he said; "I won't go down there alone; I'll cling fast to you as long as there's life in me!"

There was a touch of contempt in Hilgate's reply:

"I wouldn't be too sure of that. I think I can take care of myself."

Harlan lay back as before, his arms under his head and his eyes on the other. And while Hilgate thought he braved him unfalteringly, he cried inwardly and bewailed his reckless rashness in entering the boat. Fool! fool! Why had he got in? To prove he was not afraid when he was afraid. He was a coward, and a fool as well; he was only more afraid of being thought afraid than of the actual peril. He had always been so. Well, was he not richly paid? Had he a right to allow his folly to involve not only his own destruction but this man's guilt of blood? And Marian—at that thought his fierce resentment sprang up again. What claim had this fellow upon his truth or to any regard? By the deceit of an implied promise to ferry him over, he had inveigled him into this snare; did such treachery deserve any greater respect? Deceit? It would be no deceit. There were things that outweighed all words. Compulsory speech or writing was held void in any court. Without any definite volition, he continued his thinking aloud:

"Do you imagine any one would be bound by such a promise under these circumstances? I suppose you have the power to make me repeat any form of words you choose."

Hilgate looked at him a minute, then answered, unchanged:

"That will do you no good. I want no form of words: if you couple your promise with any such proviso, it will be the same as a refusal. I simply want you to assure me in your own way that you will do as I require."

"And do you believe I should keep such a promise made under threats against my life?"

And after a pause Hilgate answered with deliberate assurance, "Yes, I do."

They faced one another gravely for a minute, then Hilgate looked down at his watch and said with a determined air:

"Think it over, now, and take your choice. There's no danger of an interruption. I'll give you fifteen minutes to make up your mind."

The commanding voice and address of the handsome fellow had from the first wrought powerfully upon Harlan; he had always been strongly affected by what is in most people an instinctive submission to the influence of certain natural leaders. Now for a time it took complete possession of him, and he gave entertainment to all manner of weak and plausible imaginings. There was no use denying that Hilgate was by far the finer fellow, every way his superior, and an infinitely fitter companion for her—rich, strong, clever, and looking it all; and, in candor, ought he to be the less admired for what he would do and risk for her sake? Was not all literature full of the glorification of such absorbing passion? He recoiled with horror from that dark, resounding gorge, and beside it in his mind came unbidden the picture of a South American valley, sunny and peaceful and beautiful as paradise. Life seemed very sweet then, and could he hesitate between death in that gorge and life in that valley when the only question was whether or not he should leave Marian free to make a better match if she chose? He had not named her nor let his thought dwell upon her in that train of reasoning till now, and at her name there leaped into his heart the remembered longing with which he had ached so many a day in that happy valley; and, at the idea of life there without even the hope that had made his exile endurable, the sunny valley turned suddenly black in his thought, as if Cotopaxi had belched forth and rained thick ashes upon it and darkness that could be felt. No, there were things worse than death!

The unflinching face and figure he confronted became inexpressibly hateful to him, and a murderous feeling swelled in him almost beyond restraint. He turned on his side and drew down his hat to shut out the hated vision. But his thoughts remained hot and resentful. What reason had this man to place him in such a dilemma? Had he any right to further the ends of his treacherous entrapper by stickling about would and would not? Why not say what the fellow demanded, and as soon as he was free deny and defy him? He had already warned him, and was not that the manly part? Truth was no matter of words but of deeds. "A man may smile and smile, and be a villain"; a man may lie and lie, and all his words be true. All men say thus and so every hour upon hearsay or half-knowledge, and have to explain or go without explaining, yet all are not false. To quibble about words in a matter of life and death was a womanish superstition. What should he say—that was all? How should he turn or rise and say it? He tried this form and that; he imagined how he would sit and look and speak. But he felt the blood come and go in his face, and his voice stick and die in his throat. His heart sank again; he knew he could not do it. The fellow's very expression of belief in his word had stirred a string in him that vibrated through all that sophistry and still rang clear. What he might be led to do in haste or sudden fear, what he might feel bound to do for another's sake, he could not tell; but there were things he could not say in cold blood for his own gain or safety. It was no matter of would or would not; he could not do it! But why should he not for her sake? Was he not hers? Were they not one? Should he let his scruple of conscience or habit of mind bring harm to her? Again at the thought of her the yearning heart-sickness rose over him; again he was swayed by the longing to go to meet her to be parted no more. But her image, that had fostered all his better part so long, stirred it now anew; and he felt by anticipation the intolerable shame of owing her welcome, her dear, pure presence always—to a lie! Yes, that was it; there was no disguising it. He could not wrong her by selling her at such a price; his first duty to her was to be true. No, he not only could not —he was far from boastful now—but out of his dread and weakness he cried to God for help to keep his resolve that he would not.

And yet, and yet!—the weak flesh shrank and recoiled. Was there no escape? Covertly he examined the cliffs with eager scrutiny; instinctively even then he would not let Hilgate see that he quailed. He peered down into the dark flood, and mentally measured his strength with it; could he row or swim against it? The inevitable answer sent his thought back at Hilgate: could he leap up and seize an oar and strike him dead! He hugged the thought for a while, but he knew he could not, and if he could it would not help him. And Hilgate sat calmly and watched the hands count the time.

Physically Harlan was as powerless as a newborn child. An active, impetuous, grown man, he lay there, and felt as if all his sinews were drawn; he could not move a finger in his own defense. But he would not, could not yield. Bone and muscle were useless, but might he not match him with his brain? Could he not yet outwit him? He thought of Sonti, the early explorer of the Northwest, with one good hand and an artificial one of metal, left alone for months among the wild tribes, with a thousand miles of primeval wilderness between him and another

white man, actually making his crippled member do tenfold service, and ruling over a savage horde by the awe of his iron hand. More aptly he remembered the man in Bulwer's novel (the name Jaspar ran in his mind) who, when beleaguered something like himself in an isolated upper room at night, pretended to write what his enemy demanded of him, wrote instead a statement of his situation, wrapped a weight in it, and tossed it from the window upon a ledge where a friendly hand would find it in the morning; and so escaped. Was it possible for him to communicate with any one? While his body lay motionless, his mind beat about the world like Noah's wing-weary dove. But it presently returned to rest, finding no point of support.

A tired, drowsy feeling crept over him, a longing to sleep and forget it all, such as comes to us after weary, anxious days. But not to wake again! To slide so into the undiscovered land whence none returns! Oh, the man could not be in earnest! Could he deliberately perpetrate such a crime? But a glance at him did not reassure; and were not the newspapers full of deadly deeds done for like cause?

He must hug no weak delusion. He must address himself to meet with such fortitude as he might the hard fate that confronted him. With an effort he turned his shrinking face to regard it. What would it be like? He felt in imagination the swift, smooth rush down the dark defile, heard the roar, felt the dashing spray, took the breathless flight and plunge. And what then? Should he sink and be smothered with water, struggle vainly for the upper air, and then slide into innnition? Should he drift, still conscious, into some deep cave, to keep thenceforth the grisly company of the ones lost there before him? Should he be dashed to death on the cruel rocks or jammed between them irretrievably? He turned from that contemplation, shuddering.

Why should he vex himself? Whatever its form, it would be short. He had always hoped for a speedy death, and resolved not to suffer it but once. And as for the dim beyond, it was no new object in his thought. He had not needed reminder of graveyard or preacher to turn him to it. Life trod always close beside death, and any step might be across the line. He had not been so fortunate as they who walk the world in the unwavering confidence that they can see behind the veil, and are solaced and inspired by the beatific vision on which they fix their eyes. But more and more he had come to see and feel that he and his life were part of the infinite order and movement of the world. He acted and must act as if free, but when he looked back he saw that his life had been shaped at every turn by forces outside of his will, and he felt under no more obligation to reconcile freedom with fate than to comprehend the million mysteries that enveloped thought and sense. Death is as life to Him who orders all; here or there we lie in his hand and perform his immutable will.

That well-tried conviction did not fail him utterly now, though flesh and spirit shrank. More palpably than ever before, he felt the resistless grasp upon his life; and he yielded himself, like a child that struggles a moment with the arms that lull it, then falls asleep. Humbly he solaced himself with the thought that he should die true, should die for the truth as really as any martyr of the past. His mind wandered back to the men who had died for every cause and religion, for liberty and for loyalty. He went over hastily the deaths he remembered of notable people: thought of Socrates calmly draining the fatal cup; of the selfish, frivolous, courtly Charles apologizing to his attendants that he was "an unconscionable while a-dying"; of the loving, reverent fortitude of William and Mary; of the false, merciless, corrupted Philip testifying that he died conscious of rectitude and of having wronged no man; of religious Dr. Johnson, with his life-long horror of death; of noble Dr. Arnold's noble end; of Wolfe and Montcalm, Nelson and Moore, and the host who have had the enviable fortune to die in the ardor of glorious victory or glorious defeat; of great-hearted Thackeray, found dead with his arms thrown up upon the pillow; of the good Macaulay dying where he had lived, in his library chair; of Dickens, struck down at his table, and lying a night and a day with that stertorous breathing that typified his life, then resting for the first time and finally; of Russell, before he went out to execution, turning from parting with his wife in the prison and saying, "Now the bitterness of death is past!" At that, with a great throb, his thought leaped back to Marian, and he cried to her out of the deep waters: "Marian! Marian! Marian!" And then, as if the flood indeed encompassed him and his ears were full of its loud lapping and bubbling, he heard Hilgate's voice sounding far off and solemnly:

"You have three minutes left to decide!"

The warning startled him vaguely, and scattered his thoughts like a stone dropped in a stream. But the strong current was only disturbed and set again in a moment; all his instincts sought and huddled about the thought of Marian. Oh yes, that was the bitterness of it! He felt that he could bear it but for that; but how could he bear that? He could not, he could not! He held her with his thought; he could not let her go. He held her long, long and fast. A mighty love filled him and lifted him bodily; he felt there was nothing he could not do or face for

her sake except to give her up. But what could he do now? Nothing but give her up, nothing but endeavor to die worthy of her.

He felt himself turning from her, felt her slipping from him as if the heart were being drawn from his breast. It grew dark; he heaved with a suffocating inward sobbing. But suddenly he was stilled. Light and clear, like the voices heard of old from heaven, he seemed to hear her now, her sweet, plaintive, reverential tones comforting him and saying:

"Yea, though I walk through the valley of the shadow of death, I will fear no evil: for thou art with me; thy rod and thy staff they comfort me."

A great stillness, a deep, sad peace and solemnity stole over him. He sobbed still, but low and subsiding. He made his peace with men, with this man; he put enmity out of his heart. He would not survive in his place. He composed himself as to sleep. He trusted God; he could leave Marian and his sister in his care. Poor Jess! poor Jess!

Half unconsciously then, he fumbled in his breast for Marian's last letter and her picture. Ha, they were gone! Could they be lost? The thought was a bitter pang. Then he remembered the two coats hanging together in the hotel; he had put on the wrong one in his haste. But what was this in the pocket? Something hard and cold. His fingers groped about it mechanically, then clutched hold of it, and though he made no sound he seemed to himself to shout till he heard the cliffs ring and reëcho. Righteous God, he held a revolver in his hand! But then he fell to trembling—if it were not loaded! He drew it out eagerly, keeping it out of sight; he pressed the spring, bent back the barrel, and the chamber fell out in his hand. It was full of ball-cartridges; he counted them with his fingers over and over, head and point. He lay still and fondled the weapon, and he thanked God for gunpowder, that makes the weak the equal of the strong and cruel!

The case of Hilgate's watch snapped short. His voice said slowly:

"The time is up. What do you say?"

Harlan put back the chamber carefully, closed it, and examined every part. Then he sat up, rested his hand on his knee with the pistol pointed, and looked Hilgate in the face. They confronted each other silently awhile.

"That was what made you so cool, was it?" Hilgate said then, steadily.

Harlan did not answer nor move his eyes or his hand.

"Well," Hilgate went on presently, "what will you do now?"

"I will ask you," Harlan answered, low and

huskily, but with a firm hand and face, "to take those oars and row me out of this. I'm not good at rowing or swimming, but I'm a practiced shot."

Hilgate said, "You will not shoot."

"You said you would believe my word," Harlan answered; "do you doubt it now?"

"You have not given your word."

Harlan's face fell before that unfaltering gaze. Should he be beaten still? He felt, with a great heart-sinking, more than ever how true it is that the man who has assurance and is without fear can do anything and go anywhere. Hilgate seemed to penetrate his consciousness. No, he did not want to shoot him. Could he, if he would, sit there and deliberately pull the trigger that would kill? His soul revolted from taking the man's blood upon it. And Hilgate, as if he followed the motion of his thought, took it up and said:

"If you were to kill me, what better off would you be?"

An overpowering despondency settled down upon Harlan. A blackness gathered about him, and he seemed sinking out of consciousness. Then suddenly he came back with a sharp rebound. He set his face and cleared his eyes. He seemed to see Marian, grieved and reproachful, looking at him mutely, as she might if he quailed from his country's defense or from hers. No, he would *not* be beaten! He was bound to use the means Heaven had so strangely put in his hands. He would use them. His face and voice were sorrowful when he spoke, but there was a determination in them not to be mistaken.

"I don't want to hurt you," he said; "I bear you no ill-will. But, if you slip that knot, I will shoot you through the heart!"

A baffled expression came into Hilgate's face then, and he bowed his head in stern meditation. But soon he raised it slowly, and looked back only more darkly than before, and spoke deep and low:

"Be careful; don't try to scare me! Don't rouse the devil in me any more than is necessary."

He put his hand under his coat, and drew out a revolver of his own. Harlan could not disguise a perceptible quivering. Hilgate said:

"You see it is an even thing yet. Throw yours away, and I will throw mine."

"I can't do it," Harlan answered, absently; "it is not mine." Then he looked up and added: "It did not make me cool; I did not know I had it till a moment ago. This is George Raymond's coat."

Hilgate sat darkly a minute or two, then bent over and laid his pistol in the bottom of the boat, equally distant between him and Harlan.

"Put yours down beside it," he said.

"Do you promise to row me out of here in safety, if I lay it there?"

Hilgate sat and looked at him a long minute before his lips could move to say the one word— "Yes."

Harlan turned aside his face and thought it over and over, finding it painfully difficult to make up his mind. But at last he turned back slowly, heaved a deep sigh, and leaned forward and laid his pistol down beside the other. He sat up again then, but he could not look at Hilgate or hide the strong trepidation that took hold of him.

But Hilgate took no notice. He sat, looking down at the pistols, thinking somberly, but not of them. Then he raised his head and put out his arms, moving stiffly. He slid out the oars.

"Reach forward and take this line," he said, coldly.

Harlan did so. Hilgate dipped the oars and began to row, increasing gradually till he pulled with his strength. And the anchor-rope sagged.

"Now jerk that loose," he said, harshly.

Harlan obeyed, and the current drew the rope rattling out of the ring and whipped it astern of them with significant swiftness.

The flood seemed to gather together and surge at the skiff with redoubled power and went seething and whirling away from them as if angrily bent upon having them to whisk down the gorge. Very, very slowly the cliffs stole back and spread apart. The frowning gateway no longer loomed above them; the heights bowed their heads by degrees; and out of the valley of death they crept with increasing pace, and then emerged from behind the island upon the placid river of light and life. Not a word was spoken, but steadily and powerfully they swept up the stream, the faint grace of the fading sunset brooding over hill and river like a heavenly benediction, and the smooth current bubbling, oh, so gratefully, against the bows!

The ferry came in sight; the boat slid in and ran close to the wharf. Hilgate steadied the skiff against the piles beside a ladder, and waited without looking at Harlan. Harlan got up slowly, took hold of the rounds and climbed out and stood on the wharf. He lingered and looked back a minute or two, finding himself dizzy; then he went away up the plank walk, crossing from side to side of it as he ascended. He passed the station and took the path he had followed the day before. He had a half-formed feeling that he was grown old, and had walked that path once when he was young. He came to the gate, and went in and up the steps.

There was a quick rustle, a patter of firm, small feet. Marian Stillfleet appeared in the doorway, stopped and looked at him, and gave a startled cry. He awoke then. He took her in his arms; he began to laugh. But he fell down on the bench, and broke out into loud sobbing. Marian's father came out hastily at the sound.

"Harlan, Ned Harlan, what is it, what is it?" he called, in helpless alarm.

Harlan stood up, staggering, still holding Marian.

"Nothing, nothing!" he cried out. "Don't mind me; don't be afraid. It is nothing; only this thy son was dead and is alive again, he was lost and is found!"

THE PINE-ROOT FENCE.

IT skirts the field for many a rood, and twines
Grotesquely, forks and antlers, baffling, thus
Crumple to leap the barrier underneath
The rain of missiles cast by ragged Jim,
While grazing the green basins of the road.
Not Carlo, though he saw within the field
The woodchuck washing, by his wood-edged den,
His whiskered face with paws hung Shaker-like,
Could pierce its web, although with quivering
    brush
And eager yelp he seeks an entrance. Scarce
The weasel could twist through. When Summer
    smiles
The blackberry-bramble here finds ready room
To hang its sable beehives. Here, too, clings
The smooth, neat blackcap, and the raspberry
    shows
Its ruddy turbans. Mingled slight with all
The delicate clematis climbs and spangles round
Its little leaves and spreads its woolly tufts
When autumn glows. In that rich season, too,
The allspice shows its crimson berries through
The maze like clustered fires ; and the wild grape
Twines its broad arbor o'er. In genial spring
The bluebird in the crannies weaves a nest,
And in the chinks the robin thrusts fresh moss
And wreathes its tiny home ; blue, speckled eggs
Tell whence the parent bird has instant flown,
As little, truant Jack steals close and parts
The verdure where she brooded. Winter sheds
His plumage till the rough, grim, frowning fence
Seems carved of pearl ; each twig and stub gro-
    tesque
Shines in pure swan's-down where the snow bird
    leaves
Its mezzotints of prints, and chirps its notes
As if to link the ear to those glad songs
That Spring sends jubilant o'er all the land.
And then the variant colors of the fence—
Some, soft and silvery, like velvet ; some,
Streaked like the agate ; some, like ebony

Sable and glossy ; some, in curly spots
Like dimples in the water, and some specked
Like motes in sunbeams. Gray in lichen here,
There, red in powdery moss, with now and then
A splinter where the thistle's plumy stars
Hung tattered, and slight, narrow openings where
The wood-tick clicked its trick-trick castanets ;
The frog below has roughed his tambourine,
While his small progeny has shrilly trilled
Like the sweet chiming of the circling bells.
Soon as the first warm days of April make
In sheltered dingles the sharp-bladed grass
Pierce sodden leaves, heave acorn-cups away,
And mosses raise slight threads of sprays, to show
The birds the rafters for their little huts,
The nooks and crannies of the fence begin
To show faint tinges from the opening buds
Of the niched brambles, and they do not cease
Until the thorns and apple-trees above
See their white trickery doubled in the fence,
Whelming its roughness in their velvet snow.

ALFRED B. STREET.

HOLIDAYS OFF THE BEATEN PATH.

BY WILLIAM H. RIDEING.

ONE or two summers ago, when a club of artists chartered a canal-boat and embarked in it for a cruise along the waterways of New York, it was looked upon by some as a novel and rather dubious experiment. They lit up the hold with the splendors of Turkish rugs, and hung it with pictures and soft tapestries ; they transferred the choicest contents of their studios into this cabin—statuettes of marble, bits of armor, and rare pottery of all sorts ; they obliterated whatever was against their sense of beauty, and succeeded in transforming the bulky carrier into barge such as never floated out of the harbor before, or perhaps anywhere in the world. All this was very charming, and would vastly enhance the pleasure of an excursion in almost any direction ; but along the canal, amid a class noted for their savagery—what attraction could there be? The club came back hilarious with success, browned by the sun, and with portfolios crammed full of studies, which, elaborated into full-grown pictures, have been answering the question at various exhibitions ever since. What attractions along the canal, indeed! There is the loveliest scenery and the quaintest character. In all the excursions we ever made, none gave us more satisfaction and pleasure than that from New York to Buffalo in a canal-boat which we made years before the Tile Club was born, and this despite the fact that we had no special accommodations, and fared with the boatmen on the simplest food.

One morning, when we were crossing the East River by Hamilton Ferry, and smoking our after-breakfast cigar (we were young then, and could smoke an after-breakfast cigar without tasting it for the rest of the day), a long tow of canal-boats, twenty or more, knitted together in the wake of one of those tow-boats which have no hulls to speak of, and an abnormal development of engine and smoke-stack, prevented us from entering the New York slip; and while we waited for them to open a passage for us, we glanced at the varied life the plain of white decks revealed. There were babies rocking in cradles, and dogs peeping out of the cockpits; women hanging clothes out to dry, and women seated in chairs sewing. The distance between boat and boat was so small that no agility was necessary to bridge it; and perhaps it is unnecessary to say that there were women paying visits who ought to have been at home, as others were, who could be observed peeling potatoes and washing cabbage, and making other preparations for an early dinner. By "home" we mean on their own boats, for each of these twenty vessels was in the after-part the abode of a small family or a few bachelors. The signs of domesticity were striking in their variety, and, as our ferry-boat impatiently drew nearer to the obstructions, we could perceive one young woman seated at a sewing-machine which she had brought under the awning on deck, while from one of the cabins we could distinctly hear the tones of a parlor organ.

"That's the thing!" said X——, who is a clever journalist with such a quick eye for fresh phases of life and its occurrences that he is constantly "beating" his contemporaries—" that's the thing! Go up the river with a 'tow,' and through the canal by one of the boats."

The suggestion was acted upon at once. We sought out an acquaintance among the producemen near South Ferry, enlisted his services in engaging berths for us with a desirable captain, and one evening, less than a week later, we lay, with belted breeches, blue shirts, and broad-brimmed hats (an unavoidable alliteration), on the deck of a boat gliding away from the city, as the sun was setting fire to every western window and weathercock.

The selection of a captain and a boat is the only difficulty in making the canal-trip. So far from being all barbarians, many of the boatmen are superior in intelligence to the average farmer by whose lands they pass, but there are some desperadoes among them who are to be avoided. Our butter-and-cheese friend was very fortunate. The boat he chose for us carried the captain's

wife and daughter with it, and had as complete a menage astern as some yachts and French flats we know of: we were provided with a little cupboard which, though not spacious enough to swing two cats in, was clean; and the captain, though by no means a saint, was a generous, good-humored, and well-behaved fellow. He assumed no virtues, and he exhibited few vices. He could swear, but his profanity was only vented when there was an unusual delay in the locks. He could drink, and was even fond of a horn of whisky, but the subtle devil of alcohol was always under with him.

Before we had been two days out of the city, and while we were still on the river following the steamer that was leading us to the entrance of the canal at Troy, we discovered that we had hit upon the very ideal of locomotion. In a steamer, on the smoothest water, there is the tremendous vibration of the engine; in a yacht each tack throws the boat at a different angle of incline; in a train the jar and noise are beyond comparison; but in a canal-boat the eye is the one sense that perceives motion, while all the others are unconscious—the frame of the boat does not quiver, the water falls away from the bow without foam or vehemence, and the deck under one's feet seems to have the stability of earth.

When we were on the canal itself, floating midway in the landscape, and gliding through it at a pace that enabled us to take in all its features, the sensation became one of ecstasy, and the long days are fixed in the memory like dreams. The silent channel that bears one fourth of all the freight coming from the West to the East threads the valley of the Mohawk, which in its softness and repose reminds us of some garden-spot in England. Far and wide the acres are cultivated, the orchards crouch in the blossom of spring, and the meadows are dyed by purple and white clover. In the wide expanse there is no tree or house whose removal would further beautify it. The river makes itself heard between the hills, and in one of the slopes that meet it the canal is terraced, embowered by foliage. Sections of the old canal are seen here and there along the route—a moss-covered lock or a patch of the towpath nearly obliterated by weeds and grass.

The interest is not permitted to lag, and the hours are unmeasured. A boat comes along with a hard-worked woman seated in a rocking-chair at the stern; a wild lily, secured from the banks of the canal is drooping in a tumbler of water on a common box, which serves as a work-table; and in an inclosure of rope and wood, like a sheep-pen, on the cabin-roof, several children are playing. By and by another boat passes, and we see a young woman pressing a tame robin to her breast, and feeding it at the end of her finger. Meyer von Bremen's pictures are realized; poetic simplicity in beautiful surroundings is not a dream.

The houses on the towpath have quaint exteriors; and somewhere beyond Amsterdam there is one that is haunted—a pretty but sad-looking cottage. The front door is not more than a stride from the water, and the windows are all battered in. The garden is a mass of weeds which have smothered the flowers, two or three hardy rose-bushes alone having struggled through with their pink-and-white blossoms. On one of the walls near the roof there is a large patch which seems to have missed the last application of paint, and the legend is that a young boatman was renovating the place for his promised bride, when some one told him that she had flown with another: the brush fell out of his hand; he came down the ladder, and locked himself in the house, out of which he never reappeared alive, though his specter still holds possession.

As evening approached the land appeared more beautiful than ever. There were level miles of velvet turf in superb condition, bounded by hills of the gentlest contours; fields of strong, young grain, curling and singing at the touch of the breeze; old homesteads hedged in with greenery, and paths winding off toward villages in the distance. The landscape seemed too calm to be American. Wells of light were hidden in the foliage and streamed out at every crevice—surely, this was an older land than ours. But above there was a sky of native splendor, of countless tints, of surpassing brilliance. When night came cool airs swept over us, and, if the horizon was interrupted at all, it was by the graceful outlines of some hill that added nobility to the prospect. As the stars made themselves known, myriads of fire-flies emulated them in the shrubbery along the banks, and flashed across the calm surface of the stream.

Each boat carries a lantern in the bow, which disperses a circle of yellow light on the watery track ahead. The tow-lines dip occasionally with a musical trill into the water, and in advance you may hear the steady thud of the horses' hoofs on the ground, or the low cry of the driver as he urges them on. At the stern the helmsman whistles or sings scraps of tunes until a lock engages him. His voice is then raised. "Lock belo-o-ow!" he calls to his mate; "Steady, ste-a-a-dy!" to the driver. There is a momentary clatter of feet upon the deck; we rise smoothly to the new level; the lock-lights fade; quiet prevails again, and we are traveling with drowsy softness toward the amber morning.

We did not suffer at all from confinement. As often as we pleased we sprang ashore, and now wandered into the neighboring woods, or sauntered through the towns and villages which we were passing. Our boat was heavily loaded, and traveled slower than others bound in the same direction, with lighter cargoes, which, by giving us a "lift"—a courtesy never refused on the canal—enabled us to overtake it even when we remained behind two or three hours. In this way we saw a good deal of Utica and its cheese-market; Syracuse and its pretty avenues and interesting salt-wells; Rochester and its handsome dwellings.

One day we moored alongside a comfortable homestead at Oneida, and this, with two or three hundred acres, was the captain's home, where we spent several pleasant hours, and were treated with great hospitality. We picked strawberries with the captain's daughters, and joined in a chase after a fiery colt; we swung in a hammock under an old-fashioned porch, and we ended the day with a contra-dance.

All along the canal we fell in with quaint characters and indigenous wit. Our helmsman overflowed with native humor, and met any thrust at his peculiarities with never-failing repartee. He prided himself on his hair, though it was scant and bristly, and he anointed it several times a day with the contents of various small bottles, the use of which he pressed upon us at the outset of our acquaintance. "Would ye like to have some of this yar hair-'ile?" he inquired, producing one of the vials, which we declined. "Well, see yar," he continued; "jest you smell of this. This yar is boss-'ile, double-distilled, extra warranted. Ef you puts one drop on your head, your hair'll suddenly have a handsome apperience, like mine." On one occasion the captain was describing the mysterious discovery of a pair of socks, buried near the canal. "They war large, and must have b'longed to a big man," he said. "Perhaps so, cap'n," his lieutenant replied; "but don't be too sure that it wa'n't a little man with a big foot!" "Wouldn't he do to fill up the last page of a comic almanac with?" demanded the captain, referring to his man. "Yes," responded the latter, "and you'd make a fortin' ef you'd sit and hev your photogram taken to beautify valingtines!"

About two weeks after leaving New York we reached the end of our journey at Buffalo, and, when we settled with the captain, our bill for board, lodging, and transportation was fourteen dollars. For this sum we had been conveyed up the Hudson in such a manner that every point of interest could be inspected: we had seen the valley of the Mohawk and parts of the Genesee; we had been treated with uniform courtesy and hospitality; we had made the acquaintance of a class possessing many characteristics which lifted them above the commonplace, and we had gained in physical strength as well as in the recreation of the mental faculties. The fare was not made up of delicacies. There was an inordinate recurrence of ham and eggs, which seemed to be more relished by the men than any other dish. But what we had was of good quality and sufficient—better, in fact, than that of most farm-houses. Our quarters were not like the cabins of modern Atlantic steamers; but we could sleep soundly in them, though we had to wash on deck. There was not one circumstance to offend us during the whole excursion, and we look back to it with unmitigated pleasure.

The mind is so governed by habit that when, with the first warm days of April or May, the choice of a vacation is discussed, only certain watering-places or mountain resorts are considered. A number of well-known routes are remembered and compared; Newport, Long Branch, Saratoga, the Catskills, and the White Mountains are mentioned, and if the projector's purse is not a long one, he is apt to sigh and dismiss these, especially if he has a family to look out for; then he thinks of some hurried excursion, perhaps through the Thousand Islands, down the St. Lawrence, and up the Saguenay; or up the Hudson, and over Lake George to the White Mountains; but, as the arithmetic of the thing steals in with second thoughts, this, too, seems impracticable; and he hesitates and vacillates until the vacation becomes a distress rather than a matter of pleasurable expectation. We recognize that there are some who can not afford to be unconventional, and others who are so abundantly supplied with riches that any suggestion as to how they may spend a summer is superfluous. But we address ourselves to those who are embarrassed by unavoidable economies; who can not enter upon an excursion without counting every item of expense, and who are obliged to shiver in contemplating the tariffs of the usual summer resorts. To these we say: Do not be limited by habit; devise new ways; explore new paths. The results may not always be satisfactory; but in exploration and experiment there is interest and recreation, while, if you are fortunate, some resources may be opened of which neither you nor your neighbors have ever dreamed. Economy in travel is a pain to some, when it is necessary to practice it where lavishness of expenditure is the custom, and this feeling is not wholly an outcome of snobbery; but in some directions frugality may be exercised without peculiarity, though not usually in the tracks of the average summer tourist. Even supposing that money is not an object, we commend the invasion of new ground as being much better than the following of paths wherein the habitual course of

living is little changed—inspiration and tranquillity come with novelty, and he who would feel little better for a season's loafing at some place where fashion sets up an inexorable formula, may acquire unwonted vitality by doing just what we propose here for persons who are not by any means wealthy. The canal-trip, as we made it, could not be done by ladies; but it would be feasible to arrange with some boatman for the whole of his cabin accommodations, and to provide for one's own table. We can imagine nothing better than that, and this is but one of many ways in which our suggestion may be realized—ways that will multiply if they are once sought for by a person of ordinary inventiveness.

One day, when we were debating with G—— as to where we could best spend a couple of weeks by the sea, he said, "Let us go to Bill Pharo's"; and, on the next morning, we embarked in the steamer for Sandy Hook, and sailed down the harbor, through a tropical haze which made every object intangible. We rushed past all the fashionable watering-places along the shore—Seabright, Long Branch, and Oceanport—and in the evening we alighted in the small and almost unknown village of West Creek. Until G—— discovered it we fancy it was outside of all geographical cognizance, but his pictures of the vividly green and undulous sedges that lie between it and the sea, and of the fishing-boats that beat through the marsh-bound channels, have given it existence among the frequenters of the water-color exhibitions at least. The summer tourist has not profaned its early simplicity, and no summer boarders have taught the natives to imitate city manners and city dress. It is half rural and half marine. The roads are overhung by dense foliage, and the gardens are luxuriant in bloom. There are no parched grasses or arid sand-hills. All behind it are dense woods, farm-lands, and cranberry-bogs. But here and there an arm of the creek runs in, and we find a sloop undergoing repairs beneath an arch of foliage, or a net spread out to dry in the meadows, and the air has a salty pungency which tells us of the close proximity of the sea. Could we reach the top of that little church-steeple, which pierces the uppermost boughs of the trees that conceal the rest of the building, we should see in the eastward prospect a verdant plain spreading out to a varying breadth, veined by narrow channels and bounded by a crisper and bluer expanse of water. Across this water is a spit of white sand, on the outer edge of which the Atlantic breaks with a reverberant force that it has at few other places on the coast. Looking one way, we are in the heart of the country; looking the other, the ocean fills more than half the view.

8

G—— is recognized at the depot, and asks for Bill Pharo. A freckled old man guesses that Bill is out with his boat; a freckled boy, wearing a hat absurdly disproportionate to the rest of him, says that he is gone over to Barnegat; a freckled girl assures us that she saw him in the village less than an hour ago, and, while we hesitate between these contradictions, the man himself appears and possesses himself of our traps without requiring any explanation of our plans. There is a good deal of Bill Pharo about the population of West Creek; he is typical of average human nature in that village, and a description of him applies, in a measure, to all the rest. The trousers he wore were of such structural peculiarity as to form a new scheme in the philosophy of clothes, ceasing to be nether garments simply, and extending far above the hips to the armpits, under which they were braced with a firmness which gave one an idea that the rest of the body was suspended from the shoulders. A few inches more of length, and a pair of sleeves added, would have made any other article of costume superfluous, except for ornament. His face was long and brown-red, two high cheek-bones pressing against two saucer-like, deep-set eyes, with a craggy forehead hanging over them, and a comical seriousness flashing in them. His conversation covered a wide variety of subjects: it was his opinion that, what is now New Jersey, was at one time the bottom of the sea; and, in proof thereof, he adduced the fact that oyster-shells had been found very much farther inland than the present coast-line.

His occupations were various. Ostensibly a fisherman, he turned his hand to many things in the course of a year; and, when the sea would not yield a living, he employed himself picking cranberries, harvesting salt hay, cutting ice, or peddling. When we met him he was idle, and was glad to engage himself to us for a cruise along the coast. His boat was neither large nor stanch, but Bill was a capital sailor, and no fears of accident troubled us.

We glided down the creek between those salt meadows, which had the soft luxuriance of a baronial lawn, and lay astern in careless happiness, smoking our pipes, and conscious only of the flapping of the sail as it "jibbed" this way or that, the rustle of the sedge, the spurt of the water as it fell away from the bow, and the bright blue of the sky contrasted with the low reach of verdure on the marshes. There could be no cynicism or morbid imaginings here. If young Brown, whose literature reflects the despondent ghastliness with which he contemplates the world, had been with us, even he must have found the cup of life becoming sparkling. For as the buffets of the world, the unequitableness

of society, and all that could distress us passed away, the warm sunshine pervaded us and stole through our veins like some potent elixir that dispels all gloom. By and by an increase of motion and sound on the water showed us that we had debouched from the creek into that gulf or strait which, with occasional breaks, lies all along the Atlantic coast, from Long Island to Cape Fear, between the mainland and an outer beach of white and almost verdureless sand. The width of this beach changes with nearly every winter's storm, which also closes up some inlets as it opens others, and the water which it incloses affords a safe passage for the smaller coasting-vessels that could not safely venture outside. The sand is so bleached and glistening that it casts up the reflected light with extraordinary brilliancy, and from a distance at sea a peculiar white haze seems to hang over it. The traffic of the coasters is supplemented by fleets of fishing-boats and by yachts belonging to the many new watering-places which have sprung up on the outer beach, for which those who are interested ingeniously claim the advantage of being not by the seaside but practically *at sea*.

The greater size of the waves and freshness of the breeze caused our own small vessel to dance and pitch with startling liveliness; but Bill held on to the sheet and, though he never ceased to talk, it was satisfactorily evident that his mind was fixed upon its duty. In an hour or two we saw long ribs of foam fretting above a reef, and the motion changed again from a rapid pitch and toss to a more dignified and slower though deeper swing. We had passed through Little Egg Harbor Inlet, and now stood out on the Atlantic itself, which, smooth on the surface, was rolling with a slumberous swell. We slowly beat southward and fell asleep, with our heads sheltered under the bows and our bodies exposed to the sun. In the evening we put into Atlantic City; and, after a glance at its multifarious gayeties, we gladly returned to the quietude of our boat.

We have not space to record all our movements during the cruise in detail. We sailed now in, now outside of the outer bar; we took all that came with absolute ease and contentment. We called at old-fashioned, little fishing villages, and at the watering-places on the beach; we chatted with wreckers, lighthouse-keepers, and life-saving men. The mornings were sometimes misty and gray, but every evening the sun went down in a lurid blaze of splendor, followed by pathetic twilights that made the world seem empty. A flock of herons flew against the sky of gold and crimson, in which the sun had left a sinuous belt of fire along the horizon. The dead calm that prevailed made the water like a mirror; and, as the sun fell closer to the blue line of woods across the salt meadows, the evening-star and a crescent moon grew more radiant in the pale, gray-blue east, and cast a reflection on the water while it still held the imprint of the more passionate orb. We were, indeed, alone in the world in these moments, and the world was motionless. There was a wan, pitiful look upon the meadows which, lying in a death-like lull, gave the scene its salience, and despite the rosy ardor of the western sky, Nature desponded and fell into a sad sleep. Sunsets at second-hand are not satisfactory, but those that we saw night after night along the Jersey coast were as individualized in their contrasted splendor and their melancholy undertones that they really seemed to belong to its topography.

We parted with Bill at Tom's River, and here we found that the whole expense of our excursion had been about three dollars a day apiece. Had there been more than two of us, the cost of the boat *pro rata* would of course have been less, and had we chosen to sleep aboard, and to have found our own provisions, a still further reduction would have been possible. But we were lazy and disposed to luxuriate; every night we laid up at some tavern, where we had supper and breakfast, usually of "planked" blue-fish and ham and eggs, the inevitable staples of country hospitality. An excellent boat, large enough to carry four or five persons, can be chartered for twenty dollars or less a week, with the services of an experienced man, and supposing that the party provided themselves with blankets and provisions, four persons could thus spend a week on our cruising-ground for less than ten dollars apiece.

"What does it cost to keep a yacht?" some one asked a rich New-Yorker who had every reason to be well posted. "Well," he said, "some people are extravagant with their yachts, but I am economical; I manage to cover all expenses with about twenty-eight thousand dollars a year." But while yachting in one way is an amusement limited to the rich, it can be enjoyed in another way by persons of very moderate means; and we recall a young man who hired a boat for five dollars a week, two dollars added to which amount covered all his expenses. He slept aboard, and his mess consisted of tea, coffee, "hard-tack," salt beef, ham, and whatever fish he was fortunate enough to catch. Does not the bill of fare attract you, dear reader? Perhaps it strikes you unsavorily, because you are pent up in the suffocating city, and your appetite needs all sorts of delicacies to tempt it; you are jaded and probably dyspeptic. But if you should put on a blue-flannel shirt, a pair of strong woolen

trousers and a broad-brimmed sun-hat, and should embark one morning in a stanch sloop and sail, as the young man in question did, out of New Bedford Harbor toward Marion, with a strong breeze fanning you, and the spray communicating its briny flavor to your lips, we venture to say that, before you reached the picturesque little island that stands off the mouth of the harbor, you would be yearning with hunger for a mug of coffee, one of the hard, brown biscuits, and a slice of that salt beef, which eight hours before repelled you as being no more edible than your boots. There are epicures who fast for two and three days, that they may resume the pleasures of the table with the keen enjoyment that surfeit has deprived them of. But no fasting is necessary to him who abandons the sedentary life of the city or university for these breezes and unsullied skies; the appetite that has been dainty and capricious springs up with a craving and relish for the simplest foods. Appetite improves, of course, with any change of air, but one thing to be coupled with our advocacy of these holidays off the beaten path is the change of life, which restores and revitalizes the bodily and mental forces when neurology has exhausted its pharmacopœia and failed. There is efficacy even for invalids in "roughing it," and in expeditions in new directions there is a sort of recreation which can not be found in familiar haunts. The tenants of "Rudder Grange" had misadventures, but whoever has read Mr. Stockton's fascinating book would no doubt be glad to repeat the experiences, advantageous and disadvantageous, which he so humorously describes.

There are scores of paths off the beaten track, and out of the common knowledge, which a little searching will reveal, and which surpass in beauty and interest those crowded by summer tourists. Over the Alleghanies from Frederick, Maryland, into Wheeling, Virginia, extends a fine highway that is scarcely ever traveled now, though once it bore nearly all the traffic between the West and Southwest and the East. The scenery has a grandeur approaching that of the Sierra Nevada, and, like that range, it includes ravine, cascade, and mountain forms, wooded from the base to the summit. Out of the many taverns that existed in former times a few remain, not too far apart for convenience, and the road, though not in the perfect condition it was formerly, is as good as country roads usually are. A summer ago we drove over it from Frederick to beyond Cumberland, and at one of the villages on the way we discovered an old, roomy, springy coach, which, though the varnish on its panels was cracked, and all its early magnificence had faded, was still fit for travel. We were so delighted with our experience that we vowed we would repeat the excursion; and then our companion, who was at the ardent age which sees nothing unless a petticoat is in the prospect, cried out: "Yes, we'll come again, and bring two or three other fellows and some girls with us; we'll charter the old coach and drive four-in-hand—that's the idea!"

If the old coach could be chartered and the inside used for commissary purposes—if the expedition could be made independent of taverns—the drive would probably have a greater charm than under more commonplace conditions. There would be ample space for tents, provisions, and cooking apparatus inside the vehicle; the travelers could choose their own halting-places, selecting positions desirable for the beauty of the outlook—the distances to be made each day might be fixed by them.

But if the conveyance were a buggy, a covered wagon, or a "buckboard"; if dependence were placed on the taverns; and if the number of the party was small or large, with or without the opposite sex, we believe that the old pike would afford a holiday that would be remembered with emphatic pleasure for many years.

The canoe and bicycle are both means of branching out and discovering features that the guide-books and the rush of travelers have missed. On the country lanes of England the latter is met in every direction, speeding with its rider through the loveliest landscapes; and with the canoe rivers may be explored up to their source in the boscage, or, like the Connecticut, followed down between banks of never-failing beauty.

Many other suggestions occur to us, but our space is limited and we come at last to an instance of how little those who are young and strong need be deterred from a holiday by reasons of economy. The example is that of six young men who spent three weeks in the White Mountains, and visited nearly all the famous resorts, at a total expense of fifteen dollars apiece, and whose experiences have been described in a small book by Mr. Frank E. Clark.

Their point of departure was Center Harbor, New Hampshire, where they hired a wagon for five dollars, a horse for a dollar a day, and a tent for four dollars. Their provisions consisted of a barrel of pilot-bread, a keg of pickles, two hams, cheese, condensed milk, salt pork, tea, coffee, and various condiments, to which they added on the way fresh eggs and milk, and brook-trout. They dressed simply, and on the first day out made seventeen miles. A march of twenty miles on the second day brought them to North Conway, where they pitched their tent in a pine-grove, a little to the east of the village, and their next camp was made near the Crawford House, three

miles from which is the famous Willey House that survived the avalanche.

"Is this the old Willey House?" Mr. Clark asked a girl standing in the doorway. "Dunno," she answered. "What!" continued the gentleman, "do you mean to say you don't know whether this is the house that escaped destruction in 1826, when all the family were killed?" "Dunno," this interesting creature again replied, and she was a type of others the travelers met on their way.

Sometimes they also fell in with crusty old farmers as irresponsive as she was—men who have lived in the mountains for half a century without ever standing upon a summit, and who, as Mr. Clark says, would mistake Gabriel's trumpet for a fish-horn! There was another species of the *genus homo* whom they met—the inquisitive and irresistible Yankee—who pursued a long series of questions despite the gruff and monosyllabic answers given: "What might I call ye?" "Trade pooty brisk down your way?" "What, ain't ye a storekeeper?" "A doctor then, perhaps?" "No? Du tell!" "You've come a pooty considerable ways, I reckon?" "Mor'n a hundred miles, hev yer?" "Ye must live somewhere near Boston then, I calculate?" "Live *in* the city, du ye?" "Know Jack Styles?" "Don't?" "Wahl!" But these characters, instead of being bores, enlivened the marches, and added that human interest to them which gave the jaunt a part of its charm.

At the White Mountain House they pitched their tent for several days, which were spent in various excursions through the neighborhood. They climbed Mount Willard and Mount Washington, spending a night upon the latter, and evading the high tariff of the hotel by obtaining the station-master's permission to spread their blankets on the floor of the depot. They visited Tuckerman's Ravine, and snowballed each other, though it was midsummer, and returning to their camp at the White Mountain House, they proceeded in the direction of the Franconias. Their next halt was at the Twin Mountain House, which used to offer the unusual attraction of "Beecher every Sunday, and dances every evening," and through the pretty village of Bethlehem they entered the heavily-wooded Franconias. Here they visited Echo Lake, the Old Man of the Mountains, the Flume and the Pool, and one day was given to the ascent of Mount Lafayette. Instead of returning home by the route which they followed in coming, they turned to the southwest, and on the second day from Franconia Notch they reached the valley of the "willow-fringed Connecticut," down which they traveled to their homes.

Their expenses, given by items, were as follows: Horse, at one dollar per day for three weeks, $21; wagon, $5; hard-tack or pilot-bread, and other provisions, $22; tent and stove hire, $4; feed for horse on the way, $12; provisions bought on the way, $15; plates and cooking-utensils, $3; incidentals, $8; total, $90; which amount, divided among six individuals, was fifteen dollars apiece.

The brief experiences here recorded will, perhaps, suggest many other trips to the reader no less economical or charming. The country is spacious, and, as we have said, there are beauties off the beaten path, the discovery of which adds the interest of exploration to the pleasure of contemplation, while even the paths followed by tourists are not unattainable to persons of moderate means, if the latter are not too proud or too feeble to be original.

HOW I DINED ON THE BOULEVARD DES ITALIENS.

By Nugent Robinson.

A GRILLING day in the month of August, 1875, found me in Paris without a centime. My vacation had melted away in Spain and with it my money. The few Isabellinas saved from Seville "burst up" at San Sabastian, and, ere I could tear myself from that *bijou* watering-place, my *impedimenta* were in pledge to the surly host of the Fonda del Corazon in the sum of one thousand reals, for the use of a very clean bed—the beds in Spain are belaced and befringed like altars—very unwholesome food, in which garlic held the pass against all comers, and desperately dubious drink combining the delicate flavor of beeswax with the unholy mawkishness of untanned leather. It was past six o'clock as I lounged along the shady side of the Boulevard des Italiens excessively fatigued, ravenously hungry, and confoundedly out of sorts. I had been to the *poste restante* (confidently expecting remittances —who doesn't expect remittances at the *poste restante?*), but a curly-headed employee, after shuffling a number of letters, as if he were about to deal a hand at euchre, with due regard to the location of the bowers, shook his head negatively, shrugged his shoulders, expressing an avalanche of No's, and, muttering something which meant to convey that I might as well have saved myself the trouble of applying to him, and have saved *him* the mental worry of replying to *me*, sank languidly into an easy-chair, and proceeded to inter himself in the naughtily illuminated pages of the "Petit Journal pour Rire."

Yes, I was hungry, hungry in the most vulgar acceptation of the term—a hunger that would have thrown over a *chef-d'œuvre* of Soyer for a dish of *bouilli*, or an idea of Francatelli for a plate of bacon and beans; a hunger that would have plunged the susceptibilities of Baron Steinmayer into the deepest mourning, and have driven my Lord Ogleby into a lunatic asylum! Having partaken of some slight refreshment at a period which now appeared to have been in the remote ages, my inner man, nailing the black flag to the mast, was in open mutiny, and Commodore Appetite threatened to scuttle the ship if his imperious terms were not forthwith complied with.

The position was extremely critical. No hotel would harbor me without money or marbles. A walking-stick and a pocket-handkerchief could scarcely be considered in the light of luggage. My watch had been abstracted during a frantic struggle to gain admittance to a bull-fight. Appearances, too, were dead against me. The mosquitoes, *et hoc genus omne*, had left my visage not unlike the interior of an unbaked red-currant tart. A Spanish barber had cropped me for a fever or a ticket-of-leave; my hat bore traces of not only one but of the four seasons, and might have been used as a soup-tureen for its general greasiness; and my garments had come to violent grief through the instrumentality of a "somebody's darling" who would persist in eating woolly bread and gluey jam all over my back during the major portion of the journey up. I had calculated upon lifting letters, and going right through to London, but the shrug of the postal Adonis in the Rue Jean Jacques Rousseau shivered my plans into smithereens, leaving me high and very dry on the flags of the French capital, and in a state of mind and body better to be imagined than described. Never did the *cafés* appear so inviting, the *menus* so seductive, the wine-lists so tantalizing. Could it be possible that, for the sake of a mere idea, I would be refused a dinner? It seemed incredible! Money was actually traveling toward me, but alas! my appetite journeyed much more rapidly. In Bayswater I was somebody, here worse than nobody—a beggar, an outcast, a coinless counterfeit. In London, I could command. In Paris, a thin sheet of plate-glass proved as formidable as the Great Wall of China. Heavens! to think that my club was awaiting me, and grouse soup, chicken turbot— The picture was too vivid! My inner man whooped and danced a frantic war-dance.

A gifted writer has observed how very uninteresting even the Boulevard des Italiens must be to the man who walks up and down it, in the hope of meeting an acquaintance from whom to borrow half a crown. How keenly I felt the truth of this observation as I stared eagerly at every passer-by, in the feeble expectation of dropping upon somebody who would stand a dinner, or the price of one!

"Hope springs eternal in the human breast," says Mr. Pope, and a slight thrill ran through mine as I read the words "English spoken here," in brazen letters upon an enormous sheet of plate-glass, which stood between me and a dish of cutlets delicately breaded, as a lady's face is powdered—a lobster, and half a dozen piquante dainties, with a background of rugged melons, and a Bacchanalian bower of grapes, flanked by golden-necked champagne-bottles coyly cooling themselves in blocks of pellucid ice.

"I can explain my position here," I reasoned; "tell them who and what I am, give them my card, and refer them to the London Directory. They must see that I am a gentleman and not a Jeremy Diddler. The thing is quite on the cards, and a little address will put matters right in a trice. Your restaurateur perceives at a glance the good money and the bad—it's his business."

It was a chance, at all events, and who can afford to lose a chance whose interior clamors for food! Taking heart of grace, I entered a sumptuously mirrored salon, where, alas! I found my seedy appearance reflected about five hundred times in as many hundred different positions, and approaching a very fashionably attired individual who was seated behind a grove of scarlet geraniums, negligently smoking a cigarette, asked if he spoke English?

"Non, m'sieur!" with a shrug and a twirl of his watch-chain.

"I wish to make some inquiries about dinner."

"Ah! Gustav! Gustav! venez ici."

Gustav, who was in attendance upon a swell-looking brace of Frenchmen with red ribbons in their respective buttonholes (what a prolific plant is the Legion d'Honneur!) reluctantly responded to the summons, and approached me in a manner which clearly bespoke his secret misgivings.

"You speak English?" I observed with what was intended for a winning smile.

"Yaas, sure. Vat vill you to vant?"

"The fact is, I wish to dine."

"Dinnare, à la carte?"

"I wish to explain to you that—"

"Does table disengage," planting a golden chair, upholstered in crimson velvet, opposite a small table snowed up in spotless damask, decorated with glittering cutlery and glasses of many shapes, and of every color in the rainbow—ay, and out of it, too.

I heartily wished myself once more upon the boulevards.

"Before I order the dinner, I—"

"No require ordare. She is prepare"; and Gustav essayed to relieve me of my battered hat and travel-stained stick.

"I wish to mention that before ordering dinner I would like you to understand—"

"I you understan' perfeck," interposed Gustav. "Me vos in Angland since tree year. You vill to dine. Dinnare is here ver goot." Here he shook the gorgeous chair, and presented the wine-card at my head in a threatening sort of way.

I saw that to avoid an interview with a gendarme I should come to the point at once.

"Gustav"—assuming a manner which upon some few occasions in my singularly uneventful career had proved irresistible—"I want a dinner, a tray-bong dinner; but I have no money paw day layong, till to-morrow."

Gustav recoiled. By a supreme effort he repressed a shriek. His glance riveted itself upon my excoriated visage. Was he counting the mosquito-bites?

"I expected to have received money to-day, but it has not arrived. It's certain to be here demang. I wish to arrange to dine here and I will pay to-morrow, and give you a five-franc piece for yourself."

This was artful, and ought to have succeeded. "Que voulez-vous, m'sieur?" exclaimed Gustav, dropping his three-year-old English, and retreating within his French fortifications, whither I could not safely follow him.

I repeated my request, laying especial stress upon the five francs for himself.

"Oui, m'sieur." This was addressed to one of the beribboned Frenchmen, who, by-the-by, had not called him at all; then, turning to me—"Vous n'avez pas de l'argent?"

I scrambled up a little hillock of the language, and boldly replied from the summit:

"Pas aujourd'hui."

Gustav winked facetiously, placed his hand gently but firmly upon my shoulder, smiled blandly, pointed to the door, and, bowing low, murmured the single word "Demain."

I would have parted with my expected remittance ten times told to have given him one, just one, kick in the region where the tail of his coat ought to have pendulated. I shook my fist in his face, and told him in good Saxon that he might thank his stars the law prevented me from breaking every bone in his contemptible carcass, in addition to which the fact of his being a miserable garçon du café placed him on so low a level as to preclude the possibility of assailing him save through the medium of contempt.

"What's the row, Mr. Foxley?" exclaimed a voice close to my ear. I turned and beheld to my unspeakable rapture a gentleman whom I had casually met in London, and one to whom under other circumstances I would have given an extremely wide berth. But now how altered my feelings! What a transition! From twenty degrees below freezing-point to ninety-five in the shade—from an icy "sir" to a gushing "Jenkins." With what sincere pleasure did I wring his hand! With what effusive solicitude did I inquire for his health and that of his family, whom I had never seen or even heard of! If I had cut him over and over again, was that a reason for continuing such stupidity now? If I had pilled him at the club—we are swells at the Rhadamanthus—that lay between the ballot-box and myself, and ballot-boxes tell no tales. If I had been uncharitable, this was the moment of compromise. Here was my safety-valve, my life-preserver, my *dinner.* No ocean-wrecked mariner espied a sail with greater delight than the joy with which I encountered the vulgar visage of Mr. Thomas Jenkins. He was evidently pleased, much pleased, flattered, at my reception of him. It would not do to mention the *casus belli;* so, in reply to his query, I merely observed: "These rascally Frenchmen, I have no patience with them. I lose my temper five times a day over their cursed self-satisfied ignorance!"

I took his arm and turned down the boulevard. If anybody had said to me a few hours previously that this would have come to pass, I would have used a forcible and full-flavored negative. *Tempora mutantur.*

"Where are you stopping, Jenkins?"

"Well, I have only just arrived, and haven't made up my mind."

He hadn't made up his mind. So much the better for me; we could both put up at the same hotel, upon his luggage.

"Where are you hanging out?" asked Jenkins. This was a poser. He was not the class of man to whom one could confide one's troubles. If he thought for a moment that I hadn't as much money in my pocket as would jingle on a tombstone, he would quietly drop me, and trump up a facetious story to be told hereafter at my expense, in a set with whom I stood high, but haughtily aloof. Born a diplomatist, my instincts prompted me to do a little Talleyrand now. By naming an hotel, he would repair thither, and my condition need not be exposed. I would be saved an ordeal of a most mortifying confusion, and, better still, I would secure my dinner.

"What do you think of the Hôtel du Louvre, Jenkins? It's very central and extremely comfortable."

"It's rather dear, isn't it?" he observed.

"Well, it's not cheap, but, 'cheap and nasty,' you know; and, after all, the difference of a few francs a day between a first- and second-class hotel pays itself."

"You're quite right, Mr. Foxley. I'll put up with you there, if you've no objection?"

"Objection, my dear Jenkins? I'm delighted at the prospect of having your company!"

"Have you dined yet, Mr. Foxley?"

Assuming an indifference that I was far from feeling, I replied:

"Well, no—not yet. It's rather early."

"By jingo, my stomach thinks that my throat's cut! I didn't touch bit, bite, or sup since we left London this morning."

A bold thought, and yet a happy one—a master-stroke! I would invite him to dine at my expense. It would not cost me much more than the sum I intended to pay at the *café,* from which I had been so unceremoniously ejected. After dinner I could borrow a sovereign from him, and later on proceed to the hotel.

"You'll dine with *me,* Jenkins! My foot is on my native heath."

"You're very kind," said Jenkins, "and, if I might venture on a suggestion, the sooner we dine the better."

"Let us turn in here. This is the celebrated Maison Dorée. One of the three best cooks in the world operates here. The Cavour at Milan possesses one, Delmonico at New York has secured the second, and the third is to be found here."

"I'm in luck!" observed Jenkins.

"And so am I," was my inner thought upon entering that celebrated restaurant with the *sang-froid* peculiar to him who comes into the market as a purchaser. "I'll show this fellow that I am inside the ropes, and that the men of the Rhadamanthus Club know how to dine," and, selecting a table commanding the boulevard, I called imperiously for the *menu.*

It was a source of intense satisfaction to me to show off before Jenkins. The fellow would brag about this dinner for the next twelve months, and of the fact of my having ordered it. So I scanned the bill of fare with a critical eye, much as a newly fledged apothecary regards an illegible prescription, pish'd and pooh'd, shrugged my shoulders, threw up my eyebrows, and betrayed considerable symptoms of mental disquietude, while endeavoring to guess at the nature of some of the multifarious and mysteriously named dishes, resplendently set forth. My pronunciation was not of the Faubourg St. Germain indeed: it was more of the "Mossoo" and "Bolong" school. Nevertheless I made a vigorous onslaught upon several inoffensive words, and succeeded at length, by dint of considerable shouting and pantomimic gesture, in selecting a feed which will be engraven upon my memory so long as that useful and necessary article continues to exist.

"What soup do you particularly like in August, Jenkins?"

"Oh! it's all the same to me," he replied, as his experience was bounded by mock-turtle and mutton-broth.

"Do name an August soup!"

"Well, then, mock-turtle" (this after considerable hesitation).

"You are jesting, Jenkins! Mock-turtle in August? Why, man, if I were to order it, the proprietor would beg of us to leave the Maison Dorée. To ask for anything out of season here is simply a crime, or, what is worse, a blunder."

"Ox-tail is prime."

"Pshaw! man, you are not in Cheapside, at 'Pym's,' or the 'Cheshire Cheese.' Will you take potage à la baie de Bisque, or potage à la Chewmoutong."

"The Bay of Biscay by all means," replied Jenkins with alacrity.

"If you will be guided by me, you'll take the other."

"All right. Anything you order is sure to be up to the mark. You know what's what."

Now, when you ask a man to dine, and especially when it is your intention to borrow the money from him in order to discharge the reckoning, the very least you can do is to order a good dinner. Independently of my own feelings on the subject, I resolved upon giving Jenkins such a banquet as would leave him no chance of finding fault with his fare; on the contrary, his food and wine should be of such quantity and quality as to make it obligatory upon him to lend me the money with a will, and as a personal favor to himself.

"Garsong! Potage à la Chewmoutong."

The waiter ticked off a soup which I had not named.

"What fish, Jenkins?"

"Oh, salmon, of course."

"Salmon in August. Are you insane, Jenkins? Why, you'll be asking for boiled mutton next!"

"Never mind me," said my abashed guest. "I'm not up to this sort of thing. You are."

"Garsong! Poison."

"Poisson? Oui, m'sieur," and he ticked off what subsequently proved to be a slice of woolly turbot swimming in buttermilk.

The entrées which I unluckily ordered were chiefly composed of baked cobwebs and potato-skins, and in one of them I discovered something

that bore a ghastly resemblance to the tail of a rat.

I descended the bill of fare with as much caution and gravity as though it were a rickety flight of stairs, pausing at each landing and scrutinizing the name of each dish without possessing the faintest idea of what the cabalistic inscriptions meant to convey. Why don't they publish a key to their menus? It would save time, trouble, and danger.

"Now, Jenkins," I cried, "you'll get a dinner such as few men know how to order and few to enjoy.—Gàrsong! the wine-list."

Wine is the gas that puffs out the bill. Sir John Falstaff's half-pennyworth of bread was a modest item compared with the sack. Yet why not come out strong upon this occasion? Had I not just escaped from the jaws, if not of peril, at least of intolerable inconvenience? Champagne let it be, and I ordered a bottle to be preceded by a pint of sherry.

The dinner was excellent, despite some secret misgivings as to the condiments, the wines good, the attendance machine-made, the entourage delightful. In the generosity of my heart I ordered a second bottle of the sparkling, and lay back in my chair lazily toying with my glass, and watching the tiny globules darting to the surface.

"I say," observed Jenkins, who had eaten for three, and whose powers of suction would have astonished a snipe—"I say, old chap, let's have 'nother bottle."

"Certainly if you desire it," I replied, although his applying for it under the circumstances was somewhat indelicate. The knife was at my throat, the pistol at my head. If he had asked for imperial Tokay or the King of Spain's sherry, he should have gotten it. Having summoned the waiter, and communicated my desire to him, he with considerable politeness gave me to understand that our consuming the wine at another table would greatly oblige, as that which we at present occupied had been engaged at an early hour by a party which had just entered. At this unexpected demand the British lion within me growled. When explained to Mr. Thomas Jenkins the noble animal fairly roared.

"What the d—l, do you mean, sir," cried my exasperated guest, upon whom the champagne had produced enlivening effects, "by such infernal cheek? If you imagine we are going to give this table up to anybody, you are in Queen Street off the Square. Let those people dine in that corner, it's good enough for them; but this is our table, and by jingo we'll not part with it!" and he banged his mottled and somewhat dirty hand among the dessert-plates and enameled glasses.

The waiter shrugged his shoulders, muttered something unintelligible, and withdrew.

"Did you ever hear of such a thing, Foxley?" "Never."

"Only imagine a waiter at the Star and Garter trying such a dodge on! Why, he'd be kicked into the Thames!"

"He was tipped, I suppose."

"Certainly! I saw that bald-headed cove whispering, 'You scratch me and I'll scratch you.' We'll stop here till midnight, just to spite them!" and he glared at the new-comers in a defiant and knock-you-down way.

"It was very politely done, however," I remarked as Jenkins's wrath was upheaving.

"A fig for their politeness—a set of beggarly Mossoo's to displace us! I'd like to see them do it, I would! This waiter won't bring the wine for an hour. This is more of their impertinence.—Garsong! garsong! hi! hi! hi!" and he commenced to ring a peal of bells upon every tangible article on the table, and to assert his British supremacy in a manner that caused me to wince.

A sort of major-domo came forward, and requested to be informed in what way he could be of service to monsieur. There was a reproof in his calmness, impeachment in his politeness.

"What is the French for wine, Foxley?"

"Vang."

"Doo vang, garsong! Doo vang, vang, vang!" shouted Jenkins, causing the glasses to perform acrobatic feats of a most complicated pattern, as he thumped the table.

Scarcely deigning to notice him, the superintendent turned to me and explained that the wine was coming *tout de suite.*

"What is the fellow saying about sweet?"

"He says the wine is coming immediately."

"I'shaw! He had time to manufacture it. Why, the meanest public-house in London wouldn't keep you this way. It's a dodge to get the table. *I'm* up to them! I'll dodge them!" and, working himself into a violent state of excitement, commenced—"Garsong! vang!—garsong! vang!" with increased vigor and energy.

Upon this renewal of hostilities, the parties who were dining at the various tables around us began to manifest impatience at so unseemly a disturbance, and cries of "Silence!" hissed from several quarters at the same moment; while a very energetic gentleman, whose hair was cropped as closely as my own, imperiously called upon the manager to interfere.

I implored of Jenkins to restrain his indignation, pointing out to him how very unparliamentary his conduct would be considered in any country, but especially in France, where such manifestations were regarded not merely as mistakes but as outrages.

"Why don't they bring the wine?" he cried. "Do you imagine I care one dump what the snail-eating, frog-swallowing duffers think? If one of them dare say a word, I'll go up to him and shout 'Waterloo' under his mustache! Ay, Waterloo!" he repeated, addressing himself to the crop-headed gentleman; "and if you don't like that, perhaps a little German sausage may be of service to you!"

My guest was intoxicated, and in his cups vulgar. I was heartily ashamed of him, and longed for money to cut the whole concern. But a cruel and relentless destiny willed it otherwise; and like Prometheus I was chained to the spot, while the vulture Jenkins gnawed at my sensibilities. In a few minutes, during which we were the observed of all observers, as the table-banging and garsong-howling continued unremittingly, the manager advanced to our table and handed me the bill.

I threw one short, sharp, feverish, electric glance at the "demnition total," and my startled gaze fell upon fifty-eight francs! I plunged at the items—the list was correct. Two dinners, twenty-four francs; sherry, five francs; champagne, twenty-six francs; service, three francs. Was I insane when ordering such a dinner? Had the emptiness of my stomach caused a vacuum in my head? A week's board, ay, and lodging too, both gone in fifty-eight minutes! Was I dreaming? No, the items spoke for themselves, and the total replied for all.

"Where's the wine?" hammered Jenkins.

"Never mind," I replied, seeing that we had received our *congé*, "we'll turn into a snug little *café* down the boulevard for brandy-and-water."

This smote Jenkins in the right place. He bounded to his feet, and seizing his hat joyously exclaimed, "The very thing!" and was about to dart into the street, when I caught him flying.

The supreme moment had come.

Now to ask him for three sovereigns.

"By the way, Jenkins," I exclaimed, with that slippery carelessness which people assume when about to borrow money, and as if the long-premeditated idea had only just come to the surface, "I find that I have no money with me. Lend me three sovereigns, will you?"

"I would with the greatest pleasure, old man, but I haven't a farthing about me," was his startling reply.

"I am in earnest, Jenkins," I said, attempting to strain out a sickly laugh.

"So am I."

"No money at all?"

"Not a shilling. My purse is in my portmanteau."

I never fainted in my life, but I must have been very near it at that particular moment. I clutched the legs of the table convulsively, and made a desperate effort to appear calm.

Here was a position. The dinner eaten, and no money to pay for it, and, to add to the embarrassment, an outraged manager to deal with.

"This is cursedly awkward, Jenkins! "

"Not a bit of it. Give 'em your card."

"Card be hanged! If it wasn't for your conduct they might have taken it."

"Give 'em your ticker. They'll snap at that."

"I lost it at a bull-fight in Spain."

Jenkins whistled, and reseated himself.

"There is nothing for it, Jenkins, and I'm really very sorry to trouble you, but I must ask you to lend me your watch and—"

"I haven't one!" he interposed.

"No watch? "

"I left it at home for Billy my brother, as I intend to buy one here; they are so much better and cheaper."

A cold perspiration burst out all over me. Feigning to examine the figures in the bill, my thoughts were racking themselves upon the red-hot wheel of ways and means. I had sown the wind, and this looked uncommonly like the whirlwind. Deception ever recoils, and I was paid in coin as good as I gave. Gathering my ideas together with a mental wrench I exclaimed:

"Jenkins! take a cab, and go at once to the station, open your portmanteau, get at your purse, and come back here as fast as ever you can. I'll wait for you."

He looked at me in a puzzled, frightened way. "I can not well do that! " he said.

"Not do it? "

"No."

"Why, might I ask? what's to prevent you? "

"I've got no luggage."

"What! " I gasped.

"Not as much as a pill-box."

Despair seized upon and shook me. I turned fiercely upon my guest.

"What the devil do you mean, by traveling without money or luggage, sir? It's monstrous, simply monstrous! "

"I will explain, Foxley."

"Hang your explanations, sir! "

"Listen to me. My luggage is coming after me. It was to have been sent to Charing Cross station by my aunt, at whose house I was stopping, but the servant didn't arrive in time although I saw her driving up as the train moved off. I forgot that my money was in my portmanteau, and all I had with me was the return half of an excursion ticket to Paris, which I bought from the boots at the Tavistock, the date of which expired this very day. So I had to come away by that train, or forfeit the ticket."

The abject despair written in my face sobered Jenkins. He now saw the precipice upon which we stood, and peered for a moment into its depths.

"Do you know anybody in Paris? " I asked, in a feeble tone.

"I do! "

"Who? "

"A man of the name of Smith! "

"Where does he reside? " and hope once more beamed in upon my shuttered soul.

Jenkins scratched his rosy head.

"I can't recollect his address."

"Try."

"It's no use. I don't think I ever knew it."

"This is a terrible state of things, Jenkins."

"Couldn't be much more unpleasant."

"It's quite likely that the police will be called in."

"I saw the waiter speaking to one just now. 'Pon my soul, Foxley, I pity you."

"I pity *you*, Jenkins."

"Oh, never mind *me*. *I* didn't order the dinner."

"You are equally implicated with me, Mr. Jenkins, let me tell you that, and—"

"Hold hard, old man," he interposed, a hopeful expression lighting up his features. "I'll tell you what *can* be done, and it's the wonder that neither of us thought of it till now. Take a cab, go to your hotel, get your money, and come back here. I'll wait for you."

Parrot-like, he traveled over my own words.

With shame I own that for the moment I felt inclined to jump at the suggestion, on the grounds of self-preservation, and never to come back, but happily the better man within me came to the rescue.

The moment had arrived for telling him everything.

"The fact of the matter is, Jenkins, I am precisely in the same position as yourself. I have no hotel."

"No hotel! then where are you stopping? "

"Nowhere? "

"Nowhere? " he repeated, mechanically.

"And where is your luggage? "

"I have no luggage. I left it in Spain."

"He left his luggage in Spain! " groaned Jenkins, thinking aloud.

"I am waiting for remittances which I expect to-morrow morning."

My guest's chin fell upon his breastbone. Once or twice he essayed to speak, but utterance failed him.

"I depended upon *you*, Jenkins, to pull me through, which made me so glad to see you."

"And I depended on you to pull *me* through, which made me so delighted to see *you*," he retorted, bitterly.

"What *is* to be done, Mr. Jenkins? " I asked,

inasmuch as the manager, finding this dramatic dialogue, carried on in a language to which he was an utter stranger, a little dull, began to exhibit very decided symptoms of disquietude.

" Telegraph," suggested Jenkins.

" Where is the money, assuming your suggestion to be worth anything, which it isn't?"

" I forgot that."

" I thought so."

By a simultaneous impulse we commenced to scrutinize each other's toilet, commencing with the shirt-collar, and winding up with the boots.

" I can't compliment you on the condition of your garments," observed Jenkins, gloomily.

" They were good once, which is more than can be said of your shoddy raiment," a howling plaid with blood-red stripes across it giving him the appearance of a crimped salmon.

" It would fetch more money than yours at my uncle's."

" What would the coat bring?"

" About fifteen shillings if my uncle was soft, ten if he was hard. The whole suit was handed down to me, ready made, for forty-two bob."

And our dinner-bill was fifty-eight francs.

The manager, sidling up to me, blandly requested a settlement.

I waved him off wildly, and, in order to diplomatize and gain time, asked if he spoke English.

" Non!" with a terrific shrug, which sent his shirt-collar to comb his back hair, a process which it needed sorely.

" Garsong, parlay Anglay?"

" Non."

" Alley ong momong."

He retired with a very bad grace, evidently with an intention of returning at an early opportunity.

" Could the English ambassador do anything for us, Foxley? He's bound to stand by Britons in distress, and he couldn't be better employed than in extricating us from this cursed dilemma."

" We'd look very well indeed going up to the embassy with such a story! No, Jenkins, there's nothing for it but the police-cell to-night, and to-morrow morning we can explain everything to the magistrate through an interpreter."

At this moment the table next to us became occupied by a young and very pretty girl, attired in the newest of new garments and in the fiercest of fierce fashion. The roses upon her cheek and the healthy sparkle in her eye would have cried " English ware " in the desert of Sahara. Unbuttoning a cream-colored glove of four buttons, she displayed with evident satisfaction the little gold ring upon the third finger of her left hand, which, from its shine and luster, bespoke not only the matron but the bride. She was joined in a moment or two by a tall, fair-haired man of

about five and twenty, possessing an air of insolent aristocracy that, outside of his particular set, would cause him to be detested. He was faultlessly attired, and wore his exquisitely fitting garments as if he didn't care a cent whether they came to grief or not. I looked at Jenkins—Jenkins looked at me. What a pair of vulgar-looking counter-jumpers we appeared beside this " thing of the purple "!

" English," whispered Jenkins.

" May Fair," I replied.

" That suit was made by Poole."

" Or Smallpage."

" Would he stand fifty-eight francs?"

" Hush!"

" You'll row up this waiter, Georgie," drawled the new-comer, addressing the lady. " Your French fits better than mine."

" Always lazy, Fred."

" Don't be down upon me, or I'll ask you to pay the bill."

She spoke French fluently, and with a charming accent.

" There's nothing for it but to appeal to this swell," observed Jenkins. " He's English to the backbone, and hang it, he won't see his countrymen sent to prison for fifty-eight francs."

There was so much of " No " in the man's appearance, that I resolved upon throwing the chance away sooner than risk it. Not so with Jenkins. He believed so firmly in the tie of country—in " Britons strike home "—that, without any previous intimation to me, he boldly plunged in medias res.

" I beg your pardon, sir—you're English, I presume?"

The new-comer slowly faced Jenkins, commenced a survey of his person with the naked eye, extracted a small glass from his pocket, wiped it carefully, screwed it into the corner of his left eye, and drawled—

" Yaas."

" So am I. So's my friend here."

" Indeed!"

" This is my card," thrusting it forward, but ultimately compelled to lay it upon the table, as the other shrank from touching it. " You see my name and address."

" What do you want?" asked the Saxon swell, without deigning to cast a glance in the direction of the pasteboard, still steadily gazing at Jenkins as if he were a wild animal or a curious piece of machinery.

" The fact is, we find ourselves without money enough to pay our bill. We've both got plenty of it, and—"

" I'm not the proprietor of this place "—and, turning to the lady, " Will you take champagne or Moselle, Georgie?"

I pitied Jenkins. He stood as if he had been petrified—his mouth still open, his right hand advanced, his neck craned into a bow. Stammering something, he drew himself together and collapsed on to a chair.

The lady possessed more of the milk of human kindness than her lord and master, for she apologetically added:

" You should explain yourself to the proprietor. He will surely arrange with you."

" But I can not, madam," blurted Jenkins. " I can not speak French."

" Does your friend speak the language ? "

" It's six of one and half a dozen of the other.—Why don't you speak out, Foxley ? "

" Foxley is a Cheshire name," she remarked inquiringly.

" We are from Cheshire, near Northwich," I said.

" There are the Foxleys of Plumsted Park."

" Frederick Herbert Foxley is my second cousin."

" The deuce he is ! " growled the gentleman, tossing off a glass of sherry.

The lady spoke rapidly to him in an undertone, to which he replied by the single word—
" Bosh ! "

" Do you know Mr. Frederick Herbert Foxley ? " she inquired, somewhat anxiously.

" I never saw him. We are the poor and insignificant branch of the family."

" You do not reside in Cheshire ? "

" No. I live in London."

" What's your club ? " asked the gentleman, much as he would demand a cabman's number.

This was indeed a chance; this was playing into my hand, as my club *was* a club, and about a hundred years old, not a mushroom proprietary public-house. To be elected to it, meant twenty years in waiting, and the death by extreme old age of three sets of proposers and seconders. The Crimean war ran me in in seven years. My own cousin, the very man of whom we had been speaking, was on the books, and likely to remain

there for several seasons to come. As a man's social status is determined by his club, it was with no small flutter of pride that I coolly replied :

" My club is the Rhadamanthus."

" The Rhadamanthus in Saint James's Street ? " he asked in some surprise—as, indeed, he might.

" *The* Rhadamanthus. I was not aware of the existence of any other than the old rookery in Saint James's Street ? " Every man speaks disparagingly of his club, and pooh-poohs it— the kitchen alone excepted.

His tone altered at once.

" Mr. Foxley, will you excuse me if I take the liberty of asking you for some proof of this ? I have a cogent reason for so doing."

" Here are proofs enough," I exclaimed, pulling out a bundle of letters which had been forwarded to me in Spain by the house steward, " and here is my card."

" And here is mine," he laughed, handing me a piece of pasteboard upon which I read, with feelings of the most profound astonishment, the name and address of my cousin :

> *Frederick Herbert Foxley,*
> *Plumsted Park,*
> *Cheshire.*
>
> 27 *Curzon Street,*
> *May Fair.*

.   .   .   .

What a laugh we enjoyed over my temporary embarrassments as we sat in the courtyard of the Grande Hotel later on, sipping our coffee!

" If it had not been for my politeness, we never would have known you," exclaimed Mrs. Foxley.

" If it had not been for me, we would have been in prison this minute," added Jenkins.

" My dear Jenkins, I owe you much," said I ; " for, if it had not been for you, I never would this day have dined in the Boulevard des Italiens."

TAKING THE BLUE RIBBON AT THE COUNTY FAIR.

BY CHARLES EGBERT CRADDOCK.

SILAS HOBBS sat on the fence. He slowly turned the quid of tobacco in his cheek, and lifting up his voice spoke with an oracular drawl:

" Ef he kin take the certif'cate it's the mos' es he kin do. He ain't never a-goin' ter git no premi-*um* in this life. Sure's ye're a born sinner."

And he relapsed into silence. His long legs dangled dejectedly among the roadside weeds; his brown jean trousers, that had despaired of ever reaching his ankles, were ornamented here and there with ill-adjusted patches, and his loose-fitting coat was out at the elbows. An old white felt hat drooped over his eyes, which were fixed absently on certain distant blue mountain-ranges, melting tenderly into the blue of the noonday sky, and framing an exquisite mosaic of poly-tinted fields in the valley, far, far below the grim gray crag on which his little home was perched.

Despite his long legs he was a light weight, or he would not have chosen as his favorite seat so rickety a fence. His interlocutor, a heavier man, apparently had some doubts, for he leaned only slightly against one of the projecting rails as he whittled a pine stick, and with every movement the frail structure trembled. The house, or rather the log-cabin, seemed as rickety as the fence. The little front porch had lost a plank here and there in the flooring—perhaps on some cold winter night when Silas Hobbs's energy was not sufficiently exuberant to convey him to the wood-pile; the slender posts that upheld its roof seemed hardly strong enough to withstand the weight of the luxuriant vines with their wealth of golden gourds which had clambered far over the moss-grown shingles; the windows had fewer panes of glass than rags; and the chimney, built of clay and sticks, leaned portentously away from the house. The open door displayed a rough, uncovered floor; a few old rush-bottomed chairs; a bedstead with a patch-work calico quilt, the mattress swagging in the center and showing the badly arranged cords below; strings of bright-red pepper hanging from the dark rafters; an endless perspective of tow-headed, grave-faced, barefooted children, and, occupying almost one side of the room, a broad, deep, old-fashioned fireplace, where winter and summer a lazy fire burned under a lazy pot.

Such was the altar of Mr. Hobbs's lares and penates. Quite contented with it all, he sat outside on the fence, sheltered from the hot September sun by the low-hanging branches of the chestnut-oak trees, and drawlingly talked to his neighbor about the coming county fair.

Notwithstanding the gaunt poverty of the aspect of the place and the evident sloth of its master, it was characterized by a scrupulous cleanliness strangely at variance with its forlorn deficiencies. The rough floor was not only swept but scoured; the dark rafters, whence depended the flaming banners of the red pepper, harbored no cobwebs; the grave faces of the white-haired children bore no more dirt than was consistent with their recent occupation of making mud-pies; and the sedate, bald-headed baby, lying silent but wide-awake in an uncouth wooden cradle, was as clean as clear spring-water and yellow soap could make it. Mrs. Hobbs herself, seen through the vista of opposite open doors, energetically rubbing the coarse wet clothes upon the resonant washboard, seemed neat enough in her blue-and-white checked homespun dress, and with her scanty gray-streaked hair drawn smoothly back

from her deeply wrinkled brow into a tidy little knot on the top of her head.

Spare and gaunt she was, and with many lines in her prematurely old face. Perhaps they told of the hard fight her brave spirit waged against the stern ordering of her life; of the struggles with squalor—inevitable concomitant of poverty, and to keep together the souls and bodies of those numberless children, with no more efficient assistance than could be wrung from her reluctant husband in the short intervals when he did not sit on the fence. She managed as well as she could; there was an abundance of fine fruit in that low line of foliage behind the house—but everybody on Old Bear Mountain had fine fruit. Something rarer, she had good vegetables—the planting and hoeing her own work and her daughter's; an occasional shallow furrow representing the contribution of her husband's plow. The althea-bushes and the branches of the laurel sheltered a goodly number of roosting hens in these September nights; and to the pond, which had been formed by damming the waters of the spring branch in the hollow across the road, was moving even now a stately procession of geese in single file. These simple belongings were the trophies of a gallant battle against unalterable conditions and the dragging, dispiriting clog of her husband's inertia.

His inner life—does it seem hard to realize that in the uncouth figure on the fence concenter the complex, incomprehensible, ever-shifting emotions of that surging flood of inner life which, after all, is so much stronger, and deeper, and broader than the material? Here, too, beats the hot heart of humanity—beats with no measured throb. He had his hopes, his pleasure, his pain, like those of a higher culture, differing only in object, and something perhaps in degree. His disappointments, bitter and lasting; his triumphs, few and sordid; his single aspiration—to take the premium offered by the directors of the Kildeer County Fair for the best rider.

This incongruous and unpromising ambition had sprung up in this wise: Between the country people of Kildeer County and the citizens of the village of Woodville, the county-seat, existed a bitter and deeply-rooted animosity manifesting itself at conventions, elections for the Legislature, etc., the rural population voting as a unit against the town's candidate. On all occasions of public meetings there was a struggle to crush any invidious distinction against the "country boys," especially at the annual fair. Here to the rustics of Kildeer County came the tug of war. The country population was more numerous, and, when it could be used as a suffrage-engine, all-powerful; but the region immediately adjacent to the town was far more fertile. On those fine meadows grazed the graceful Jersey; there were bred sundry long-tailed colts with long-tailed pedigrees; there greedy Berkshires fattened themselves to abnormal proportions; and the merinos could hardly walk, for the weight of their own rich wardrobes. The well-to-do farmers of this section were hand-in-glove with the town's people; they drove their trotters in every day or so to get their mail, to chat with their cronies, to attend to their affairs in court, to sell or to buy—their pleasures centered in the town, and they turned the cold shoulder upon the country, which supported them, and gave their influence to Woodville, accounting themselves an integral part of it. Thus, at the fairs the town claimed the honor and glory. The blue ribbon decorated cattle and horses bred within ten miles of the flaunting flag on the judges' stand, and the foaming mountain-torrents and the placid stream in the valley beheld no cerulean hues save those of the sky which they reflected.

The premium offered this year for the best rider was, as it happened, a new feature, and excited especial interest. The country's blood was up. Here was something for which it could fairly compete, with none of the disadvantages of the false position in which it was placed. Hence a prosperous landed proprietor, the leader of the rural faction, dwelling midway between the town and the range of mountains that bounded the county on the north and west, bethought himself one day of Silas Hobbs, whose famous riding had been the feature of a certain dashing cavalry - charge — once famous, too — forgotten now by all but the men who, for the first and only time in their existence, penetrated in those war-days the blue Alleghany hills fencing in their county from the outer world, and looked upon the alien life beyond that wooded barrier. The experience of those four years, submerged in the whirling rush of events elsewhere, survives in these eventless regions in a dreamy, dispassionate sort of longevity. And Silas Hobbs's feat of riding stolidly—one could hardly say bravely—up a sheer precipice to a flame-belching battery, came suddenly into the landed magnate's recollection with the gentle vapors and soothing aroma of a meditative after-dinner pipe. Feeling " the future in the instant," and quivering with party-spirit, Squire Goodlet sent for Hobbs and offered to lend him the best horse on the place, and a saddle and bridle, if he would go down to Woodville and beat those town fellows out on their own ground.

No misgivings had Silas. The inordinate personal pride characteristic of the mountaineer precluded his feeling the shrinking pain other men would have suffered at the prospect of being presented, a sorry contrast, among the well-

clad, well-to-do burgher class, to compete in a public contest. He did not appreciate the difference—he thought himself as good as the best.

And to-day, complacent enough, he sat upon the rickety fence at home, dangling his low-spirited jean legs, and oracularly disparaging the equestrian accomplishments of the town's noted champion.

"I dunno—I dunno," said his young companion, doubtfully. "Hackett sets mighty firm onto his saddle. He's ez straight ez any shingle, an' ez tough ez a pine-knot. He come up hyar las' summer—war is las' summer, now? No, 'twar summer afore las'—with some o' them other Woodville folks, a-fox-huntin', an' a-deer-huntin', an' one thing an' 'nother. I seen 'em a time or two in the woods. An' he kin ride jes' ez good 'mongst the gullies and bowlders like ez ef he had been born in the hills. He ain't a-goin' ter be beat easy."

"It don't make no differ," retorted Silas. "He'll never git no premi-um. The certif'cate's good a-plenty fur what ridin' he kin do."

Doubt was still expressed in the face of the young man, but he said no more, and, after a few minutes' silence, Mr. Hobbs, perhaps not relishing his visitor's want of appreciation, dismounted, so to speak, from the fence, and slouched off slowly up the road.

Jacob Dicey still stood leaning against the rails and whittling his pine stick, in no wise angered or dismayed by his host's unceremonious departure, for social etiquette is not very rigid on Old Bear Mountain. His suit of brown jean, which is the universal wear in the hills, only differed from that incasing the lank frame of Silas Hobbs in that it was well filled by a symmetrical and finely-developed figure, and displayed, besides the ornaments of patches, sundry deep grass-stains about the knees. Not that he was pious enough to spend much time in the lowly attitude of prayer, unless, indeed, Diana might be accounted the goddess of his worship. The green juice was pressed out when kneeling, hidden in some leafy, grassy nook, he heard the infrequent cry of the wild turkey, or his large, intent blue eyes caught a glimpse of the stately branches of an antlered stag, moving majestically in the alternate sheen of the sunlight and shadow of the overhanging crags, or while his deft hunter's hands dragged him by slow, noiseless degrees, through the ferns and tufts of rank weeds, to the water's edge, that he might catch a shot at the feeding wood-duck. A leather belt around his waist supported his powder-horn—for his accoutrements were exactly such as might have been borne a hundred years ago by a hunter of Old Bear Mountain—and his gun leaned against the trunk of a chestnut-oak.

Still he stood outside of the fence, aimlessly

lounging, it seemed, although there was a look on his face of a half-suppressed expectancy, which rendered the immobile features less statuesque than was their wont—an expectancy that showed itself in the furtive lifting of his eyelids now and then, enabling him to survey the doorway without turning his head. Suddenly his face reassumed its habitual, inexpressive mask of immobility, and the furtive eyes were persistently downcast.

A flare of color, and Cynthia Hobbs was standing in the doorway, leaning against its frame. She was robed, like September, in a brilliant orange. The material and make were of the meanest, but there was a certain appropriateness in the color with her slumberous, dark eyes and the curling tendrils of brown hair which fell upon her forehead and were clustered together at the back of her neck. No cuffs and no collar could this costume boast, but she had shown the inclination to finery, characteristic of her age and sex, by wearing around her throat, where the orange of her dress met the creamy tint of her skin, a row of large, black beads, threaded upon a shoe-string in default of an elastic, the brass ends flaunting brazenly enough among them. She held in her hand a string of red peppers, to which she was adding some newly-gathered pods. A slow job Cynthia seemed to make of it.

She took no more notice of the man under the tree than he accorded to her. There they stood, within twelve feet of each other, in utter silence, and, to all appearance, each entirely unconscious of the other's existence—he, whittling his pine stick; she, slowly, slowly stringing the pods of red peppers.

There was something almost portentous in the gravity and sobriety of demeanor of this girl of seventeen; but, indeed, a sedate propriety of manner is noticeable in all these mountain women, young and old. Cynthia, however, manifested less interest in the young man than her own grandmother might have shown.

He was constrained to speak first. "Cynthy—" he said at length, without raising his eyes or turning his head. She did not answer; but he knew without looking that she had fixed those slumberous, brown eyes upon him, waiting for him to go on. "Cynthy," he said again, with a hesitating, uneasy manner—then, with an awkward attempt at raillery — "ain't yer never a-thinkin' 'bout a-gittin' married?"

He cast a laughing glance toward her, and looked down quickly at his clasp-knife and the stick he was whittling. It was growing very slender now.

Cynthia's serious face relaxed its gravity. "Ye're foolish, Jacob," she said, laughing. After stringing on another pepper-pod with great delib-

eration, she continued: "Ef I war a-studyin' 'bout a-gittin' married, thar ain't nobody round 'bout hyar ez I'd hev." And she added another pod to the flaming red string, so bright against the orange of her dress.

That stick could not long escape annihilation. The clasp-knife moved vigorously through its fibers, and accented certain arbitrary clauses in its owner's retort. "Yer talk like," he said, his face as monotonous in its expression as if every line was cut in some tenderly-tinted marble—"yer talk like—yer thought ez how I—war a-goin' ter ax yer—ter marry me. I ain't though, nuther."

The stick was a shaving. It fell among the weeds. The young hunter shut his clasp-knife with a snap, shouldered his gun, and, without a word of adieu on either side, the conference terminated, and he walked off down the white, sandy road.

Cynthia stood watching him until the laurel-bushes hid him from sight; then, sliding from the door-frame to the step, she sat motionless, a bright-hued mass of red and orange, her slumberous, deep eyes resting on the leaves that had closed upon him.

She was the central figure of a still landscape. The mid-day sunshine fell in vertical effulgence upon it; the homely, dun-colored shadows had been running away all the morning, as if shirking the contrast with the splendors of the golden light, until nothing was left of them except a dark circle beneath the wide-spreading trees; the whole world now seemed quite motionless, so slowly did it turn from the noonday skies to the great, red west, waiting for it somewhere below the horizon. No breath of wind stirred the leaves, or rippled the surface of the little pond. The lethargy of the hour had descended even upon the towering pine-trees, growing on the precipitous slope of the mountain, and showing their topmost plumes just above the frowning, gray crag—their melancholy song was hushed. The silent masses of dazzling white clouds were poised motionless in the ambient air, high above the valley, and the misty expanse of the distant, wooded ranges.

A lazy, lazy day, and very, very warm. The birds had much ado to find sheltering shady nooks where they might escape the glare and the heat; their gay carols were out of season, and they blinked and nodded under their leafy umbrellas, and fanned themselves with their wings, and twittered disapproval of the weather. "Hot, hot, red-hot!" said the birds—"broiling hot!"

Now and then an acorn fell from among the serrated chestnut-leaves, striking upon the fence with a sounding thwack, and rebounding in the weeds. Those chestnut-oaks always seem to unaccustomed eyes the creation of Nature in a fit of mental aberration—useful freak! the mountain swine fatten themselves on the plenteous mast, and the bark is highly esteemed at the tanyard.

A large cat was lying at length on the floor of the little porch, watching with drowsy, half-closed eyes the assembled birds in the tree. But she seemed to have relinquished the pleasures of the chase until the mercury should fall. " *Toujours perdrix !* " quoted the cat.

Close in to the muddiest side of the pond over there, which was all silver and blue with the reflection of the great masses of white clouds, and the deep azure sky, a fleet of shining, snowy geese was moored, perfectly motionless too. No circumnavigation for them this hot day.

And Cynthia's dark-brown eyes, fixed upon the leafy vista of the road, were as slumberous as the noontide sunshine.

" Cynthy! whar *is* the gal ? " said poor Mrs. Hobbs, as she came around the house to hang out the ragged clothes on the althea-bushes and the rickety fence. " Cynthy, is yer a-goin' ter sit thar in the door all day, an' that thar pot a-bilin' all the stren'th out 'n that thar cabbige an' rous' in'-ears? Dish up dinner, child, an' don't be so slow an' slack-twisted like yer par."

Great merriment there was, to be sure, at the Kildeer Fair-grounds, situated on the outskirts of Woodville, when it became known to the convulsed town faction that the gawky Silas Hobbs intended to compete for the premium to be awarded to the best and most graceful rider. The contests of the week had as usual resulted in Woodville's favor; this was the last day of the fair, and the defeated country population anxiously but still hopefully awaited its notable event.

A warm sun shone ; a brisk autumnal breeze waved the flag flying from the judges' stand; a brass-band in the upper story of that structure thrilled the air with the vibrations of popular waltzes and marches, somewhat marred now and then by mysteriously discordant brass tones; the judges, portly, red-faced, middle-aged gentlemen, sat below in cane-bottom chairs critically a-tilt on the hind-legs. The rough, wooden, circular edifice, a bold satire on the stately Roman amphitheatre, was filled with the rosy rural faces of the denizens of Woodville and the country people of Kildeer County ; and within the charmed inclosure the competitors for the saddle and bridle to be awarded to the best rider, were just now entering, ready mounted, from a door beneath the tiers of seats, and were slowly making the tour of the circle around the judges' stand. One by one they came, with a certain nonchalant pride of demeanor, conscious of an effort to dis-

play themselves and their horses to the greatest advantage, and yet a little ashamed of the consciousness. For the most part they were young men, prosperous-looking, and clad according to the requirements of fashion which prevailed in this little town on the mountain-bench. Shut in though it was from the pomps and vanities of the world, by the encircling chains of blue ranges, and the bending sky which rested upon their summits, the frivolity of the mode, distorted and belated, found its way and ruled with imperative rigor. Good riders they were undoubtedly, accustomed to the saddle almost from infancy, and well mounted. A certain air of gallantry, always characteristic of an athletic horseman, commended these equestrian figures to the eye as they slowly circled about. Still they came—eight—nine—ten—the eleventh, the long, lank frame of Silas Hobbs mounted on Squire Goodlet's " John Barleycorn."

The horsemen received this ungainly addition to their party with polite composure, and the genteel element of the spectators was silent too from the force of good breeding and good feeling; but the Great Unwashed, always critically a-loose in a crowd, shouted and screamed with derisive hilarity. What they were laughing at, Silas Hobbs never knew. Grave and stolid, but as complacent as the best, he too made the usual circuit with his ill-fitting jean suit, his slouching old felt hat, and his long, gaunt figure. But he sat the spirited " John Barleycorn " as if he were a part of the steed, and held up his head with unwonted dignity, inspired perhaps by the stately attitudes of the horse, which were the results of no training nor compelling reins, but the instinct transmitted through a long line of high-headed ancestry. Of a fine old family was " John Barleycorn."

" Take care, my friends," said the annoyed Squire Goodlet to a group of stamping, yelling, young blackguards on the outskirts of the crowd, who were proceeding to offer, with no takers, fantastic bets against the candidate of the country faction. " You may find Hobbs is a singed cat—better than he looks."

A deeper sensation was in store for the spectators. Before Hobbs's appearance most of them had heard of his intention to compete, but the feeling was one of unmixed astonishment when entry No. 12 rode into the arena, and, on the part of the country people, this surprise was supplemented by an intense indignation. The twelfth man was Jacob Dicey. As he was a " mounting boy," one would imagine that, if victory should crown his efforts, the rural faction ought to feel the elation of success, but the prevailing sentiment toward him was that which every well-conducted mind must entertain concerning the ill-conditioned individual who runs against the nominee. Notwithstanding the fact that Dicey was a notable rider, too, and well calculated to try the mettle of the town's champion, there arose from the excited countrymen a keen, bitter, and outraged cry of "Take him out!" So strongly does the partisan heart pulsate to the interests of the nominee! This frantic petition had no effect on the interloper. A man who has inherited half a dozen violent quarrels, any one of which may at any moment burst into a vendetta—inheriting little else—is not easily dismayed by the disapprobation of either friend or foe. His statuesque features, shaded by the drooping brim of his old, black hat, were as calm as ever; his slow, blue eyes did not, for one moment, rest upon the excited scene about him, so unspeakably new to his scanty experience; his fine figure showed to great advantage on horseback, despite his uncouth, coarse garb; and, as far as the interests of the picturesque control us, the mountaineer, in his brown jean, was more acceptable than those exponents of Woodville fashions about him who, in solid fact, were immeasurably his superiors in station, education, and breeding. He was mounted upon a sturdy, brown mare of obscure origin, but good-looking, clean-built, sure-footed, and with the blended charm of spirit and docility; she represented his whole estate, except his gun and his lean, old deer-hound, that had accompanied him to the fair, and was even now improving the shining hour by quarreling over a bone outside of the grounds with other people's handsomer dogs.

The judges were exacting. That delightful sense of supremacy incident upon a little brief authority makes hard drivers of the best of us—we pit the mettle of our muscles against the mettle of the steed, and hang on to the reins to the last lingering gasp of our ability. The riders were ordered to gallop to the right—and around they went. To the left—and there was the spectacle of the swiftly-circling mounted figures, all leaning close to the ground as if another round would fling them upon it. They were required to draw up in a line, and to dismount; then to mount, and again to alight. Those whom these manœuvres proved inferior were dismissed at once, and the circle was reduced to eight. An exchange of horses was commanded; and once more the riding, fast and slow, left and right, the mounting and dismounting were repeated, and the criticism of the judges mowed the number down to four.

Free speech is conceded by all right-thinking people to be a blessing. It is often a balm. Outside of the building the defeated aspirants consigned, with great fervor and volubility, all the judicial magnates to that torrid region unknown to polite geographical works; and George Jones, rising in his stirrups, swore that he would be "dad - burned if them judges knew which e-end of a horse a rider oughter face—a reg'lar lay-out o' darned fools they air—or I'm a pelican of the wilderness!" This no one could suppose George Jones to be; the alternative was evident. The other vanquished competitors were afforded much comfort from his outspoken views; they acquiesced with cordial profanity in their comrade's sentiments, and, after hitching their steeds, found as potent consolation in taking a drink all round.

Of the four horsemen remaining in the ring, two were Silas Hobbs and Jacob Dicey. Another round left only the mountaineers and Tip Hackett, the man whom Jacob had pronounced a formidable rival. The circling about, the mounting and dismounting, the exchange of horses were several times repeated without any apparent result, and excitement rose to fever-heat.

The premium and certificate lay between the three men. The town faction trembled at the thought that the substantial award of the saddle and bridle, with the decoration of the blue ribbon, and the intangible but still precious secondary glory of the certificate and the red ribbon, might be given to the two mountaineers, leaving the crack rider of Woodville in an ignominious lurch; while the country party feared Hobbs's defeat by Hackett rather less than that Silas would be required to relinquish the premium to the interloper Dicey, for the young hunter's riding had stricken a pang of prophetic terror to more than one partisan rustic's heart. In the midst of the perplexing doubt, which tried the judges' minds, came the hour for dinner, and the decision was postponed until after that meal.

The riders left the arena, and the crowd transferred its attention to unburdening hampers, or to jostling each other in the dining-hall. There were humbler baskets of refreshments belonging to a different class, and sometimes among the "mounting folks" would be produced a "tickler" filled with a strong article of whiskey, made nobody knew how nor asked where. Those minions of fortune who dwelt in Woodville and the immediately adjacent region slaked their thirst from time to time with that antique beverage known to the favorite imbibers as old Bourbon, which was poured into tumblers and measured with large, indulgent fingers.

Everybody was eating dinner but Cynthia Hobbs. The intense excitement of the day, the novel sights and sounds utterly undreamed of in her former life, the abruptly-struck chords of new emotions, hitherto all unstrung, and suddenly set vibrating within her, had dulled her relish for the mid-day meal; and while the other members of the family had repaired to the shade of a tree outside the grounds to enjoy that refection, she still stood leaning against one of the large pillars which supported the roof of the amphitheatre, still gazing about the half-deserted building, with the smoldering fires of her slumberous eyes newly kindled.

To other eyes and ears it might not have seemed a scene of tumultuous metropolitan life —with the murmuring trees close at hand dappling the floor with sycamore-shadows, the fields of Indian corn across the road, the exuberant rush of waters down the slope just beyond, the handful of rustics who had intently watched the events of the day—but to Cynthia Hobbs the excitement of crowd, and movement, and noise could no further go.

By the natural force of gravitation, Jacob Dicey presently was walking slowly and apparently aimlessly around to where she was standing. He said nothing, however, when he was beside her, and she seemed entirely unconscious of his presence. Her orange dress was as stiff as a board, and as clean as her strong, young arms could make it; at her throat were the shining black beads; on her head she wore a limp, yellow-calico sunbonnet, which hung down over her eyes, and almost obscured her countenance. To this article, and her attachment to wearing it, she perhaps owed the singular purity and transparency of her complexion, as much as to the mountain air, and the scanty and chiefly vegetable fare of her father's table. She wore it constantly, notwithstanding it operated almost as a mask, rendering her more easily recognizable to their few neighbors by her flaring attire, than by her features, and obstructing from her own view all surrounding scenery, so that she could hardly see the cow, which so much of her time she was slowly poking after.

She spoke unexpectedly, and without any other symptom that she knew of the young hunter's proximity. "I never thought, Jacob, ez how yer would hev come down hyar, all the way from the mountings to ride agin my par, an' beat him out'n that thar saddle an' bridle."

"Yer won't hev nothin' ter say ter me," retorted Jacob, sourly.

A long silence ensued.

Then he resumed didactically, but with some irrelevancy, "I tole yer t'other day ez how yer war old enough ter be a-studyin' 'bout gittin' married."

"They don't think nothin' of yer ter our house, Jacob. Par's always a-jowin' at yer." Cynthia's candor certainly could not be called in question.

The young hunter replied with some natural irritation : "He had better not let me hear him, ef he wants to keep whole bones inside his skin. He better not tell me, nuther."

"He don't keer enough 'bout yer, Jacob, ter tell yer. He don't think nothin' of yer."

Love is popularly supposed to dull the mental faculties. It developed in Jacob Dicey sudden strategic abilities.

"Thar is them ez does," he said, diplomatically.

Cynthia spoke promptly and with more vivacity than usual, but in her customary drawl and apparently utterly irrelevantly :

"I never in all my days see no sech red-headed gal ez that thar Becky Snipes. She's the red-headedest gal ever I see." And Cynthia once more was silent.

Jacob resumed, also irrelevantly :

"When I goes a-huntin' up yander ter Pine Lick, they is mighty perlite ter me. They ain't never done nothin' agin me, ez I knows on." Then after a pause of deep cogitation, he added, "Nor hev they said nothin' agin me, nuther."

Cynthia took up her side of the dialogue, if dialogue it could be called, with wonted irrelevancy : "That thar Becky Snipes, she's got the freckledest face—ez freckled ez any turkey-aig" (with an indescribable drawl on the last word).

"They ain't done nothin' agin me," reiterated Jacob, astutely, "nor said nothin' nuther—none of 'em."

Cynthia looked hard across the amphitheatre at the distant Alleghany hills shimmering in the hazy September sunlight—so ineffably beautiful, so delicately blue, that they might have seemed the ideal scenery of some impossibly lovely ideal world. Perhaps she was wondering what the unconscious Becky Snipes, far away in those dark woods about Pine Lick, had secured in this life besides her freckled face. Was this the sylvan deity of the young hunter's adoration?

Cynthia took off her sun-bonnet to use it for a fan. Perhaps it was well for her that she did so at this moment; it had so entirely concealed her head that her hair might have been the color of Becky Snipes's, and no one the wiser. The dark-brown tendrils curled delicately on her creamy forehead; the excitement of the day had flushed her pale cheeks with an unwonted glow; her eyes were alight with their newly-kindled fires; the clinging curtain of her bonnet had concealed the sloping curves of her shoulders—altogether she was attractive enough, despite the flare of her orange dress, and especially attractive to the untutored eyes of Jacob Dicey. He relented suddenly, and lost all the advantages of his tact and diplomacy.

"I likes yer better nor I does Becky Snipes,"

he said, moderately. Then with more fervor, "I likes yer better nor any gal I ever see." The usual long pause ensued. "Yer hev got a mighty cur'ous way o' showin' it," Cynthia replied.

"I dunno what ye're talkin' 'bout, Cynthy."

"Yer hev got a mighty cur'ous way o' showin' it," she reiterated, with renewed animation —"a-comin' all the way down hyar from the mountings ter beat my par out 'n that thar saddle an' bridle, what he's done sot his heart onto. Mighty cur'ous way."

"Look hyar, Cynthy." The young hunter broke off suddenly, and did not speak again for several minutes. A great perplexity was surging this way and that in his slow brains—a great struggle was waging in his heart. He was to choose between love and ambition—nay, avarice too was ranged beside his aspiration. He felt himself an assured victor in the competition, and he had seen that saddle and bridle. It was on exhibition to day, and to him its material and workmanship seemed beyond expression wonderful, and elegant, and substantial. He could never hope otherwise to own such accoutrements. His eyes would never again even rest upon such resplendent objects, unless indeed in Hobbs's possession. Any one who has ever loved a horse can appreciate a horseman's dear desire that beauty should go beautifully caparisoned. And then, there was his pride in his own riding, and his anxiety to have his preëminence in that accomplishment acknowledged and recognized by his friends, and, dearer triumph still, by his enemies. A terrible pang before he spoke again.

"Look hyar, Cynthy," he said at last; "ef yer will marry me, I won't go back in yander no more. I'll leave the premi-um ter them ez kin git it."

"Ye're foolish, Jacob," she replied, still fanning with the yellow-calico sun-bonnet. "Ain't I done tole yer, ez how they don't think nothin' of yer ter our house? I don't want all of 'em a-jowin' at me, too."

"Yer talk like yer ain't got good sense, Cynthy," said Jacob, irritably. "What's ter hender me from hitchin' up my mare ter my wagon an' yer an' me a-drivin' up hyar to the Cross-roads, fifteen mile, and git Preacher Rice ter marry us? We'll git the license afore we start down hyar ter the Court-House. An' while they'll all be a-foolin' away their time a-ridin' round that thar ring, yer an' me will be a-gittin' married." Ten minutes ago Jacob Dicey did not think riding around that ring was such a reprehensible waste of time. "What's ter hender? It don't make no differ how they jow then."

"I done tole yer, Jacob," said the sedate Cynthia, still fanning with the sun-bonnet.

With a sudden return of his inspiration, Jacob retorted, affecting an air of stolid indifference: "Jes' ez yer choose. I won't hev ter ax Becky Snipes twict."

And he turned to go.

"I never said no, Jacob," said Cynthia, precipitately. "I never said ez how I wouldn't hev yer."

"Waal, then, jes' come along with me right now while I hitch up the mare. I ain't a goin' ter leave yer'n standin' hyar. Ye're too skittish. Time I come back yer'd hev done run away I dunno whar." A moment's pause and he added: "Is yer a-goin' ter stand thar all day, Cynthy Hobbs, a-lookin' up, an' around, an' a-turnin' yer neck fust this way and then t'other, an' a-lookin' fur all the worl' like a wild turkey in a trap, or one o' them thar skeery young deer, or sech senseless critters? What ails the gal?"

"Thar 'll be nobody ter help along the work ter our house," said Cynthia, the weight of the home difficulties bearing heavily on her conscience.

"Thar's chillen enough thar, 'bout yer, Cynthy, more 'n enough ter help along. An' what's ter hender yer from a-goin' down thar an' lendin' a hand every wunst in a while? But ef ye're a-goin' ter stand thar like yer hedn't no more action than a—a dunno what, jes' like yer par, I ain't. I'll jes' leave yer a-growed ter that thar post, an' I'll jes' light out stiddier, an' afore the cows git ter Pine Lick. I'll be thar too. Jes' ez yer choose. Come along ef yer wants ter come. I ain't a-goin' ter ax yer no more."

"I'm a-comin'," said Cynthia.

There was great though illogical rejoicing on the part of the country faction when the crowds were again seated, tier above tier, in the amphitheatre, and the riders were once more summoned into the ring, to discover from Jacob Dicey's unaccounted-for absence that he had withdrawn and left the nominee to his chances.

In the ensuing competition it became very evident to the not altogether impartially disposed judges, that they could not, without incurring the suspicions alike of friend and foe, award the premium to their fellow-townsman. Straight as a shingle though he might be, more prepossessing to the eye, the ex-cavalryman of fifty battles was far better trained in all the arts of horsemanship. The strength of "John Barleycorn" would have been of no avail if exerted to unseat him; the saddle seemed as much his accustomed perch as the rickety old fence at home—he was as appropriately placed as the bird on the nest. Every nerve, every muscle, every fiber, was adjusted to the movement of the horse, and whether galloping in great leaps, or walking, or trotting, or gently cantering, the rider seemed never to move—the sweeping, smooth motion was the steed's.

A wild shout of joy burst from the rural party when the most portly and rubicund of the portly and red-faced judges advanced into the ring and decorated Silas Hobbs with the blue ribbon. A frantic antistrophe rent the air. "Take it off!" vociferated the bitter town faction—"take it off!"

A diversion was produced by the refusal of the Woodville champion to receive the empty honor of the red ribbon and the certificate. Thus did he except to the ruling of the judges. In high dudgeon he faced about and left the arena, followed shortly by the decorated Silas, bearing the precious saddle and bridle, and going with a wooden face to receive the congratulations of his friends.

The entries for the slow mule-race had been withdrawn at the last moment; and the spectators, balked of that unique sport, and the fair being virtually over, were rising from their seats and making their noisy preparations for departure. Before Silas had cleared the fair-building, being somewhat impeded by the moving mass of humanity, he encountered one of his neighbors, a listless mountaineer, who spoke on this wise:

"Does yer know that thar gal o' yourn—that thar Cynthy—?"

Mr. Hobbs nodded his expressionless head—presumably he did know Cynthia.

"Waal"—continued his leisurely interlocutor, still interrogative—"does yer know Jacob Dicey?"

Ill-starred association of ideas! There was a look of apprehension on Silas Hobbs's wooden face.

"They hev done got a license down hyar ter the Court-House an' gone a-kitin' out on the Old Bar road."

This was explicit.

"Whar's my horse!" exclaimed Silas, appropriating "John Barleycorn" in his haste. Great as was his hurry, it was not too imperative to prevent him from strapping upon the horse the premium saddle and inserting in his mouth the new bit and bridle. And in less than ten minutes half of the crowd assembled in Woodville was also "a-kitin'" out on the road to Old Bear, bent on running down the eloping couple, with no more appreciation of the sentimental phase of the question and the tender illusions of love's young dream than if Jacob and Cynthia were two mountain-foxes.

Down the red-clay slopes of the outskirts of the village "John Barleycorn" thundered with a train of horsemen at his heels. Splash into the clear fair stream whose translucent depths told of its birthplace among the moun-

tain-springs—how the silver spray showered about as the pursuers surged through the ford leaving behind them a foamy wake!—and now pressing hard up the steep ascent of the opposite bank, and galloping furiously along a level stretch of road, with the fences and trees whirling by, and the September landscape flying on the wings of the wind. Past fields of tasseled Indian corn, with yellowing thickly-swathed ears, leaning heavily from the stalk; past wheat-lands, the crops harvested and the weeds having their day at last; past "woods-lots" and their black shadows, and out again into the September sunshine. Past rickety little homes, not unlike Silas's own, with tow-headed children, exactly like his, standing with wide eyes, looking at the rush and hurry of the chase; sometimes in the ill-kept yards a wood-fire was burning under the boiling sorghum; or beneath the branches of the orchard near at hand a cider-mill was crushing the juice out of the red and yellow, ripe and luscious apples. Past homeward-bound prize-cattle—a Durham bull, reluctantly permitting himself to be led into a fence-corner that the hunt might sweep by unobstructed, and turning his proud blue-ribboned head angrily toward the riders as if indignant that anything except him should absorb attention; a gallant horse, with another floating blue streamer, bearing himself as becometh a king's son—almost crushing sundry grunting porkers impervious to pride and glory in any worldly distinctions of cerulean decorations—having to draw up and wait until a flock of silly over-dressed sheep, running in frantic fear every way but the right way, could be gathered together and guided to a place of safety.

And once more, forward; past solid, red-brick houses with porches, and vine-grown verandas, and well-tended gardens, and groves of oak, and beech, and hickory trees—"John Barleycorn" makes an ineffectual but gallant struggle to get in at one of the large white gates of these comfortable places, Squire Goodlet's home, but he is urged back into the road, and again the chase sweeps on. Those blue mountains, the long parallel ranges of Old Bear and his brothers, seem no more a misty, uncertain mirage against the delicious indefinable tints of the horizon. Sharply outlined they are now, with dark, irregular shadows upon their precipitous slopes which tell of wild ravines, and stone-lined gorges, and swirling mountain-torrents, and great, beetling, gray crags. A breath of balsams comes on the freshening wind—the lungs expand to meet it. There is a new aspect in the scene; a revivifying current thrills through the blood; a sudden ideal beauty descends on prosaic creation.

"'Pears like I can't git my breath good in them flat countries," said Silas Hobbs to himself, as "John Barleycorn" improved his speed under the exhilarating influence of the wind. "I'm nigh on to sifflicated every time I goes down yander ter Woodville" (with a jerk of his wooden head in the direction of that imposing village).

Long stretches of woods on either side of the road now, with no sign of the changing season in the foliage save the slender, pointed, scarlet leaves and creamy plumes of the sumach, gleaming here and there; and presently another panorama of open country. More brick houses, and gardens, and a number of humble log-cabins, and a dingy little store, and the Cross-roads were reached. And here the conclusive intelligence met the party that Jacob and Cynthia had been married by Preacher Rice an hour ago and were still "a-kitin'," at last accounts, out on the road to Old Bear.

The pursuit stayed its ardor. The fun was over. As Jacob had appropriately remarked, "jowin'" now was of no avail. On the auspicious day when Silas Hobbs took the blue ribbon at the county fair and won the saddle and bridle, he lost his daughter.

They saw Cynthia no more until later in the autumn when she came, without a word of self-justification or apology for her conduct, to lend her mother a helping hand in spinning and weaving her little brothers' and sisters' clothes. And gradually the *éclat* attendant upon her nuptials was forgotten, except that Mrs. Hobbs now and then remarks that she "dunno how we could hev bore up agin Cynthy's a-runnin' away like she done, ef it hedn't a-been fur that thar saddle an' bridle."

A WESTERN ADVENTURE.

By C. H. Jones.

MANY years ago—upward of twenty-five, I find on counting them over—when the eyes of nearly all adventurers in the States were attracted to the newly acquired Mexican possessions, and when wild stories were afloat of the fortunes to be made, and the power to be acquired, in those little known but strangely fascinating regions, I found myself in the vanguard of what promised to be a movement of population toward the southwest, similar in character, if on a smaller scale, to that which was at the same time pressing overland to California. I was a young man then, and, though making a fortune was, of course, uppermost in my mind, I was nearly as much influenced by the desire for adventure; and this it was, perhaps, that caused me to turn my steps toward the far south-

ern frontier rather than to California. Stories were already coming back from the Golden State of disappointment and overplus of population and famine; and it occurred to me that New Mexico —where, as I had heard, the early Spanish conquerors found the richest mines—gave surer promise both of easily acquired wealth and of more romantic and unique experience.

I will confess at the start that, like most of the components of the vast caravan then surging westward, I little thought what a journey across the Plains meant. That it involved hardship I knew, and that it was not less perilous than difficult; but of the precise nature of the obstacles to be encountered I was, fortunately or unfortunately, in entire ignorance. It is necessary to remind the reader that what is now known as the "Plains"—stretching from the Missouri River to the Rocky Mountains, and from the interior of Texas to the boundary-line of British America—was at that period a great open space on the maps, across which was written the legend "Great American Desert." Geographers had in this case followed their immemorial usage of stigmatizing as uncanny any region with which they are unacquainted; and mysterious terrors, borrowed from the experience of African explorers, brooded over some of the fairest portions of the continent. Genuine terrors there were in plenty, as the reader will presently see; but I can never recall without a smile my primitive idea of the vast wastes which lay between me and my then eagerly desired goal.

The foregoing paragraphs will explain under what influences and for what objects I found myself in St. Louis early in the year 1850. The little city had suffered from several paroxysms of the "California fever," and was just beginning to settle down upon the conviction of its own brilliant destiny. Strangers were there in great numbers from all parts; but I soon discovered that nobody knew anything of the country "beyond the settlements" in the direction I wanted to go. At first I thought of descending the Mississippi to New Orleans, and then striking westward, and this I had far better have done; but I finally concluded to proceed to Fort Smith, on the extreme western border of Arkansas, procure a guide, and push directly for New Mexico.

The journey to Fort Smith, though tedious, was not difficult; and I had the good fortune, almost immediately on arriving there, to fall in with an experienced trapper and plainsman, who was more than willing to "git away from the settlements," and make venture in new fields. This guide was a noteworthy character in his way. His name was James Mitchell; but he was almost universally known as "Surly Jim," a *sobriquet* which he had acquired by reason of his morose temper and repellent ways. I have never seen on a human countenance such an expression of grim and pervading discontent as he carried when I first met him, and he could certainly behave ugly enough when he chose; but I am convinced that his surliness was simply the spontaneous and irrepressible expression of his disgust at being crowded out of his hunting-grounds and scarcely less dear solitude by the slowly rising tide of population. As soon as we had left civilization behind us, the crust vanished like frost before the morning sun, and I have seldom had a more cheerful, entertaining, and good-natured companion than Mitchell proved himself during the trip about to be described. The sole point of misunderstanding between us was my pocket-compass, for which I entertained a perhaps exaggerated respect, while Mitchell felt for it the aggressive contempt characteristic of old plains-men. It always provoked his wrath when I consulted that little monitor upon our route, though the service which it subsequently rendered in two or three emergencies compelled him to recognize that it was not altogether a device of the evil one.

Our preparations for the journey were soon made. I was already the possessor of a good horse; Mitchell had one for his own use; and I bought two pack-mules for the transportation of our "kit," which consisted of a small wall-tent, a very few cooking-utensils, and a supply of such articles of food as we were least likely to be able to obtain en route. To these I added a collection of such trade-goods as I thought most likely to be in demand in a new country unacquainted as yet with American manufactures. None of the animals was heavily burdened, and we expected to make, and in fact did make, good time. The first stage of the journey, from the Arkansas to the Red River, lay through the reservations of the Choctaw and Chickasaw Indians, occupying the southeastern portion of what is now the Indian Territory. It was traversed rapidly and with little difficulty, the Indians being even at that early date initiated into all the ways of civilization, and living in a manner scarcely different from that of their white neighbors down East. They treated us amicably, though somewhat suspicious of our intentions; often gave us what we would willingly have bought; and seemed as eager as ourselves to speed us on our journey.

We crossed the Red River about twenty miles above the mouth of the Big Wichita, and then, bearing a little south of west on a course nearly parallel with the latter stream, entered upon the unknown "Desert" region of the maps. We were now in a country where we were liable to any moment to fall in with roving or wild Indians, and I was speedily initiated into all the

mysteries of plainsmen's craft. Mitchell, who had hitherto jogged along like any ordinary traveler, now became so extremely cautious in selecting our path and so incessantly alert and watchful, that it kept me at first in a constant fume of anxiety and alarm, which was only dissipated after several days by my becoming used to it and in a measure infected by it. Not a speck on the remote horizon, nor the faintest film of mist, nor the most insignificant mark on the ground, escaped his minute and careful scrutiny; and, whenever we approached a slight elevation in the boundless and nearly level expanse of plain, he made me remain behind with the horses, and, creeping forward alone to the summit, swept the horizon in all directions. An hour before sunset, if a favorable spot could be found, it was our custom to halt, picket the animals for grazing, and kindle a fire of dried buffalo-chips (which produce scarcely any smoke) for the preparation of our supper. As soon as it was dark, Mitchell carefully obliterated all traces of our fire, and, saddling our horses, we went forward a mile or two to some sheltered locality, where we pitched our tent and settled down for the night. So much depended upon our horses that we spared no pains in securing their safety. Mitchell's horse was an old stager, and only needed to have his halter attached to a wooden stake driven in the ground, near the tent. My own horse and the two mules, besides being attached firmly to stakes, were provided with "side-lines," tying together the two legs on the same side, and completely disabling them from running.

Much of this painstaking seemed to me superfluous at the time, and I confess that I rather fretted under it; but I have had some experience of Plains-life since then, and I am convinced that it saved our scalps. Without knowing it, we were exactly crossing the track of the great buffalo-migration from the south to their summer grazing-grounds on the northern plains. Though the movement for that season was wellnigh finished, we saw great numbers every day; and, as the Indians always follow the buffalo-route, in order to secure their summer hunts, the wonder is that we did not run into their clutches a dozen times. On several occasions, indeed, we came upon indications of their close proximity, and often saw their signal-smokes on the horizon, but only once did we actually fall in with them. It was about the middle of the afternoon, and we were slowly ascending a gentle slope, when, on arriving at the crest, we saw on the other side, and coming almost directly toward us, a party of nine mounted Comanches. They were not more than six hundred yards off, and it would have been impossible to avoid the meeting; but, even if we had intended making the effort, it would have been thwarted, for immediately on sighting them one of our mules gave out a most prodigious bray, which brought them all instantly to attention. Halting a moment to consult, they dashed off at a gallop in an oblique direction to our right, yelling like demons, and brandishing their weapons. They evidently suspected there were more of us behind the slope, and wanted to gain its crest at a safe distance, instead of coming directly upon us. My first natural impulse, on seeing that there was to be a fight at such odds, was to seek a sheltered position, and I urged Mitchell to enter a rocky thicket, which lay a short distance to our left. Instead, he shouted to me to keep close up, and galloped back about a quarter of a mile on the track we had come, to a broad and perfectly level space. In the center of this he dismounted, put the side-lines on the horses, tied their heads close together, and then, taking his gun on his arm, sat down on the ground between them and the Indians, telling me to do the same. Seeing this, the Indians consulted together again, and, forming into a compact body, galloped furiously toward us, uttering such yells as I had never before heard, and giving me the impression that they would ride right over us. When they were about two hundred yards away, Mitchell raised his rifle, and instantly each man threw himself on the side of his horse, and circled back to the starting-point. This manœuvre was repeated about half a dozen times, until, contrary to Mitchell's orders, I fired and wounded one of the ponies. This inspired them with such respect for our weapons that they did not again come within range, but divided into groups, and examined the ground on every side, in search of some point where they could approach under cover. Finding none, they again came together, watched us intently for a while, and then, turning tail, galloped off. I supposed we had done with them, and wanted to resume our journey; but Mitchell only made the horses more secure, and quietly resumed his position. In about half an hour the Indians reappeared on the part of the crest nearest us, and dashed down, yelling worse than ever, and shaking blankets and buffalo-robes. The object of this manœuvre was to stampede our horses; but Mitchell had rendered this impossible, and, speedily discovering the fact, the rascals galloped off once more and disappeared.

It was growing dark by this time, and, knowing how easy it would be to creep upon us under cover of the darkness, I fully expected a night attack; but Mitchell rightly assured me that Indians would not attack at night, and that we had seen the last of them. I could not understand this at the time, and my trusty guide could tell me nothing beyond the mere fact; but I have

since learned that one of the common superstitions of the Plains Indians is that a man killed in the dark will dwell in darkness throughout eternity. This is for the white man a most fortunate belief, for the characteristic Indian qualities are precisely of the kind which make night attacks terrible.

Another quality of the Indians, which is fortunate for their white antagonists, is also exemplified in the foregoing anecdote. If we had taken to cover, as I wished, we should probably have been scalped in ten minutes; for his knowledge of the ground, and his wonderful skill in profiting by its inequalities, give the Indian overwhelming advantages in such a contest. While adventurous enough, however, in availing himself of any advantages which his superior craft gives him, the Indian has no relish for a fair, stand-up fight, in which blood is certain to be shed on both sides. Superiority of numbers seems to have no effect in diminishing this repugnance, for each Indian thinks that *he* is the one that will be killed, and an Indian has no more fondness for being killed or wounded than a white man. The raising of a single rifle is often sufficient to stop a party of thirty or forty charging in full career; and only the largest war-party will run directly upon two or three well-armed men, who have taken a favorable position in the open. Such a party they consider "bad medicine."

Four or five days after our adventure with the Indians, we found ourselves approaching the eastern border of the Llano Estacado or Staked Plain, and were congratulating each other on the excellent progress made, when a catastrophe occurred which put a peremptory end to our westward journey, and seemed more than likely at the time to put an end to our lives. We had halted as usual for supper, and then pitched our tent just on the verge of a deep, wide, and somewhat precipitous ravine, at the bottom of which ran a small stream of water. Mitchell's horse was picketed just in rear of the tent; mine and the mules about a dozen yards off. We sat up rather late that night, and when I turned in I took less than the usual care to have my gun, etc., convenient, but by a great piece of good fortune kept on my coat, vest, and socks. Shortly after midnight, Mitchell shook me by the arm; and sitting up and obeying his injunction to listen, I heard a low, continuous roaring sound like the noise of a distant cataract, but steadily increasing in volume. I was utterly bewildered, and we lost many precious moments in trying to make out what it was; but at last Mitchell rushed from the tent, and drawing on my boots I followed. The roar was much more distinct now; and, turning toward the broad prairie whence it came, we could see a wavering black line approaching rapidly, and steadily increasing both in width and blackness. One appalled look revealed to us the nature of the phenomenon—an immense herd of stampeded buffaloes was rushing directly upon us with tremendous speed and irresistible force. The advance line was not more than three hundred yards distant, so there was no time even to think of a plan of escape, much less to carry it out. For myself I could only gaze at the surging mass with a sort of horrid fascination, and I scarcely saw Mitchell as he flung down his gun and ran to the tent, striking matches as fast as he could and applying them to the grass and tent-cloth. Fortunately the grass was very dry and the cloth inflammable, and almost instantly the entire tent was in a blaze. Then seizing me by the shoulder, Mitchell dragged me to the verge of the bluff directly in front of the tent, and we both fell rather than jumped to a ledge just beneath. As we went over, my powder-can in the tent exploded with a prodigious report, and a moment afterward the first ranks of the buffalo plunged down the declivity, not ten yards distant on each side of us. Every moment for what seemed hours I expected to feel the fatal tramp of the huge beasts as they rushed over the bank above our heads; but the fire and the noise of the explosion had split the frantic herd scarcely twenty yards away, and the two divergent streams thundered harmlessly by into the darkness. Swift as were their movements, they were upward of five minutes in passing, and Mitchell himself estimated that there could not have been less than five thousand animals in this stampede.

When the tumultuous roar had subsided again into a faint and rapidly vanishing murmur, we clambered up the bank; and the scene which met our eyes might well strike us with dismay. On the spot where our tent had stood was a glowing bed of embers and ashes; while scattered about in every direction, whither they had been driven by the explosion, were pots, kettles, and the hardware truck with which I had designed to trade. Of our blankets and clothing hardly a vestige remained; every item of our ammunition had been destroyed; and the woodwork of my gun and pistol was completely burned away. Mitchell's rifle had fallen in the track of the buffalo and was trodden into a shapeless mass of iron. Flour, salt, coffee, all had fed the flames; and the sole residue of our stock, not discovered till the morning, was a large tin box full of crackers (biscuits). Saddest of all, our animals were also lost. Mitchell's horse lay dead just behind the tent, killed probably by the shock of the explosion. My horse and the mules, paralyzed with fright and unable to break away,

had been trodden by the buffaloes into an unrecognizable mass of pulp.

As if Fortune had not already done her worst, Mitchell was apprehensive lest the fire and smoke should bring the Indians upon us, and dragged me down to the densest thickets at the bottom of the ravine, where, strange to say, I at once fell asleep, and slept soundly till sunrise. In the morning we made two important discoveries: first, that five buffaloes had been killed in the desperate scramble across the ravine; second, that a large tin box filled with crackers had preserved its contents unharmed. As soon as we made these discoveries we sat down to consider our situation, and to decide upon our future course. Between us and our contemplated destination in New Mexico lay the great Staked Plain, utterly impassable to any one on foot. To retrace our steps toward the Red River was to invite almost certain death by starvation and to run terrible risks from the Indians, now on their summer migration northward. It was finally decided that our best chance lay in pushing southeast for the settlements in northern Texas. The chief danger in this direction, as we estimated it, lay in our utter ignorance of the intervening country and the probable scarcity of water; but an effort must be made, and this seemed to promise better than any other.

Our resolution being formed, it only remained to devise the ways and means of carrying it out; and the first step was to secure, if possible, an adequate amount of food for the journey. The crackers would last but a few days if we depended on them alone; and, having no weapon of any kind except a couple of hunter's knives, we could not depend on getting any game en route; but that the dead buffaloes seemed to offer ample store of food if we could only utilize them; and here Mitchell's knowledge of Plains-craft was once more of inestimable advantage. The Plains Indians live almost exclusively upon buffalo-meat, which they procure in their summer hunts, and prepare by drying it thoroughly in the sun, pounding it to powder between two stones, and packing it away in air-tight skins. We could not spare the time for this process, for every day of a meager and limited diet would diminish our strength, while every hour increased the danger of being discovered by passing Indians. Under Mitchell's direction, therefore, we contrived a more expeditious method. Selecting the leanest and juiciest meat, we cut it into long and thin strips, spread it in the sun upon a rudely constructed platform, and built under it a fire of green wood, which kept it constantly enshrouded in smoke. By this means we had at the end of two days and nights about fifty pounds of tolerably well-preserved meat, which, if dry and tough and flavorless, would at least sustain life. In the mean time we had recovered several uninjured bottles from the wreck of the tent; and these, for the purpose of carrying water, Mitchell covered with buffalo-skin tied on with raw-hide thongs; so that on the morning of the third day we were ready to start with about five pounds of crackers, as much dried meat as we could comfortably carry, and a gallon or so of water.

A detailed account of our journey would not be without interest, perhaps, if I could recall it with sufficient vividness, but it was singularly free from adventurous episodes; and, though infinitely fatiguing and not without privations, involved less of downright suffering than was to have been expected. Suffice it to say that, after a fortnight's somewhat devious wanderings, we found ourselves approaching the frontier settlements, and before reaching them fell in with a body of United States troops *en route* from Texas to New Mexico. I easily obtained permission to accompany them; and so at last, in a roundabout way, reached my original destination. Mitchell preferred to return to Arkansas, where, as I have heard, he entered the government service, and rendered valuable aid to the army as scout and guide.

I may observe, in conclusion, that the adventure I have described was not an altogether exceptional one. For many years after the period of which I write, buffalo "stampedes" constituted one of the characteristic dangers of travel on the Plains. The barbarous slaughter that has been going on since 1871, however, has not only completely eliminated this danger, but has rendered it certain that the American bison will soon be as extinct as the other strange animals whose fossil remains are found throughout the whole length and breadth of the Plains.

LIFE ON A CALIFORNIA RANCH.

IT became the fortune of the writer to leave San Francisco in September, 1878, and, after crossing Santa Clara Valley one of the richest in the State—to ascend by a fine stage-road into the very heart of a spur of the Santa Cruz Mountains. This road begins at a little village at the foot of the hills, and creeps gradually higher and higher, turning this bluff and that spur until, after a league, the traveler looks down into the glowing valley, and, if timid, shudders in secret at the depth.

The path thus leading away from the inhabited valley, full of men and towns, into the quiet

seclusion of the land among the hills, finally comes to a fair, broad region, where the "ranchmen" plant their acres with vines and fruit-trees, and where a stranger may live without ever wishing for the world of commerce, or thinking of it. There are high hills upon every side except toward the west. In that direction the land sinks in alternate ridges and ravines toward the ocean, and the great redwoods line the horizon. The houses are made of inch redwood-boards and building-paper, and are accordingly somewhat rude structures, but they sufficiently answer the purpose in this agreeable climate.

There is no stone fit for walls, like those with which the New England farmers separate their fields, and so the inhabitants split the trunks of the redwood pines into rough pickets, three inches square and five feet long; and, after driving them into the soil in lines, bind them close together at the top with strips of board. The fence thus constructed is cheap, quickly made, effective, and durable. There is little concern for appearances; the soil of many years remains undisturbed upon the wagon-wheels; no flower-garden is well cared for; they mend the harnesses with bits of ropes; and they trust little or nothing to the vanity of paint. You see no vegetable gardens, no patches of potatoes, lettuce, peas; no little areas carefully fenced and carefully cultivated in odd moments, when greens are in season. It does not pay to be at the trouble, and for this reason—the warmth of the soil and the early heat of the sun tend to force the vegetables into premature ripeness, and thence into coarseness of fiber.

The grapes that grow in this favored place are wonderfully large and fine. They are much better than those of the valleys, and are eagerly sought for by those who use the better kinds. A neighbor to me grew sixty varieties last season, though it is probable that not more than twenty kinds went to market. Every one's vines are prosperous, and the yield is enormous. The plants grow lying upon the ground; the dryness of the summer preventing the rot which attacks them in regions where rains are more frequent. It is quite a common thing to go out in the cool of a delicious morning, and cut off bunches of these grapes, and devour them three or four at a time, gazing meanwhile at acres more of the same kind. A certain ferocity develops in the reveler after a few weeks' indulgence in this sort of repast. One would lose the respect of all his friends were he to write down faithfully what his capacity for grapes at length becomes. In number, in weight, in kinds, the result is alike prodigious.

The ranchmen make boxes out of the clear redwood, and pack twenty-five pounds of grapes in each—all honestly picked, and decorated with the leaves of the vines. These are carried in wagon-loads to the valley below or to Santa Cruz on the coast. Now and then you perceive a most delicious odor in the roadway, and, after a while, it is seen that the dust has received a slight sprinkling. You walk on, half intoxicated, charmed by the soft air, the scenery, and the shade of the overhanging trees, and you overtake a wagon laden with grapes *en masse*—a purple sight, rich and tempting. They are on the way to some wine-press. Nearly every ranchman fills a few casks yearly with the juice of some of his grapes, thinking that he is laying up a claret which will be fine some day. But he has his labor for his uneducated pains, and produces only an acrid liquor the reverse of palatable.

The California ranchmen have wonderful aptitude for driving, and one sees some pretty good examples among these hills. The road down the mountain-sides is entirely unguarded upon the outer edge, and the descent in most places is precipitous. A balky horse, or a fractured wheel, or a slight carelessness in handling the reins, might easily send a carriage-load of people to destruction—and an awful destruction, too. The path is wide enough for one pair of wheels only, but at intervals, in favorable places, it broadens so that teams may pass each other. To drive in such a manner as not to meet another traveler midway between these places is a special branch of the art. The huge lumber-teams, which carry wood from the mills in the mountains to the yards in the valleys, being unwieldy and very heavy, are especially hard to manage. Yet the drivers always seem easy and nonchalant. First, there is a large, four-wheeled, oaken truck, with a seat in front ten feet above the ground; behind it is another truck, something shorter, but still enormously stout. These are fastened together, and loaded with from ten to fifteen tons of freshly sawed lumber—boards and joists. This mass is drawn by six or eight mules or horses, guided by reins and a prodigiously long whip. The first wagon has a powerful brake, worked by a long iron lever by the driver upon his seat. The driver is a man of nerve and courage. His skill must be of the highest order. It will not do for him to take fright even if in imminent danger, and he must know almost to a hair's-breadth where he can go and where he can not. Towering up far above the road, overlooking the most stupendous depths, and guiding with a few slender lines a tremendous force, he must needs be an adept, and a tireless one. But a beholder, ignorant of the danger that constantly surrounds him, would say his work was simple, and that he managed matters with ease. True, he seems so. With his broad-brimmed hat shading his sunburned face, his sinewy hands holding the reins with careless-

ness, his legs outstretched, with one foot feeling the all-important brake, he jogs onward with his monster charge without trouble or concern; the bells upon the horses' breasts jingle a little tune; the great wheels crush the stones in the path; the load creaks like a ship's hull in a sudden gust; wild birds sweep down into the hazy, sunny depths below—yet the driver seems to take no heed. But let a "scare" take place; let a herd of runaway cattle appear at a bend and set the horses wild, and then see what will happen. The day-dreamer will become a giant of strength. He is up in a flash; he shortens his hold upon the reins, and, feeling his wagon start up beneath him, places a foot of iron on the brake. The horses snort and rear and surge; the harnesses rattle, the dust arises, the load shrieks again, and the huge wheels turn fatally faster and faster. An instant may hurl the wagon down into the valley with its struggling train—a mad rush to the other side of the way may end all in one horrible plunge. Muscle, eye, brain, skill, are then brought to work so splendidly together, that the peril is averted, and the looker-on, who knows not the ways of the land, regards the teamster with profound respect thereafter.

The horses that are used in the country are mostly of the mustang sort. A mustang is a creature which has indeed the form of a horse, together with certain characteristics of his own —namely, a bad memory, which permits him to shy at a harmless shrub twenty times a day, if he sees it as often; ingratitude, which permits him to kick and injure his best human friend; absence of mind, which permits him to run furiously after it has been made clear to him that he is expected to walk; and a power to develop energy with great rapidity, which enables him to change in a twinkling from a simple, trustworthy looking nag into a snorting, biting, kicking demon. With these vices he has the one virtue of being enduring as so much brass.

There is a peculiar dress worn by the out-of-door folk of this land among the hills that deserves to be introduced into other lands, so fit is it for the wear-and-tear of farming. It consists of pantaloons or overalls, and jacket, made of canvas, colored brown, and fastened in all important places with small copper rivets. It wears astonishingly well. The hunters wear a "jumper" of the same material, filled with pockets inside and out for their innumerable wants, while the lower part forms a game-bag of considerable size.

Trees of various kinds, such as oak, cherry, etc., form an agreeable variety, where so much "redwood" predominates. The redwoods have become famous for their size and height all the world over, the *Wellingtonia gigantea* of Calaveras belonging to the family. They usually grow in fraternal groups of three or four, and it is impossible not to feel impressed by their solemnity when walking among them. The ground at their feet is covered with their browned spines, and their trunks rise one hundred and fifty feet before putting forth a branch. Many are ten feet in diameter at ten feet above the ground, and a few are so large that speculators hew and burn cavities in the bases when the road runs conveniently near, and therein set up a kind of restaurant for the benefit of the thirsty traveler.

The writer had hoped to leave at least the dust behind, and derive from the tall trees and the cooling streams a little of the summer comfort which had been so signally denied him in the region below. Disappointment, however, was his lot. On reaching the hills he found the brooks dry, and their courses marked with bowlders, upon whose nether sides one could light a match. The depths of the woods were airless ovens, where in a moment the hands and face ran with perspiration. There was not a blade of grass to be seen. The earth was brown, powdery, and hot. The dust in the roads was astonishing for its depth. It arose in obedience to the slightest breath, and, after a little acquaintance with the sunburned region, one foretold that a friend was coming by seeing a moving cloud over the top of the hill. For twenty yards on each side of the highways and lanes the underbrush was whitened. When people went to ride, they pulled linen coats over their better garments, and tied their wrists and collars. For the first mile or two the traveler snorts the dust out of his nostrils, and at intervals surveys his powdered clothing with dismay. Through his blurred eyes he barely sees the features of his neighbor upon the same seat; the horses are entirely beyond his view; a sense of suffocation overcomes him; and all sounds are drowned as they are in a snowstorm. At length, however, instead of being annoyed at the quantity of dirt which settles upon him, he refrains from shaking himself, and with a certain amused interest wonders how high the pile upon the back of his glove will grow before the journey comes to an end. The dust is a feature of the land, and strangers who have heard of it regard it with curiosity, as they do their first gold-mine.

This persistent recurrence of dry days, the everlasting pouring down of yellow light upon the parched, yellowish landscape, the breathing of hot air from all quarters, the absence of flourishing crops and greenery from the fields, soon dry up the soul of the new-comer, and weary out his patience.

At the close of October the skies were yet clear, the atmosphere a little hazy, the mornings and evenings enjoyably warm, and the nights refreshingly cool. The fruit of the orchards had been marketed long since, and the grapes were two thirds gathered. The affairs of the year were winding up; two or three weeks in November would give the farmers ample time to clear away their tardy crop, and then the winter might fall, and welcome. One bright day succeeded another; the "verdelo" ripened, yielding sweet, pale-green grapes; and piles of newly made redwood boxes stood in every yard ready for their luscious burden. At length there came a moment when further effort became useless; when the summer, with its fruits and its glories of color, went out, and winter, like a "spook" in a pantomime, came suddenly in.

In California, the two seasons end and begin respectively with the same event—a shower of rain. Autumn does not intervene; there is no fall of the leaf, no augmentation of the winds. Last year the summer ran on until the 1st of November. At eleven o'clock in the forenoon a few drops fell. After that the people spoke of the winter as having arrived. Everything seemed taken by surprise; the rain had come; the horses gazed strangely about them; the children ran out with wild noises, and stood bareheaded and laughing in the thick of the storm; the men leaned in the doorways with their hands in their pockets, silently pleased; the dust turned slowly into mire; the leaves of the madrones, the cherry-trees, and the oaks lifted themselves up and glistened in the pale light, and rills began to murmur everywhere. The yearly adjustment had begun; the other side of the balance had started downward, and the land rejoiced. Everything was changed out of its old course. The choppers, with their axes upon their shoulders, came out of the deep recesses of the woods, the mills put out their fires, and the grape-gatherers came down from the vineyards. The teams ceased to traverse the roads, stages were exchanged for wagons, and letters and papers came but rarely. A sense of being thrust out of the world, a notion of common ill fortune, made good neighbors of the people in the foot-hills, and a lively interchange of visits between ranch and ranch soon followed the beginning of the rains.

Rain followed rain in quick succession, always coming from the Pacific, and nearly always attended with a degree of cold that made it uncomfortable to stop in the open air even if thickly clad. The ranch upon which the writer lived was some eighteen miles from the nearest salt-water; yet, even as far inland as this, there were none of those calm, gently dropping showers that fall in England—those soft rains that gather the odors of the gardens, and instill the senses with so much that is grateful. Here the rain always came on the wings of a tempest, and poured down furiously. But, given a pleasant day in the midst of this California winter, and the discomfort of the rain and its attendant gloom vanishes, and the dweller in these parts goes forth charmed. The very early morning of one of these incomparable days is truly a wonder of softness and gentleness. The geniality of those few early hours is inexpressibly soothing; one is not exhilarated, but quieted; not wrought up to saddle his horse and ride a race, but impelled rather to sit in some sunlit spot and watch the world awaken in tranquillity. By the latter part of November the farmers are out with their plows, and the toil of the sower begins. The fields grow dark with the subsoil, and then change, and grow verdant with the grain. Rye-grass springs up on the brown hillsides that have been dry all summer, and the streams in the deep, wooded gulches make a low roar that never ceases. The flowers gather themselves up and show their faces, and the almond-trees put out their clouds of fragrant blossoms. On the oaks, whose branches are hung with mistletoe, a gray-green moss gathers and sways to and fro above the head. Numberless bluebirds dash across the fields, and now and then a meadow-lark lifts up its clear, sweet voice, and turns December into August. Quail, rabbit, and deer are abroad, and in the night-time the coyotes howl and bark in the forest.

The ranchman's one amusement is dancing, which he enthusiastically avails himself of. No matter if the night be stormy—no matter if the host's house be a board-cabin a mile from a road, and deep down in a gloomy ravine where the sun and moon rarely penetrate—the ranchman is bound by all the instincts of his nature to be on the spot, and to stand up in every quadrille in which he can find a place. Wood-choppers, farmers, teamsters, miners, squatters, together with a number of wives and daughters, some remarkably pretty, and some remarkably ugly—get together at an hour's notice, and keep up reels and polkas until a very late hour next morning. A single violin is the motive power. No matter if a cloud of dust arises from the ill-cleansed floor of the woodman's shanty—no matter if few appear upon the scene who have not danced together hundreds of times—the fun abates not; and at the breaking up there is no one who will not promise to be on hand " to-morrow night," in case to-morrow night is to be marked with another similar festivity.

DOGS I HAVE KNOWN AND LOVED.

By a Lady.

THE first dog of any note that my father possessed was a black Newfoundland. He was a very powerful and intelligent animal. My father trained him well, and taught him to go from our country place to the town with a basket fastened round his neck, with notes inside for the different tradespeople, who understood that he would readily give them up, and, if required, would bring anything sent, safely back. He was often dispatched for a car to an hotel about a mile distant. Hector would go into the yard, and the hostler knew at once what was wanted. One day there was a strange man in the yard, who could not understand what Hector meant; but the dog would not be baffled. He went straight to the bar, and gently barked to gain attention. "Ah!" said the girl, "Hector wants a car," which settled the business.

At that time it was very dangerous to walk at night in the country roads. It was before the rural police were appointed. When my father was absent of an evening, Hector was always sent to meet him. A spiked collar was put on, to protect his throat. He was told to wait at a certain place, and he never failed to be there.

One evening I was walking home with my father; it was so dark we could scarcely see anything. My father said: " We ought to have met George by this time. I told him to come with the lantern."

We walked on a few yards, and Hector met us. He was half a mile ahead of his accustomed waiting-place. My father was a strict disciplinarian, and spoke sharply to the dog, scolding him for coming on. But I begged him not to do so, thinking there might be some good reason for his coming. When we reached the stile to cross the fields the dog was restless, and growled savagely.

" Back, Hector, back!" said my father; but the dog would not obey him, and bounded over first. " There is something the matter," said my father, as he took out his clasp-knife, and opened it, whispering to me: " We may have a fight. Be sure you do not lay hold of my arm." He then struck a light with his flint and steel, whereupon a man sprang up and moved on before us.

" Mind yourself, father," said I; " Hector will take care of me." The dear creature came close to my side and put his nose into my hand.

I knew he would fight for us to the death; for though as gentle as a lamb to those he loved, he was fierce as a lion in defense of them. My father was a very powerful and fearless man. He had his daughter to protect, and his spirit was thoroughly roused; but he knew it would be well to trust to the sagacity of the dog, and see what he would do. When we reached the stile he stood still and growled. My father said: "Come, you fellows, come at once over this stile. I know you are there. Come at once, or I will set my dog upon you, and he will show you no mercy."

There was a movement, and one, and then another man came grumbling. Hector stood firm, uttering a low, continued growl. "Come along," exclaimed my father; "there are more of you. You had better be quick." Another came, saying "that he had as much right to the road as we had."

Still the dog would not cross the stile. "There is another of you. If you do not come at once, my dog will kill you." He saw the animal's patience was wellnigh exhausted. The last then slunk over, and the dog bounded over the stile into the lane. Then we knew the brave creature had saved us. When we came to the public-house, George, our man-servant, was sitting comfortably in the porch waiting for us with the lantern. He had seen *two* men, and was afraid to come on!

I could tell many interesting stories of this noble animal. His end was sad. When we were removing to another house, he was taken to protect some of the things that were put in the loft above the stable; the stupid man who put him there tied him up; the poor creature's feet had slipped, and, when the door was opened next morning, our faithful friend was found strangled.

We had at the same time with Hector my Blenheim spaniel Flora. She was a lovely little creature, perfect in beauty; and was very fond of Hector, whom she delighted to patronize. He was roaming about the fields one day, when espying Flora in the pond he jumped in, and took her safely to the bank. This liberty the spaniel resented by barking and scolding, after which she leaped into the water again. Hector looked very humble; but still he seemed to think he must be there, lest any harm should come. A happy thought occurred to him, and walking into the water, he quietly waited till Flora climbed upon his back, and enjoyed herself, while he swam about. When she was tired, she walked quietly home. But after this, it was a constant source of amusement to let Hector loose with Flora upon his back in the water.

We had also two terriers—one a black and tan smooth-haired; the other a wire-haired, one

of the bravest, most honest dogs I ever knew. The smooth-haired was called Tan. He was a thorough aristocrat, proud and haughty; very good and clever in a rat-hunt when excited and others were working too. But he was a perfect contrast to honest-hearted Tip. Near our house was a farm occupied by a strange sort of man, low, vulgar, and savage. This Farmer Oldacre had a dog the counterpart of himself, that was the terror of the neighborhood. One day he was loose, and by some means he got hold of poor Tip and almost killed him. We saw him torn and bleeding in the yard. Everything that could be done for the poor animal was done. It was a pretty sight to see little Flora sitting by the side of and comforting her injured friend; and many a delicious morsel was given to her to take to her patient. In about six weeks Tip was better and able to run about. One day our man-servant, who had been to a distance to fetch some hay, informed us on his return that he had seen Tan on the road, and that, on whistling, Tan took no notice of him. In the afternoon we suddenly heard a noise of barking dogs. Off started Flora, and joined them. There had assembled about twenty of all sorts, who proceeded to Farmer Oldacre's, flew at his dog, and tore it to pieces. Our man-servant, who followed them for Flora's sake, told us she in her revenge was the last to be taken off from him, while Tip sat looking quietly on, taking no share in the attack. Must not those animals have communicated with each other, and thus punished with death the savage brute? These dogs had been collected together from a radius of five miles, and it was quite evident that information regarding the farmer's savage dog had something to do in gathering them together.

Tip was one of the most faithful animals. He devoted himself to our old gardener Willy. At haymaking-time he was employed to take charge of the basket of food and the beer that were sent into the field for the laborers. No one but Willy was allowed to come near while the animal guarded Willy's coat. His faithfulness, however, cost him his life. One evening in October a sudden sharp frost set in while Willy had left Tip in charge of his coat in the garden. The old man had been persuaded to go to the public-house, and was so intoxicated that he could not return home; but the dog remained still faithful to his charge. My father went to the dog to try to get him home; but he would not come. He covered him up with a thick horse-cloth; but next morning poor Tip could not walk. He was almost paralyzed; and was in such agony that they were compelled to have him shot.

Flora was so clever that I professed to teach

her the multiplication-table. I used small biscuits; and without any mistake she would answer my questions by pushing the right number of biscuits with her paw. Of course I never tried high numbers; and as a reward at the end of her lesson I used to say, "Now, Flora, we will play at subtraction." She would put her pretty head on one side, and—if there were, say, four biscuits upon the table — I would ask: "Now, Flora; four from four, how many?" In a moment all the biscuits disappeared. Whereupon she would give a happy little bark, and run away well pleased with her performance. She was devotedly attached to my father, and in a severe illness he had would never leave him except to take a short run in the garden. One day she was taken from his room into another where the servant did not observe that the window was open. She had become so susceptible to cold from her long confinement in a warm room, that she caught a severe chill, which ended in rapid consumption.

I will now conclude with an account of Juno, the most singular dog I ever knew. When we were in Staffordshire, some years since, a female puppy was given to one of my daughters. She was a month old when we brought her home. She was partly of the hound and Lyme Hall mastiff breed, and developed into an animal of rare beauty. Her color was a light golden brown, with jet-black muzzle, and a little white upon her throat. Her eyes were large and lustrous, resembling a fawn's. Hydrophobia being very prevalent in our neighborhood, we were afraid of her coming in contact with any other dogs; and, as she grew up, the fear of losing her compelled us to be very careful, so that she never went out without a leash. When she came to us we had a kitten, to which she attached herself; and they were constant companions until the little creature was accidentally killed. Some time after this she saw a cat, and ran up to play with it. But puss flew at Juno and scratched her severely on the ear. She never forgot this; waited her opportunity, and killed it. From that time all cats were doomed that she could lay hold of; and our back-yard, which had been much infested by them, was kept clear of their presence for years.

Juno soon became so completely identified with us, that she did not care to associate with any other dogs. She was a most affectionate and loving creature to us all, and also formed strong attachments to various friends.

She was remarkable as a watch-dog; indeed,

she became quite "a terror to evil-doers." We felt quite secure from burglars, though the houses of many in our neighborhood were attacked. She never barked unnecessarily. When the gate was left open for the early-morning men to empty the ash-pit, it was quite sufficient to tell her so before retiring for the night, and then she never uttered a sound. Her sense of smell was so keen that it was impossible to administer any medicine to her. Once only was this done, and it required such severe measures that those who witnessed the scene in the yard of the veterinary surgeon have never forgotten it. One summer she was very unwell, suffering from an eruption of the skin—we supposed from a fight she had had with a cat. It occurred to me that ripe pears would do her good. She ate them with a thorough relish; and in the course of three weeks she was completely cured!

Her love for me was very great, though it was to her master she evinced the deepest devotion. When he was absent from home, she would eagerly watch for the postman, and fetch to me her master's letter, without touching any other. I had a severe illness, and while confined to the house she was my constant companion. One day I was very depressed, and had been weeping. She came to me, looked into my face, whined, patted me with her paw, and licked my hand. Seeing this had no effect in drying my tears, she snatched my handkerchief, and ran away with it to the other end of the room. When she saw me smiling, she came slowly back again, and, after a little coaxing, returned it to me. Though so brave and fearless, she was highly nervous, and suffered dreadfully in a thunderstorm. If I were near her, she would hide her head in the folds of my dress. When alarmed, her face perceptibly paled. We saw a remarkable instance of this one day when my husband returned from a funeral. Juno hearing his voice, as usual ran to meet him; but started back as if in horror when she saw him with a long black silk hat-band, and a scarf of the same material across his shoulders. Her color left her, and it was some minutes before she recovered.

It has often been to me a matter of inquiry how much of reasoning power as distinguished from instinct is to be found in animals. The more I have studied them, and watched their various ways and acts, the more I am convinced that they are not so far in this respect removed from man as some would have us believe. Their sense of humor is great, and we all saw this frequently in Juno.

FIFTH AVENUE ON AN AUGUST NIGHT.

Midnight Reveries of a Lonesome Stockbroker.

NEW YORK AT THE SEASIDE.

Mrs. Darling endures the pangs of separation from her Husband, during the Dog-days, " Solely on account of the Children, my dear ! "

"THE HAMMOCK."

By O. W. H.

A FEW years ago one might have published a Summer Book and left out all allusions to the hammock without comment being made on it, but not so now. So completely has it become interwoven into our out of-door summer life that to ignore it is to pass by one of the prime necessities to the full enjoyment of the summer season. To quote a recent writer, whose soul was touched by the poetry that his sensitive nature discovered in its "deft union of simplicity and comfort":

"If summer brought nothing else, it might justly be credited with a completed mission in supplying the proper conditions for the hammock. What other device of civilized life can compare with it in its deft union of simplicity and comfort; what other reveal so subtile an inspiration in its adaptability to the finer sense of men? No rigid lines chafe; no unyielding forms oppress him. The hammock anticipates the whims and humors of its occupant. It follows the turnings and contortions of his body, adapting itself like a loving nurse to each new position, and holding him gently and without a protest in whatever ridiculous attitude hot weather fancies or fatigue may lead him. It may be enjoyed in the sleeping-room or on the veranda, but its natural and most appropriate place is between two stalwart elms or maples. These are the best, but, if not available, almost any domestic trees will do. Then it is ready to give the most exquisite enjoyment to all who can accept the invitation to its cooling embrace. Wrapped in a hammock, man is like a bird—a rather inert and drowsy bird, perhaps, but that is because he has the advantage of the tribes of the air in being obliged to put forth no exertion to keep himself afloat. The cool currents of air dash over him on every side. He is buoyed up by an almost invisible power, and he bathes in the breezes, and inhales a tonic that strengthens as well as exhilarates. But that is only the framework of the poetry of the hammock. The world takes on a delightful though almost unreal glamour to the happy prisoner in its meshes. The trees, the flowers, and moving animate objects, become mingled with vacant thoughts and form a part of them, or upon the azure background of the sky the cool and playful clouds arrange themselves in a quick-succeeding, ever-varying tableaux that, touched with a little imagination, may bring before the fascinated watcher this whole great world in an afternoon. If city men and women sigh for homes in the country, let them make haste to swell their bank account so that they can buy each two trees, about twenty feet apart, and the land on which they grow, and then, like the orioles, let them swing their hammocks and be happy."

This poet—if poet he surely is—touches the key-note of the "poetry of the hammock." Who will gainsay what he has written, or say that more than the full meed of praise has been accorded to it? Surely not those who have ever owned one, provided it met the proper conditions of the hammock; and this leads us to remark that care should be taken in choosing a hammock, for, since their use has become so general, so many kinds have been put upon the market that a little advice on this point may not be found amiss. Some of them, especially the grass and manila imported hammocks, are not as flexible, and consequently not as comfortable, as some others. Those made of "Union Web," by the Union Hammock Co., of Gloucester, Massachusetts, are the best we have found, as they avoid the rigidity of the grass ones, and, being knotted at short intervals, are indestructible.

Shade-trees are, of course, to be preferred to hanging a hammock to. That these are not available is often the case, when a less satisfactory position is substituted. One large tree may be made available for several hammocks, by setting stout posts around it at convenient distances, to which one end of each hammock may be attached, and the other end to a chain placed around the tree. Care should be taken that hammocks are well secured, and that stones and other hard substances are removed from under them.

In hanging a hammock, six feet or more of rope should be used, and, if intended for a seat or swing, both ends may be hung the same height from the ground. For use as a hammock, the head should be five feet three inches from the ground, and the foot three feet three inches, the longest stretch of rope being used for the latter.

By following instructions, in the first place buying a hammock that is reliable, and using it in a common-sense way, more real enjoyment and unalloyed comfort can be procured than with any other device we know of.

APPLETONS' GUIDE-BOOKS.

Appletons' European Guide-book.

Containing Maps of the Various Political Divisions, and Plans of the Principal Cities. Being a Complete Guide to the Continent of Europe, Egypt, Algeria, and the Holy Land. To which are appended a Vocabulary of Travel-talk—in English, German, French, and Italian—an Hotel Appendix, and Specialties of European Cities. *Completely revised and corrected up to date.* Handsomely bound in two volumes, in red morocco, gilt edges. Price, $5.00.

Appletons' General Guide

TO THE UNITED STATES AND CANADA. An entirely new work. With a Railroad Map of the United States and Canada, and Thirteen Sectional Maps, including "The Adirondacks," "Yosemite Valley," and "Yellowstone Park"; and Plans (with References) of Fourteen of the Principal Cities—especially prepared for the work. Illustrated. This work is compiled on the plan of the famous BAEDEKER HAND-BOOKS of Europe. COMPLETE IN ONE VOLUME. 500 pages, 16mo, pocket form, bound in roan, price, $2.50; or separately:

> THE NEW ENGLAND AND MIDDLE STATES AND CANADA. One vol., 264 pages, 16mo, bound in cloth, $1.25.
>
> THE WESTERN AND SOUTHERN STATES. One vol., 234 pages, 16mo, bound in cloth, $1.25.

The leading idea which has governed the preparation of the above work has been to combine fullness and precision of information with the utmost attainable economy of space; to present the information in such a manner as to be most easy of use; to furnish a hand book for the traveler that will supply the place of guides in a land where *couriers* or professional guides are unknown. All the important cities and great routes of travel in the United States and Canada are carefully and minutely described, and also every locality which is sufficiently visited for its own sake to entitle it to a place in such a work.

Appletons' Hand-book of Summer Resorts.

Illustrated. Large 12mo. Paper cover, 50c.; cloth, 75c.

Appletons' Railway Guide.

Paper cover, 25 cents. Published monthly. Revised and corrected to date.

Appletons' Dictionary of New York and Vicinity.

A Guide on a New Plan; being an alphabetically arranged Index to all Places, Societies, Institutions, Amusements, and innumerable matters upon which information is daily needed. With Maps of New York and Vicinity. Square 12mo. Paper, 30c.; cloth, 50c.

New York Illustrated.

With 102 Illustrations and a Map of the City. The illustrations and text fully delineating the Elevated Railway system, Post-Office, and other Public Buildings, Churches, Street Scenes, Suburbs, etc., etc. 4to. Paper cover, price, 60 cents.

Scenery of the Pacific Railways and Colorado.

With Maps, and 71 Illustrations. Paper cover, 75 cents; cloth, $1.25.

Appletons' Hand-book of American Cities.

Large 12mo. Illustrated. Paper cover, 50 cents; cloth, 75 cents.

Appletons' Hand-book of Winter Resorts.

For Tourists and Invalids. With 47 Illustrations. Paper cover, 50 cts.; cloth, 75 cts.

** Either of the above sent by mail, post-paid, to any address in the United States, on receipt of the price.

D. APPLETON & CO., Publishers, 1, 3, & 5 Bond Street, New York.

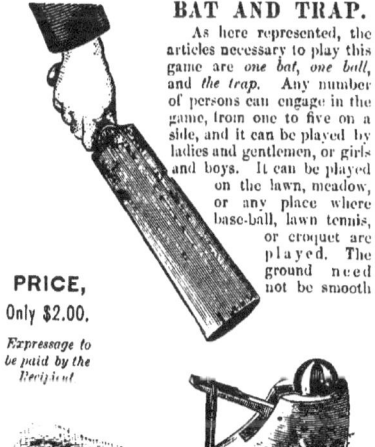

CHARLIER INSTITUTE,

FOR BOYS AND YOUNG GENTLEMEN,

108 WEST FIFTY-NINTH STREET,

(Opposite Central Park, New York City).

The Advantages claimed for this School are:

1. *Its location, equaled by none in New York City.*

2. *A new building, erected purposely, with as perfect ventilation and accommodations as science can make them to-day.*

3. *An experience of* **Thirty Years.**

4. *Experienced Teachers, and a course of studies preparing pupils for*

College, Business,
West Point,
Naval Academy,
OR ANY

Scientific School
IN THE UNITED STATES
OR ABROAD.

5. *There is a special department for youths who desire to go to college, and wish to learn Latin and Greek rapidly. Special preparation for Harvard, Yale, Columbia, Princeton, etc.*

6. *Modern Languages, especially French, German, and Spanish, are taught by native teachers, and spoken with them.*

For testimonials, details, terms, etc., send for a Prospectus of the School.

Professor ELIE CHARLIER, Director.

The twenty-sixth School Year begins September 20, 1880.

THE MASSASOIT HOUSE,

SPRINGFIELD, MASS.

M. & E. S. CHAPIN, Proprietors.

The Massasoit House, near the Railroad Stations, was established in 1843. It has been twice enlarged, making it three times its original size, and thoroughly remodeled and refurnished. The large, airy sleeping-rooms, furnished with hot and cold water, are excelled by none in the country. Special attention paid to ventilation and all sanitary improvements. The proprietors are determined that the world-wide reputation of the Massasoit shall be maintained in all respects.

THE HYGEIA HOTEL,

OLD POINT COMFORT, VA.

Situated 100 yards from Fortress Monroe, at the confluence of the Chesapeake Bay and Hampton Roads, being the first point of land lying westward between the Capes of Virginia, about fifteen miles north of Norfolk and Portsmouth; all passenger-steamers running to and from those cities touch at the pier, going and returning, with the United States mails, landing only twenty rods from the Hotel, which is substantially built and comfortably furnished. Has hydraulic passenger elevator, gas and electric bells in all rooms; water, rooms for bath (including hot sea), and closets on every floor, with the most perfect system of drainage of any Hotel or public building in the country; and as a resort for the pleasure-seeker, invalid, or restin-place for tourists on their way to Florida or the North. Seven hundred guests present inducements which certainly are not equaled elsewhere as a summer resort or cold weather sanitarium, the invigorating atmosphere and mild temperature being especially adapted to that class who seek the genial winters of the South and cool summers of the North. For sleeplessness and nervousness, the delicious tonic of the pure ocean air, and the lullaby of the ocean waves rolling upon the sandy beach but a few feet from the bedroom windows, are most healthful soporifics at the Hygeia.

For further information, address, by mail or telegraph,   H. PHŒBUS, Proprietor.

ST. LOUIS HOTEL,

ST. LOUIS STREET, QUEBEC.

This Hotel, which is unrivaled for size, style, and locality in Quebec, is open throughout the year, for pleasure and business travel. It is eligibly situated near to, and surrounded by, the most delightful and fashionable promenades—the Governor's Garden, the Citadel, the Esplanade, the Place d'Armes, and Durham Terrace—which furnish the splendid views and magnificent scenery for which Quebec is so justly celebrated, and which is unsurpassed in any part of the world.

To Durham Terrace has been added what will be called Dufferin Terrace, an extension of fourteen hundred feet, with an average width of eighty feet, to a point directly under the flag-staff of the Citadel, with steps leading from the Terrace up to the inclosure of the Citadel, thus forming one of the finest promenades in the world, and being two hundred and fifty feet above the river.

The Proprietors, in returning thanks for the very liberal patronage they have hitherto enjoyed, inform the public that this Hotel has been thoroughly renovated and embellished, and can now accommodate about five hundred visitors; and assure them that nothing will be wanting on their part that will conduce to the comfort and enjoyment of their guests.

THE RUSSELL HOTEL COMPANY,

PROPRIETORS.

WILLIS RUSSELL, President.

"TRAVERS" AMERICAN HAMMOCK.

Patented July 29, 1879.

New Style: Perfection in Shape; Beauty and Strength; Brass Mounted; Cardinal Binding.

TESTED TO BEAR OVER 1,000 lbs.

Sample, $3.00.   Postage, 50 cents.

Suitable for the Piazza, Camp, Grove, etc.

Discount to Camp-Meetings, Clubs, Picnics, etc.

AGENTS WANTED.

Twine House established 1845.

J. P. TRAVERS & SON,

46 Beekman Street, N. Y.

DUNCAN A. GRANT,

879 BROADWAY,

IMPORTER OF

Rich Passementeries,

Gimps, Fringes, Buttons,

Ornaments, Etc., Etc.

PONGEE AND FRENCH EMBROIDERIES,

FOR SUMMER USE.

Capes, Scarfs, Breakfast-Caps,

Bows, Fichus, Mantles,

Handkerchiefs, Fans, Etc.

Collarettes, Capes, and Caps, made up in the most
becoming and attractive styles, at
very Low Prices.

MAIL-ORDERS PROMPTLY ATTENDED TO.